&

Soul Searching

Beth Hanggeli

&

Soul Searching is a work of fiction. Names, characters, places and incidents either are the product of the author's imagination or are used fictitiously. Any resemblance to events, locales, or actual persons, living or dead, is entirely coincidental.

ISBN: 149911964X
ISBN-13: 978-1499119640

www.bethhanggeli.com

For what is a man profited,

if he shall gain the whole world,

and lose his own soul?

— Matthew 16:26

~ *1* ~

A house can't cry.

Even a house that has sat abandoned for too many years with no one to protect, or to protect it.

The wind moans as it rushes around lonely corners. Raindrops slip down empty windowpanes like teardrops. The roof droops, and the porch sags. The brittle floors groan.

But a house can't be sad.

It used to stand tall and proud. It used to protect the soul of a family. But now it is slowly surrendering to the devastation of time. Already shutters fall, wood rots, paint peels. Already it begins to admit defeat.

But a house can't fail.

The air around it is still. Even the birds are silent, waiting for someone to return and save it. Although it might already be too late.

A house can't cry. But it can hope.

~ 2 ~

It was time.

Tara Davies' palms were slick on the steering wheel as she sped through the winter night. She was late, which made it worse. He didn't like it when she was late.

She had been working toward this night for months, gathering her courage so that when the time was right, she'd finally be able to ask her father the question she longed to ask for years. And she decided the time was right tonight.

They were supposed to meet at his house in Portland, so when he asked her to come to Surfside, Tara was confused. As far as she knew, Ethan didn't know anyone in the tiny coastal town.

Having the conversation on neutral ground instead might work in her favor. Sitting in her father's house among the dusty books and musty drapes was too nerve-wracking. There were too many ghosts reminding her of why she left at 17, swearing never to return.

She rehearsed the words as she drove the winding roads to Surfside, searching for the perfect combination that would unlock their past, and her future. Everything depended on Ethan's response. Her last chance for a normal life hinged on his forgiveness.

She traveled the dark roads, following his directions. The specific turns to take, since the road signs were hard to see at night. The exact mileage to the driveway. The retired engineer had carefully drawn it out for her, down to the two green reflectors on the mailbox post.

Tara rounded a corner and was blinded by the high beams of a car heading straight for her on the wrong side of the road. She threw up her hand to shield her eyes and slammed on the brakes, jerking the wheel to the right. At the last second, the car veered back into its own lane and zoomed past, stereo thumping.

She pulled onto the shoulder and sat for a moment, heart pounding. Then, hands shaking, carefully steered back onto the road and continued following the double yellow line.

&

Tara finally found the green reflectors and followed the driveway up a steep hill. At the top, her headlights shone on a garage, a flagstone path, and a wraparound porch. Her father's Ford Explorer was parked in front of the house. There were no lights on outside. No lights on inside.

What was he doing in a dark house?

She pulled her flashlight from the glove compartment and pressed the switch. Nothing. She smacked it against her leg and tried again. This time it worked, but the yellow light told her she'd be in the dark again before long.

Tara hurried through the cold drizzle down the path to the stairs and climbed to the porch. The flashlight illuminated a gaping hole in the third tread, which she carefully stepped over. She knocked on the front door and waited.

The light was growing dimmer. She knocked again, harder, and heard the sound echoing through the house. Still no answer.

This was ridiculous. She tried the doorknob, but it was locked. She shone the light through the bay windows on the right side of the door, and saw a dining room and what might be a study behind it.

There were matching bay windows on the other side of the door, so she crossed the porch and peered through them. She could make out an overstuffed couch and chairs in front of a massive brick fireplace with a chimney that soared to the rafters.

She swept the light around the rest of the room, afraid that it would go out before she found her father.

Maybe it would have been better if it had.

Although the beam was dying, it was still strong enough to illuminate two figures lying motionless on the hardwood floor. One was a woman. The other was Ethan — Tara's father.

~ 3 ~

Maybe it was the lateness of the hour, or the desire to avoid questions he wasn't supposed to answer. But the deputy driving Tara to Portland didn't say a word to her. Once he settled her into the rear of his ultra-clean Crown Victoria police car, he seemed to forget that she was there.

The car was quiet, almost peaceful, after the chaos at the house. The screaming sirens, the kaleidoscope of red and blue lights, the roar of the MedEvac helicopter flying her father to Portland. The crime scene cordoned off with yellow tape. The deputies sipping coffee from Styrofoam cups, wisps of steam dissipating in the glow of their headlights.

The paramedics tended to her father with quiet efficiency before sending him to the hospital, attended by a deputy. Tara shuddered when the investigator said the deputy was there in case her father made a dying declaration.

And finally, as the crime scene cleared, the coroner's van silently carrying the woman's body to the morgue.

Tara peered through the mesh screen separating her from the driver. When Deputy Knowles introduced himself, she almost expected him to salute. He could have come directly from Central Casting: tall, broad shoulders, ash blonde buzz-cut. Cookie-cutter cop. He was young, and too concerned with maintaining his tough-guy image to remember to be human.

As the night slipped past the rain-spattered windows, Tara tried to collect herself. She closed her eyes as soon as she saw the bodies, but the image of her father lying on the floor was burned into her brain. She didn't know who the woman was; hopefully she wouldn't show up in Tara's nightmares, too.

She was grateful that the deputy drove her to the hospital, especially after the paramedics said there wasn't room in the helicopter for her. Deputy Knowles held her back as it lifted off, and practically dragged her to his car as she sobbed. Maybe that was another reason he wasn't talking to her.

She perched on the hard vinyl seat, reminding herself to breathe.

&

Compared to the steady, slightly chaotic pace of the rest of the hospital, the Intensive Care Unit at Legacy Emanuel resembled a morgue. A very bright morgue. But Tara quickly suppressed that thought as she entered her father's room.

Ethan Davies seemed to have shrunk since they met for cocoa last week. Her cheerful, robust father was a shadow of his usual self: eyes hollow, cheeks sunken, complexion pallid, as though the machines were draining his spirit.

Tara studied the strands of graying hair on his forehead, the oversized ears — his Dumbo Jumbo ears, he called them — the startling blue eyes, like hers, behind his closed lids. IV lines and wires bound him to the machines clustered around the bed and a green screen beeped annoyingly overhead. But that annoying sound meant he was still alive, so she forced herself to ignore and even appreciate the steady beeping.

Monitoring devices bound his right hand, while his left lay motionless on the crisp sheet. She stroked his wedding ring, the gold band worn thin. Wondering at the devotion he showed her mother for so many years. Wondering why she couldn't do the same.

A doctor paused outside the room to speak with a nurse, and Tara slipped out to join them. "Excuse me. I'm Tara Davies, Ethan's daughter. Could you tell me how he is?"

"Dr. Chambers," the young woman said, extending a slim hand. "I'm afraid I don't have much to tell you. His vital signs are stable, but weak. There are signs of blunt force trauma to the head, so there is the possibility of brain damage. We'll continue to monitor his condition, and let you know if there's any change."

Tara thanked her and returned to her father's room, her footsteps echoing in the sterile hallway. She lowered herself into the olive green recliner next to her father's bed.

"Daddy?" she whispered. "Can you hear me? I don't know who did this to you, but you need to wake up. We have things we need to talk about. We have things we need to do." She buried her face in his limp hand and cried silently.

&

After the nurses promised they'd call her if his condition changed, Tara allowed Deputy Knowles to escort her back to his car. He rode quietly in the front seat on the trip back to Surfside as she rode silently in the back.

When they approached the outskirts of town, he finally spoke. "My sergeant needs you to stop by the office tonight, ma'am."

"Tonight? It can't wait until tomorrow?" Tara was in no mood to face anything tonight except her pillow and blanket. And once he dropped her off in Surfside, she still had to drive home to Merrow Bay.

"He said tonight."

Recognizing a battle she wasn't going to win, she sighed and leaned back against the hard seat.

At the sheriff's station, Deputy Knowles guided her down the wet sidewalk, his hand stiff on the small of her back. Maybe he was afraid she would pass out; maybe he was merely following Chapter Two, Section Five in the Pacific County Sheriff's Manual outlining the proper procedure for escorting hysterical women. Either way, he was obviously uncomfortable with the human contact. What he would do if she fainted, forcing him to choose between catching her and maintaining his impeccable carriage? Hopefully she wouldn't find out.

He steered her toward a chair in front of a metal desk almost hidden behind a half-dead rubber plant. The once-red cushion was cracked, its yellowed stuffing oozing like cream from an éclair. Hollywood had it wrong: the sergeant's office didn't have smudged windows, crooked venetian blinds, and a door with his name etched on a tarnished brass plate. Just institutional furniture, and the reek of stale coffee and fear.

"My sergeant will be back in a minute," he said. "Sit. Please. Here."

Tara sat and he disappeared, probably back to his insulated squad-car world. She stared unseeing at the sad plant.

Footsteps. A tall man approached with two steaming mugs. Unlike Deputy Knowles, this man was *not* from Central Casting. Brown hair hung in shaggy strands over his light blue eyes. His uniform was wrinkled, his tie crooked, and he needed a shave. Pens bulged from a shirt pocket stained with splotches of green ink. But his smile was open, even innocent. She thought she remembered seeing him at the house earlier.

"Ms. Davies?" He wedged the mugs between the towering stacks of paper, ballpoint pens, and a cracked keyboard on the desk. Murky liquid splashed onto the cluttered surface. "I'm Sergeant Wells. I thought you might like some coffee. I hope you don't mind it black; we're out of creamer. I haven't been able to shame anyone into going to the store."

Compared to Deputy Stoneface, Sergeant Wells was a regular chatterbox.

"Black is fine, Sergeant. Thank you." She reached for a chipped white ceramic mug with "I heart Cannon Beach" on it in red letters, and took a sip. The bitter liquid tasted like diesel fuel and burned her tongue.

She wished she was back in Paris, sitting at a sidewalk café on St. Germaine in the morning sun, reading the International Herald Tribune, sipping café au lait, a warm baguette dripping butter on the small table in front of her. Now *that* was coffee.

The sergeant spoke and Paris vanished. "I'm sorry about your father," he began, dropping into his chair and raking the hair from his eyes with ink-stained fingers. "I hope he recovers soon."

Tara nodded her thanks.

"I need to ask you a few questions," he continued. He shifted and his chair creaked, the sound echoing through the empty office.

Questions. Where should she begin? Years of running, after she escaped. Years colored by guilt. Then finally, the promise of a new start. The chance to heal her wounds, to find what she'd been seeking for so long. It was just within her reach. Or had been, until tonight.

"I told the investigator everything I know," she said.

He balanced his half-empty mug on the corner of the desk. "I understand and I'm sorry, but I really need you to go over it again."

She sighed and once again related the details leading to finding her father and the woman on the living room floor. Sergeant Wells scratched notes on a yellow legal pad he pulled from one of the stacks.

"Who could have done this?" Tara asked him when she was finished.

He kept his eyes on the legal pad. "The evidence suggests that your father was responsible."

"My father? You think my *father* did this?" Tara stared at him. "My father can't kill the moles that eat his garden every summer; there's no way he could kill a person. Besides, he obviously didn't put himself into a coma. That's ridiculous."

"I can't go into the details at this point," Sergeant Wells said, finally meeting her eyes. "I'll give you more information when I can. But until we find evidence to the contrary, he's our only suspect. And will be charged with murder as soon as he regains consciousness."

"But…" She wanted to defend her father, to tell the sergeant he was crazy. But she was too tired to be coherent. It probably wouldn't help, anyway. She closed her eyes and dropped her head into her hands.

Sergeant Wells shifted in his chair and it creaked again. "I need your help with one more task."

"Now what?" Tara had lost her manners somewhere in the long night.

"I need you to identify the woman," he said.

"The woman? Why? I don't know any of my father's friends."

"She wasn't his friend, Tara." His use of her first name was jarring, and she looked up. "She was your aunt."

&

"My aunt?" Tara said. "I don't have an aunt."

"Her driver's license identified her as Deirdre McCarthy, who we believe is your mother's sister." He chewed on his pen, leaving a green mark on his lower lip.

"Deirdre? Are you sure?" Tara frowned. "She disappeared years ago. We thought she was dead." He didn't need to know the part Deirdre had played in Tara's life.

"Apparently not." He raked the hair from his eyes again, a little more impatiently. "Anyway, you're her closest relative. I don't mean to be insensitive, but it's late. They're waiting at the morgue." He reached for the phone.

"Please, could you give me a minute?" she asked, and he released the receiver and leaned back in his chair.

Tara rose and paced around the silent office, its regular occupants at home with their families this late at night. She stopped at a window and pressed her nose against the cold glass, staring at the empty parking lot below as it glistened in the yellow glow of the streetlights.

Deidre, alive after all. All this time…

Her mother didn't talk much about her sister. When she did, her words were laced with anger. Tara would never be angry with her sister, if she had one.

Deirdre gone. Her father slipping away. Tara's stomach began to churn as the loneliness threatened to engulf her.

No. She couldn't fall apart now. She'd think about it later. Burying her emotions, she returned to the wounded chair. "I've only seen pictures of her as a teenager," she said. "But I'll try."

He nodded and reached for the telephone again. Tara leaned back in the chair and finished the lukewarm coffee in one acrid gulp.

&

The morgue technician had to have a bottle of tequila hidden in his office; Tara couldn't imagine doing this job sober. Bearing the weight of people's grief as they saw their loved ones for the last time, naked on a plastic tray, stripped of all dignity. The families could probably use a shot themselves.

You couldn't tell day from night in the viewing room. There were no windows, just a small television monitor and a camera bolted to the wall. Muzak droned from hidden speakers and a chemical smell that Tara hoped was disinfectant hung in the air.

Plastic flowers balanced on a plastic table and a faded Thomas Kinkade print hung on a scarred wall. Everything needed dusting.

The monitor flickered and a dark-haired man waddled into view. He approached a wall of what looked like filing cabinets, but Tara knew better. She took a steadying breath. She saw a body once, but it was years ago. And at the time, she didn't know that she was dead.

"Are you ready, Ms. Davies?" the technician asked, his voice tinny through the speakers. Tara nodded. He wiped his forehead on the sleeve of his lab coat, pulled open a drawer, and unzipped the bag that held the woman who fueled Tara's fantasies.

She had never met her aunt; Deirdre disappeared shortly after Tara was born. Good riddance, Mary said, although Tara believed that Deirdre's leaving hurt her mother far more than she would admit. Mary said her sister was a jetsetter, living a carefree life, traveling the world while she stayed behind and bore the burden of maintaining a family and a home. But after years passed with no word from her, Mary declared that Deirdre was dead. So to find that she had been alive after all, and living in Surfside, was overwhelming. To lose her so horribly, without ever getting to meet her, was even worse.

As a child, Tara prayed that her long-lost aunt would someday reappear and save her from the nightmare that was her life. Deirdre would fling open the door of Tara's silent home, wrap her in a mink jacket, and bundle her into the sleek black limo waiting to whisk them to the airport. A private jet would be preparing to take off, and as soon as they settled into the sumptuous leather seats the plane would soar into the azure sky, leaving her parents far behind. Then they'd realize what they had done. Then they'd be sorry.

Even as she traveled the world as an adult, Tara watched for a tall redhead with emerald eyes and a dimple swinging through Gatwick Airport, or feeding pigeons in St. Mark's Square. She dreamed Deirdre would call and they'd meet in Rome… Bangkok...Barcelona. Although she knew Deirdre probably wouldn't be meeting her anywhere, she still clung to the fantasy. Sometimes fantasies were all Tara had.

Once, when her mother went into town to run errands — buy vodka, in other words — Tara snuck into her room and found a box of black and white photographs hidden under the bed. Toasting the anonymous photographer with sweating bottles of beer, the bikini-clad sisters looked fresh and young, untroubled by the burdens that life would soon force upon them. They could have been twins except for their hairstyles: Deirdre wore long tresses, while Mary kept hers short. And Deirdre's dimple, which gave her an impish air that her solemn sister could never hope to match. Tara barely recognized her mother without the scowl that alcohol and disappointment had since carved into her countenance. She slid the box back into its hiding place, and wondered how life had turned the carefree teens into disillusioned adults.

Tara took a deep breath and fiddled with an object suspended from a thin gold chain around her neck as she forced herself to look at the woman in the monitor. There were bruises on her neck and an angry red mark on her temple, but her face was unmarred. Tara wondered how she died, but quickly dismissed the thought; this wasn't the time or place to think about that.

She could see the resemblance to her mother. Same long thin nose, same high forehead, same slanted eyes, thankfully closed. Although Deirdre's red hair was streaked with gray; Tara made sure Mary's was dyed regularly.

"Is…is there a dimple…in her left cheek?" she stuttered, and the technician looked down at the figure and nodded.

He needed no further confirmation when Tara dropped her head into her hands, and he started to zip the bag back over Deirdre's face.

"Excuse me," Tara said. He paused and glanced at the camera. "Do you think I could…could come in and…maybe…?" She hesitantly extended her fingers toward the monitor.

The technician looked at the clock over his head; it was well after midnight. Then he nodded once and pointed at a door behind him. Tara hurried out of the viewing room and down the hallway, the sound of her steps echoing off the silent walls. She peered through the small window as she tapped on the door, and he opened it. The room was freezing, and she wondered why the man was sweating so profusely. Hangover, perhaps? Too many cheeseburgers, more likely.

"I'm not supposed to do this," he said, "but no one's here but me. Just make it quick, okay?"

"I really appreciate it. It'll only take a second."

Tara moved to the body lying inside the drawer. She tentatively brushed a stray curl from her aunt's face and recoiled when she touched the icy skin, even though she knew it would be cold. Then she reached out again and softly stroked the pale cheek. Tears slid down her face like raindrops on a windowpane.

"I'm sorry, Deirdre," she said. "I'm so, so sorry."

The technician cleared his throat and Tara looked up at the clock. How had fifteen minutes passed? She nodded at him, and took one last look at her aunt.

He zipped the bag over Deirdre's face and slid the drawer back into the wall. Tara watched her aunt disappear, and felt another door of her life slam shut.

~ 4 ~

Safely back in Merrow Bay, Tara didn't seek the shelter of her cozy cottage, in spite of the late hour and the cold December winds. Instead, she wrapped an old patchwork quilt around her shoulders, collapsed into a wicker chair on the front porch, and watched the stars emerge one by one through the storm clouds lingering in the indigo sky. She wished it were spring instead of winter; she missed the heady scent of lilacs drifting through the yard.

There were too many thoughts careening through her head to focus on any one. Deirdre alive, and now dead. Deirdre and her father together, in Surfside. And worst of all, her father comatose in a hospital in Portland, charged with Deirdre's murder.

Ethan had always been there for Tara, when she was a child. Although Mary and her needs consumed most of her father's attention, he still found time to attend her school plays, buy her bell-bottom jeans and platform shoes, and read her Winnie the Pooh stories at bedtime.

But over the years, as Mary worsened, they lost sight of each other. Her mother's disease became his. When his need to maintain the illusion of normalcy became more important than his need to nurture his daughter, Tara ran, seeking stability, survival. Seeking escape.

She spent years traveling the world, never staying in one place for very long. Never really sure what she was looking for, or running from. And never returning to Oregon. In her case, absence didn't make the heart grow fonder.

Then, a year ago, Mary left. Once he adjusted to his wife's absence, Ethan bloomed, discovering talents and passions he never had time to pursue while caring for her. He went fishing with friends. He carved a lush garden out of the damp Portland soil, each bed carefully laid out in geometric patterns. He designed intricate birdhouses, working up detailed blueprints for the tiny structures. And he and Tara slowly began to rebuild their relationship. She moved back to Oregon, to Merrow Bay, to be closer to him. But not too close.

After years of loneliness, Tara allowed herself to hope. To believe they could find safe ground with each other, in spite of their rocky past. That he would forgive her, and they could finally be a family again.

But now those fragile dreams were in danger of dying, as her father fought for his life.

Without his forgiveness, Tara had nothing.

&

Dawn approached, the sun gradually peeking over the slate gray roofs of Merrow Bay. The sky shifted from indigo to fuchsia to a violent purple. Tara rose from her chair and stretched, bones chilled and back aching from the long, cold night. It was time.

She faced the rising sun, closed her eyes, and grasped her necklace.

Good morning, Emma. I'm sorry you aren't here to see this beautiful day. I'll try to make you proud of me today.

Opening her eyes, she released the necklace and opened the door to her cottage, wondering how to start rebuilding her shattered life.

&

The hardwood floors creaked as Tara paced. She had spent the last two days at the hospital, sitting with her father in half-hour increments. A few of his friends sent flowers and cards, but otherwise were noticeably absent. Tara wasn't sure if that was due to the restricted visiting hours of the ICU or the circumstances under which he was there. The story was front-page news in Surfside; in Portland, it had been relegated to page six, below a story about two boys rescuing a pig from an icy pond.

Eventually, the nursing staff convinced her to go home and rest. She would be spending enough time with him over the coming weeks — maybe months — and should probably take breaks while he was still unconscious.

If Ethan remained in this state for very long, she would need to pay his bills, maintain his house, etc. And would need legal permission to do so, which meant having power of attorney.

She needed to get into his house to find his attorney's name, and see if such a document existed. Not to mention discussing the legal defense he'd need, once he woke.

But she didn't have a key. And although she had grown up there, Tara didn't feel comfortable in his house. There were too many memories she didn't want to revisit. A woman named Marge cleaned it every two weeks, but Tara didn't know how to contact her.

Now what? Her shaky world lay in pieces at her feet. If — when — Ethan recovered, there could be permanent physical and mental damage. He faced a lifetime in prison for a crime he didn't commit. And she couldn't do anything about it.

Tara saw her life being consumed with too many details, responsibilities, and tasks. She looked around her tiny cottage and felt its safety evaporating.

As always, when her world threatened to crash around her, she sought solace in the one world she *could* control, where no one judged her. The one place she could find peace. She opened the door to her office and entered another life.

In this case, the life of Bessie and Arthur Morgan.

&

Her cell phone rang. Tara looked up from the worktable and checked the display. It was a Surfside number. She suddenly was very popular in Surfside.

"Miss Davies?" A stranger. She didn't give her number to strangers.

"Yes?"

"This is Wilson Edison. I am — was — Deirdre McCarthy's attorney."

"Deirdre had an attorney in *Surfside*?"

Mr. Edison chuckled. "Believe it or not, there are a few of us practicing law out here on the wild frontier."

"I'm sorry," Tara said. "I didn't mean to imply that... "

"I'm sure you didn't," he interrupted. "I'm teasing you, my dear. Many people don't realize that we have many of the same amenities in Surfside that the larger cities offer."

"I'm sure you do. What I meant was, I'm surprised Deirdre has an attorney in Oregon instead of closer to her home."

"This *was* her home. At least it was recently. But we can discuss that when you come in."

"Come in?" Tara asked.

"Ah, there I go again, getting ahead of myself. Forgive me, my dear. As Ms. McCarthy's attorney, it is my unenviable duty to summon her relations to the reading of her last will and testament."

"Her will?" Tara felt like a parrot, repeating everything he said. "I'm sorry. Why would *I* need to be at the reading of her will?"

"I have a list of people to contact, and your name is on that list."

Tara sighed. Obviously, her life wasn't going to get back to normal any time soon. Whatever 'normal' was. "All right, tell me when and where and I'll do my best to be there."

"Are you familiar with Surfside?"

"No, I'm afraid not. But I hear it's really…nice," she ended lamely. Surfside ranked somewhere below Siberia on the list of places she planned to visit before she died.

Mr. Edison laughed. "Hopefully you will grow to love it as we do." He gave her directions to his office, and they agreed to meet the next morning.

As she returned to her work, she wondered why the lawyer thought she'd love Surfside. There was no reason for her to spend any time there. She felt safe in Merrow Bay, which really wasn't a town at all, so it was an easy place to hide. Surfside would have more people, and thus more chance of being discovered.

Why would she need to attend the reading of Deirdre's will? Maybe she left her a million dollars. Tara laughed. And her imagination took flight, carrying her far from her shaky reality to a world that didn't involve morgues and ruined dreams.

~ 5 ~

Downtown Surfside was dressed up for the holidays. The cobblestone streets glistened in the early morning drizzle, and the Christmas lights hanging in the trees surrounding Lewis and Clark Square sparkled in the gray morning light.

Tara was late. She crept along impatiently in the holiday traffic, circling the square twice before she found a place to park. Her parallel parking skills were nonexistent, but she eventually squeezed her little blue pickup truck into a space, only hitting the curb once and barely nudging the Volkswagen Beetle in front of her. She pulled a baseball cap low across her face and slipped on a pair of sunglasses before getting out of the truck.

The hem of Tara's coat flapped against her legs as she hurried past a bakery oozing the aroma of fresh-baked bread, a women's boutique, and an antique store before she came to the door marked 'Wilson Edison, Esq.' The yellowed shade banged as she closed the glass door, and she found herself in a modest reception area with an empty desk and an antique couch, upholstered in green silk. Lush houseplants, mingled with red and white poinsettias, perched on every surface. Classical music whispered in the background. And a neon-hued sailfish mounted on a varnished wooden plank stretched the length of the far wall.

Tara swore the beady plastic eye followed her as she moved closer to study the colorful fish. For a moment she was back in Mexico, sipping margaritas at a white plastic table shoved into the sand at the water's edge, the music of a mariachi band drifting on the warm breeze. She could almost taste the salt on the rim of the glass and the sharp tang of lime, as the waves tickled her toes.

"Quite a specimen, isn't he?"

She turned as an elderly man entered the room. His neatly combed white hair framed a face whose wrinkles spoke of more smiles than frowns, and his brown eyes sparkled.

"You could say that," she said, Mexico fading. She pulled off her cap and shoved it into her pocket. "I've never seen anything like it. Well, except in pictures. Is it real?"

"Not quite. The colors on the real ones fade with time. It's fiberglass: an exact replica of the one I caught off the coast of Baja California many years ago." He nodded toward his right hand, which was hidden in the pocket of his navy suit coat. "He put up a good fight. Cost me the use of my hand, but I don't begrudge the loss. I took his life in return."

It seemed wasteful to kill such a magnificent creature, but Tara didn't think it was prudent to express that opinion. Especially if the man had lost his hand in the process. Seemed like a high price to pay for a fish, though.

The attorney extended his left hand. "Wilson Edison. I'm very pleased to meet you." His grip was strong, though his hand shook a little. "Come in, come in. Nasty weather we're having this morning. But at least it's not snowing!" He chuckled as he ushered her through a door and into his office.

"Please sit," he urged, motioning toward two wooden chairs in front of an imposing desk. "I apologize for the severity of the seating, but many of my clients are elderly and have difficulty rising from softer, although admittedly more comfortable, chairs."

Tara settled into one of the old-fashioned armchairs and caught a whiff of leather polish. The scent reminded her of her father's office, and she blinked away the tears that fell too easily these days.

"I understand your father was injured at the same time we… lost…Ms. McCarthy. Please let me know if there is anything I can do to help during his recovery."

Tara nodded her thanks. It was hard to keep a secret in a small town. She wondered what else the man knew.

He cleared his throat, and continued. "Ms. McCarthy's funeral will be held at two o'clock this afternoon at Oceanview Cemetery. It's three miles south of town on Route 101, across the highway from Lee's Place. There will be a brief graveside service before the interment."

"But I don't..." She started to say she hated funerals, thought better of it. After all, who liked them? The least she could do was pay her respects.

"Who planned the funeral?" Tara knew the next-of-kin usually was responsible for that painful task.

"Ms. McCarthy took care of everything before she passed."

"She knew she was going to die?" Tara asked.

"We all do, my dear. We just don't know when."

She was silent for a moment, too many questions running through her head to focus on one. Why would Deirdre plan a funeral in Surfside? And when did she make the arrangements? No one had heard from her in over 30 years. It seemed like an unusual coincidence that she arrived in Surfside just in time to die.

"Why would my aunt have an attorney in Surfside, of all places?"

He chuckled. "Believe it or not, there are a few of us practicing law out here on the wild frontier."

"I'm sorry, I didn't mean to imply that..."

"I'm sure you didn't, my dear," he interrupted. "I'm teasing you. Surfside is a small community, so many people don't realize we offer many of the same services larger cities do."

"I'm sure you do. But what I meant was, I'm surprised Deirdre had an attorney in Oregon, instead of one closer to home."

"Surfside was always her home." Mr. Edison removed the Ben Franklin glasses from the top of his head and balanced them on his nose. His right hand remained under the desk. "Now then..."

"Isn't anyone else coming?" Tara asked.

He smiled sadly. "No, my dear."

"She didn't have a husband, or children?"

He toyed with his glasses, not meeting her gaze. "You are the only person who will be present for the reading." Mr. Edison placed the glasses back on his nose and began reading before Tara could ask any more questions.

He ran through the usual boilerplate, where Deirdre swore she was of sound mind and body, over the age of eighteen, and not acting under duress. He flipped to the next page.

"'To my niece, Tara Marie Davies, I leave my home. It is where her mother and I were born and raised, so it's only right that she become the new owner. But it's been neglected for many years and will need to be restored before she can live there comfortably.'"

Tara started to speak, but Mr. Edison held up the index finger of his good hand and continued.

"'I have opened an account in her name at the Surfside branch of Oregon State Bank, with the stipulation that she have no access to it until the necessary repairs are made to the house. And Tara must do all of the work herself.'"

He continued. "She ends with a rather cryptic statement. 'The house will help you find what you seek, but the price can be steep. Be sure you are prepared to pay that price.'" He laid the will on the blotter, removed his glasses, and placed them on the corner of the desk. "You have questions." It was a statement.

"Yes, I do," Tara said. "Let me see if I've got this right. I've inherited an abandoned house in Surfside, but I have to restore it before I can live in it. There's a bank account waiting for me, but I can't use the money to do the repairs. And somehow this house will help me find what I seek, as long as I'm careful what I ask for." Tara looked at the attorney. "Does that sound as strange to you as it does to me?"

He smiled. "I actually hoped you would be able to explain it."

"Not a friggin' clue. Oh, sorry." She blushed.

"Completely understandable. These old ears have heard much worse." He put his glasses back on. "So, my dear, I need your signature on a few documents, and then you may claim your inheritance."

"But I didn't even know her!" Tara burst out. "Why did she leave me her house?"

"I'm afraid I can't answer that question," he said, smiling. "Maybe the house can."

"I'm beginning to wonder about the sound mind part," Tara said.

&

She had inherited a house. An old, abandoned house. Tara didn't know anything about repairing houses.

And what did the last line mean, find what she was seeking? Deirdre didn't know anything about Tara or what she might be looking for.

She needed answers, but there wasn't anybody to ask. Stopped at a traffic light, Tara rested her head on the steering wheel and asked the gods why they had added yet another burden to her already-full plate.

A blast from a horn behind her made her jump. She slammed the truck into gear and continued through town.

The last thing she wanted was to own a house, let alone restore one. Even if it had been in her family for generations. Her handyman skills were limited to replacing burnt-out light bulbs, and she usually broke those.

Her year in Merrow Bay was an aberration. After college, Tara moved regularly, always seeking something, if only anonymity. Owning a house was limiting, confining. Too much responsibility. Yet one more thing at which she would fail. Heck, she couldn't take care of a house. She couldn't even take care of herself — or those she loved.

No, she decided, toying with her necklace, no house. Not now. Probably not ever.

But as she reached for her phone to call Mr. Edison and tell him that she didn't want it, something stopped her. It was a strange sensation — a need to see the house, as soon as possible.

Well, she could at least look at it before rejecting it, out of respect for Deirdre, if nothing else. What could it hurt?

She could always sell it. She might have to, to pay the inheritance taxes. While her business covered her expenses, it certainly couldn't pay for a house she didn't even want.

Tara pulled to the side of the road and opened the envelope Mr. Edison had given her. As she withdrew her copy of the will, she sliced her finger on the flap and blood oozed from the cut.

Sucking her finger and grimacing at the metal taste, she scanned the pages for the address. Seven Chinook Road. She would drive out before the funeral and take a quick look at it, and then call the attorney. It couldn't be that hard to find.

&

Tara Davies stared at the 'Road Closed' sign and sighed, wondering when the gods were going to give her a break.

The windshield wipers squeaked in time to the song murmuring on the radio. Maybe trying to find the house before the funeral wasn't such a good idea after all. But the strange sensation that started when she left the attorney's office that morning — the need to see the house as soon as possible — wouldn't stop. It was as if the house were calling to her, demanding her attention.

Which was, of course, crazy.

Maybe if she took a quick look at the place, the sensation would go away. But after an hour of wrong turns and backtracking, she was out of both patience and time. Calling hours at the funeral home began in twenty minutes and not only did she not know where Chinook Road was, now she didn't even know where *she* was.

The story of her life. Always choosing the wrong road. Just like decisions. If there was a wrong one to be made, Tara made it. Jobs, apartments, lovers. She was always apologizing to someone — even if it was just to herself — for her lousy choices.

Enough whining. She wasn't going to find the house, or the cemetery, by sitting at the end of this dirt road. Tara shifted her little blue pickup truck into gear and started driving again.

And in a few moments, she found a paved road with a yellow line, which eventually led to a bigger paved road with a bigger yellow line. And finally, on her left, a sign.

Chinook Road. She shook her head and turned onto the road. How did she miss it before?

The first mailbox she passed said 'Nine.' And the next, 'Eleven.' So she turned around and continued down the road until she saw the mailbox with 'Seven' on it in white reflective letters, perched on a rotting wooden post at the foot of a gravel road that disappeared into the silent forest. A length of shiny chain lay coiled in a pile next to the post; Tara wondered if it was supposed to be blocking the driveway and if so, who had moved it.

She stopped in front of the mailbox. The sensation was getting stronger. She was almost being pulled up the hill.

But as she turned the truck into the driveway, a loud *beep* startled her.

Tara stared at her watch, Winnie the Pooh frolicking across the dial, and jabbed at the button to turn off the alarm. Then she looked up again to study the driveway through the rain-spattered windshield.

It wouldn't take long. She'd miss calling hours, but she'd be there for the funeral. Then again, what did it matter if she missed the whole thing? It's not like she knew her.

Then her conscience kicked in.

Of course she couldn't skip the funeral. What would her father think? Especially if she were the only person there. And it would be embarrassing, not to mention rude, to show up late.

She had no choice. She needed to be there. For Deirdre's sake. The house would have to wait.

Damn.

Tara sighed and looked at the directions scribbled on the back of a Taco Heaven receipt. *Oceanview Cemetery, south of town, across from Lee's Place.* Then she slowly pulled back onto the highway and, with a final glance over her shoulder at the driveway, headed south.

~ 6 ~

Lee's Place wasn't south.

Tara came to the colorful "Welcome to the Village of Cannon Beach" sign and realized she had gone the wrong way. Again.

She swung her truck into an illegal U-turn, barely missing a rusty sedan that blasted its horn as it zoomed past, and sped north, one eye on the clock and the other on the road.

Tara saw the simple *Lee's Place* sign at the same time she saw the cemetery. Breathing a sigh of relief, she swung into the tree-lined lane, cutting the turn a little too wide and narrowly missing an ancient oak. She parked behind a white hearse, and hurried across the damp carpet of decaying leaves toward a small brick building perched at the edge of the graveyard.

She pulled open the heavy wooden door and found herself in a musty foyer, with doors on either side. A guest book rested on a metal stand by the door on the left; a nametag with "Deirdre McCarthy" written in calligraphy was taped to the top of the stand. The pages of the book were blank. Tara signed her name in a shaky scrawl, and slowly opened the door.

The room was empty except for a simple mahogany casket, surrounded by lush arrangements of white roses and blood red carnations. She walked past the bare wooden pews and approached the open casket. The scent of the flowers was almost suffocating in the small room, and she wondered who had sent them.

Taking a steadying breath, Tara stepped to the casket and looked at Deirdre for the last time. Tears slid unnoticed down her cheeks and onto the white silk lining of the casket as she gazed at her aunt. She couldn't see any bruises or abrasions; the undertaker had done a good job of covering up any evidence of her struggle.

"I'm sorry we didn't know each other, Aunt Deirdre," Tara whispered. "I wish I knew why you left me your house, and what you think I'm searching for. And why you think I'll find it there.

"I'll try to make you proud of me today."

Someone in the back of the room coughed, and Tara looked up. A man in a dark suit stood by the door. "The graveside service will begin in a few moments, ma'am," he said.

"Oh, thank you." She glanced at her watch. How had half an hour passed? She leaned down to kiss her aunt's smooth forehead and whispered, "Goodbye."

Tara glanced over her shoulder as she left the room, and watched the man slowly lower the lid of the casket over Deirdre's face. Suddenly, she couldn't breathe. She almost fell through the front door as she shoved it open and rushed outside. Leaning against the side of the building she gasped, dragging the crisp winter air into her lungs, waiting for the panic to subside.

Once her heartbeat slowed, she walked to the gravesite and stood under the blue canopy next to Mr. Edison. She nodded at the gray-haired priest standing silently at the head of the grave; she could smell the freshly turned earth. Cold raindrops trickled down the neck of her wool coat, and she wished she hadn't left her cap in the truck; she hadn't thought she'd need it here. The casket was already in place over the gaping hole.

A man stood next to the priest, staring at the casket. A well-loved leather jacket shielded his broad shoulders and chest. He wore a trim goatee and mustache, and damp blond curls tumbled from beneath the brim of his cap. Wraparound sunglasses masked his face, even though the sun wasn't shining. Tara wondered what he was trying to hide behind those glasses, and then caught herself. Why was she being so suspicious? Maybe he was hiding his tears.

He looked up at her, and she thought she saw him flinch. After acknowledging her with a nod, he lowered his eyes and continued staring at the casket.

The service was brief, which was fine with Tara; the drizzle had turned into a steady rain, and her fingers and toes were numb. After the final prayer, the priest invited the mourners to place a white rose on the casket, which would be lowered into the grave after they left.

Mr. Edison gently laid his rose on the polished wood and patted the casket before returning to stand beside Tara. The stranger stood for a long moment gripping his rose, then threw it on the ground and strode away.

Tara pricked her thumb on a thorn as she accepted the rose from the priest; a drop of scarlet blood welled unnoticed. A lifetime of dreams lay in the simple box before her: the mysterious woman who had fueled Tara's fantasies, whose exotic life gave Tara hope that someday she would escape her troubled childhood and begin life again, somewhere else. But she never knew the woman. And now, never would.

"I'm sorry, Deirdre," she said. "I'm so, so sorry."

She slipped a few delicate petals into her pocket, not noticing the blood smeared on them, and lifted the rose to her nose. After breathing its sweet scent for a long moment, she carefully slid it into one of the arrangements, making sure it blended perfectly with the other blooms. Tara stood with her head bowed, stroking an object suspended from a thin gold chain around her neck and listening to the tap of the rain on the canopy. And felt another door of her life slam shut.

She didn't notice the man in the leather jacket standing in the distance, watching her.

&

Tara turned up the heater to thaw her frozen fingers and toes, and pulled out of the cemetery parking lot, wiping her eyes. The damned house was still calling her; it was almost screaming. She might as well see it before she headed back to the hospital. Maybe then it would leave her alone and she could get back to her normal life. Or at least what passed for normal these days.

Once again she headed south, toward Seven Chinook Road.

&

Tara sat at the foot of the driveway and studied the winding road, more mud than dirt, as the rain pounded the ground around her. Something about it was familiar — and not because she had been here earlier that day.

She shrugged, shifted her truck into gear, and held her breath as she drove up the steep incline, half-expecting whoever had moved the chain to leap out of the woods and stop her. But she crested the hill without anyone accosting her, and laughed at herself as she emerged from the dense forest into a clearing.

In front of her was a house. A house with a garage, a flagstone path, and a wraparound porch. There were also Styrofoam cups, sterile gauze packets and soggy cigarette butts scattered on the ground, a small scrap of yellow crime scene tape knotted around one of the porch columns, and a Ford Explorer parked in front of the garage.

Her father's Ford Explorer.

Tara hit the brakes. No wonder the place looked familiar.

She sat in the truck and stared at the house. Why hadn't she recognized it sooner? Even though it had been nighttime, she should have remembered the roads she took to get here, or at least the green reflectors on the post. Hell, even the driveway. She must have pretty been distracted not to remember any of it.

She shuddered at the thought of entering the house. How could she, after what happened? If she closed her eyes, she could still picture Ethan and Deidre lying on the living room floor.

As for actually living here…well, she couldn't even begin to imagine how she could do that.

She shook her head. *Get a grip, Davies.* The house didn't attack her aunt and father. It would be stupid to refuse to live in a house because something awful happened in it. She had overcome worse things in her life.

Then there was the strange calling sensation. Maybe if she walked through the house, it would go away.

And someone needed to clean up the mess the sheriff's department had left.

She turned off the engine and studied the house as gusts of wind swept through the trees around the clearing, tossing the naked branches. It had gray weathered clapboard siding and a gingerbread-trimmed porch that cried for a swing. A dark green metal roof shielded the house from the elements. Two bay windows gazed across the dormant lawn and empty flowerbeds. Emerald shutters hung askew from the windows in the second story dormers, where panes of leaded glass reflected the weak afternoon light. Surprisingly, the glass was still intact.

Unlike most empty houses, this one didn't feel abandoned. Instead, it seemed to be waiting. Watching. Biding its time until someone returned to care for it.

A clang made Tara jump. She saw a brass bell hanging by the front door, banging in the wind, and she giggled nervously.

Checking her watch in the fading light, she was surprised to see that an hour had passed. She still needed to see the inside; she hadn't been in any condition to notice specifics the last time she was here. She would dash in and look around, and then head home and be done with it.

She would, that is, if she had a key.

Damn! She didn't have a way to get into the house. Why hadn't she gotten a key from Mr. Edison?

Oh well, at least she could look through the windows. Tara dashed through the rain up the flagstone path and climbed to the porch, hopping over the hole in the third step. She tried the doorknob in case the police had left it unlocked. They hadn't.

Wet hair plastered to her forehead, she peeked through the bay window on the left and saw the living room and the kitchen behind it. She could see the dining room through the other bay window, and the study behind it.

As she stood on the porch, the cold wind tugging at her coat, the strange sensation changed. Now it felt as though the house was whispering to her, asking her to live there, to repair it, to care for it. Or was it saying that it would care for her?

Ridiculous. Houses didn't talk to people. She was tired, and her imagination was working overtime. She obviously needed to get some perspective. And some sleep.

As she ran back to her truck, Tara decided she would call Mr. Edison in the morning and arrange to pick up a key. Then she could come back and explore the house. There must be at least two, if not three, bedrooms upstairs, and who knew what was in the basement, if there was one. She could set up her office in the study; working from home had its benefits. Maybe there were built-in bookshelves; Tara loved built-in bookshelves. She always wanted to collect books, but they were too heavy to move. Shelves rising to the ceiling, full of...

Wait a minute. Tara stopped fastening her seat belt. She was acting like she was going to actually keep the house. *Ridiculous*. She shook her head and headed down the hill.

Driving into town, she reminded herself of the many reasons she didn't want to own a house. The responsibility, the work, the expense. Home ownership would get in the way of her traveling. Make her accountable. She would have to buy stuff, and stuff tied you down. She didn't want to be tied to anything or anyone; she couldn't be trusted to take care of those ties. Her history of disappointing people spoke for itself.

And there was the small detail of Deirdre dying in the house. She still didn't know how she'd deal with that.

Her aunt said Tara would find something here — something she'd been searching for. Even Tara wasn't sure what she was searching for; what drove her to travel, never staying in one place very long. She blamed her constant moving on needing to escape her reputation, having to leave every time someone figured out who she was. Although she knew that wasn't the only thing that kept her on the road.

But how did Deirdre know she'd been searching? Obviously, her aunt hadn't followed Tara as she bounced from shoddy apartment to shoddier house, boxes and bags filled with memories and regrets.

Tara didn't know what she could possibly find in an abandoned house in Surfside, Oregon that she couldn't find anywhere else in the world.

Stomach grumbling, she pulled into the parking lot of Taco Heaven and waited for a break in the storm before she dashed into the restaurant. The smell of refried beans and deep-fried potatoes made her mouth water.

Maybe she could stay for a month or two, she thought as she munched on a taco. Fix up the house, then sell it and move on. She'd have cash in her pocket and a clear conscience, knowing she had fulfilled Deirdre's last wish.

Maybe she'd find that she liked having roots, as long as they were shallow ones. She'd establish a routine, walk on the beach, find a local market for her work. Stop looking over her shoulder, waiting for her past to catch up with her.

Maybe this was her chance to succeed at something, after a lifetime of failure. She felt for her necklace. Maybe Emma would be proud of her for making the right choice for a change, instead of the easy one.

Maybe she was just losing her mind.

Tara adjusted the chain around her neck. "Go home," she told herself. "Go back to Merrow Bay. Tomorrow, pick up the key. Look at the place. Then decide." She was too tired to think any more. She was certainly too tired to drive to Portland. She was wet and cold, and wanted to snuggle under her warm quilt in her warm bed with a good book. And later, escape into a dream world where there were no lies, tears, or death. Where no one was to blame.

~ 7 ~

"Hello." The greeting sounded like an afterthought.

"Hello? Is this Mr. Edison's office?" Tara asked, resting the phone between her ear and shoulder.

"Sure is!" the woman replied.

"Is Mr. Edison available?"

"Sure ain't!"

Silence.

May the gods give her strength, Tara thought. "Um, will he back soon? This is Tara Davies, and…"

"Sorry, honey," the woman said, "it's not my week to watch him." She cackled, and Tara wondered why Mr. Edison let this woman answer his phone.

Tara tried again. "I need a key for a house I inherited, and I was hoping Mr. Edison had one."

"A key? He's not a locksmith, honey." And cackled again.

Enough. "Never mind. I'll try him again tomorrow."

"Don't bother. He won't be here then, either. He's gone to the Bahamas for a week. Or is it two? Deep-sea fishing. Thaw out those ancient bones of his."

"Two weeks?" Tara's heart dropped. "I can't wait that long. Isn't there anyone else who can help me find a key?"

"Not a soul. Did you look under the doormat?" It sounded like she was eating potato chips; Tara imagined greasy fingerprints on the woman's telephone, and could almost smell barbecue sauce.

"You're a big help. I'll look there. Thanks." She didn't add, "for nothing."

"You got it, sweetcheeks." And the line went dead.

Tara stared at the phone. Mr. Edison went on vacation and left his business in the hands of a crazy lady who chewed with her mouth open. A crazy lady who didn't have a key to the house.

Now how was she supposed to get in?

&

There wasn't a doormat. Not that Tara expected to find one, especially with a key tucked underneath it, but that would have made things a lot easier.

She searched the usual places people hid keys: under a paving stone, on top of the doorframe, in a fake rock in the sleeping garden. Even inside the brass bell. Nothing. The garage was locked, so she couldn't look for a key hanging on a nail. She jiggled every door handle. Tried to pry open every window. No luck.

She really didn't want to break into the house, even if she did own the place. It felt…wrong. But unless she wanted to wait until Mr. Edison came back, breaking in was her only option. And the calling sensation was becoming unbearable; she didn't think the house would wait much longer.

Brushing the dirt off her hands, she studied the back door. It was made of solid steel, with a glass insert divided into small panes. People in the movies broke windows all the time; how hard could it be?

She selected a fist-sized rock from the flowerbed and, with a silent apology to Deirdre and a promise to fix the window, threw the rock at the pane closest to the door handle. It bounced off the frame, narrowly missing her. She tried again, and this time the rock bounced back and hit her in the arm.

"Ouch!" That would leave a bruise. Maybe this wasn't going to be as easy as she thought.

Her arm throbbing, Tara grabbed the rock again, and smashed it against the window. The glass shattered, littering the stoop with sharp fragments. She tossed the rock back into the yard and carefully reached through the broken window to unlock the deadbolt.

Something in the woods screeched, and she flinched. And a shard of glass attached to the frame jabbed deep into her wrist.

"Ow!" she said. "Damn it!" Blood streamed warm down her arm, tracing a trail of scarlet drops down the leg of her jeans. She grabbed her wrist, putting pressure on the cut to staunch the flow, and stumbled around the front of the house to her truck.

A plastic bag filled with clothes destined for the women's shelter was stuffed behind the seat. Tara pulled out a T-shirt and wrapped the bright yellow cloth around her wounded wrist. Feeling light-headed, she wobbled to the porch and sat on the steps in the winter sunshine, her head between her knees.

After a few moments, she peeled the shirt away from the cut. The gash was small, but deep. And still bleeding.

She needed a first aid kit. Or a kindly neighbor. But she didn't have either: the house was tucked deep in the woods, with no other homes in sight. There was no reason to look in her father's SUV for a bandage; she nagged him to carry emergency supplies, but he just laughed.

There might be a first aid kit in the house, although she doubted forty-year old bandages would still be any good. But she might as well try. Tara circled around to the back of the house, carefully reached through the broken window with her good hand, and unlocked the door. It swung open easily, as though someone had recently oiled the hinges, and she stepped into the laundry room, where she caught a whiff of something salty, like a fresh sea breeze.

Maybe the wind was blowing from the west. Although she hadn't smelled it outside. And the house should be musty and airless, after being closed for so long. It shouldn't make her think of barquentines and beaches.

Her wrist throbbed, and she forgot about the ocean breeze and started opening cabinets. But they were empty; much emptier than they should be. No dead bugs, dead rodents, or dead dust bunnies.

Then she noticed the clothes folded on the dryer. Jeans, blouses, lacy underwear.

That didn't make any sense. Her wrist throbbed again, reminding her that she really needed to find a bandage. So she continued into the kitchen, where red tile floors and golden oak cabinets gave the room a warm, cozy feel. A brick fireplace reminded Tara of the early settlers cooking their meals over stone hearths. Which they would have eaten at the scarred maple table in the center of the room, sitting on the eight ladderback chairs gathered around it. In contrast to the old furniture, the matte black appliances looked modern, almost new. She opened each cabinet, the doors creaking, but found only canned goods and a few dishes.

The worn pine floors creaked as Tara walked from the kitchen into the hallway. The aged plaster walls could use a coat of paint, and a wrought iron chandelier with a lone bulb dangled at the foot of the curved staircase. She noticed something unusual about the banister, but didn't take time to study it as she climbed the stairs, noting that one of the steps gave a little when she stepped on it.

Upstairs were two smaller bedrooms, one decorated in green and the other in pink, and a guest bathroom. She checked the bathroom for first aid supplies, but found nothing.

A bright red stain continued to ooze through the yellow shirt. She hoped she hadn't severed an artery or anything like that.

At the end of the hallway was the master suite. Tara hurried through the bedroom furnished with solid mahogany pieces — the queen-sized bed facing the floor-length windows, the mirrored bureau pushed against the wall, the massive chest of drawers centered between the windows — and into the master bath. She studied the blue and white tile walls, and the claw-foot tub nestled below an expansive window. Tara imagined soaking in the tub, chin-deep in steaming water and lavender bubbles, gazing up at the full moon or into the dark forest below.

Her head swam. *Focus, Davies, focus.* Once again, she checked the drawers and cabinets. And finally, success. A white plastic box with a red cross on the lid held bandages, antiseptic, butterfly closures, and a roll of medical tape. Everything she needed to patch her wounded wrist. All relatively new.

There were other things in the bathroom that she didn't need. Like makeup, a toothbrush, perfume, and a hair dryer.

Mr. Edison didn't mention that anyone was living here. Then she remembered his words: *Surfside was always her home.* She thought he meant it figuratively, since Deirdre grew up there. But maybe he meant it literally. Maybe all those years that Tara thought Deidre was traveling the world, she was actually living in Surfside. Although considering the condition of the house, she hadn't lived there in a long time.

Tara didn't know why Deirdre had been in Surfside. She thought it was just a coincidence; she was passing through, or arranged to meet Ethan here for some reason — maybe to discuss renovating the house. But now she realized that Deirdre actually was *living* here.

Her eyes filled with tears. It was hard enough being in her aunt's house; knowing she had actually been living here made the pain of losing her that much more acute. Then again, that knowledge might bring Tara some comfort in the coming days, if she decided to live here herself.

Once she bandaged her wrist, Tara returned to the master bedroom. A few items hung in the closet: dresses in bright reds and yellows, silky shirts, an old wool coat. Tara ran her fingers through the clothing, thinking about the woman who had worn it. The perfume on the bureau was exotic, musky and unfamiliar; she sprayed a small amount onto a tissue and breathed the rich scent, then slipped it into her pocket. Strands of red hair were tangled in the bristles of a silver-backed hairbrush. Silver bangle bracelets. A pair of earrings, hammered silver and turquoise, suggesting a southwestern origin: maybe New Mexico, maybe Central America.

And another set of earrings that was strangely out of place among Deirdre's silver. They were ornate, crafted from what looked like antique gold, studded with rubies and emeralds. Probably costume jewelry; Tara wondered what the story was behind them. She slipped the hooks into her pierced ears and studied her reflection in the mirror. They were heavier than she thought they'd be, but she liked how the jewels shimmered in the afternoon light.

She laid the earrings on the bureau and walked back down the hallway. The pink and green bedrooms were simply furnished with four-poster beds, graceful nightstands and mirrored bureaus. Sunlight streamed through the windows, making the rooms feel warm and cozy.

Downstairs, Tara knelt to take a closer look at the staircase banister. The handrail and balustrades were simple, fashioned from polished oak. But the main support post was far from simple. It was an intricate carving of a woman — or at least part of one. She had a full mane of long curly hair that flowed back from her face, as if blown by the wind. Her features were strong yet wistful, her chin uplifted, her eyes gazing into the distance.

Her slender neck stretched down to her full breasts, hands clasped over them as if in prayer. But her body ended below her breasts in a jagged line, which had been smoothed to fit into the stair tread below.

The carving was old, much older than the rest of the banister. Probably older than the house, for that matter. Stepping back, Tara studied it, and realized it was the figurehead of a ship. She ran her fingers across the rough wood fibers, swollen from years of exposure to salt water. Traces of color remained, like the woman's emerald eyes and the deep blue shawl draped over her shoulders. What a sight she must have been, proudly gracing the bow of a ship.

"Where did you come from, my lady?" Tara whispered, tracing the carved features with a single finger. "What are you looking at? And how did you end up here?" She imagined the places the figurehead had been, and the adventures had by those who sailed with her. Then she noticed something in her hands. Although age had dulled the edges, it looked like a comb and mirror. An image flashed across her mind: a woman perched on a rock, running a comb through her long tresses.

A mermaid?

Could the missing section of the figure's body be a tail?

Her great-great-whatever grandfather must have had a connection with the sea, to include a piece like this in a house perched on a rocky hill. But where did she come from?

Tara put the question aside to think about later. Fighting her uneasiness, she continued into the living room, quickly walking past the place where she found her father and aunt. She had already seen the fireplace, nestled in a hearth of river rock with a chimney that soared to the tongue-in-groove pine ceiling. The crown molding around the edges of the room echoed the Victorian theme of the rest of the house.

A bench seat nestled beneath the bay window, facing the clearing and the dark woods beyond. An upholstered sofa and matching chairs clustered around the fireplace, with fragile-looking tables scattered around the room and a threadbare Persian rug spread on the floor. The wallpaper was faded, but she could still make out the lacy leaf pattern.

She walked across the hallway and into the dining room, where she found the same well-worn pine flooring and another bay window with a bench seat, this one with a tattered green velvet cushion. Wrought iron sconces on the walls matched the light fixtures at the foot of the staircase and in the living room. A cherry dining table with matching chairs waited patiently for an elegant dinner. Wallpaper the same as that in the living room, although in navy instead of burgundy.

Behind this room was a cozy study, paneled in mahogany with French doors that looked over the expansive side lawn. A leather couch stretched the length of the room, with a solid oak desk and swivel armchair facing the window. Bookshelves towered from floor to ceiling. Another faded carpet covered this floor, an intricate blue and red pattern woven in the silk threads.

Tara was surprised at the condition of the furniture, considering how long the house sat abandoned. Deirdre must have taken it out of storage when she moved back into the house. Or somehow it survived the years unscathed. Maybe the metal roof protected more than just the building. She imagined how much homier the house would feel with paintings on the walls and knickknacks on the shelves. A vase of flowers on the dining room table.

There were other things, like holes in the walls, missing baseboards, and mouse droppings on the countertops. But for now she chose to overlook that, hoping that the culprits had long since moved on to a more hospitable residence.

After so many years, what brought Deirdre back to Oregon? She couldn't have lived here for very long; in the will, she said the house had been neglected for many years. But she must have been here long enough to repair any major damage that occurred while the house was empty, like replacing broken windows and cleaning up debris.

Tara slipped off her sneakers and curled up in the chair at the desk, cold feet tucked under her, aching wrist resting in her lap. Maybe it was the fact that Deirdre had been here recently, a thought that was becoming more comforting than uncomfortable. Maybe it was knowing that the house had been in her family for generations. Or maybe it was whatever called her to the house. But for the first time in years — maybe ever — Tara felt at home.

There was something soothing about the place — even the knowledge that Deirdre had died here was bothering her less and less, the longer she was in the house.

It would be habitable, once she did a thorough cleaning and made the needed repairs. She didn't have much handyman experience, but how hard could it be? She could ask questions, and was a quick learner. And there was always the Internet. She would have to hang curtains, although since there weren't any neighbors, maybe she didn't really need them. Buy some throw pillows, hang a few pictures. She could stop renting the cottage in Merrow Bay and live in the house while she restored it. Once the project was finished she could sell it, take the money, and get back on the road again.

It wasn't as though she had any other obligations: just her work, and her father. It'd be a longer drive to Portland from here than from Merrow Bay, but hopefully he'd be home soon. Although she wasn't sure which home he'd be going to. Unless he went to prison…but she didn't want to think about that. Maybe she'd learn more about Deirdre. And figure out what it was that she was supposed to find.

She could do this. She wanted to do this.

She *needed* to do this.

Tara settled deeper into the chair and gazed through the French doors, watching black-headed chickadees hop through the rain falling softly on the sleeping flowerbeds. She felt at home. And, for the moment anyway, she felt safe.

~ 8 ~

The lights of Lee's Place glowed warm and welcoming through the late afternoon drizzle as Tara drove past. On a whim, she swung into the half-filled parking lot. She'd treat herself to a cold beer to celebrate her big decision. Besides, after spending the afternoon with Deirdre's ghost, she wasn't excited about facing another evening alone.

The building was long and low, tucked into a thick grove of coastal pines. The cedar siding had weathered to a light gray, and colorful neon signs in the windows advertised microbrews and Coronas. A wide deck extended to the left, where picnic tables and benches clustered beneath bright red umbrellas. Whiskey barrels sat at regular intervals across the front of the building; were they filled with gaudy blossoms in the summer, or trash?

The sign by the road read *Lee's Place*. But a hand-carved plaque over the door warned, *Abandon hope, all ye who enter here*. She recognized the quote by Dante. Whoever Lee was, he — or she — must have a sense of humor.

Tara studied the tavern, wondering if high-backed barstools spun at a gleaming bar; if the tables held red candles or vases filled with sprigs of lavender; if the lighting was bright or cozy.

Then she laughed at herself. The place was probably full of drunks, reeked of stale beer and cigarette smoke, and served pork hocks and pickled eggs. She parked her truck and crossed the parking lot to the building.

To enter Lee's Place, one must first navigate Lee's Door. If Tara had asked in town, they would have warned her about the front door.

Warned her that it didn't have a handle.

She tried pushing on the massive wooden door with her good hand. Forcing her ragged fingernails into invisible crevices. Even uttering magic words, but none of the usual ones worked.

Finally, she backed up and stared at the door. To hell with it. She didn't need the stupid beer anyway. As she turned to leave, the door suddenly opened and a rotund man stepped out of the building.

"Trying to get in?" he asked.

"No, selling Avon. Ding, dong." Stupid questions brought out Tara's sarcastic side.

The man laughed, a sound that started in his toes and bubbled out his wide mouth, as he held open the door. "Ask Lee," he said as she ducked under his outstretched arm. He continued toward the parking lot, still chuckling.

Tara stood in an entryway. She waited for her eyes to adjust to the dim light, and saw another door in front of her. She pushed hesitantly, and was relieved when this door opened easily. She crossed the threshold and bumped into an elephant.

Her scream bounced off other animals in the room: a giraffe, bending down to gaze at her with liquid brown eyes. Four antelopes lined up like Rockettes without their tap shoes. A sleek-coated zebra with a white belly and narrow black stripes. And the elephant, with a plastic garland of holly draped around her neck.

"African," said a voice behind her. "You can tell by the size of her ears."

"What?" Tara spun around.

"The elephant. She's African. Loxodonta africana, the Savanna Elephant." A man crossed the room and flipped a switch. A row of track lights blinded her.

"What is this?" she asked.

"The building or the animals?" he asked as he continued toward her. Tara took in the blonde curls, the trim goatee, and the broad shoulders that she last saw at the cemetery, covered by a well-loved leather coat.

"It's you," she said.

"Yes, it is," he replied. "And you must be…you."

"Well, of course I'm…" Then she realized he was teasing her, and laughed. "Right now I'm not sure who I am. I'm certainly not sure where I am."

"We'll start with the easy stuff. I'm Lee Dillon, and you're in my place." He held out his hand, and Tara reached for it. "And you are…"

"Oh, sorry. I'm Tara," she replied, finally grasping his extended hand. She noted clean, trimmed fingernails. No rings. "Tara Davies."

"Nice to meet you, Tara Davies." He nodded at the elephant. "And you've already met my sweetheart, Miss Gertrude. Or Gertie, for short. Named for Gunpowder Gertie, the Pirate Queen of the Kootenays."

"Why do you have dead animals in here?" Then she groaned. "I'm sorry, sometimes my mouth has a mind of its own."

"No harm done. Come. I'll tell you all about them." He moved toward a door behind the zebra, Tara following close behind him. As she passed the giraffe, she could have sworn its soulless eyes followed her. She reached out a tentative finger and touched the black nose, half-expecting it to be warm and wet. And was almost disappointed to find it cold and plastic.

Once through the door, Tara found herself in a traditional tavern. Pine paneling, green-shaded lights suspended from a beamed ceiling, painted wood floor. Bowls of salty nuts on the bar top. Tables and chairs scattered around the dimly lit room. The air smelled of damp wool coats, fried onions, and fermented hops. And the distinctive odor of wet dog.

The bar itself was beautiful. Hand-carved cherry, stretching the length of the back wall, bedecked with twinkling gold Christmas lights. The bar top was sleek with countless coats of polyurethane, and the brass foot rail gleamed. Figures were carved into the columns that framed the oversized mirror at the back; they looked like benevolent gargoyles, with their cherubic cheeks and demonic fangs.

Tara was relieved that the only animals in this room were the two-legged kind, except for a sheepdog snoring softly in the corner. Half of the high-backed stools were occupied. She chose an empty one and sank onto the padded seat, draping her wet coat across another. She pulled down the brim of her cap so that it cast a shadow across her face.

"What's your pleasure?" Lee asked from behind the bar.

"Corona, please."

"With fruit?"

"Huh?"

He grinned. "Fruit. You know, lemon, lime."

"Oh, sorry. Do you have oranges?" Lee raised an eyebrow, but folded a slice of orange and wedged the fruit into the neck of a sweating bottle, muttering something about ruining good beer. Tara laughed and felt some of the tension in her shoulders ease.

He opened a bottle for himself, and raised it. "To fallen comrades."

The cold bottle slipped a little in Tara's fingers. "To fallen comrades." And loved ones, she added silently, reaching for her necklace.

"What happened to your wrist?"

Tara glanced at the bandage. "Sliced the heck out of it," she admitted sheepishly.

"On purpose?" He was staring at her intently.

"Why would I…" She paused for a moment, and then laughed. "Oh, no, I wasn't trying to kill myself." Although some days, that didn't sound like such a bad idea. "Nope, just sheer clumsiness."

Lee continued to study her, and she grew uneasy under his direct gaze. Did he think she was hiding something? And wouldn't he be right. She adjusted her cap again.

"This bar is beautiful," she said, changing the subject. She ran her fingers across the top. "You don't find this kind of craftsmanship any more." The beer was cold and smooth sliding down her throat, a hint of orange lingering on her tongue. Maybe she'd have another one. Maybe it would help her forget.

"True enough. I love old stuff. Shipped this beauty from Chicago. Saved her from the wrecking ball when they razed our neighborhood bar. City thought we needed another fucking parking lot." He idly spun the bottle in his hand, and told her about Lee's Place.

The business began as a gas station in the 1950's. The owner, a Swede called Ole, added to the place as the years passed: first a general store, then a café.

"Eventually he retired and his kids took over. Turned out he always had a secret dream to be a big game hunter. So, he headed to Africa; the family thought he was joking. Until crates started arriving. Big crates. First the antelope. Next, the zebra. When the giraffe showed up — that one came in two crates — his wife sent a telegram, suggesting that he come home.

"Rumor has it that when the elephant arrived, she flew to Africa and dragged his ass home. No more crates." He took a long swig from his bottle, wiped his mouth, and flashed a brilliant smile. "I love that story."

The dog stood, stretched, and shook vigorously. Ears flapping, she showered the nearby patrons with a spray of dirty water before flopping into the corner again with a heavy sigh. "Thanks a lot, Zelda," a man in a dark suit said, scooting his stool down the bar, away from the damp dog.

"So how did *you* end up here?" Tara asked.

"Ole's kids grew tired of the long hours and the rain. The timing was right; I was looking for a new line of work. Made a few changes. Kept the critters, though. They're good company. And great conversation starters."

A raucous group entered the room and Lee moved down the bar toward them. In the background, Bonnie Raitt sang of margaritas and stars shining above Laredo.

Tara stood; this was more socializing than she had done in a long time. Lee noticed the movement and returned. "Leaving already? Hope I didn't chase you away. Next time, tell me to shut up."

She shook her head and smiled. "Nope, it's just time for me to go."

"Glad you stopped by. Come again."

She smiled and reached over the bar to shake his hand. He held hers a beat longer than she expected, his hand warm as it enveloped her smaller one.

"I will."

As she ran through the rain to her truck, Tara mentally smacked herself in the head. She forgot to ask Lee what the secret was to opening the damned door. How was she supposed to get in next time? Assuming there was a next time.

&

As she drove back to Merrow Bay, Tara realized she also forgot to ask Lee why he was at the funeral. The animals distracted her, as did Lee himself.

And that door. If she had to stand outside and wait for someone to open it, she might not go back. And she wanted to go back. Maybe Lee's would be a place where she could hide. Maybe it could be her neighborhood bar.

Owning a house, hanging out at a bar…what was next? Throwing a Tupperware party? Going out on a date?

Her vision blurred and her throat tightened, the light-hearted moment lost. No dating. Not yet.

~ *9* ~

Click. A door swings shut, and locks. *Clank.* Flakes of rust fall onto a cold hearth as the damper drops into place. The roofline looks straighter, the porch sturdier. Windows gleam, cushions straighten, lights twinkle a little brighter before blinking off.

An armchair moves six inches to the right. The coffee table scoots an inch closer to the couch. Wrinkles in the worn Persian rug disappear.

Emerald eyes watch, overseeing the preparations. A whiff of sea air floats down a hallway and ruffles the fringe of a blue shawl.

It's been a long wait. But now, everything is ready.

&

There's no sense of time in the ICU. Shifts change, doctors come and go, weary family members pace the hallways. There are no windows to mark the passage of the hours. Whether Tara arrived at nine in the morning or six in the evening, the time was always the same. Time to worry.

The disinfectant smell was stronger than usual today; a combination of ammonia and Tropical Passion burned her nose as she stepped off the elevator. A Muzak version of "Rudolph the Red-Nosed Reindeer" played softly in the background. She stopped at the nurses' station, where they told her there was no change in her father's condition. A young blonde who sounded like Minnie Mouse explained that 'no change' was good news, but Tara had a hard time seeing it that way.

She pointedly ignored Deputy Knowles, who she had nicknamed Stoneface, sitting on a straight-backed chair outside the door, who pointedly ignored her in return, and lowered herself into the olive green recliner next to her father's bed. She tossed her cap on the bedside table.

"Daddy?" she whispered. "Daddy, it's Tara. Can you hear me?" She squeezed his hand. Nothing. Not that she expected anything. But she needed to try.

"I have bad news, Daddy." She took a deep breath. She hadn't told him what happened, afraid it would upset him. Assuming he could hear her, that is. But it had been days since the attack, and she couldn't hide the truth any longer.

"Aunt Deirdre is dead. Whoever attacked you, killed her. I wish you could tell me what happened. Why you were there. And who did this to you." She heard a noise and turned to see the doctor standing at the door.

"I'll be right back," she said, rising and walking into the hallway. She should have worn her sneakers; the new loafers were rubbing blisters on her heels. "Good morning, Dr. Chambers," she said.

"Please call me Karen. I see you more than I do my own family," Dr. Chambers said.

"You're married?" Tara asked, noticing a small diamond on the doctor's left hand.

"Yep, John and I have two boys, Jesse and Justin. They're five and three. I'd show you a picture, but…" she motioned to her white coat and shrugged.

"It must be hard to be a doctor and have a family, too."

"Sometimes. I feel like I'm missing so much of their lives." Dr. Chambers absently toyed with the simple ring. "I didn't want to choose between dreams — being a mother or a doctor — so I have to make it work. Anyway, I wanted to see how you are."

"Me?" Tara asked. "I'm fine. Hoping for some kind of change." She looked at the figure lying motionless beneath the starched white sheets. "Anything to show he's still…in there."

"Well, this shows his brain activity," the doctor said, pointing to a monitor, "so we know he's 'in there.' Physically, he's holding his own. But as far as progress, I don't have any good news for you. We'll keep him here as long as we feel it's necessary, but we'll eventually have to discuss long-term care options, if he doesn't regain consciousness." She looked down at the chart in her hand, and coffee-colored curls fell across her face. As she tucked them behind her ear with a graceful gesture, she said, "As his next of kin, those decisions will fall to you."

"What do you mean, 'if he doesn't regain consciousness'?"

Dr. Chambers studied her. "He's in a coma, Tara. There's no way of knowing how long he'll be in that state. Our primary responsibility is to treat his injuries; we can't keep him here indefinitely. But I wouldn't worry about that now. He has a long way to go before we have to make those decisions."

"I know you're doing all you can. It's just hard to see him so helpless." Tara pictured him humming as he meticulously weeded his daylilies, and fought back tears.

Dr. Chambers slipped her arm around Tara's tired shoulders. "We'll let you know if there's any change. In the meantime, you're doing all you can. Even though it may not feel like it, your being here does help. You'd be surprised what comatose patients remember when they wake up."

If they wake up.

Once the doctor left, Tara returned to her father's bedside. "Anyway, like I was saying, the sheriff…well,…they think you killed Aunt Deirdre. But I know you're not a murderer." She knew all about murderers.

Grabbing his hand, she whispered fiercely, "I won't let them do that to you, Daddy. Now it's my turn to protect you."

One of the machines started beeping. Minnie Mouse ran into the room and scanned the machines. "What did you do?" she snapped.

"Nothing. I was just…just talking to him." Wide-eyed, Tara stared at her father and back at the nurse.

Minnie twisted a dial, checked Ethan's pulse, and turned to Tara. "I'm sorry; I didn't mean to bark at you. Nothing's wrong. His heartbeat changed, that's all. I just wondered what caused the increase."

"I said something that might have upset him," Tara said. "So does that mean he *can* hear me?"

"Don't get your hopes up. It was probably a coincidence."

Tara didn't believe in coincidences.

&

The pickup truck sat in front of the house, stuffed with Tara's worldly possessions.

After she had emptied the cottage, Tara stood at the front gate and thought about the hopes and dreams she brought to Merrow Bay. The town had been a safe haven, and she would miss it. Hopefully, this time she was moving toward something, instead of running away. She had run one too many times, and the scars were getting harder to hide.

Sometimes Tara longed for the trappings of roots: a soft leather loveseat, a lush garden with bees buzzing among the fragrant blossoms, a wide porch to lounge on at sunset. Planning to replace the roof in two years. Painting the kitchen walls in vivid reds and golds. Watching neighborhood children grow.

But then, fear set in. Roots were chains, binding you to predictability, to boredom. People began to expect things of you, want to be your friend, learn about your past. And eventually, they'd find out. She couldn't risk that. So she kept moving, avoiding getting too close to anyone.

Knowing that, how could she commit to staying here long enough to restore the house?

She needed to try. She owed it to Deirdre. She owed it to herself.

Since she still didn't have a key, Tara walked around to the back door, her sneakers crunching through the glass that littered the stoop. A cold breeze whipped strands of auburn hair into her face. She tucked them behind her ear and stretched her arm carefully through the broken window to unlock the deadbolt as she did before, trying to avoid scraping her wrist against the frame.

She couldn't reach the lock.

That didn't make any sense. Her arm hadn't gotten shorter overnight. She wiggled the remaining shards of glass out of the frame and forced her arm through the small space until her fingertips brushed the deadbolt. Straining, she was able to twist the knob and open the door.

She walked through the cold house to the front door and propped it open. Wishing Mr. Edison would catch his limit and come home early, Tara started unloading her truck.

&

She couldn't do it.

Tara stood in the doorway of Deirdre's room with her suitcases. It made sense for her to use the master suite. After all, the house *was* hers. But that meant she'd have to move Deirdre's things, and she couldn't do it. It felt disrespectful, not to mention downright strange. So she carried the bags down the hall to the green room instead, and started unpacking. The smaller room would be just fine.

Shirts and shoes in the closet, her favorite little black dress stashed in the back, just in case. Jeans and underwear in the drawers. Her collection of baseball caps, gathered over the years on her travels. And a much-loved Winnie the Pooh on top of the bureau, reclining against the mirror.

The day passed quickly. After turning up the heat, Tara washed the linens she found in the laundry room and made her bed, stopping to bury her face in the hot sheets and breathe their warm, clean scent. There were towels and washcloths in the linen closet; it looked like Deirdre planned to stay for a while. But why?

Soon her precious books were lined up on the shelves next to the fireplace in the living room. Toiletries in the shower and dishes in the kitchen. The study laid out as her office, laptop in the center of the desk and work materials organized on the bookshelves. Tara silently thanked the metal roof for protecting the house from the elements for all those years. And Deirdre, for cleaning it enough for her to live there.

If indeed Deirdre was the one who made the house habitable again. Maybe she hired someone to maintain it for her while she was gone, to keep the critters and the ravages of time at bay. Maybe she even came back from time to time, although Tara's parents never mentioned it.

Regardless of who cared for the house over the years, Tara was grateful. Not that she was squeamish, but the thought of moving into a house that stood empty for that long was creepy. Because the house truly would not have been empty. Whole families of critters would have made their homes in there. In fact, she had already scrubbed the kitchen counter that morning, after finding mouse droppings scattered across the Formica surface. She might be lonely, but that kind of roommate she didn't need.

What she did need was a cat. That would solve the unwelcome roommate problem without having to use traps; she couldn't stand the thought of killing something herself. She added 'visit animal shelter' to her mental to-do list. She wasn't really a cat person, but it'd be nice to have company. Well, feline company, anyway. She could always find a home for the cat when she finished the house and moved on.

That evening, she sat on the front porch sipping cocoa, watching the stars come out. They were so much brighter than she was used to, having spent most of her life in big cities. She could smell the pungent spruce and the smoke from a neighbor's woodstove. Somewhere in the forest a coyote yipped and a chorus of his friends joined him; they sounded mournful, and a little otherworldly. Tara shivered and wrapped her hands tighter around her mug.

Her first day in the house had gone well; she tried not to think about her father and Deirdre as she unpacked and settled in. She had already decided that she would *not* be squeamish about what happened. If she was going to fulfill her plan, she had to feel safe living here. A lifetime of managing the unmanageable would serve her well; as with everything else, she'd tuck the pain and fear into a mental cubbyhole, and deal with it when she had the strength. Although that cubby was getting pretty full.

A page torn from her journal lay on the kitchen table, listing the repairs she needed to make — at least the ones she could see. She was sure there were more, but the list was already overwhelming; she wasn't in a hurry to add to it. She took another sip of the spicy chocolate and looked up into the sky.

What do you think, Emma? Can you believe I have a house?

&

Two young girls, identically dressed, playing with dolls on a worn Persian rug. The older child is putting on a show for the younger. Malibu Barbie hits GI Joe.

'You're an idiot!' Barbie shouts. 'Why don't you ever listen to me? I wanted steak, not chicken!' Slap. 'You can't do anything right!' Slap.

'I'm sorry, honey,' GI Joe says. 'I'll make you a steak.'

'Don't bother,' Barbie says. 'I don't want to eat. Get me a drink.'

GI Joe hands an invisible glass to Barbie, who drinks from it and falls to the floor. He carries her to her pink bed, then sits on the pink couch and stares at the pink wall.

"Mommy sick?" the younger girl asks.

"No, Barbie just has a headache," the older girl replies. "We have to be quiet and not bother her. She'll be better tomorrow."

The girls silently move furniture around the dollhouse as GI Joe sits and Barbie sleeps.

~ 10 ~

Tara awoke to pain. A headache lurked just behind her eyes, which was strange; she never had headaches. She pulled the down comforter over her head, the silky cover sliding across her cheek, and blocked out the sun streaming through the windows. The acrid taste of pain made her nauseous.

Fragments of a dream lingered at the edge of her consciousness. She remembered something pink, and children playing with dolls. But she didn't think it was a good dream.

Tara went over the list of tasks in her head as she showered, hot water beating on her neck, hoping it would relieve the tension that must be causing the headache. Or maybe it was stress; there *was* a lot on her plate — or stuffed in that mental cubbyhole. She even tried aromatherapy, lathering her body first with lemongrass soap and then rosewater lotion, but nothing eased the pain.

Staying busy would keep her mind off her problems. Busy is better than bored. Although some days boredom looked pretty darn appealing.

She dripped on the neon pink rug she bought at Costco — she thought the bright color would cheer her up — as she got ready for the trip to Portland.

&

Tara never had a home. Not as an adult. And certainly not as a child, she thought as she stared at her father's house, silent under darkening skies.

After stalling for a few minutes — rubbing her temples to ease the headache that hadn't gone away, pulling on her leather gloves, winding her fuzzy purple scarf around her neck, adjusting her cap — she crawled out of her truck and plodded up the cement steps to the front door. She wrapped her arms tightly around herself, trying to stop the shivering.

In the summer, purple, red and white petunias exploded along the steps and the sidewalk, filling the yard with their pungent perfume. Now the blooms were gone, the beds barren and cold.

She considered driving the Explorer from Surfside so it would be waiting for her father, but she didn't have a key, or a way to get back home. Not to mention feeling weird about driving his vehicle. Even though chronologically she was an adult, in some ways she'd always be a child, needing his permission. His approval.

Tara reached behind the 'Welcome Friends' plaque next to the front door and found the house key right where Ethan's housekeeper Marge said it would be, when she called Tara a few days earlier. Almost as secure as hiding it under the mat. The key turned easily, and the glossy blue door swung open with a groan.

The house was cold and gloomy. Tara crossed the living room and flung open the curtains, coughing on the dust, to let in what little light the gray day offered. There were enough ghosts in the house already: she didn't need to scare herself even more by creeping around in the dark.

Marge agreed to continue taking care of the house until Ethan returned, or someone else took responsibility for the place. All Tara needed to do today was check messages, find his attorney's name and number, and get back home.

Home. Interesting that she already thought of Deirdre's house as home. It wasn't very homey. No pictures on the walls or plants on the windowsills. But compared to this place, where she *did* live at one time, the empty house on Chinook Road was a comfy, welcoming nest.

Tara looked around at the possessions her pack rat father collected during his sixty-six years of living, and vowed to go home and throw away half of everything she owned. She didn't want to end up a prisoner of her belongings.

Like the rest of the house, his office was a mess; Ethan hadn't taken to bachelorhood very well. Marge must clean around the clutter. Tara studied the piles on the desk, the files stacked on the metal cabinet in the corner, the papers scattered on the beige carpet. Her obsessive need for order obviously didn't come from him. She sat in the oversized chair at his desk and, feeling like a small child again, gingerly chose a folder from the nearest pile. The sooner this was done, the better.

Half an hour later, fingers numb, wrist sore, and stomach grumbling, Tara had found the information that she needed. And a lot that she didn't.

She called Tom Daugherty, her father's attorney, but his secretary said he was out for the day and took a message.

She found a key for the Explorer hanging on a hook in the kitchen and slid it into her pocket along with a Post-It note that was stuck on the refrigerator door, with 'peanut butter' and 'tuna fish' in her father's handwriting. The light on the answering machine was flashing red. Tara found a pen and notepad, and pushed the 'play' button.

She listened to the usual hang-ups, telemarketers, and calls from his friends wanting to meet for coffee — obviously they hadn't heard. A reminder about a dentist's appointment. A recorded message from a local politician, inviting Mr. Evan Dennis to contribute to his campaign.

One message, though, puzzled her. The woman spoke low and fast, and a bad connection made her difficult to understand.

"I know…taking over where Mary left off…protect her. Don't think about hurting…tell sheriff…make you pay…watching you…."

Tara played the message a number of times, but couldn't make it out. It was probably a wrong number, although the woman did mention her mother's name. But she could just as well have said Larry or Carrie. She unplugged the machine and put it by the front door to take home with her; maybe the cryptic message would make more sense later.

Passing the foot of the staircase, she thought about checking out her old room. She hadn't been up there in years.

Her parents hadn't done much socializing. By the time most parties started, Ethan was already pouring Mary into bed. And on the rare occasions when they did go out, they were fighting by the time they got home.

As soon as she heard their car, Tara would retreat to her bedroom closet. She had pushed the clothes to the far end, stacked pillows in the corner, dragged a blanket from the sweet-smelling cedar chest in the spare bedroom, and bought a flashlight and batteries with her allowance. She called the closet her library, but it was really her sanctuary. Her hiding place. Like a rabbit in a car's headlights, Tara believed that if she didn't move, if she couldn't be seen, she'd be safe.

But as the carcasses on the highway prove, staying still never saved anyone.

Shaking her head, she decided some memories were better left alone and started closing up the house, her necklace heavy around her neck.

&

Tara was elbow-deep in drywall mud, patching one of the many holes in the walls of her new home, when she heard the doorbell chime over Bob Seger belting out "Turn the Page" on the CD player.

"Damn!" she muttered. "Who could that be?"

She called "Just a minute!" as she hurried to the front door, wiping her sticky hands on her jeans and wishing she hadn't forgotten to buy rags when she was in town.

She opened the door — and looked down. A girl in a pink sweatshirt and blue jeans sat in a wheelchair in a patch of sunlight. Her short brown hair looked as though someone cut it with dull scissors, and her wide smile revealed three missing teeth.

"Hi!" the girl said. "Who are you?"

"I'm Tara. Who are you?"

"I'm Mariah," she said, holding out her hand. Tara shook it solemnly, hoping she had gotten most of the drywall mud off her hands.

"Nice to meet you, Mariah." Tara looked over the girl's shoulder for a car. "Um, how did you get here?"

"Up the driveway. Can I come in? It's cold out here."

How did she get up the steep driveway alone? Tara glanced at the tires on the wheelchair to see if they were knobby, like mountain bike tires, but they were normal smooth ones.

Not comfortable with her coming in, but not wanting to be rude either, Tara opened the door wider and the girl bumped over the threshold.

"What's that?" Mariah asked, pointing at the figure carved into the banister.

"I think she's a mermaid. I've been calling her Ariel, like in the movie." Tara rested her hand on the coarse hair of the silent woman.

"She's cool," Mariah said. "How long have you been here, anyways?"

"I just moved in this week," Tara replied, following the girl into the living room. "How did you know I was here?"

Mariah was peering up the chimney, so took a moment to answer. "I come up here sometimes," she said, her voice muffled. She pulled out her head and looked up at Tara, eyes anxious, a black smudge on her cheek. "Am I in trouble?"

"Oh no, not at all," Tara said, turning down the volume on the CD player. "Although you might want to be careful. Some people call that trespassing, and might not like you wandering around their property."

"I don't mean to cause any problems. I just like checking things out. Do you have anything to drink?"

Tara smiled at the girl's nonstop chatter. "I have water and orange juice. And coffee, but I doubt you want that." She forgot to buy cocoa on her last trip to the Stop 'N' Shop.

Mariah grimaced. "No way! Coffee's gross. Got any juice?"

Tara walked into the kitchen, the girl following close behind.

"Ooh, you have a fireplace in the kitchen, too! I love fireplaces." And she rolled over to inspect the chimney as thoroughly as she had the one in the living room. "Boy, it's dark up there."

Tara hoped she didn't get her head stuck in the chimney.

Mariah abandoned her tour to drink her juice, her eyes roaming around the kitchen. "This house is a dump. Why do you live here?"

Tara laughed. Dark circles ringed the girl's violet eyes, but her smile was infectious.

"Good question. My great-great-whatever grandfather built this house. I inherited it from my aunt, but she hadn't lived here in a long time. So I have to fix it up."

"Wow, you know how to do that?"

"Not really, but I'm learning." Tara leaned against the kitchen sink, her left foot propped on her right shin.

"It's a cool house, even if it is a mess." Mariah spun the empty glass on the table and a few drops spattered onto the surface.

Nothing like the candor of a child. "Thanks. I think so, too," Tara said. "The cool part, anyway." They both laughed. "Why aren't you in school?"

"We're on vacation," Mariah said. "Thanks for the juice. It was delicious. I better go." She opened the front door, rolled to the far end of the porch and dropped onto the path, and waved as she disappeared beneath the sun-dappled canopy down the driveway.

Tara watched her leave, thinking it was a little early for school to be out for Christmas break. And hoping the girl didn't make a habit of dropping by unannounced. Tara didn't really like unexpected visitors.

She sighed, picked up her trowel, and returned to the hole in the hallway.

~ 11 ~

Tara stood on the porch in her flannel nightgown, watching the winter sun creep over the treetops. She closed her eyes and raised her face to the rosy light, necklace in hand, lips moving in a silent prayer.

Her back ached. She couldn't raise her arms. But she had patched every hole in every wall. The next step was to sand and paint, but that could wait. At least now she didn't have to walk past the holes and wonder what was lurking in their dark cavities. Maybe she wouldn't find mouse droppings in the kitchen now; she hoped she had been dreaming when she felt something scurry across her pillow last night. She really needed a cat.

She headed for the kitchen, ready for a cup of coffee and a blueberry muffin; she was still out of cocoa. The aroma of the coffee drifting through the house was making her hungry. Then she stopped in front of a hole in the hallway wall.

A hole she patched the day before. Or at least thought she did.

Tara studied the hole, trying to remember if she repaired that one. Eventually she shrugged. She must have missed it.

So much for being finished with the patching project. She put 'patch hole' back on her to-do list and poured a cup of coffee, the pot hissing as she slid it back onto the hot burner. And as she took the first sip of the day, called the hospital.

&

While Tara was talking to Dr. Chambers, her phone beeped, signaling another call coming in. It was a Portland number, but not one she recognized. When she finished with her call, she dialed the number.

"Legal Associates, how may I help you?" the voice droned. It came out as one long word: howmayihelpyou.

"This is Tara Davies. Someone at this number just called."

"Did they leave a message?"

"No. If they had, I would know who called." Another winner. If the woman called her sweetcheeks, Tara was hanging up.

"One minute, please." And she put Tara on hold. Which lasted for what felt like hours, but was probably only a couple of minutes. Finally, a male voice interrupted the Muzak.

"Tom Daugherty."

Then Tara realized who she was calling.

"Mr. Daugherty, this is Tara Davies."

"Yes?"

"I believe you're my father's attorney?"

"And your father would be…?"

"Ethan Davies." She could swear he was chewing gum. And blowing bubbles.

"Don't recognize the name. Are you sure he's my client?"

"Of course I'm sure!" She was starting to wonder why her father chose this man.

"Assuming he is my client, what do you expect me to do about it?"

Tara spoke slowly and clearly. "My father has been attacked, and is in a coma. He has also been charged with murder, and will be arrested as soon as he regains consciousness. I need to discuss his defense, as well as find out who he assigned Power of Attorney to when you did his will."

"I don't know who you're talking about. I don't have any clients named Davis." Chew. Pop.

"Davies! With an E. Davies. Not Davis. Ethan Davies."

"Davies? I thought you said Alan Davis."

Tara wanted to reach through the phone and strangle the man. "Ethan. Davies. Do you need me to spell it for you?"

"Oh no, I think I've got it now. Ethan Davies…wait, isn't he the guy who killed his girlfriend in Surfside?"

Tara shook her head. The man was the picture of tact. "Actually, no. She wasn't his girlfriend; she was my aunt. She was murdered by an intruder. The same person who injured him. Unfortunately, the sheriff believes my father was responsible for the attack."

"Ah, gotcha. Wow, that's a totally different story. How about I take a look around and see what I can find? You wanna hold?"

Tom Daugherty's accent had changed from stuffy attorney to street urchin.

"I'd like nothing better." She was afraid if she hung up, she'd never hear from the man again. Although she regretted wasting her cell phone minutes. And there was no Muzak to entertain her this time; he laid the phone on the desk without pushing the 'hold' button. She could hear file drawers opening and closing, papers shuffling, and an occasional "Shit!"

Tara emptied her cold coffee into the sink and refilled her mug. The coffee was strong and bitter after simmering all morning, and she made a face when she took the first sip. Then he returned. "Mrs. Davis — sorry, Davies — are you still there?"

"Ms. Davies. Yes, I'm still here."

"Guess what? I found his file!"

"Good for you." She mentally rolled her eyes.

"You asked about Power of Attorney." She could hear him flipping through pages. "Nope, nothing here."

"Are you kidding? You did his will, yet you didn't discuss assigning Power of Attorney with a man in his sixties? How on earth could you miss that?"

He cleared his throat. "Right. Well. Um. Guess we should have done that, huh?"

"Yes, you should have. I can't pay his bills, access his accounts, handle his business, anything, without that document. I don't suppose you have any suggestions as to what I'm supposed to do now?"

After a long, uncomfortable silence during which Tara could almost hear him sweat, Tom Daugherty said, "I…don't have a clue. Maybe he'll wake up…or something."

"That's a big help. And his legal defense?"

There was another pause. "Well, if he's in a coma, I guess you won't need to get him out on bail!" He started to chuckle, then stopped short. "Um. Well, I can't do much until he wakes up. When that happens, call me, and I'll jump right on it."

Tara said, "Don't hold your breath," and hung up. She'd run naked through Surfside before she'd call that man again. Ethan retained a real attorney when he owned his engineering business; she wondered why he didn't have him do his will.

Now what? At least her father wouldn't need legal representation until he woke up. Not that she'd be calling Mr. Useless, Esq. again. She could make medical decisions as his next of kin, but she couldn't take care of anything else. And she certainly couldn't pay his bills out of her own meager bank account. All she could do was hope he regained consciousness before his creditors turned him over to a collection agency. What a nice mess that would be for him to wake up to.

She walked out to the porch and flung her cold coffee into the empty flowerbed.

&

The doorbell rang as Tara slapped mud on the hole in the hallway wall. Again. Her muffin was in the trash, tossed there after she found a corner nibbled off — and mouse droppings on the counter around the plate. Luckily, she noticed the missing corner before she took a bite. But black coffee and a granola bar wasn't much of a breakfast. And her wrist still hurt.

She hoped the visitor wasn't Mariah again; the girl could become a nuisance. Wiping her hands on her jeans and muttering about rotten timing, she opened the door and something black streaked past her into the house.

"What the…" Tara looked behind her, and then at the man standing on her porch. "What was that?"

"A cat. He was waiting at the door. Isn't he yours?"

"Nope." She wasn't sure what she should do first, chase the cat or find out who this guy was.

"You looked surprised when you opened the door," he said. "Even before you saw the cat."

"You're not who I thought you were going to be." She glanced over his shoulder at the gold Corvette convertible parked in front of the garage. The sun reflecting off the perfect paint job was blinding. She didn't hear him pull up, but maybe that was because her stereo was blasting her favorite REO Speedwagon song, "Roll with the Changes."

"My ex-wife said the same thing," the man replied, smiling. His front tooth was chipped. "Craig Morris." He extended his hand and Tara did the same, comparing her ragged, unpolished nails to his manicured ones. She chewed them when she was stressed; at this rate, she'd be lucky to have any fingers left by the end of this project. As she took his hand, he slipped a business card into hers.

Craig Morris, Developer. A Surfside address. But a California phone number.

Californians were taking over the Northwest, showing up with wads of cash, raising housing prices and taxes. Locals could no longer afford to buy homes in their own hometowns. And developers were the worst, clear-cutting the forests to build ticky-tack houses that other Californians would buy, and rent to the locals at outrageous rates. The whole situation pissed her off.

A Californian. Strike one. And a developer. Strike two.

"Tara Davies," she said, slipping the card into her pocket.

"Tara? Like in *Gone with the Wind*?"

"Not quite. It means "hill" in Gaelic. Or "star," depending on who you talk to. My forefathers were Irish. What brings you to Oregon?" Besides trying to make a quick buck.

"My mother was born here," he said, stuffing his hands into the pockets of his Burberry raincoat. "She died when I was a baby. I thought I might find out something about her or her family, although I don't have much more than her name to go on."

"Well, good luck. What can I do for you?" she said, glancing back over her shoulder into the house. Where did that cat go?

"I wanted to welcome you to the neighborhood." He beamed, jingling the change in his pocket.

"How did you know I was here?"

"It's a small town. Word gets around."

No one knew she was living here. Mr. Edison was still in the Bahamas. She hadn't found the nerve to do any shopping in town. She hadn't even asked the Post Office to forward her mail yet; it was still being held in Merrow Bay. So far, her attempt to keep a low profile in Surfside was working. The only person who knew she was here was Mariah.

"Do you know a girl in a wheelchair?" she asked.

"Wheelchair? No. Why?"

"Never mind." She doubted Mariah would know someone like this, anyway. "I appreciate the welcome, but I need to get back to work." She indicated her stained jeans and chalky hands. "And find that cat."

"Looks like drywall compound. Messy stuff." He peered over her shoulder into the hallway and studied the drop cloth, bucket, and trowel. "You a do-it-yourselfer?"

"No, but I'm learning. Thanks again." She started to close the door, but Craig held up his hand.

"Wait." His green eyes clouded. "I did have another reason for coming."

Tara waited, one eyebrow raised, one white hand on the doorknob. The December air oozing through the open door was cold on her bare ankles.

"I wanted to express my condolences on the passing of your…mother?"

"Aunt." It popped out before Tara could stop herself.

"I'm sorry. Your aunt. Such a terrible tragedy." He looked at the broken step and sagging porch, the paint peeling on the railing, and the bird's nest wedged in the rafters. "You've got a lot of work on your hands. But the place has a lot of potential. There's something unusual about this house…"

"Did you know my aunt?" She already knew the answer.

"No, I'm afraid I didn't."

She advanced, and he took a step backward. "So how did you know she was dead?" Another step forward. Another step backward. Almost a dance.

"I…uh…saw the story in the newspaper."

Aha.

Tara backed him to the top of the steps. He grabbed one of the columns to steady himself as he balanced on the edge of the porch, the breeze tossing his perfectly styled auburn hair.

"So you came up here to visit the grieving family? Thought we'd give you a good deal on her house, to get it off our hands?"

"Now, wait a minute, I…"

"Get off my property!" She grabbed the flagpole from the bracket by the door and swung the metal rod like a baseball bat. Craig jumped down the steps before the rod struck the column he was hanging onto. It made contact with a satisfying *thunk.* "How dare you take advantage of people in pain?"

He ran for his car as Tara swung again, and again made contact with the column. *Thunk.* This time the rod left a dent in the aged wood.

"Asshole!" she screamed as he sped down the driveway. She stood for a moment, shaking, watching him disappear. Then she replaced the flagpole in the bracket and ran her fingers over the dent in the column.

"So maybe I overreacted," she said. "Maybe I have anger issues." She couldn't afford to lose her temper like that. She wanted to avoid attention, not attract it.

She added 'fix column' to her list, right below 'get a grip.' Rubbed her wrist. And went inside to look for the cat.

&

"Okay, kitty, you can come out now." She searched and called, but found no sign of the black streak. If Craig hadn't seen the cat too, she might think she imagined it. "If you don't show yourself soon, I swear I'll throw you back out into the cold, cruel world when I do find you. I don't have time to play hide and seek."

Since threats and pleading weren't working, she finally sat at the foot of the staircase and listened for unusual sounds. Besides the creaking of an old house.

And it worked. A soft mewing echoed down the staircase and Tara crept along the hallway, following the sound to Deirdre's room. Where a shivering, bedraggled black cat peeked out from underneath the bed.

"Poor kitty," she said, crouching just inside the door, trying to look non-threatening. "I didn't mean any of those nasty things I said. I'm really a very nice person." The soothing chatter seemed to reassure the cat and he slowly approached Tara's outstretched hand, placing one oversized black paw on the hardwood floor, followed by two tentative white ones.

"You're a mess, cat." She stroked his filthy fur and could feel his bones. "Poor baby. I don't think anyone's taking care of you."

She would put ads in the paper and contact the humane society, but she didn't think anyone was looking for this cat. Funny that he showed up just when she needed him.

"What shall we call you? Nothing as obvious as Socks or Boots. How about Sneakers? That's a little more creative." He crawled into her lap and started purring frantically, and she decided this was his way of agreeing with her. "Okay, Sneakers it is." She added more items to her mental shopping list, like cat food and kitty litter, as she cuddled the little cat.

"I just hope you're good at scaring away mice."

~ 12 ~

Her cocoa was cold. Her stomach was in knots. She knew she couldn't put it off any longer. She should have done it days ago.

Dread slowed her every move. She didn't have a choice. She needed to do it. But she'd do anything to avoid it.

Maybe she could tell her on the phone. Or maybe they'd tell her instead. Someone there must like her. Her mother wouldn't dare treat them like she treated Tara.

She trudged to the sink. Washed her mug. Dried it. Placed it carefully in the cabinet. Straightened the other mugs so they were in a perfect line. Walked to the table and selected an apple from the woven basket, and smelled the sharp tang of its skin. Bit into it, savoring the juicy flavor and crunchy texture. Then meticulously dropped the core in the trashcan.

Enough stalling. Just get it over with.

She reached for her phone, stared at it for a long moment, and then made the call.

"Good morning, Fairhaven Manor," the smooth voice answered.

"This is Tara Davies. I have to…I mean, I need to talk to my mother."

"And who is your mother?"

"Mary Davies."

There was a pause. "Ah, here she is. Number fifteen. I'll transfer you."

"No, no, wait! I don't want to talk to her. I just want to make sure that it's okay to visit her." Although talking to her mother on the phone would be a lot easier, Tara didn't know if she still knew how to use one.

"You don't need permission, dear. You just come on down any time between nine and seven. You can join us for dinner at five, if you'd like. Our residents enjoy having company during their meals."

It'd be a cold day in Hell when she'd stay a second longer than she had to. But Tara said, "Thank you. I appreciate the invitation. I'll be there this afternoon."

She closed the phone. Done. Although that was the easy part.

Tara headed for the shower, wishing for the thousandth time for a normal mother, a normal childhood, a normal life. But she destroyed that, a long time ago.

&

A black Labrador wanders up a sunny gravel road. Tail wagging, nose twitching, following a delicious scent: maybe rabbit, maybe fox, maybe something even more fun. He loves to chase his furry friends because he's sure someday he's going to catch one and it'll play with him. He stops to munch a snack of round deer yummies before continuing his journey.

The rabbit — he's sure it's rabbit, it smells like grass and white tail and long funny ears — must have hopped up the road and across the big grassy area, through the flowerbeds, and under the porch of the people building. He can smell new people, but can't see them.

He sniffs around the porch and finds the perfect place to tell everyone that this spot is his, right on the corner, on the wood that smells of time.

As he lifts his leg, tongue lolling, tail wagging, a metal pipe pulls away from the building and crashes to the ground next to him. He jumps and bolts and runs down the road, furry friend forgotten. When he looks back, he sees the pipe on the wall, right where it was before.

&

The hospital staff continued to be encouraging, but their eyes told a different story. Tara could see pity in those eyes each time she visited her father.

As she pulled into the parking lot, she saw an official car parked in the fire lane, and Deputy Knowles walking down the steps of the building. They had avoided speaking to each other up until this point, but maybe he might have news about the case.

So, Tara decided to break her self-imposed silence, and strode up to him.

"Good morning, Deputy." She even removed her cap in a show of respect, hoping it might help.

He loomed over her, his face registering no emotion; he'd make a great poker player. "Good morning, Miss Davies."

"I take it you've been guarding my father?" 'Guarding' sounded better than 'making sure the murderer didn't escape,' which was probably what he thought he was doing.

"My sergeant asked that I check on the status of the accused."

Tara winced. "As you can see, there's no change. He's still in the coma." And still not guilty.

"I spoke with the staff and they updated me on his condition. Now if you will excuse me…" He turned to walk toward his car.

"So you don't have any more information on who was really responsible for the attack?"

"As I said, Miss Davies, I was checking on the accused." He jingled the keys in his right hand.

"My father is a peaceful man. There's no way he did this! Besides, if he's the murderer, how did he end up in a coma? It doesn't make any sense…"

The poker face stared back at her, and Tara realized she was wasting her breath. "Never mind. Thank you for your time." The man clearly had no heart. And probably no life outside of his job. She could almost feel sorry for him, if he showed an ounce of humanity.

He nodded once, and opened the driver's door on his car. And Tara noticed a small hole in his earlobe. So, Deputy Stoneface wore an earring when he wasn't playing Deputy Stoneface.

Maybe there was a human being inside that uniform, after all.

&

As Tara perched on the edge of her father's bed, rambling about nothing, nurse Minnie Mouse came into the room carrying a Styrofoam cup. The tag on the pocket of her uniform read 'Sophie,' and had a tiny Santa Claus clipped to it.

"He's not going to get any better, is he?" Tara asked, accepting the cup and sipping the lukewarm coffee, which tasted pretty much like she thought it would — like dirty socks.

Sophie glanced down the hallway, where another nurse and doctor were deep in conversation. "Sometimes they do," she said in a low voice. "There have been cases of patients waking up from comas after 5, 10, 20 years. But," she looked toward her coworkers again, "there's always some kind of damage; you can't be unconscious for that long without having major problems.

"I'm not supposed to tell you this," she continued, and Tara nodded. "I'm supposed to be positive and encouraging. But it's hard to watch you sit here, knowing you're probably wasting your time. You should be saying goodbye, instead of waiting for him to wake up."

"Thanks for being honest with me. But I need to believe he's going to get out of here. I promise I won't live in a fantasy world forever. It's not my nature."

Sophie nodded as Dr. Chambers entered the room. "Let me know if I can do anything else for you," she said, and left.

"Hi, Dr. C.," Tara said. "I know. No news is good news."

"Well, I do have news, and it's more good than bad. We're moving your father. He's stable enough that he doesn't need to be in the ICU any longer. He'll still get the same degree of attention, but he'll be able to have visitors. And our other wards are less…severe…than the ICU."

"I'll take that as progress. Thank you."

A shrill beeping interrupted them. The doctor pulled a pager from the pocket of her white coat. "Sorry, duty calls," and smiled briefly before hurrying out of the room.

Tara perched on the edge of the bed. He might be stable medically, but her father appeared to be collapsing in on himself, shrinking and fading more each time she saw him.

"I'm going to see Mama, Daddy. Hopefully she's stopped hating me. If she even remembers me. Wish me luck." She leaned down to kiss his pale cheek, missing the smell of his Old Spice aftershave, and headed to Fairhaven.

&

It was a beautiful prison.

A rambling brick structure, Fairhaven Manor sat back from the road in a grove of birch trees, their leafless branches rustling in the winter breeze. Benches, bird feeders, and play areas for visiting grandchildren were scattered throughout the manicured grounds. Gravel paths meandered across the lawns, encouraging the residents to spend time in the fresh air. But the high fence surrounding the property and the front gate manned by a uniformed guard served as reminders that this was not a normal retirement community.

Alzheimer's robbed people of their memories, their ability to function and eventually, their lives. Fairhaven offered a homey environment, staffed by caring individuals who tried to create an atmosphere of success rather than failure for the residents. But it was still an institution, and the staff employees, not family.

The facility hadn't changed much since Tara brought her mother there a year earlier, after her doctor diagnosed Alzheimer's and not alcoholism as the cause of Mary's erratic behavior. It took weeks for Ethan to forgive Tara for intervening, even though he was the one who called her when Mary came at him with a knife.

"You didn't have to send her away," he complained after they left Mary chatting in the community living room with a catatonic gentleman in a plaid vest. "I can still take care of her."

"Daddy, it was time," Tara snapped, overtired from a week of parenting her parents. "The next time she could hurt you. Or herself. Set the house on fire. Wander down the road and get hit by a truck."

She took a deep breath. "We agreed that this is best for both of you. You did all you could — for way too long. Now she's in good hands, and you can get back to your life."

"She is my life," her father answered.

And once again, Tara felt like an outsider in her own family.

After stopping at the reception desk, she crept along a hallway bedecked with festive garlands and dancing angels. "Silent Night" played over the PA system, and the pine scent from the evergreen boughs at each door masked the faux-lemon disinfectant smell. The soles of her sneakers squeaked on the shiny linoleum.

There should be a bar in the lobby. Dim and dark, with a bartender known for his generous pours and minimal conversation. A shot of fiery tequila might make this visit easier. Then again, alcohol was what ruined her relationship with her mother in the first place. Or at least made it worse, after she killed Emma.

She stopped at the door marked '15' and studied the plastic nameplate: *Mary Davies.*

Grasping her necklace for strength, Tara peeked into her mother's room. A dark-haired woman sat in a straight-backed chair by the window, tracing random patterns on the foggy glass.

Mary wore a long black skirt and crimson top that brought out the color in her cheeks. She had a weekly appointment at the beauty parlor down the hall, where they washed and styled her silky hair. Her wedding rings were on her right hand, and a battered Betty Boop watch Ethan gave her as a joke on her left wrist. Simple pearl earrings completed the outfit. Looking at her, Tara could almost forget anything was wrong with her. Almost.

The staff helped her bathe and made sure she wore clean clothes. Otherwise, she'd use her underwear as a washcloth, or wear the same outfit for weeks. Some days the toilet confused her; on others, she searched frantically for children who didn't exist. Each month she lost more — her ability to complete simple tasks, her memory, her personality.

Years of drinking had devastating results; once she stopped, Nature stepped in to continue the slow erosion of everything that was Mary. Maybe somehow she called the dementia down upon herself to destroy the memories that she couldn't drown.

"Mama?" Tara said, and Mary turned with a confused stare.

"Who are you?" she asked. "What you want?"

"Mama, it's Tara," she said, stepping into the room. It had to be ninety degrees in there; she shed her long wool coat and draped it on a chair near the door along with her cap, easily accessible in case she needed to make a quick getaway. "I came to see you."

"Well, that's nice," Mary said, no recognition in her vacant brown eyes. She gestured toward a chair, searching for the right words. "You…?"

"Thank you." Tara perched on the edge of the worn cushion and searched for a way to start the conversation. Her mother's gaze drifted to the television in the corner, where *It's a Wonderful Life* played silently. Tara wasn't sure why there was a television in the room; even if Mary watched a program, she didn't understand what was going on. Without memory, there could be no comprehension. Her mother was a resident in a foreign country where she didn't speak the language and couldn't read the signs.

"Sorry I haven't visited, Mama," Tara began. Her mother continued to stare at the television. "I'm working a lot, and it's a long drive, and…" she trailed off. She was a terrible liar. And had stopped caring what her mother thought of her a long time before. At this point, she was just trying to avoid any more pain.

"Anyway, I have bad news." She took a steadying breath. "There's been an accident, and…well...Daddy's hurt. He's unconscious, Mama." She watched for a reaction. Nothing.

"And…Aunt Deirdre came back. Remember your sister, Deirdre? She was living in Surfside, and someone attacked her. And now she's…dead."

"Dee?" Mary said. She stared at Tara. "You came back? You came back!" She stood unsteadily and swayed toward Tara, who rose to catch her. Mary wrapped her fragile arms around Tara's slender waist and leaned heavily into her, tears rolling down her wrinkled cheeks.

"Where you been? Why you leave me alone with them?" she sobbed, burying her face in Tara's chest. She patted her mother's back stiffly; Mary hadn't shown her much affection as a child, let alone as an adult, so Tara wasn't quite sure what to do with this. She could smell her mother's hairspray, and the underlying odor of sweat and age.

"It's okay, I know you sorry. I did it anyway, for you, I did it. But it hurt, Dee, it hurt. You didn't need to leave. I didn't tell. No one knows."

What was she talking about?

"Sorry I couldn't take both. One was hard enough." She stopped crying, reached up and stroked Tara's cheek. "Secrets safe. House take care of them."

"Secrets, Mama? What secrets? What house?"

"Everything safe." Mary nodded emphatically. "House knows." Then she wiped her eyes. "You were gone so long," she pouted. "Why did you go? Why you not take me with you?"

Mary must be referring to Tara leaving her at Fairhaven. But she called her 'Dee.' And acted as though Tara was the one who left.

Finally, it dawned on her.

Mary thought she was Deirdre.

Tara didn't know what to say. Should she try to convince her mother that she wasn't her long-lost sister? Or go along with her and try to figure out what the hell she was talking about?

"I couldn't take you with me," Tara finally said. "You needed to stay and take care of the house. And the…secrets."

"They're safe," Mary whispered, glancing toward the door. "No one find them. House protects them." She leaned close to Tara's ear. "Go back now. It's been alone too long."

"Okay, I'll go back. But maybe you should tell me where the secrets are, just in case the house forgets."

"Same place. But lots more now. House knows. House will tell you." Mary released Tara and returned to her chair, falling heavily into it. "Tired. So tired."

Tara knelt next to her mother. "Mama, Deirdre is gone. Daddy's hurt. I'm the only one left. And I don't know what you're talking about."

But her mother had returned to her silent world, lost in the flickering screen.

&

Secrets.

Tara sat on the back stoop with a bowl of Moose Tracks ice cream, licking gooey fudge from the spoon as she replayed the conversation with her mother.

Mary was upset that Deirdre left. But Tara already knew that. She never hid her anger at her sister's disappearance.

Mary did something for Deirdre that hurt, and she expected Deirdre to be sorry about it.

And, most of all, a house was protecting secrets.

What kind of secrets could Mary — and apparently Deirdre — have? Mary made it sound as though the house was actively doing something, which was crazy. And which house was she talking about? Mary was born in Surfside, but lived most of her married life in Portland.

None of this made sense. Obviously, Mary's mind was failing faster than Tara realized. She should probably call the doctor and see if he could change her medication.

A house protecting secrets. Her mother was definitely nuts.

Tara stood and stretched, gazing at the moon overhead, a few days from full. A sheen of moisture glistened on the sleeping lawn. If the temperature dropped much further, that sheen would turn to ice. Sneakers was slinking through the damp grass, intent on invisible prey. The little black cat looked better already: amazing what a few good meals could do.

Although she couldn't see it clearly in the moonlight, Tara knew the outside of the house needed as much work as the inside. She had to hop over the hole in the third step each time she climbed to the porch. The windows might be intact, but the shutters were barely holding on. The siding needed a coat of stain. Sections of clapboard needed replacing, as did a number of floorboards on the porch. Not to mention the path, the driveway, the garage, the lawn, the flowerbeds: the list was mind-boggling.

She had enough to worry about without trying to figure out her mother's ramblings.

If the weather held, she'd start on the outside projects tomorrow. Maybe she'd find a chest filled with gold doubloons buried in the back yard. With a laugh that echoed off the fir trees towering around the house, she called to her cat and walked inside.

~ 13 ~

Tara felt her presence before she saw her. There was a warmth in the bedroom that wasn't there a moment earlier.

She opened her eyes and saw a young woman perched on a straight-backed chair near the foot of the bed. The trees around the house shielded the window from all but a few slivers of moonlight, so Tara couldn't make out specific details or colors. She sensed, more than saw, the features of the woman sitting in front of her.

Long curls cascaded to her waist and her eyes gleamed in the moonlight, flashing as she glanced around the room. Her smile had a devilish hint. She wore a long flowing skirt and beaded peasant blouse: the uniform of youth in the Sixties.

Tara was relatively certain the woman sitting at the foot of her bed wasn't real. Was she dreaming, or being visited by a hippie ghost?

If she was a ghost, she wasn't rattling chains or moaning like ghosts were supposed to do. Instead, she was cradling a small box. Tara heard a metallic creak as the woman slowly opened the lid. Bracelets jangled on her wrists. Her face reflected the golden light coming from the box as she peeked into it. Then she closed the lid and cupped her hands around it, as if guarding a precious treasure.

Tara leaned forward, trying to get a better look. The woman noticed the movement and turned toward her. When she saw Tara watching, she rose and moved toward the head of the bed, stopping just out of Tara's reach — a safe distance for both of them. She motioned at the box and looked at Tara as if to ask, 'Do you want to see inside?'

Tara nodded and held her breath, hoping a very small, vicious creature wouldn't jump out and attack her. Like a ghost weasel.

The woman cautiously came closer, as though she knew a sudden move could change Tara's attitude. And just as cautiously, lowered herself onto the edge of the bed. Tara could feel the mattress shift as it bore the added weight. She smelled a hint of heady perfume: plumeria, perhaps, or gardenia.

Dream…ghost…real.

Tara wanted to reach out and touch her shoulder, but she fought the urge. She wasn't prepared to deal with the possibility of her hand going *through* the woman's shoulder.

As they sat side by side, Tara felt something pass between them. It was a kinship of sorts — a shared history.

Who was she?

"You know who I am, Tara," the woman replied. Tara didn't realize she had spoken her thoughts aloud. Then wondered if she truly did.

"The box, Tara. Come see what's inside the box." She opened the lid slowly, and Tara leaned over to peer inside.

A galaxy of golden stars danced in the inky darkness. They reminded Tara of Tinkerbell, the fairy from Peter Pan. A thousand Tinkerbells. It felt as though she were looking into the depths of the universe, a Milky Way inside a tiny box.

"What are they?" she asked in awe, unable to tear her eyes away from the dancing lights.

"When you are ready, you will understand."

"Ready for what?"

The woman continued, ignoring Tara's question. "The house protects the secrets. It will help you find what you seek, but the price can be steep. Be sure you are prepared to pay the price."

"What house? You mean this house? The price for what?" Why did those words sound so familiar?

The woman lowered the lid and Tara's heart wrenched as the glow vanished. She wanted to see the stars again. Needed to see them. The woman stood, clutching her prize.

"Wait!" Tara said. "Please, don't go. I don't understand."

The woman smiled sadly, and then Tara knew. She'd been given a gift, and now must decide what to do with it. She nodded at the woman, who moved toward the window and disappeared through the glass into the night.

The room turned bitter cold.

&

The moon had set, taking its comforting light with it. Tara stood at the window and studied the stars overhead, comparing them to the ones in the box. She wiped a clear spot on the foggy glass; the real stars paled in comparison to the dancing lights. She started to sit in the chair the woman had used, but there wasn't one.

If it was a dream, she needed to stop eating Moose Tracks for dinner. A box full of stars. Definitely too much ice cream.

But what if it *was* a ghost — one with a message for her? She said Tara knew who she was, but Tara couldn't see her features. She did look familiar, though. Or at least she *felt* familiar. Tara stared out the window and thought about the sense of loss she felt when the woman closed the box.

Suddenly she realized why the woman's words sounded familiar. Mr. Edison read those very phrases. They were in Deirdre's will.

She traced patterns on the window with a single finger. Could the ghost have been Deirdre? She *did* resemble the woman Tara saw at the cemetery.

Ghosts were supposed to be lost souls. If that were true, why would Deirdre's soul be lost?

The house will help you find what you seek. Tara had spent her life searching for something, although she never really knew what. But how could what she was looking for be in this house?

Maybe the box was a symbol of something hidden in the house. Something that held the family's secrets. Something the house was protecting. If she discovered the secrets, maybe they would reveal the answers about her own life.

Tara sighed and turned toward the bed, and stepped on something hard. "Ow!" She rubbed her foot, then turned on the lamp on the nightstand to look at the object. It was a glass bead. What was it doing here? Then she remembered.

The ghost was wearing a beaded shirt.

It had probably been there for years. Or maybe it was Deirdre's. But Tara hadn't seen any beaded clothing in Deirdre's closet, and she had swept the bedroom floor that afternoon.

She tossed the bead into a small dish next to the lamp and crawled under the comforter, closing her eyes with a sigh.

She didn't see the gold star hovering above her head before it danced across the room and disappeared through the foggy windowpane.

~ *14* ~

Tara adjusted her cap as she opened the fingerprint-smudged doors of Surfside Hardware. The beauty of small towns was that most of them still had an old-fashioned hardware store. The do-it-yourself chains lurked on the edge of town, but they couldn't match the level of service the smaller stores offered.

If you needed one specific-sized bolt to fit one specific-sized nut, the big box stores weren't much help: you had to buy a carton of twenty-five and hope they were the right size. But at the local hardware store, the clerk would not only find the bolt, he'd ask if you needed a washer, and make sure you had the right wrench for the job, too.

Which was a godsend for Tara. She needed to repair the broken glass in the back door. The piece of cardboard she taped over the hole wasn't very secure, especially since whoever attacked Ethan and Deirdre was still out there somewhere. Although the door couldn't have been very secure to begin with, if *she* could break in. But she didn't want to think about that. With real glass in the door again, she could pretend to feel safe.

There must have been a sale on Christmas CDs at the dollar store; every business in town was playing the same tired Muzak carols. Tara wandered through aisles smelling of dust and chainsaw oil until she found a clerk helping a family in the garden department. Once they left, he stepped back onto his stool and returned to straightening items on the shelf.

"Excuse me?" Tara said, always uncomfortable admitting that she didn't know how to do something. The clerk was middle-aged, thin bordering on skeletal, with a nervous habit of pulling on the hem of his red vest as if trying to cover his non-existent rear end.

"Yes, ma'am," he replied, staring down from his perch. "How can I help you?"

"I need to replace a pane of glass in a door."

He stepped off the stool, but still towered over her, dwarfing her 5’8” frame. “What happened to it?”

She blushed. “I had to break into my house. I forgot my keys.” It was easier to tell a white lie than to explain what really happened. Not that it was any of his business. She pulled her cap lower across her face.

“Are you new in town?”

The fist began tightening around Tara’s bruised heart.

“Yes, I am. Just moved here from Merrow Bay.” Hopefully that made her more of a local and therefore, less suspicious.

“Where do you live?”

“Out on Chinook Road. I think I need a piece of glass eight inches square. I guess I should have measured it, huh?” She laughed nervously.

He took a step closer. Tara took a step backward. “I heard someone moved in up there,” he said. “Kind of lonely, a woman living by herself.”

Impatience was quickly replacing fear. Besides, how did he know she lived alone? “Not really. Do you have a piece of glass that size?”

“Bad doings on the Chinook Road last month. I suppose you heard?” He was fishing, and Tara was tired of being bait.

“Yes, I did, actually. Someone attacked my father and murdered my aunt. Now I’m living in that house, and I’d like to make sure that whoever assaulted them doesn’t come back and slash my throat in my sleep. So can you help me or not?”

“I thought so,” he replied. His hard eyes narrowed as he studied her. “Funny that you would worry about someone killing you. Paybacks are hell, aren’t they?”

The fist released her heart to tear at her lungs. She couldn’t breathe.

Tara spun around and searched for the door. A maze of gaudy Christmas displays surrounded her. She hurried toward the front of the store and passed a fish that began singing “Jingle Bells” at full volume. She dropped her purse, and a cascade of items rolled across the scuffed floor. Kneeling to pick them up, tears blurred her vision.

She had to get out.

Tara grabbed everything she could see, and almost knocked over another display as she stood. People were starting to stare. Maybe because she was crying in a hardware store, but more likely because the clerk was already spreading the word.

They knew.

She pushed past an elderly couple whispering to each other, and she thought she heard the word 'murderer.' Every face closed as she approached, every body stiffened as she passed.

Finally, she rounded a corner and saw the winter sun framed in the dirty glass door.

Out.

Hide.

Tara burst through the door, jabbing the button on the remote as she ran toward her truck. She fumbled the key into the ignition and sped out of the parking lot. She didn't know where she was going; she just needed to escape.

What had she been thinking? Moving to Surfside was a mistake. She should have stayed hidden in Merrow Bay.

She drove blindly down the twisting roads. When she saw a parking lot she swung in and stopped under a spruce tree. Her hands shook, her heart pounded. She took deep breaths, trying to calm herself. Even with her baseball cap and sunglasses, she still hadn't been prepared. She had been found out.

Tara buried her face in her hands and wept.

&

A sharp rap on the window startled her. Tara looked up and saw a man peering at her with a frown. They both jumped. Recognized each other at the same time. And laughed.

Lee pantomimed rolling down the window. "I didn't mean to scare you."

Tara wiped her eyes and smiled ruefully. "Sorry. I didn't know where I was."

"Bad morning?"

"You could say that." But it would be an understatement.

"Buy you a cup of coffee? Looks like you need one."

"Only if you have arsenic to put in it."

He laughed. "Sorry, out of arsenic. Plenty of Baileys, though."

"That'll have to do." She rolled up the window and crawled out of the truck. Maybe a cup of coffee — with plenty of Baileys — would get her mind off her problems. She didn't realize she was in Lee's parking lot. She shouldn't have been driving when she was that upset; she didn't realize she had driven that far out of town.

Lee was holding the door open for her. As she passed the silent menagerie, she patted the elephant's leg. The wrinkled skin felt rubbery, like an eraser. "Hey there, Miss Gertrude," she said, not noticing that Lee was watching her.

She settled onto a stool and he filled two mugs. He pushed one toward her, and coffee sloshed over the rim.

"Sorry," he said as he mopped up the mess. He tossed the stained towel behind the bar and settled onto another stool. "So, you want to tell the klutzy bartender all about it?" His tone was light, his eyes kind.

Tara shrugged. "An old ghost came back to haunt me today. I thought I exorcised that particular one, but apparently I haven't." She inhaled the rich aroma and took a sip, barely noticing the hot liquid burning her tongue. "Funny how one little thing can cut you off at the knees. I'm embarrassed you caught me, though."

Tara felt something gently bump her leg and looked down. The sheepdog nudged her with a cold, wet nose. She stroked the soft head and floppy ears, and the big dog collapsed at her feet with a contented sigh.

"Forget it. I didn't recognize your truck, so thought you were someone wanting to sell me something. Or a customer who didn't make it home last night. I was relieved it was you. Although I can't help but wonder what kind of ghost could shake you up like that." He sat quietly, neither pressing nor retreating.

Tara studied her coffee. It wasn't something she talked about.

But she was tired. Tired of hiding. Tired of running. Of living with the shame. The scene in the hardware store had pushed her over the edge.

He'd know soon enough, anyway; the story would be all over town in a matter of days. He might as well hear it from her first. She didn't know him very well yet, so it wouldn't be that awful when he kicked her out. Although she'd be sorry because she was starting to like him.

Tara took a deep breath and said the words that had haunted her for thirty-one years.

"I murdered my sister."

&

She waited for the usual outburst of indignation, the look of disgust.

Instead, Lee nodded. Which puzzled, then irritated, her.

"If you're waiting for more, that's it. Isn't that enough?" she said, standing and pulling on her gloves.

"Aren't you going to finish?" he asked.

"Finish what?"

"Your coffee."

"My coffee?" Tara looked down at her mug and back at him. "You want me to finish my coffee?"

"Yep, that's the gist of it. Although we forgot the Baileys." He slipped around the back of the bar and pulled a brown bottle from the cooler. "Need a warm-up first?"

Tara stared at him. "Didn't you hear me?"

He filled her mug, more Baileys than coffee, and then his own again. "I heard you. I'm waiting for the rest of the story." He returned to his stool. "Drink up. It's a shame to waste Baileys."

Of all of the reactions she'd experienced, this was a new one.

"I'm sorry. I'm kind of at a loss. Normal people don't offer me a drink when they find that out." She sank onto her stool and dropped her gloves back onto the bar.

"So I'm not normal. Not the first time I've heard that. Does that mean you're not going to tell me the rest of the story?" He took a sip from his steaming mug.

"I've never told anyone the real story. I don't think I even know how."

"Then this would be a good time to practice." He leaned closer. "Tara, we all have secrets. Don't assume yours are worse than anyone else's. Everyone has a story. We're not always lucky enough to hear them.

"I'd like to hear yours." He looked at his watch. "I don't open for a couple of hours. Is that enough time?"

Enough time? To tell this stranger about the disaster that was her life? To describe the pain, the sorrow, the loneliness? To risk rejection from someone who could be a friend?

"I don't know where to start," she said softly.

"Try the beginning," he replied, just as softly.

&

Tara is eight and Emma, five. Mama and Daddy are in the living room. Mama is in one of her moods, so Daddy tells them to play with their dolls in the study and not bother her. He doesn't let them play in the study very often.

Tara loves the dark walls and shelves full of dusty books. Sometimes she sneaks one off the shelf and carefully opens it, lowering her face into the pages and breathing the smell of old words.

Someday she'll read all of these books, but now she is supposed to take care of her little sister. Sometimes she wishes Emma would just go away, so she wouldn't have to watch her any more. Emma wants to play dolls when Tara wants to play Candy Land or Life. But because Emma is the baby, Tara has to do what Emma wants. Someday she'll get to do what she wants. Someday Emma won't get all of the attention.

She can hear her parents in the other room: Daddy's quiet voice, Mama's loud one. Mama's mood is worse some days than others. Those are the days Tara and Emma play in their bedroom, whispering. You don't want to make Mama mad when she's in one of her moods. Emma's cheeks are always sore from Mama 'slapping that look off her face.' Emma has a way of doing or saying the wrong thing at the wrong time; she hasn't learned when to shut up and smile like Tara. Sometimes she thinks Emma makes Mama mad on purpose, though she doesn't know why.

Mama never hits Tara, but that doesn't mean she doesn't hurt her. Mama's yelling hurts as much as her blows.

Tara likes it when it is just her and Daddy, when Emma is asleep in her trundle bed and Mama is in her room with the door closed. They sit on the porch and eat cherry popsicles and Daddy points out the constellations — Tara thinks he says constipations — the Big Dipper and Cassiopeia the Queen on her throne and her favorite, Orion the hunter. He asks her how school is, and listens to her stories about Miss Morton and the boy who pulls her hair and the black and white hamster in the smelly cage in the back of her classroom.

Tonight, Mama is louder than usual. Daddy is rumbling more than usual. And Emma won't be quiet.

"Emma, shut up," Tara whispers as her sister plays with the dolls. "Daddy said if we're not quiet, we can't play in here."

"You're not the boss of me!" Emma says. She starts singing, "You can't make me, you can't make me."

"Emma!" Tara says, louder, "you're going to get us in trouble. Do you want Mama to hit you again?"

"I don't care!" Emma screams, throwing Las Vegas Barbie at Tara. But Tara ducks and Barbie bounces off a vase on the table next to the couch. The vase crashes onto the floor. A really loud crash. Blue glass, water, and flowers fly everywhere.

Tara grabs Emma by the arm and drags her away from the mess. "Look what you did! Now we're going to get in trouble. Why can't you listen for a change?" She shakes Emma, knowing that her mother will do a lot worse when she comes in. "Why do you always have to make her mad at you?"

Tara shoves Emma, and Emma falls onto the couch. Her head hits the corner of the table with a crack. She slides onto the floor, leaving a thin trail of blood on the caramel-colored cushions.

"Emma!" Tara says, staring at the blood. "Oh no, Emma. Wake up!" She shakes her sister, but Emma doesn't wake up.

"I'm sorry, Emma, I'm sorry, I'm sorry," she keeps repeating to the too-still figure. Kneels next to her, patting her face like she's seen people do in the movies. "Wake up and I'll play Barbies with you any time, I promise. I won't let her hurt you any more. Please, Emma, please wake up."

The door opens and their father enters the room. He looks at the girls, the glass and the flowers, and the blood.

"Stand back, Tara," he says, bending to pick up his daughter.

"I didn't mean to, Daddy. She hit her head. I didn't mean to hurt her. I would never hurt her."

He carries Emma out of the room. A drop of blood splashes onto the hardwood floor. Tara wipes it up with the corner of her new yellow sweater. Then she gathers the dolls and puts them in their carrying case. She carefully picks up the shards of glass and drops them in the wastebasket. There is another vase under the sink in the kitchen; she fills it with water and puts the flowers in it, then carries it carefully into the study and sets it on the table. She gets a towel from the kitchen and dries the water on the floor. With the wet towel, she scrubs at the blood on the cushions, tears rolling down her face.

Then she sits on the caramel-colored couch and waits.

&

"He called an ambulance," Tara said flatly, staring into her empty mug, the smooth taste of Baileys lingering on her tongue. "But it was too late. By the time they got there, she was gone." She glanced up at Lee, tears in her eyes. "I never saw my sister again. They wouldn't even let me go to her funeral."

"And all of these years, you've blamed yourself?"

"Who else should I blame? It was my fault. I pushed her. I should have called my father earlier. Maybe he could have saved her." Her hand went to her necklace.

"You were eight years old," Lee argued. "You didn't know how badly she was hurt. And you certainly didn't do it on purpose. How can you blame yourself for that?"

"People did." She didn't say which people. "Even though there are rules that are supposed to protect children, one of the tabloids discovered where we lived. They staked out the house. They branded me 'child killer,' 'sister slayer,' and my personal favorite, 'baby basher.'" Lee flinched as Tara spat out the words. "They made me out to be a monster. And my parents did nothing about it. I've been running from my reputation ever since."

"So what happened today?"

"I didn't run fast enough." She rose. "I should get going. I need to feed my cat. Besides, you don't want to be seen associating with me; it'll be bad for business." The dog stood and stretched, too.

"Fuck that," Lee said. "I've never chosen my friends according to popular opinion, and I don't intend to start now."

"You don't know me. Why would you be willing to risk anything for me?"

"Maybe I know you better than you think." He stood and looked down at her. "Like I said, we all have secrets. Maybe one of these days I'll tell you mine." He smiled and rested his hand on her shoulder. It felt warm and safe. "You okay to drive?"

"Yes, I'm fine. Thanks for the coffee. And for not having any arsenic." She smiled ruefully. "And for not kicking me out. It feels weird to talk about it, after all this time." She looked up at Lee, wondering what was going on behind those hazel eyes.

"Maybe you'll find word doesn't spread as fast as you think it does. Or that people are more forgiving than you give them credit for."

He walked her to the door, the sheepdog plodding behind them. "Put me in your phone. Just in case." She punched in the number, and nodded her thanks. "By the way," he said, "what's with the necklace?"

Tara fingered the child's ring suspended from the slender gold chain. There were silver patches on the band where the gold plating had flaked off, and the blue stone was nicked and battered.

"It was Emma's."

"Ah."

"It reminds me of what I lost." *What I killed.*

"And helps you continue to feel guilty that you're alive and she isn't?"

She looked up at him. "Of course not!" But deep inside, she knew he was right.

&

The little black cat padded softly up the staircase and down the hallway, pausing to sniff at spots on the hardwood floor. He disappeared into the master bedroom, emerging a few minutes later to continue his meticulous tour.

He poked his head into the pink room, but didn't find anything intriguing enough to go in. Then on to the green room, which smelled much more interesting. He wandered in and crawled under the bed, only to discover the fringe on the white bedspread, which he batted happily with an oversized paw. Then leapt onto the bed and paced across the mattress, leaving tiny indentations.

As he started to curl into a ball in the midst of the pillows, he glanced at the nightstand and froze, and then crossed to it, his gaze fixed on something. He snaked past the lamp and clock and arrived at his destination: a bead nestled in a glass dish.

With one swat of his paw, the bead flew across the floor. He chased it around the room, leaping, rolling, pouncing. Then suddenly, it was gone.

The cat stopped and studied the spot where he last saw it, and then sat in the middle of the room, looking puzzled.

~ *15* ~

Tara breathed the rich odor of the man whose body covered hers: part aftershave, part sweat. Her fingers knotted in his curls, pulling his mouth down to meet hers. She was lost in the sensations flooding her, the taste of his skin, the feel of his lips, the urgent need for him to bury himself inside her. He seemed to know exactly where to touch her, now fast, now slow. The words to whisper into her ear that would both soothe and excite her. Her breath came in gasps as they writhed between the tangled sheets, struggling to pull each other closer. Their limbs tangled together as they stroked and touched, urged and teased, rising together, and then finally falling.

Later, by the light of a single candle, she stroked his damp skin as he slept, tracing the intricate pattern that wound around his body. How had she been so lucky to find this man who knew exactly what she liked, what she needed? Who accepted her for who she was — in spite of who she was. She snuggled into his arms, spent and satisfied, knowing she'd never be alone again.

&

Tara awoke and stretched, pointing her toes, arching her back, pressing her palms against the smooth wood headboard. The memory of the night before was too sweet to ruin it by opening her eyes. Besides, there wasn't much to see; it was still dark.

She reached for the man curled in the bed next to her. Hopefully he liked morning sex, too. But her hand touched soft fur instead of a warm, hard body. She turned on the bedside lamp and looked around. No clothes scattered around the room. No candle burning on the bureau. No handsome man with blond curls in her bed. She was alone. Except for Sneakers, snoring softly on the side of the bed where her lover should be.

Tara fell back onto the bed. *Damn*. It was only a dream.

But boy, what a dream. Her skin still tingled from his touch. She sighed and rolled onto her side, tucking her arm under her pillow. Of course it hadn't been real, considering her luck with men. But for a few moments, she felt cherished and desired. It was a wonderful — though unfamiliar — feeling.

Where in the heck did that come from? Maybe telling Lee her story opened a gate in Tara's memory, a gate that she usually kept locked. Next thing she knew, she'd be sharing intimate details of her sex life with total strangers. Well, her imaginary sex life, since she didn't have a real one. But with dreams that vivid, who needed a real one? She wondered who this mystery man was, and hoped he'd return to spend the night with her again.

Tara crept out of bed. She needed a shower. A very cold one.

&

Rain slicked the French doors in the study. The wind must be blowing; Tara could hear the tap-tap-tapping of a branch on one of the windowpanes. She woke early, intending to work in the yard, but the weather dictated otherwise. So she decided to research mermaids, being curious about her taciturn housemate. If she could get online, that is. Internet service was sketchy at best this far south of town. Especially when it rained.

Today was no exception. Tara turned on her laptop and saw the "no connection" message.

Damn.

After two phone calls to her Internet provider and twenty minutes of cursing, she was finally online. Crossing her fingers, she typed 'mermaid' into the search engine and started reading.

After a couple of hours, she leaned back in her chair and stretched. Ariel was indeed a mermaid. Unlike other female figureheads, mermaids were traditionally depicted with a comb and a mirror, symbolizing their deadly beauty.

Legend claimed that mermaids lured sailors to their deaths, although it wasn't certain if they did it out of spite or because they forgot their beloved humans couldn't breathe underwater. They longed for immortal souls, which they could only gain by marrying a human, and in return would grant him three wishes.

They also were associated with Aphrodite, the goddess of fertility — the perfect woman.

Tara walked down the hallway and crouched next to the carving, which now wore a lei of scarlet and yellow silk flowers, and traced her flowing curls with a single finger. "What stories you could tell, Ariel. How many luckless sailors fell prey to your lethal beauty? Or were you just lonely?"

The beaches of the Oregon coast were littered with remnants of shipwrecks. As a child, Tara clambered around the rocks with her father, searching for treasure. She loved the tidal pools with their slimy sea creatures, and sometimes even found a starfish half-hidden in the sand. But it was rare to find anything this size, and in such good condition.

Then she remembered the bell hanging by the front door. Although she hadn't examined it very carefully, it looked nautical; maybe the two were connected. She shivered as she opened the front door and the damp coastal air rushed into the warm house.

The brass bell was tarnished from years of exposure to the weather. Tara was surprised that no one had stolen it. Then again, she was surprised that most everything in the house was still there and in decent shape, considering how many years the place sat empty. It was almost as if it had somehow been protected.

Tara examined the bell and found something etched into the surface. She ran her fingers across the brass, thinking the marks might be letters. But she'd have to polish it to find out. 'Brass polish' went on the shopping list once she was back inside, after giving the bell one final tap to hear its soulful ring.

"Well, wherever you're from, thanks for sharing your home with me," she said to Ariel as she walked toward the kitchen. And once again, caught a whiff of salt air. She stopped and glanced over her shoulder, but the mermaid gazed silently into the distance.

Outside, the bell swayed in an invisible breeze, clanging softly.

&

Tara and Mariah sat side by side in the study drinking cocoa, after spending the afternoon hanging loose shutters; well, Tara nailed the shutters into place while Mariah kept up a steady stream of girlish chatter. The smaller shutters Tara could do alone, but the larger ones were going to be a challenge; she'd worry about them later.

"You made this?" Mariah asked, studying a memory book. "It looks like a picture album." The steady beat of the rain on the windows, along with the ever-present tapping of the branch on the glass, made the room feel like a cozy haven in the storm.

"Well, yes, it's sort of like a photo album. Only a little fancier. People give me pictures, birth announcements, anniversary cards, stuff like that. They tell me where the pictures wee taken, and about the people in them. I add my own touches. I find leaves from the tree in one picture, sand from the beach in another. Voice clips from grandparents. Sometimes perfume or an earring. Whatever helps people remember their family. Then I put them into a book."

"You get paid to do this?"

"Believe it or not," Tara answered, smiling. Sometimes the amount people were willing to pay for her books amazed her. Although they were much more than scrapbooks; she infused them with the very soul of a family, and her clients often marveled how she brought their loved ones to life on the page.

Tara was discovered after she created a book for a Portland artist, who showed it to a friend in the media. Soon her work was being touted as a highly prized art form and she was earning national recognition — under a fictitious name, of course. Although she refused requests for pictures and televised interviews, magazine, newspaper and Internet articles brought in more business than she could handle. Tara earned enough to pay her bills, and still have some left over for traveling.

And she loved the work. She could lose herself in the lives of other people and, for a while, forget about her own.

With the added expense of repairing the house, she really needed to take on more work, but she didn't have time because she was repairing the house. A vicious circle. At least she didn't have a family to care for.

Talk about making lemonade out of lemons.

"Would you like me to make a book for you?" she asked.

Mariah shook her head. "I don't have many pictures. Who's this?"

As Tara identified the people in the pictures, she thought about her own family, and wondered if the people in her books truly were as happy as they looked. Pictures could hide a multitude of truths. And lies.

There was a box of photographs in her closet, most of which were taken when Emma was alive. After she died, everything changed, including recording her family's history. Looking at the people posing with their black and white smiles, you couldn't see the sadness or the anger, the fear or the neglect. Or the silence. The silence that was worse than the yelling. The silence that sent Tara running to her closet, hoping her father could divert her mother before she found her. She bore the scars from the times that he couldn't.

"Why don't you have many pictures?" she asked Mariah.

"Oh, there are probably some from before I lost my legs."

"Lost them?" Tara looked down at Mariah's blue jeans and beat-up sneakers.

The girl shrugged. "People acted weird when they saw that my legs stopped at the knees. So I stuffed my jeans with rags and found these sneakers in a garbage can at school. Now no one can tell. I'm pretty creative for 13, huh?" She patted the lower half of her leg proudly, and Tara saw that it indeed was soft. It *was* creative. And kind of eerie.

"Yes, you are. How did you lose them?"

"Bacterial meningitis." The words rolled off her tongue like old friends.

"That can be fatal, can't it?"

"Yep. I was lucky." Mariah licked her finger and methodically turned a page. Tara marveled that she could define her situation as 'luck.'

"Don't you have artificial legs?"

"Nope. My parents don't believe in them. They didn't believe me when I told them I was sick, either. The doctors said if they had waited much longer to take me to the emergency room, I would have died. But I can't stay mad at them forever; that just hurts me."

"You're a pretty understanding person," Tara said. How could Mariah forgive her parents for behavior that impacted her life so severely?

Mariah shrugged. *Whatever.* And continued studying a picture of a family gathered around a holiday table groaning with a golden turkey and all the trimmings. "Why don't you have kids?"

"I'm not very comfortable around children." Tara couldn't tell Mariah that she didn't trust herself around children. That she longed for a family, but vowed never to endanger another child's life. So she remained childless. And single, since most of the men she met wanted a family, and disappeared when she told them she wasn't interested. Imagine how fast they would disappear if she told them *why* she wasn't interested.

The purring of a car engine interrupted their conversation, and they glanced out the French doors toward the driveway.

"Looks like some sleazy guy," Mariah said.

Tara recognized Craig Morris's convertible. "Yep, he's sleazy, all right. How can you tell?"

"Only sleazy guys drive cars like that." Mariah gave Tara a quick hug and wheeled her chair through the dining room. "I'll go out the back door so you don't have to explain who I am."

"I don't care…" Tara began, but Mariah was already in the laundry room, tugging on her yellow slicker.

"Thanks for the cocoa. It was delish. See you later." She disappeared through the back door.

Tara pulled on her sweatshirt and opened the front door. Craig sat in his car, talking on his phone. The rain had stopped, but his wipers still squeaked across the windshield. He looked up and made a 'just a minute' motion, and she sighed and picked up one of the emerald shutters. He must not be very bright; attacking him with a flagpole should have been a pretty clear indication that he shouldn't rush back.

As she struggled with the shutter, a pair of hands appeared from behind her and pinned it to the side of the house. "Is this where you want to put it?" Craig asked.

"Well, it's not my first choice." Her sharp tongue was going to get her into trouble one of these days. "But yes, that's fine. Thanks." She nailed the shutter in place, the blows of her hammer echoing through the still afternoon air, and allowed him to help with the others.

When they were finished, he wiped his hands on his raincoat, leaving dirty streaks. "You need help with anything else?"

"No thanks." She rolled the hammer around in her hand. He stood in front of her, almost expectantly.

"Okay, what do you want?" Tara said. "I appreciate the help and all, but I thought I was pretty clear that you aren't welcome."

"I checked to see if you were packing the flagpole before I got out of my car," he said with a wry grin.

Tara tried not to smile, but failed. "Oh, it's handy, if I need it. Will I need it?"

"I hope not. I came to apologize."

"For what?" she asked. Even the birds stopped singing, as if waiting for his response.

"For being a jerk the other day. I wasn't very smooth."

"Not by a long shot. I'm surprised you had the balls to come back."

He looked down at his polished loafers. "This is going to sound really weird, but I didn't have a choice. This damn house keeps calling me."

That got her attention. "Calling you?"

"I don't know how else to explain it." He tried to brush the dirt from his coat. "I can't get this place off my mind. It didn't stop until I pulled into the yard. Believe me, I wasn't that excited about seeing you again, either."

"That shows you do have *some* decency."

"I actually do." He smiled. "Anyway, I'm embarrassed that I let my business sense overrule my common sense. I've never done that before, and I promise it won't happen again. "

Tara didn't believe him, but wanted to be fair. "Okay. I forgive you. Especially since you helped me with those stupid shutters. They're a handful for one person. And Mariah isn't much help, obviously."

"Mariah?"

"The girl you passed in the driveway."

"I didn't see a girl."

"Are you blind? Wheelchair, bright yellow raincoat?"

"Sorry," Craig said, shaking his head.

"That's strange." Maybe she took a shortcut through the woods. But Tara hadn't seen a path wide enough to accommodate Mariah's chair.

"Anyway, I just wanted to apologize. I truly am sorry for your loss." He extended his hand, this time without a business card.

Tara hesitated for a second before taking it. "Thanks."

He turned to walk down the steps, and Tara realized he was heading for the hole. "Watch out!"

Too late. His foot crashed through the third tread and he pitched forward, grabbing for the handrail. Which also gave way, sending him face first down the steps.

"Are you okay?" Tara jumped off the porch and knelt next to him, as he lay motionless on the wet ground. "I am *so* sorry!"

"I think your house hates me," he groaned. He slowly struggled to a sitting position.

"I should have warned you about that step." With her luck, he'd sue; she hadn't gotten homeowner's insurance and couldn't afford to pay medical bills, let alone damages or court costs.

He crawled to his feet and glanced down at his wet, dirty clothes. "I'll be fine. I'm a rock climber; this is nothing compared to how I feel some Monday mornings." He ran his tongue over his chipped tooth.

"You're being very gracious."

"It's no big deal. Forget it." He waved half-heartedly and limped to his car, rubbing his shoulder.

Tara watched him drive away, and walked back inside. Maybe he was a decent guy, after all. Although she wasn't ready to forgive him just yet.

It was strange, though. Why would the house call to him, too? So much for feeling special. Hopefully a stream of folks didn't show up at her door, answering the house's summons.

As she walked through the hallway, Tara tripped. Reaching out to break her fall, she shoved her hand through the newly repaired hole in the wall. And tore open the cut on her wrist.

"Ow! Damn it!" she yelled, staring at the hole, and the cut, which was once again bleeding all over her jeans. "I do not believe this!" She looked down to see what she tripped on, and found the trowel she used to patch the wall. Which she left on the staircase when she finished filling the hole. Maybe it fell...although it would have taken a small earthquake to move the tool clear across the hallway.

Tara picked up the trowel and studied it. She was beginning to think the house didn't want that hole repaired. And she was only half kidding.

&

A young Mary holds a crying baby. Her arms are stiff, all elbows and wrists, as she tries to manage the squirming bundle.

"Ethan!" she calls. "Did you find her?"

Ethan enters the room, holding a piece of paper. He looks at Mary. "She's gone."

"Gone? What do you mean, gone?" She jiggles the baby awkwardly and the screams increase.

"Gone as in left, as in no longer here." He reads the note, raising his voice over the child's cries. "'Mary: I need to tie up some loose ends. I'll be back in a couple of days, promise. Please take care of my little girl, Lil Sis. Love, D.'" The page is wrinkled where he grips it.

"'Tie up some loose ends?'" Mary stares at her husband, her eyes wide. "She can't be serious."

"There must be a party somewhere." He looks at the baby, red-faced and bawling. "Can't you make her stop?"

"No, I can't," she snaps. "Maybe she's hungry. I don't know when Deirdre fed her last." She pushes the bundle into her husband's arms. "Take her. I'll find a bottle."

"I don't know what to do with a baby."

"You think I do?" Mary snaps. She stumbles into the kitchen. Ethan looks down at the baby, who begins to hiccup.

"She's going to figure it out," he says under his breath, gazing into her startling blue eyes. "It won't take her long. She'll figure us out."

~ *16* ~

"Damn it!"

Tara was beyond frustrated. She had worked on the downstairs bathroom all morning. After she patched the hole in the hallway *again*, this time adding an extra layer of mud. She was starting to wonder why the house didn't want that hole covered.

Sometime in the past forty years, something in the upstairs bathroom had overflowed, destroying the ceiling and walls below. Tara hoped it hadn't been the toilet. She tore out the rotten plaster, choking on the dust that swirled around the tiny room. Then she pulled down the ceiling tiles, and years of dead spiders and mouse droppings cascaded onto her head.

"Yuck!" Tara screamed and ran into the kitchen, and stuck her head under the faucet to rinse the filth out of her hair. "This is just plain disgusting," she muttered to herself, drying her hair with a daisy-covered dishtowel. 'Mask' and 'scarf' went onto her shopping list.

Now, wet hair tickling her neck, Tara tried to fill the gaps in the walls. No one at the do-it-yourself store warned her about the weight of a sheet of drywall, or that a jack would make the job a lot easier. For the hundredth time, she cursed the nasty clerk at Surfside Hardware; now she had to drive miles to a box store and deal with high schoolers who didn't know a ball peen from a ball bearing. Not that she did, either, but she wasn't being paid to know.

Her shoulders ached. The cut on her wrist burned. There was plaster dust in her mouth. The sheet of drywall she was trying to hang kept slipping. She didn't know how she was going to fix the ceiling: her shoulders were so sore she could barely lift her arms over her head, let alone hold tiles and a hammer, too.

The sheet of drywall slipped again, this time breaking a corner as it bounced off the toilet she was kneeling on.

"Damn!"

Tara awoke with another headache that morning. She could still hear a baby screaming and felt a deep sense of loss, although she couldn't remember the dream.

After breakfast, she drove to Portland. In spite of Dr. Chambers' optimism, Tara felt like her father looked less like himself each time she saw him. She was afraid that one day she would arrive to find a stranger in his bed, every characteristic that made up the man she knew as 'father' gone.

On the way home, she stopped at the hardware store for more building supplies, and then at her father's house. His mailbox was full and newspapers littered the porch. Another thing she hadn't done; Tara made a mental note to stop the paper and have the mail forwarded to her house. The brown lawn was covered with dead leaves and garbage from an overturned can across the street. She picked up the papers, the mail, and the garbage, and hoped the winter wind would blow away the leaves. Although the neighbors probably wouldn't be too pleased when they ended up in their yards.

She planned to stop at the Stop 'N' Shop on the way home; it'd be nice to put up a Christmas tree, even a little Charlie Brown one. But her truck was full and her wallet was empty. The restoration project was quickly depleting her savings and, once again, she cursed Deirdre's untouchable bank account. Not that she wanted the inheritance; she just needed the money to fulfill her aunt's wishes. Right now, she didn't care if she ever fixed the stupid house. The whole thing was just pissing her off.

Sitting on the broken toilet, staring at the broken wallboard, Tara asked herself if she *really* needed this bathroom. She could close the door and pretend it was a closet.

Maybe food would help her mood. She brushed unidentified creepy stuff from her T-shirt and stumbled into the kitchen. After piling crackers onto a plate, she opened the cabinet where she kept the peanut butter. But it was empty. She searched the kitchen, finally finding the jar in the refrigerator.

She never stored peanut butter in the refrigerator; it was too hard to spread. But she was too mad to wonder how it got there.

As she ate her lunch, crumbs on her T-shirt and peanut butter on her fingers, she noticed a door in the far corner of the kitchen that she hadn't seen before. Although it obviously had been there the whole time: doors didn't appear out of nowhere. Holding a cracker in one hand, she walked to it and turned the knob. Locked. Of course.

Carrying the cracker around the kitchen, she began looking for the key. She found a desiccated mouse carcass and a tarnished 1945 wheat penny, which she pocketed for good luck. But no key.

Tara checked the clock on the microwave. The day was flying by and the bathroom still wasn't finished, not to mention the list of other projects waiting for her. She rattled the doorknob once more and gave up. The door wasn't going anywhere. She'd look for the key later.

She licked the peanut butter off her fingers, brushed the crumbs off her shirt, and plodded back into the damned bathroom to deal with the damned drywall.

&

Her pocket buzzed.

Tara sat on the porch, legs dangling over the edge, picking a splinter out of her finger. A hawk screeched overhead, making lazy circles on invisible thermals, but she was too tired to notice. The drywall in the bathroom was finally in place, but the ceiling tiles would have to wait until her arms stopped hurting and her temper cooled. And she had the right equipment. So she moved outside, fixed the handrail, and was in the middle of replacing the broken step when she jammed a splinter under her fingernail.

It just wasn't her day. She flinched as she picked at the elusive piece of wood with a pair of dull tweezers. Hell, it wasn't her year. The phone in her pocket buzzed again and Tara checked the display. The call was from Fairhaven. Hopefully it wasn't bad news about her mother. But why else would they call her?

"Ms. Davies? This is Doris from the business office at Fairhaven Manor. I apologize for disturbing you, but we haven't been able to reach your father. And your number is listed as the emergency back-up."

The woman must be the only person in Portland who didn't read the newspaper. "My father was seriously injured, and is in the hospital in intensive care."

"I'm so sorry, Ms. Davies. I hope he's going to be okay."

"Thank you," Tara said, not wanting to go into details about Ethan's condition. "You mentioned an emergency. Is something wrong with my mother?"

"Oh no, nothing like that. In fact, I hesitate to even mention it, considering all that you must be going through with your father's accident…"

"No, please, go ahead. What's the problem?"

"Well, we haven't received this month's payment, and wondered if there was a problem. Your father is usually very prompt."

That was better news than her mother being ill. But not much. "I'm sorry, I don't know anything about it. I can't get into my father's house, so I can't handle any of his business. But I should have that situation resolved in a few days, and will see what I can do about the payment then."

There was a moment of silence. "I'll make a note in her file, but we'll have to charge a late fee. And if it happens again, we will reconsider your mother's ability to remain at Fairhaven. Which would be a great tragedy, considering how well she's doing here."

"You can't kick her out because we missed a payment!"

More silence. Apparently they could.

"I'll do what I can," Tara said. She didn't have the energy to argue with the woman.

"Thank you. Please give your father our wishes for a speedy recovery."

Tara closed her phone and slid it into her pocket. She still held the tweezers, but now the splinter didn't seem nearly as important.

Great. Just what she needed, one more thing to worry about.

It wasn't bad enough that she was trying to restore an abandoned house on a limited budget. That her aunt was dead and her father in a coma. That her hopes for her father's forgiveness, for leading a normal life, were on hold. Her wrist hurt and her heart hurt, and she was tired of patching walls and living alone and looking over her shoulder as her past relentlessly pursued her.

Now, on top of everything else, she had to deal with her mother's future. Talk about one small thing pushing you over the flipping edge.

She couldn't afford Fairhaven's regular fee, let alone late charges. Mary living with her was out of the question. Way, way out of the question. And without power of attorney, she couldn't access her father's checking account to make the payment.

Tara went back to digging in her finger, cursing her father's incompetent attorney. Thinking about escaping to a sun-drenched island in the Caribbean, a handsome cabana boy rubbing coconut-scented lotion into her tanned skin. And a salt-rimmed margarita.

Maybe two.

&

Although a bitter wind still blew around the corners of the house, the sun had finally come out, so Tara decided to take a quick walk, hoping it would clear her head. She pulled on a baseball cap and down jacket, and hiked down the driveway.

What would her life be like if she hadn't killed Emma? She pictured her mother sober and her father relaxed, sipping espresso at the kitchen table as they planned a Colorado ski vacation. Emma crossing a stage to accept her college diploma, flashbulbs popping, a huge smile on her sweet face. Tara in a white satin gown and fingertip veil, gliding down the aisle on Ethan's arm, a handsome man waiting at the altar. The annual family portrait, smiling generations gathered around a fragrant Christmas tree.

An engine roared behind her, interrupting her daydream, and she jumped toward the edge of the highway. But instead of passing her, the car slowed. Tara pulled down the brim of her cap and kept walking, hoping that if she ignored whoever it was, they would go away. Then a horn beeped and she whirled around, her heart pounding. A Corvette idled behind her.

Craig Morris.

The passenger window slid open. "Need a ride?" he asked.

"Just enjoying the sunshine," Tara said. But then she realized the sun was setting, and her fingers and nose were getting numb. "But if you insist." She slid into the warm car, noting the soft leather seats and luxurious interior, breathing the 'new car' smell. A little different from her well-loved pickup truck.

"Out for an afternoon spin?" she asked as the car purred back onto the road.

"Just had the engine tuned and wanted to make sure they got the kinks out. Rocky's a good mechanic, if you need one; he owns the garage on the corner of Oak and Front Streets. Don't know if you've noticed the place. Looks kind of run-down on the outside, but they know their stuff. I wouldn't trust this baby with anyone else in town, that's for sure."

"I'll keep that in mind. Thanks." Tara prayed her truck wouldn't need work for a long time, doubting that Rocky would accept a memory book as payment for truck repairs.

"Nice hat, by the way," he said. Tara pulled off the baseball cap to see which one she was wearing. Ah, one of her favorites. The Denver Broncos.

"Thanks," she said. "Are you a fan?"

"Seahawks," he said.

"Too bad," she replied with a smile.

The sleek car roared up the driveway, and Craig stopped in front of the house. Tara turned to face him. "I'd invite you in, but the place is a disaster. Although the steps are safe now." She smiled a little, hoping he found the humor in his last visit instead of preparing legal papers.

"That's a relief. The bruises are healing fine, by the way," he replied, smiling back at her. "How are the repairs going?"

She still didn't trust him, but the question seemed harmless. "Like I said, it's a disaster. There's so much work to be done, especially working alone. Some days I'd be happy to hand over the whole mess to someone — anyone."

"Maybe you've bitten off more than you can chew. This is a big project for a woman. I mean one woman — one person," he added, but it was too late.

"So, women aren't capable of handling big projects?" Ice slipped into her voice.

"That's not what I meant. You said it was a lot to do alone, and I agreed with you. I offered to help, remember? I told you, I feel a connection with the house. One that keeps getting stronger. I just can't walk away from that."

"I'm not sure I can help you," Tara said. "Maybe you should consider counseling." She cringed. Why couldn't she be nice to this man?

He stared at her, his eyes hardening, his smile frozen. "I didn't think of that, but thanks for the suggestion. What I have thought of, however, is buying the place from you."

"Why? So you can raze it and build ticky-tack cookie cutter houses?" She was wringing her hat in her hands, wishing it were his neck.

"Actually, I was thinking of condos," he snapped, matching her tone. "It wouldn't take too much to finish gutting the place; after all, it *is* a disaster."

Tara sprang out of the car and slammed the door behind her. "My home is not for sale. Especially not to you!" She ran up the steps and reached for the doorknob, but Craig was there first.

"Will you listen to me for a minute?" he said, his face inches from hers. "Why do you insist on turning every conversation into a battle?"

"How did you expect me to react, threatening to turn my home into condos?" She stepped toward the flagpole, the flag whipping in the breeze.

Craig grabbed it first. "Oh no, you're not taking batting practice at me again." He tossed the pole into the yard, where it rolled across the dead grass. "Can we please discuss this like adults?" He crossed his arms and leaned against the front door, his loafer-clad left foot propped against his right shin.

Tara crossed her arms and leaned against the railing, same foot propped against same shin.

"I'd make you a fair offer. You could take the money and get back to your real life — whatever that is. Why do you care what happens to this place, anyway?" he said.

"Why wouldn't I?" she replied. "This house has been in my family for generations. Now it's my home. So thank you for the offer, but I'm not interested." Her fingers drummed a silent beat on her arm.

Something inside the house crashed and Craig jumped, but Tara ignored it. He pulled a folded piece of paper from his pocket and handed it to her. "This might change your mind. The property taxes are overdue. Way overdue. In fact, in a matter of weeks, the tax collector will own this place." He watched as Tara studied the page, the color leaving her face.

"This can't be right! Why are they so high?"

"Prime real estate. Of course, the bill was a lot less before they added penalties, interest and fees."

"Where did you get this?" The paper trembled in her hand.

"Matter of public record. Anyone can look it up. I figured you probably hadn't seen the certified letters, so thought I'd warn you before the county acquired the deed." He shoved his hands into the pockets of his raincoat, and Tara noticed a stain on the left lapel: ketchup, maybe. "See, I'm not a complete monster."

"Thank you," she said, struggling to keep her voice even. "I appreciate the information. Now, if you will excuse me, I have things to do." Like curl up in a ball and die.

Craig took two steps across the porch, and his foot plunged through a rotten floorboard. He reached out to catch himself and his hand struck one of the newly hung shutters, which bounced off his arm before crashing to the floor. The brass bell clanged once, and fell silent.

"Ow! Shit!" he cursed, pulling his arm into his body: the same arm he had injured the last time. He tried to pull his foot out of the hole, but lost his balance and sat heavily on the fallen shutter. The nails that failed to keep it attached to the house were now exposed, and he leaned squarely on them.

"Damn!" He sucked his punctured hand. "I told you, this house doesn't like me!"

"What do you expect, threatening us like that?" Tara extended her good hand to help him up, but he ignored it and crawled to his feet, after retrieving his loafer from somewhere inside the porch floor.

"The offer still stands," he said, once he was standing safely on solid ground. "But not for long. They'll auction this place and I'll be able to buy it for a lot less. I'm being pretty generous, all things considered."

She swallowed a snort. "Yeah, you're a saint." But realizing he *did* have the upper hand, she tried to be civil. "Thanks. I'll call you."

Craig limped to his car and eased into the driver's seat. As he started down the road, a large branch crashed to the ground in front of him. He swerved to miss it and sped down the driveway, gravel flying.

Tara looked at the shutter, the branch, and the hole in the floor. Then she looked up at the house, looming silently over her. "Could you really be doing all of these things?"

She laughed uneasily. She was losing it, thinking a house could have a mind of its own. Then she shook her head, suddenly exhausted. She needed pizza, beer, and a soft bed. And tomorrow, she needed to come up with a plan to save the house.

Tara stepped over the shutter lying in front of the door and walked inside.

~ 17 ~

Money woke Tara the next morning. Or worrying about the lack of it, anyway. As she greeted Emma and brushed her teeth, she added numbers in her head, trying to figure out how she was going to pay for the repairs, Fairhaven, and her living expenses. There was no way she could pay the overdue taxes, too.

Sitting at the kitchen table, Tara sipped her orange juice and grimaced at the bitter taste; she should have brushed her teeth *after* breakfast. She thought about Craig's visit. He mentioned certified letters. What could have happened to them?

Then she remembered the mailbox. *Damn!* She hadn't checked it since she moved in. They were probably stuffed in there, along with a million other pieces of mail. Great. What other important details was she forgetting — or unaware of?

The sun was already up, but it was a pale winter one. Still, better than the chilly drizzle that fell earlier in the week. She decided to walk to the mailbox; it would be faster than warming up the truck.

Tara pulled on her down coat, baseball cap and a pair of thick gloves and headed down the driveway, Sneakers padding silently behind her. Swallows darted overhead, calling to each other as she passed under the canopy of branches that sheltered the road. The birds reminded her of her father's birdhouses.

The thought of him took her breath away. It felt like someone punched her in the stomach, the sense of loss was so strong.

Every time she called or visited the hospital, it was the same story: no change. And even though she tried to be optimistic, she was starting to admit that her father was never going to get better. That she was going to be alone forever.

She still didn't know how to convince the sheriff that he was innocent. Nor could she afford to hire a private detective to do the investigation the sheriff's department wasn't doing.

Salty tears slipped across her lips as she stumbled over sharp rocks and dead branches. She tripped on an exposed root and fell forward, landing hard on the heels of her hands. After crawling to her feet, she studied her torn jeans and scraped knees. What else could go wrong?

But by the time she reached the mailbox, she stopped crying. If she let herself fall apart, she might never be able to pull herself back together again. Sniffling, she opened the shiny black box and startled a small brown spider spinning a futile web in the back corner. But otherwise, the mailbox was empty.

Maybe they didn't deliver mail out this far. Maybe her aunt had a Post Office box. Tara doubted the U.S. Postal Service would give her Deirdre's mail without some kind of official authorization, though. And besides, she really didn't want to drive all the way into town.

As she stared into the empty box a horn tooted, and a Chevy Blazer with a plastic wreath wired to the grill and a 'U.S. Mail' sign propped in the window stopped next to her.

"Morning!" The driver sat in the passenger's seat, but the steering wheel was on the driver's side.

"I never have figured out how you do that," Tara said.

The man smiled. "Just like getting to Carnegie Hall."

Tara frowned. "Excuse me?"

"You must be too young for that joke," he said, setting the emergency brake. "Fella's strolling down Broadway in New York City when a tourist walks up and asks, 'How do you get to Carnegie Hall?'

"'Practice, man, practice.'" The mailman laughed, and wiped the sweat from his bald head with a bandana. "That's an oldie. I can't believe you haven't heard that one."

Tara smiled. "Maybe I just wanted to hear you tell it."

"A girl after my own heart. Are you living here?" He nodded toward the driveway.

"Yes, I am. I inherited the house from my aunt."

He stuck a beefy paw out the window. "I'm George. Been running this route for 10 years. My old dad ran it before me for 15. Nothing happens on Chinook Road we don't know about." He winked.

"Nice to meet you, George. I'm Tara Davies." She grasped his large hand and peeked out from underneath the brim of her cap, waiting for her name to elicit a response. He looked pensive for a moment, and then smiled.

"Nice to meet you, Tara Davies. I'm sorry about your aunt." He folded his hands across his barrel-shaped belly. "A bad deal all around."

"Thank you. I was just checking to see if she had any mail. But the box is empty, so she must pick it up at the Post Office."

George shook his head. "I've been holding it. Didn't want anyone rifling through her stuff after…well, after what happened. There's a pile waiting back at the office, safe and sound."

"Oh, that's great, thank you. I'll pick it up the next time I'm in town."

"Sorry, you won't be able to do that. Once it's out of the box, it's out of my hands. You need authorization to receive another person's mail, even when it's a relative. You'll have to present a copy of her will or other legal document that names you as her representative." He looked around, and lowered his voice. "But until then, if you want, I can flip through the stack and find anything special you might be looking for. Not that I can give it to you, you see, but just so's you know it's there."

She smiled. "Thanks, but that's not necessary. I'm not looking for anything in particular, just tying up loose ends. She left a lot of them."

"I guess she didn't plan on dying that day, huh?" George said.

"I guess most of us don't." She thanked him and waved as he disappeared down the road, and wondered what other surprises were lurking in Deirdre's unopened mail.

Tara looked around for her cat, but he had vanished. She trudged back up the hill to the house and reached for the doorknob, when she noticed that the shutter had moved. She remembered stepping over it to enter the house the night before; now it was leaning against the wall next to the door. Underneath the flagpole, which was also back in its bracket instead of lying on the lawn where Craig tossed it.

"Hello?" she called, but the only reply was her voice echoing off the trees that surrounded the clearing. "Is anyone here?"

Maybe Mariah snuck up her secret forest path. She could have dragged the shutter away from the door. But she couldn't reach the bracket to replace the flagpole.

Tara was really starting to wonder about the house. Things were happening that defied logic. And physics. As much as she didn't want to believe the place was haunted, something — or someone — was causing very strange things to occur.

She didn't believe in ghosts. But if there *was* a ghost, maybe it moved the shutter and the flagpole. And the trowel. Maybe even put the peanut butter in the fridge.

Tara laughed. It was sad that a ghost moving things was a more plausible explanation than a house moving things. Talk about the lesser of two evils.

She looked at the second story windows gleaming in the afternoon sun. What was the house — or ghost, or whatever was doing this stuff — trying to tell her? Then she shook her head. It was telling her that she needed a vacation. She didn't know how she came up with this stuff. And in the light of day, no less. Obviously, someone moved the flagpole and shutter. They came up the hill through the woods and left the same way. Because …

There was no 'because.' There was no reason for anyone to do any of this.

Tara sat on the porch steps and put her head in her hands, suddenly afraid to go inside. The flag rippled in the breeze. A tree trunk squeaked as it rubbed against another in the forest. She thought about crying. But instead, realized that she was angry. No, she was furious.

She stormed to the front door and flung it open.

"Listen up!" she yelled. "I don't know what's going on, but it's got to stop. Tell me what you want from me, or leave me the hell alone! I have had *enough!*" She slammed the door on the last word, stomped to her truck, and sped down the driveway.

She didn't see the mud, spread double thick on the hole in the hallway, tumble onto the floor in a cascade of dust and small white chunks.

&

Tara glared at the massive wooden door, studded with antique iron rivets.

She hadn't planned to come to Lee's Place, but once she reached the main road, it sounded like a good idea. Alcohol was her mother's answer to her problems. Why couldn't it be hers?

But she forgot about the door.

A red Jeep Cherokee sat at the far end of the lot, so someone must be inside — hopefully Lee. Because she didn't feel like admitting to a stranger that she didn't know how to open the damned thing.

To hell with it. She pounded on the door with her gloved fist.

Pound pound pound. A robin burst out of its hiding spot in the rafters with a flurry of feathers and she jumped, heart racing. Then she tried again: *pound pound pound*, harder this time. As she raised her fist over her head a third time, her patience gone, Tara heard the creak of metal on metal and the door swung open.

"You give up too easily," Lee said, wiping his hands on a dishtowel. Then he saw the look on her face. "Ok-ay, maybe today isn't a good day for door lessons." He held open the heavy door and she ducked inside.

As Tara walked toward the bar, Lee said, "You're so pissed you can't say hello to my sweetheart?"

She turned to glare at him, and realized he was referring to her greeting the elephant the last time she was there. She didn't realize he had noticed.

"Sorry, Miss Gertrude," she said, stroking her trunk. The coarse hairs tickled her hand. "I didn't notice her eyes before. They're —"

"Plastic."

"Very funny. I was going to say they're kind. But maybe that's just my wanting to humanize her."

"Anthropomorphism," Lee said.

"Huh?"

"Giving animals human characteristics. But you're right; their eyes usually *are* kind. People picture them rampaging through the jungle, trampling small children and razing villages. But elephants have an advanced family structure. Their social life revolves around raising their babies. And I'm sure you know how they mourn when a member of the herd dies.

"But," he continued, eyes flashing, "did you know that they actually recognize themselves? Researchers have installed mirrors in their exercise yards. Elephants spend more time in front of the mirror than any other part of the yard, pulling their ears, waving their trunks: generally inspecting and observing themselves.

"They've also found that elephants can tell whether specific people are friends or foes. They literally can smell danger. Wouldn't that be a nice talent to have? Yet we continue to consider them dumb animals and kill them for jewelry. Makes me sick." Lee shook his head. "Sorry. I go on sometimes."

"That's okay. It's interesting." And much better than thinking about haunted houses and bankruptcy.

They took their usual places at the bar, Billie Holiday crooning softly in the background. Lee reached for the coffee pot.

"I'll have a beer," Tara said. "Without fruit."

Lee released the handle of the coffee pot. "Another bad day?"

"Seems like I have a lot of those, huh?"

"Or maybe you just end up here when you do. Not that I'm complaining." He smiled. "There are worse ways to blow off steam than drinking a beer."

"Like drinking ten?"

"Yes, that would be one of the bad ways, especially for someone your size. If you were a linebacker, it'd be a different story."

"Two is my limit." Lee didn't need to know about her mother. Or why Tara drank beer and not vodka.

He opened a Corona and placed the bottle on the bar in front of her, and opened one for himself. "Can't let a good customer drink alone."

"I'm not sure I qualify as a good customer yet." She looked down at the holes in her jeans. Her knees weren't bleeding, but they were filthy. And they hurt.

"Call it a hunch." He deftly slit a lime wedge in half and squeezed it around the blade of the knife, letting the tart juice drip into the narrow neck of his bottle before pushing the wedge in with the tip of the knife.

"Looks like you've done that before."

He laughed. "Read about it in Esquire, believe it or not. I'm one of those guys who *does* buy those magazines for the articles." He raised his bottle. "To better days."

"Better days." She took a long swig and relished the cold liquid sliding down her throat. Now, if the alcohol would just kick in. It was sad when a building could drive you to drink. Especially before noon.

"No cap today?" he asked.

Tara reached for her cap, and realized that she left the house in such a hurry, she hadn't put one on. Good thing there weren't any other customers. Well, good for her. Not so good for Lee.

"Is this 'bad day' related to what we talked about last time?" he asked.

How much did she want to tell this man? Although he didn't judge her when she told him about Emma, Tara wasn't sure what he'd think if she told him her house was out to get her.

"Home repairs," she replied instead, glancing at her wrist.

"Let me guess. Drywall?"

She looked up, surprised. "Among other things. But how did you know?"

"Everyone hates drywall. Everyone thinks it'll be easy, so they refuse to pay someone to do the work. And everyone is always sorry."

"Why do you know so much about this stuff?"

"Secrets, my sweet. Secrets." He winked and took another swig of beer. "As I said before, everyone has them. Some don't matter to anyone but you. Some can change the world. They can rule your life, if you let them. And ruin it.

"I keep mine locked up where they can't hurt anyone, especially me. Because there's a difference between where you hide the key and where you hide the bodies."

"Bodies?" Tara choked, and Lee laughed and patted her back.

"Sorry. I didn't mean that literally. I mean, secrets are just that: secret. You don't have to share them with anyone. Why should your secrets matter to anyone else?"

"Well, if you have bodies buried in your back yard, that would matter to someone," Tara said. "Like their relatives. Or the police."

"So you're saying that if my secrets involve something illegal, I have an obligation to tell someone?" He carefully rolled up the cuffs of his denim shirt, making sure each sleeve was the same length.

“Of course.” But suddenly Tara wasn’t sure. “Wait a minute. How did this turn into a philosophy discussion?” She remembered the Dante quote over the door.

Lee smiled. “Most of mine do. It’s a character flaw. You’ll find that when you get to know me better.”

“Again, you’re making an assumption.”

“Again, it’s a hunch.” He drained his bottle. “Ready for another?”

Spending the day drinking with Lee and Billie sounded pretty good. But then she decided, “I’d better not. It’d be too easy to sit here with you and ignore my responsibilities.”

“That’s a bad thing?”

She reached for her wallet, but he shook his head. She nodded her thanks and looked around. “Where’s your dog?”

“Zelda? Play day at a friend’s house.” He shrugged. “Sometimes a dog needs other dogs, even ones who think they’re human.”

He walked her to the door. “I’m glad you stopped by. Good luck with the drywall.”

Tara groaned. “I forgot about that. Thanks for reminding me.”

“If you need help, let me know.”

“What, you moonlight as a handyman?”

He laughed. “No way. I know someone who does, though.” As he opened the door he added, “Just remember: sometimes what you think is secret really isn’t. And sometimes you should leave things alone. Don’t go searching for secrets that should remain just that.

“Secret.”

&

Tara sat in her truck, her fingers drumming on the steering wheel. She didn’t want to go into the house.

She knew she was being silly. There were rational explanations for everything that had happened. Some were a stretch, but they were still possible. Not probable. But possible.

But, suppose something otherworldly *was* going on. Say the house was possessed, or inhabited by a ghost. Or somehow had a mind of its own. And an agenda.

So far, nothing bad happened to her except cutting her wrist, which she couldn't really blame on the house. Craig, on the other hand, had been hurt twice. Then again, he wanted to gut the place and build condominiums. Which the house, or whatever was protecting it, probably wouldn't like.

Tara, on the other hand, was trying to restore it. She was living in it and taking care of it. Which, she assumed, were good things. So maybe that's why the house hadn't really harmed her. So far, anyway.

A commercial blared on the truck radio and she wrenched the knob to turn down the volume.

Maybe the house was just trying to get her attention.

But she was also trying to find its secrets. Maybe her mother wasn't speaking figuratively: maybe the house *was* actively protecting something. So maybe it was trying to scare her away so she'd stop looking.

This was crazy. She was trying to use logic to explain illogical things.

Whatever was going on, something had to change. She couldn't be scared of her own home.

Tara climbed out of the truck and stood on the flagstone path with her hands on her hips. She was glad she'd had the beer; the alcohol flowing through her bloodstream was the only thing keeping her from running back to Merrow Bay. The ever-present wind whipped her coat around her legs; it always seemed to blow harder in the afternoon. The bell clanged, reminding her that she still hadn't bought brass polish.

"Okay, whoever or whatever you are, let's call a truce," she said. "I'm sorry I lost my temper, but this is getting ridiculous. I promise to pay better attention to whatever message you're trying to send me. But in return, could you please stop screwing with my mind?"

She stepped onto the first tread, and stopped. "Oh. Thank you." She bobbed her head, climbed the steps, and reached for the door handle.

The shutter leaning against the house crashed to the porch. And when she opened the door, she saw the chunks of drywall mud on the floor, and the hole once again gaping in the wall.

Tara sighed. "I'll take that as a 'no'."

On a whim, she marched to the hole, which seemed to grow every time it reappeared, and shoved her head into the wall. But, of course, it was dark in there. She found a pack of matches in her purse — from Margaritaville in Key West — lit one, held it in the hole, and peered over the edge again.

And, far below, saw something shiny. She blew out the match and stuck her good hand gingerly into the hole, but couldn't reach anything except cobwebs.

Tara was determined to find out what was down there. She swung the hammer at the wall. Bits of white plaster flew through the air and stuck to her black coat, but she didn't care. It was partly frustration and partly wanting to solve at least one of the house's mysteries. And it felt good to smash something.

After a few minutes of pounding, the hole was bigger. Much bigger. It was going to take a lot of mud to patch the damn thing now. Tara dropped the hammer, reached deep into the wall, and touched something hard and cold. She wrapped her fingers around it and pulled it out, and was surprised to find that she was holding a sword. A very old sword, wrapped in a very old rag.

Her fingers grew tacky as she unwound the oily rag. The sword was a little over two feet long and curved, with a rounded handle. It was sheathed in a leather sleeve that looked as if it might disintegrate at any moment, so she carefully slid out the sword and placed the sleeve on the floor. The steel blade was scuffed and marred, but otherwise whole. And oiled. No rust, no pitting: whoever hid the sword took great pains to make sure it was protected from the damage that time could inflict upon it.

The handle was the most interesting part of the weapon. Once ornately detailed, most of the engraving was worn away. From what she could see, it looked like the outline of a woman.

Tara traced her fingers along the sleeve, dark leather with tarnished brass accents, also very old. She slid the blade back into it, wrapped the rag around it again, and carried it into the dining room. She placed it gently on the table, then wiped her hands on her jeans and stood back to study it.

No wonder the damned hole wouldn't stay covered.

Tara didn't know where the sword came from, or why it was hidden in the wall. Maybe one of her forefathers put it there. Or someone else, during thc years the house was empty. Although that didn't make a lot of sense.

This must be what Mary meant by the house protecting secrets. Not something intangible, but concrete items that could actually be found.

And sold.

This might be the solution to Tara's money problems. She could sell the sword and pay some of her bills. No more sleepless nights. No more worrying about making ends meet.

She was kidding when she wished for treasure buried in the back yard. Who could have guessed that she'd find it in the walls of the house? Maybe she should wish for a winning lottery ticket. Or a boyfriend.

Now all she had to do was find someone honest to help her figure out what the sword was worth, and sell it. But those were small things. The main thing was, she found the secret. And it was going to help her sleep at night.

Tara felt a huge burden lift from her shoulders. She thanked the gods, Deirdre, and the mysterious person who hid the sword in the wall for solving her problems. At least the financial ones.

Now she could get back to work on the house and her memory books, and stop spending so much time searching for secrets.

And maybe now the house would let her fix the stupid wall.

~ 18 ~

"Please be back," Tara whispered into the phone. Sneakers slept in her lap, his soft snores keeping time with the soft music playing on the stereo.

"Wilson Edison," said the voice on the other end of the phone.

"Oh, thank God," she said.

"I don't usually elicit that response, but I'll take it as a compliment," Mr. Edison said, chuckling.

"I'm sorry. I'm just relieved that it's you and not your assistant." Tara spun a ballpoint pen in circles on the kitchen table. Mariah's juice drops, which she had forgotten to clean up, were now a sticky mess.

"Beg your pardon?"

"The last time I called, the woman who answered told me you were deep-sea fishing in the Bahamas, but she didn't know when you'd be back. Actually, she wasn't any help at all. I hope you don't pay her very much."

"One detail at a time, please. With whom am I speaking?"

"I apologize again, Mr. Edison. This is Tara Davies."

"Ah, Miss Davies. Good morning. Now, you say a woman answered when you called?"

"Yes, a week, ten days ago. I forgot to get the key to the house when I was in your office, so I called to see if you had one." She stopped spinning the pen and began drawing connecting squares on a yellow legal pad.

"I do not employ either a secretary or an assistant. She told you I was in the Bahamas?"

"Yes, she did."

"I surely wish I had been vacationing in the Bahamas, my dear. Unfortunately, my deep-sea fishing days are over, if you recall. I was right here in Surfside, enjoying our brisk winter weather."

"You were here the whole time?" Tara looked at the wound on her wrist and thought about the broken window, and the cut, and the blood. "Are you kidding me?"

"Indeed I am not. I find myself at a loss to explain whom you might have spoken with. I can't imagine my housekeeper answering the phone in such a manner."

"I'll check my phone and make sure I dialed the right number." She could have called the wrong number. But she knew she hadn't. "I still need a key, though."

"I'm sorry, I don't have one. Wasn't there a key in Ms. McCarthy's personal effects?"

"No, there wasn't. Speaking of which, what am I supposed to do with her clothes and other things?" The squares grew darker as she pressed the pen harder into the paper. She didn't mention the sword.

"Those items weren't addressed in her instructions. You can dispose of them as you will."

"Thank you. I'm sorry to have bothered you."

"I am, as always, happy to be of service. Please let me know if I can do anything else for you. I have no plans to go to the Bahamas again any time soon." He hung up, chuckling.

The cat yawned and watched as Tara ripped the page off the pad, wadded it up, and threw it toward the trashcan in the corner. The yellow ball bounced off the rim of the can and into the corner behind it. She sighed and got ready for the drive to Portland, wishing she were going to the Bahamas instead.

&

Tara wandered toward the dining room, munching on a tomato sandwich, thinking about how old her father looked that morning. The corners of her mouth burned; maybe she used too much hot mustard.

She noticed a movement outside, and glanced out the window as Mariah rolled into view. Tara was surprised the girl continued to visit after they discussed her not being comfortable around kids. But she also had to admit she was getting used to having the girl around, and even looked forward to her company. She opened the door before Mariah could knock.

"You have mustard on your mouth. Why is that shutter lying on the porch?" Mariah asked as she rolled through the hallway.

Tara followed, wiping her mouth on the sleeve of her sweatshirt. "I think the house threw it at the guy in the convertible."

Mariah sighed as only a thirteen-year old could. "You realize that's nuts, right?" They continued into the kitchen.

"I know, but I can't come up with a better explanation."

Mariah sat back in her chair and crossed her arms. "This I gotta hear."

So Tara told her about everything that had happened.

"Maybe you're tired and are imagining things," Mariah said.

Then Tara told her about the ghost.

"That was just a dream," Mariah said. "You know there's no such thing as ghosts. And you know the house can't be doing stuff. It's a *building,* for cripes' sake. Buildings don't throw things. They just…sit there." She shook her head. "Don't tell this stuff to grown-ups because they'll send you to the funny farm."

Tara sighed. "You're probably right. Maybe I'm spending too much time alone. And I *am* pretty tired." She flopped into a chair and absently flicked crumbs across the table and onto the floor.

Mariah smiled. "That's why I'm here: to keep you company. But you really should find some old people to hang out with. Especially since you don't like kids." She rolled to the refrigerator and pulled out a can of soda.

"Old people, huh?" Tara smiled. "Thanks a lot. Okay, since you're here, do you want to help me look for something?"

Mariah popped the top of the can and took a sip. "Like what?" she said, and burped. And giggled. "Sorry."

"A couple of things. I need to find a key ring full of…well, keys. I've looked everywhere and I can't find the darned thing. I'm tired of leaving my doors unlocked."

"You said a couple of things. Is the other thing more interesting than keys?'"

"There's some kind of treasure hidden in the house. I already found one thing, but I think there's more. The ghost showed me a box about this big." She held up her hands to indicate the size.

Mariah's eyes lit up. "There's treasure in the box?"

"Actually, I think there's something that looks like a bunch of stars in the box. But I don't know where to start looking for it."

"I'll search the short places and you search the tall ones." Mariah rolled into the living room and started tapping on the walls, and Tara followed her. She smiled as she watched the girl dash from room to room.

Tara was concentrating on a hollow-sounding section of wall in the living room when she heard a thump. She rushed into the study and found Mariah sprawled on the floor.

"Mariah! Honey, are you okay?" She ran toward her, but stopped when the girl laughed.

"Of course I am. I can't reach the floor from my chair. Sometimes things are hidden under floorboards, you know." She scooted around the room on her rear end, knocking on the floor.

"Tell me again how old you were when you lost your legs?" Tara said, leaning on the doorjamb while she waited for her heart to stop pounding.

"I was five," Mariah said, wedging her fingers into a crack.

"Do you remember much about it?"

She shook her head. "I remember a bright place, like a tunnel. And people all around. Like they were waiting for me. I guess it must have been the emergency room." She lifted a corner of the worn Persian carpet, grimaced at the debris underneath and dropped it, then wiped her fingers on her thigh. "I remember eating ice cream, but my parents tell me I didn't. I have a vivid imagination."

It sounded like Mariah was repeating something she'd heard many times. Tara fought the urge to hug her. She didn't want to get too close to her. People died when they got too close to her.

"Your parents are probably wondering where you are. We can treasure-hunt more the next time you're here."

"No, they aren't, but I'll get out of your hair." She hoisted herself back into the chair and Tara was once again amazed at her self-sufficiency. Had she been that independent at thirteen?

Of course; she didn't have a choice.

"Just remember," Mariah said as she rolled to the front door, "don't tell anyone else what you told me. There's a reason for everything; you just have to figure out what it is." She looked at the pile of drywall mud on the floor. "You should clean that up. It's gross."

"Thanks for the housekeeping advice." Tara waved as the girl rolled toward the driveway, and then slowly closed the door. She wasn't going to find the box by banging on walls. And if she did find it, it obviously wouldn't be filled with stars. She needed to search the house completely and if she didn't find anything, then she'd decide what to do next.

Damn! She forgot to ask Mr. Edison about Deirdre's mail. Her father's mail was still scattered across the floor of her truck. By now, there was probably more in his mailbox. And her mail would soon start arriving from Merrow Bay — with more bills.

She walked into the kitchen and sat, rested her forehead on the table, and pictured spring skiing on Aspen Mountain. Slicing through the corn snow in blue jeans and a T-shirt. The sky a deep blue, that close to the heavens. Her nose burnt by the late winter sun. She could smell the pine trees and the smoke from the grill at that restaurant halfway up the mountain — she forgot the name of it. Anyway, a warm brownie — they made the best brownies — and an icy glass of milk, after one final run down Copper.

Tara traveled to fill her memory banks with good times. When things got bad, she could pull from this reserve, and forget who and where she was for a while. But she was afraid her banks were going to be empty by the time this project was over, and she could get back on the road again.

The taste of brownie fading, Tara lifted her head and began searching for the box again. Until the phone rang.

"Ms. Davies? It's Sophie at Legacy. Your father has suffered an attack. You need to get to the hospital as soon as possible."

"What happened? He was fine this morning!" Tara ran through the house searching for shoes, coat, purse.

"I'd rather the doctor explain it to you in person."

Tara was already in her truck, thanking the mobility of cell phones. "I'm over an hour away, but I'll get there as fast as I can."

"Hurry." One word never sounded so sinister.

As she sped along two-lane roads blessedly free of traffic, scenes from Tara's childhood tumbled through her mind. Ethan pushing her on a swing in their backyard. Attending her Brownie troop's Parents Day in the elementary school cafeteria, where he sat at a miniature table with his arthritic knees tucked under his chin, singing with the other equally uncomfortable parents in his off-tune monotone. Waiting outside the dressing room as she tried on her first bra, and asking a saleswoman to make sure it fit properly since her mother couldn't make the trip to the mall. "She's having one of her headaches," he explained to the saleswoman, who raised an eyebrow at a coworker, but said nothing.

And hurrying into the living room after they returned from a party, whispering, "Your mother is in one of her moods, Squirt. Why don't you read in your room tonight?" Those were the nights she wished for a lock on her bedroom door.

Sometimes Tara caught her father gazing at her with a strange look, and wondered what he was thinking. Was he questioning the choices he made in his life, or was something deeper bothering him? But he never said anything, and she didn't have the nerve to ask.

For the umpteenth time, Tara wondered what her life would have been like growing up in a normal family instead of her wounded one. Were it not for her father, she might not have grown up at all. "Hang in there, Daddy," she whispered as the miles disappeared under her tires. "Don't leave me now."

Just as she thought she was going to make the trip in record time, the taillights of a log truck appeared in the distance. It was a winding section of highway with no passing lanes. So for five tortuous miles, Tara was trapped behind the truck as it swayed and groaned down the road, hauling a load of freshly cut Doug fir to the mill. She wished the nurse had given her more information; were the last minutes of her father's life ticking away as she dodged flying bark behind this lumbering beast?

Finally, the log truck moved onto the shoulder. She flashed her lights in acknowledgement and squeezed past, relieved that he couldn't hear her cursing him. She pushed her truck to its limit, praying the police were chasing real criminals instead of issuing speeding tickets.

At the hospital, Tara ran up the stairs instead of waiting for the glacial elevator. The ward was silent and for a moment, she thought she was too late. She hurried down the hallway toward her father's room, but Dr. Chambers stopped her at the nurses' station and steered her into the waiting room.

"Can I see him?" Tara asked, gasping for breath.

"In a minute." The doctor almost pushed her into a chair.

"Why can't I see him now?"

She put a calming hand on Tara's shoulder. "It's okay, Tara. Relax. They've taken him downstairs for some tests."

"What happened?"

"We think it was just a reaction to a new medication. He's stable now, but we'll keep a close eye on him. He dodged a bullet, as my dad would have said." Dr. Chambers smiled, and Tara appreciated the attempt to put her at ease.

"Is your dad a doctor, too?"

"No, a big John Wayne fan. We lost him last year."

"I'm sorry," Tara said, and the doctor nodded her thanks.

"You can wait in his room. But don't stay too long; you look pretty beat." They rose and walked down the hall.

"As do you," Tara said. "When are you going home to your boys?"

"Soon. They're in bed already, so there's no rush." Tara detected a sad note in her voice, and wondered how much luck the young doctor was having, balancing her dreams.

It was long after midnight when Tara finally left the hospital and slowly drove home through the misty night, satisfied that her father was once again stable, but also painfully aware of how tenuous his hold on life truly was.

&

The girls could be twins, except for their hair: one red, one dark. Eyes that normally twinkle are somber as the auburn-haired man fixes the girls with his direct gaze. "Daughters, 'tis time we talked about the house."

The girls are still young enough to worship their father, but old enough to pretend that they don't. He tolerates their bored looks and theatrical sighs as they lounge carelessly on the porch.

"This house is special," he continues. "'Twill always protect ye, be ye 'neath its wings. But the house protects more than just

this family." He kneads the knuckles on his work-worn hands, toughened by years of pounding nails into fir and chipboard.

"Humans are fragile beings, bound together by souls. Lose a piece, and the soul grieves until 'tis found again.

"Pieces sometimes are ripped away, and sometimes discarded without thought. But the greatest loss is when we hold anger against those who wrong us. When we refuse to forgive the transgressions of others, we lose a piece of our souls."

"What do you mean, Da?" the dark one, his younger, asked. "How can we lose them?"

"Do ye not feel a pain when someone hurts ye?" She nodded. "And if ye do not forgive that hurt, do ye not continue to feel that pain?" Again, she nodded.

"That is ye'r soul, missing its piece. Keepin' anger just hurts ye, darlin', not the one ye anger at. But forgive the sinner and ye will be at peace, for ye'r soul will be whole."

He stands and gazes up at the house. "When me great-great grandfather built this house, he charged it with protectin' his family. But the house also protects the pieces of souls that find their way here. When he died, that duty passed to me, to help the house fulfill its charge. As will happen to ye, when I'm gone."

"Where are you going?" the older asks. His dreamer, his flighty one.

"Nowhere yet, my pet, God be willin'. But one day, when I'm called home, ye and ye'r sister will remain. And the duty will pass on to ye.

"'Tis a sacred duty, not to be taken lightly. The house will help ye, but it will also need ye'r help. Just as it needs the souls."

The girls stir, uneasy with their father's somber tone. "Be gone with the both of ye," he says, smiling. "We'll talk upon this later." They disappear through the front door, their father's words already fading.

"They will learn. But will they survive the carryin' of the burden?" He rises slowly and follows them into the house.

~ 19 ~

Tara slept reasonably well, now that she wasn't listening for the pitter-patter of tiny feet. Hopefully Sneakers convinced the critters to move to a more charitable abode and hadn't eaten them for a midnight snack. Either way, the mice were gone.

She tried not to worry about the intruder returning to attack her. It was something called cognitive dissonance: an inconsistency between belief and action. If she thought she wasn't safe in the house, she couldn't live there. So, something had to give. The attacker was after Ethan or Deirdre, although she had no idea why, so there was no reason for him to come back and harm her. Maybe she was being naïve, but at this point, she didn't have any other options. She already lived in fear; what was a little more?

Tara rose early and, after taking yet another aspirin for yet another headache, started tackling her to-do list, grateful for her overdeveloped sense of organization. A characteristic of the oldest child of an alcoholic. Along with being the perfect child, the peacemaker, the family hero. Although when Emma died, she lost her hero status.

After a quick bowl of oatmeal, she called the sheriff's department and left a message for Sergeant Wells. She needed to find Deirdre's personal effects, and wanted to know if there was any new information on the real killer, despite Deputy Stoneface's dire pronouncement.

She dashed through the freezing drizzle to grab her father's mail from her truck. Luckily there wasn't anything urgent, other than the overdue notice from Fairhaven. She turned on her laptop, found the U.S. Post Office's website and set up a forwarding order for her father's mail.

She was on a roll. She left a message on Mr. Edison's answering machine, asking him about accessing Deirdre's mail. She needed to find out when the house would go to auction if the tax bill wasn't paid, but she couldn't call the county offices this early in the morning. Hopefully there was a provision in Deirdre's will that would allow her to access the bank account in an emergency.

Of course, there was Craig's offer. She could sell him the house and he could worry about the property taxes, while she paid the inheritance taxes and banked the rest.

But Tara wasn't going to give up that easily. In spite of the strange happenings, the house was growing on her. She was getting used to working in the peaceful study with the sun shining warm through the French doors. Slipping between soft flannel sheets at night to watch the stars appear one by one in the midnight sky. Sitting on the porch in the early morning, the haunting sound of the Tillamook Rock foghorn echoing off the forest around her, sipping cocoa and watching the chipmunks chattering across the lawn. She hoped Sneakers didn't like chipmunk.

She was surprised that she was actually considering staying in Surfside. There hadn't been any more unpleasant scenes on her trips into town. Maybe the rumors had died; maybe the scene at the hardware store was merely a product of her overactive imagination. In any case, the thought of staying here for more than a few weeks wasn't as scary as it once was.

Those decisions were a long way away, though. She needed to resolve some of her legal and financial issues before she could plan her future. Which still hinged on her father's recovery.

Sneakers padded into the kitchen, stretching and yawning.

"Good morning, sleepyhead. I've been up for hours. Where have you been?"

The cat looked at her as if to say, 'Do you mind if I eat my breakfast first?' and continued to the corner where he munched on cat chow, tail swishing. After a quick bath, he explored the kitchen while Tara balanced her checkbook. When he came to the door in the corner he froze, fur on end, and began to growl.

Tara had never heard a cat growl. "What's wrong, Sneakers? It's just a door. A locked door. See?" She walked over and twisted the doorknob to prove her point. And the door opened.

She froze. Musty air oozed through the opening. Sneakers kept growling. "There's no reason to be scared," she said, pretending to reassure the cat. "Maybe the door was stuck when I tried to open it before, and the change in the weather loosened it."

Her phone rang and she jumped, and then laughed at herself. *Get a grip, Davies.* It was Mr. Edison, assuring her that he would contact the Post Office and arrange for them to resume delivery of Deirdre's mail. He also agreed to examine the will for any loopholes allowing access to the bank account, although he wasn't optimistic.

"I will get back to you, my dear, but don't count on my being successful. The will is rather specific regarding the funds."

"I understand, Mr. Edison. It's just that without them, I may not have a house to restore." She briefly outlined Craig's plans.

"Oh my, that would be a shame. Well, I'll see what I can do."

She thanked him and hung up, then looked at the door, which was still open. But the cat had vanished.

"Kitty? Sneakers? Where did you go?" She eased the door all the way open. A staircase disappeared into the darkness, but she wasn't very excited about descending it.

Now what?

An echoed 'meow' made the decision for her. If her cat was brave enough to go down there, then she was, too. She felt along the wall for a switch, found one, and flipped it.

Nothing.

She was *not* going downstairs in the dark. And the batteries in her flashlight were dead.

Matches. Where did she put her matches?

Tara fumbled through M&Ms, loose coins and sticky stuff in the bottom of her purse before she found the book of matches. She lit one and looked down the staircase, and caught a glimpse of an empty light fixture before the match burned her fingers.

"Ouch!" She dropped it and sucked on her fingers, then unscrewed one of the bulbs from the bathroom light fixture. Lit a few more matches to find her way down the stairs to replace the bulb. Tried the switch again, and this time the light blinked on.

Tara crept down the staircase, her desire to find the little cat making her brave. The basement was dark: either there weren't any windows down there or they were so filthy, the winter light couldn't work its way through them. Halfway down the staircase she tripped, and grabbed for the handrail to steady herself. But there was no handrail. Luckily, she regained her balance before falling headfirst down the rickety wooden stairs, and continued at a much slower pace.

"Sneakers?" she called softly at the bottom, her slippers stirring up the dirt floor. The only answer was her voice echoing in the dark, empty space. "Here, kitty kitty."

A black streak zipped past her and up the stairs. Tara caught a glimpse of a long tail disappearing around the corner into the kitchen, and she followed it. If Sneakers didn't want to be down there, she didn't, either.

At least not in the dark. She added 'buy flashlight batteries' to her list. And looked for the cat, finding him huddled in his basket in the bedroom.

"What scared you, Sneak?" she asked, kneeling to stroke the shivering cat. "Maybe you're just a scairdy cat." At least she hoped that was the case; Tara really didn't want to believe there was something sinister in the basement.

She decided to run into town for the batteries. After all, the box could be in the basement. Hopefully that was all that was down there.

Tara pulled on her Denver Broncos baseball cap, poking her ponytail through the back and pulling the brim low over her eyes, and shrugged into her denim jacket. Luckily the rain had stopped and the sun was trying to shine, so she could wear sunglasses and not draw strange looks.

Disguise complete, she walked to her truck, stopping to try the garage door as she passed it. The basement door unlocked itself, so maybe this one did, too. But it was still locked. Although it wouldn't surprise her if the damned thing was open when she got home.

&

As Tara drove through town, past light poles decorated with colorful holiday banners, she noticed the antique store next to Mr. Edison's office; maybe they'd know something about the sword. The worst that could happen was they'd tell her she should give it to a kid for his Halloween costume. She parked in front of the store, pulled on her cap, and walked in.

Tara didn't have much experience with antiques, or antique stores, for that matter. This one looked as she imagined it should: dark and dusty, cluttered with piles of what her father called junk. "One man's treasure is another man's junk," he'd say as they drove past yard sales on Saturday mornings. Tara thought it would be fun to try and find something valuable in the piles scattered across the green lawns, but her father never had time.

The price tags on the items in this store said someone thought pretty highly of their junk. She checked a few as she weaved through the narrow aisles, and gasped at the amounts. Maybe she *would* have found treasure at those garage sales, if this stuff was worth this much.

Tara turned a corner and bumped into a life-sized crucifix. The detail bordered on gruesome: the torn flesh, bloody streaks, and agonized expression. His black eyes bored into hers, asking questions she wasn't ready to answer. She stumbled backwards, unable to look away.

"Good morning!" a voice echoed through the store. "I know you're in here somewhere!"

"Hello?" Tara replied, grateful for the interruption. "I *am* here. Somewhere."

"Aha!" A woman popped around the corner of an ornate china hutch, and Tara jumped. She was much shorter than Tara, with a riot of jet-black curls, blue eyes, and a mischievous grin. A streak of pure white shot through the curls over her left ear, where a row of small gold hoops dangled.

The woman nodded toward the crucifix. "Gives the term 'sell your soul' a whole new meaning, huh? Anyway, what can I do for you, now that I've scared the pants off you?"

"Well, I found a sword, and I want to know more about it."

"Like how much it's worth?" the woman asked. Tara caught a twinkle in her eye. Was she teasing her?

"Well, sure. But also what it is, and why someone would hide it in my house."

"You'd be amazed at the places we find stuff. Everyone has their own opinion of what's valuable, and where's a safe place to hide those treasures. I could tell you stories…" she laughed. "But anyway, I might be able to help. Come on back."

As they made their way toward the counter at the rear of the store, Tara was amazed by the sheer volume of items lining the aisles and walls. "Where do you find all of this stuff?"

"Oh, here and there. My uncle started the business, pack rat that he was; I helped him on weekends and summer vacations. Watch that rug, everyone trips on it. Anyway, when he retired, he turned the business over to me. I guess I have a nose for finding the treasure in the trash."

"So is this the treasure or the trash?" Then Tara realized what she said. "Oh, I'm sorry. I wasn't calling your stuff trash." She blushed the trademark hue of a redhead, trying to think of a way to pull her foot out of her mouth. *Good one, Davies.*

"No worries. A lot of valuable stuff looks like trash. You have to know what you're looking at." The woman motioned to an armchair next to the counter, circa 1940s. "Grab a seat and tell me about your sword. I'm Bonnie, by the way." She extended her hand; it was soft and warm, holding Tara's for a long beat. A puff of dust sifted into the air as Tara sat on the embroidered cushion, making her cough. She described the sword to Bonnie, down to the leather sleeve and engraved handle, and where she found it.

Bonnie explained that the weapon was probably a cutlass, the sleeve was called a scabbard, and the handle a bell guard.

"So is it worth anything?" Tara asked.

"Hard to say. They've been making quality replicas for years, since the real thing is very rare and very expensive. I would have to look at yours to know if it's real or not. But even if it is a fake — sorry, an imitation — I would think it'd have some sentimental value, since someone cared enough about it to hide it in the first place."

The phone rang and Bonnie excused herself, disappearing through a door behind the counter.

A fake. Tara's heart dropped. That wasn't what she wanted to hear. She couldn't pay her bills with sentimental value. It *had* to be real.

She wiped the dust off the seat of her jeans and wandered around the shop, studying the displays. One in particular caught her eye. It was labeled 'Pirate Loot,' with items scattered on a purple cloth in a glass case. A framed magazine article was propped in the rear of the case titled 'Oregon Pirates,' and in the article was a picture of Tara's sword. Or one just like it, down to the engraving on the bell guard and the brass accents on the scabbard.

Tara quickly scanned the article, which was about the pirates from the Spanish Main who cruised the North American Pacific coast in the 1700s on their way from the Philippines to Mexico, and the common belief that they hid stashes of treasure along the coastline to resupply their coffers. The article said the sword in the picture was found in the wreck of a Brigantine called the Bruja del Mar and that her sister ship, the Alma del Mar, was rumored to have gone down somewhere off the Oregon coast.

Pirates? In Oregon?

Bonnie returned. "Sorry. One of those days." She nodded at the display. "Local history," she said. "Not many people know that pirates sailed our coast back in the day."

Tara pointed at the sword. "That's what my sword looks like."

"Lots of swords are similar to that one. It's a pretty popular design, with the enlarged bell guard. But most antique scabbards were made of wood and the guards were considerably smaller. And rarely engraved so intricately."

"No, I mean mine is *exactly* like that one."

Bonnie stared at her. "Really? Maybe you should bring it in, so I can take a look at it."

"Thanks, I'll do that. Heck, by the time I get back into town, who knows what I'll have found in those walls!" Tara laughed and, after a moment, Bonnie joined her. Then Bonnie asked where she lived and Tara told her about the house. The short version, anyway.

"I'm on Chinook Road, about five miles past Lee's Place," she ended.

A shadow crossed Bonnie's face. "Have you met Lee?"

"I've stopped in a couple of times. He seems like a nice guy."

Bonnie shrugged. "People can fool you. There are folks who wouldn't trust him to water their plants, let alone serve them a beer. Be careful.

"Anyway," she continued, "I live in Cannon Beach. I can stop by your place on my way home, instead of your having to come back here. That way I can see your other goodies." Her eyes twinkled.

"Oh, I haven't found anything else yet."

"Yet?"

"My aunt thought I would find something special in the house. But that's a long story." Although she liked this feisty woman so far, Tara wasn't ready to trust her.

"Don't get your hopes up," Bonnie said. "But I might be able to find someone to buy your sword, even if it isn't real."

"I hope so. A fake sword might be pretty, but I could use the cash."

Tara gave Bonnie directions to her house and left the store smiling, liking the impish woman and looking forward to seeing her again. It was about time she made some friends. Maybe Bonnie would be her first, since now she wasn't so sure about Lee.

&

Her next stop was the library. If there were something historically significant about the house, maybe the city fathers wouldn't let Craig destroy it. There had to be something about the figurehead in the local history books; something that unique couldn't have gone unnoticed all those years, nor should it be allowed to be wantonly destroyed. Because as time went on, Tara grew less confident that she was going to be able to save the house.

She hurried through the town square, the sun shining through the trees and tracing patterns on the wet sidewalk, past the statues of the explorers Lewis and Clark standing solemnly next to a nativity scene, and up the steps of the small brick building.

The quiet enveloped Tara as she passed through the glass doors, and she felt the tension in her shoulders ease. There was something calming about a library, being surrounded by old books and comfy armchairs. Tara remembered the joy she used to feel, breathing in the dust of the books in her father's study, and her excitement about the adventures waiting between their worn covers. But today, as much as she wanted to nestle into an overstuffed chair and lose herself in a good book, she was on a mission. She needed to find a reprieve.

As she approached the reference desk, balancing her sunglasses on her cap, the low hum of a male voice caught her attention. She rounded a corner and saw Craig Morris reading to an elderly woman in a flowery dress and blue sweater. Her eyes were closed, her hands clasped in her lap, a contented smile on her face. Tara ducked into an aisle and peered through the shelves at them.

The bastard had a heart after all. Although she was hesitant to completely forgive him; maybe the woman owned a house he wanted to raze.

As Tara turned back toward the desk, she heard a gasp. She glanced over her shoulder and saw the elderly woman crumpled on the floor next to the low table between their chairs.

Tara ran toward them. Craig was on his knees, leaning over the unconscious woman.

"Evelyn! Are you okay?" He looked around frantically and saw Tara. "Call 9-1-1! I think she hit her head!"

Tara pulled her phone from her pocket, but couldn't get a signal. *Damn!* She ran outside and made the call, then hurried back inside. A group of people had gathered, and Tara had to push her way through them to get to Craig. His jacket was folded beneath Evelyn's head and he was smoothing wispy hair from her face.

"Is she okay?" Tara said, kneeling next to them. She caught a whiff of perfume: Chanel No. 5, her mother's favorite. Scents bring back powerful memories, and this one made Tara's stomach flip, but she forced herself to ignore it.

"I don't know," he said. "I can't get a response out of her."

A siren screamed, and then fell silent. Emergency personnel rushed into the room. They quickly examined Evelyn, and then loaded her onto a gurney and out into the ambulance. When Craig tried to follow her, one of the paramedics asked if he was a relative.

"No," he responded. "Just a friend."

"Sorry, you'll have to drive yourself." He slammed the doors in Craig's face and they pulled away.

"I'll take you," Tara offered.

He stared at her. "You will?"

"Sure. But I don't know where the hospital is." They dashed through the parking lot as the skies opened.

"Why are you being so nice to me all of a sudden?" he said, once they were in her truck. "Did I miss something?"

"I'm a sucker when someone needs help. Besides, I'm really a nice person, believe it or not."

"Underneath all that hostility?" he asked.

She glanced sideways at him. "Be careful. I can make you walk."

He watched the rain pounding on the windshield. "Good point."

They pulled into the hospital parking lot and ran toward the emergency room entrance. Inside, the volunteer at the reception desk directed them to the waiting room and assured them a doctor would be with them shortly.

"You don't have to stay," Craig said. "I can catch a cab back to my car."

"Cab? You mean that rusty minivan that limps up and down Main Street with 'Taxi' spray-painted on the driver's door?"

He almost smiled, and brushed the wet hair out of his eyes. "Yep, that's the one. Life in a small town."

Tara shook her head. "I'll stay for a bit. You could probably use the company."

"Yeah, I could. Thanks." He sank onto a vinyl couch sandwiched between a plastic rubber plant and a table piled with tired copies of People Magazine. A middle-aged man in a wrinkled suit snored in a chair in the corner.

Tara filled two Styrofoam cups with lukewarm coffee from a pot that teetered on a rickety table. "So," she said, sitting next to him, "is Evelyn a relative? Did you find her while you were looking for your mother?"

"I haven't had much luck with that search. No, she's my landlady." He took a sip of the coffee and made a face, and sat the cup next to the magazines.

"Why do you read to your landlady? Does she give you a break on the rent?" Tara wanted to kick herself; she just couldn't seem to be nice to this man.

"Well, she can't see very well," he said, "so she doesn't read much any more. I ordered a CD player for her so she can listen to audio books, but it hasn't arrived. Believe it or not, I'm really a nice person, too. You bring out the worst in me."

"What do you expect? You're trying to take my home away from me." Her whisper went up a decibel.

Craig glanced at the man sleeping in the corner. "I'm trying to help you," he whispered back.

"How is stealing my house helping me?" Up another decibel. The man stirred.

"Will you keep it down?" Craig said. "This is a hospital, remember?"

Tara realized they were arguing when Evelyn was lying somewhere, seriously injured. "I'm sorry." She sipped her now-cold coffee. "You bring out the worst in me, too."

"How about we call a truce? I promise we can yell at each other later." He extended his hand and Tara shook it.

"Deal." She smiled at him as a doctor in green scrubs entered the room. He glanced at the sleeping man, and came over to where Tara and Craig sat. "Are you with Mrs. Chapman?"

"Yes," Craig said.

"I understand she hit her head, and was unconscious for a time. She is awake and responsive, but we'll keep her overnight for observation. Considering her condition, I thought it prudent."

"Her condition?" Craig asked.

"Yes. The brain tumor." He noted the shock on Craig's face. "I'm sorry, I assumed you knew. She indicated that she's known for a few months."

"I can tell she's in pain, but she refuses to admit it. So I'm not surprised. Just sad." Craig's shoulders slumped. "Can I see her?"

The doctor shook his head. "I've given her a sedative. I'd prefer that you wait until morning."

After the doctor assured Craig someone would call him when Evelyn was ready to go home, Tara drove him back to the library in silence. She stopped in a patch of sunshine at the edge of the parking lot. Typical Oregon weather — if you don't like it, wait five minutes and it'll change.

"Thanks," Craig said, but didn't get out of the truck.

"Any time. I'm sorry."

He brushed a piece of dust from the dashboard. “She’s a good person. I’ll miss her.”

“She’s lucky to have you taking care of her.”

He shrugged. “She doesn’t have anyone else. I know what that feels like.” He reached for the door handle. “Thanks for driving. And the company.”

“If you need anything, call.” Tara scribbled her phone number on a scrap of paper and handed it to him. Craig thanked her and got out of the truck; she watched him trudge through the puddles, and felt bad about the new burden that he carried.

She was blocks away from the library when she realized she hadn’t done any research on the mermaid. But now she wasn’t sure that she needed to. Although she didn’t completely trust Craig, he had gone a long way toward redeeming himself.

Tara continued home, thinking about life and death, and how they laid bare what was important and what just wasn’t.

~ 20 ~

As Tara drove past Lee's Place, she saw him balancing on a ladder cleaning out rain gutters, and pulled into the parking lot. Zelda was buried headfirst in the dripping rhododendron bushes at the side of the building, her stubby white tail keeping time to an internal beat.

"Couldn't you pick a nicer day to do that?" Tara called from the bottom of the ladder. The sun might be out, but it was still chilly and damp from the morning's rain.

He looked down at her. "You mean one of the countless warm, dry, sunny days we have here in December?"

She laughed. "Point taken. Need any help?"

Lee climbed down, wiping his hands on a grimy rag. "Nope, just about done. It's really a one-man job. Thanks anyway."

Realizing her person was back on solid ground, Zelda hurtled around the building, barking frantically. She hit the brakes too late, sliding into Tara and almost knocking her off her feet.

"Zelda! Chill!" Lee snapped.

"It's okay," Tara said, pulling a rawhide chew out of her pocket and offering it to the dog. She sniffed it suspiciously, and looked to Lee for approval. When he nodded, she daintily took it from Tara's fingers and ambled to the deck, flopped in a sunny corner and gnawed contentedly, making snuffling noises.

As Lee lifted the back of his worn T-shirt to shove the rag into his rear pocket, Tara noticed something on the small of his back. "Is that one of your secrets?" she asked.

"What?"

"Your tattoo."

He smiled. "You peeked. I don't show that to just anyone, you know."

"What is it?"

He pulled up the edge of his shirt again to reveal part of an intricate, colorful design. "I don't know you well enough to show you the rest. Yet." And he winked.

Tara thought she could make out what looked like scales. But why would Lee have a fish tattooed on his back? Suddenly she remembered her dream, the man with the tattoo wrapped around his body. Her face flushed as she thought about his mouth on hers, their legs entwined, the smell of his skin. Why would she have dreamed about Lee?

He folded the ladder with a crash, jolting Tara back to the present. "Did you come by just to harass me, or do you have time for a cup of coffee?" he asked.

"Pure harassment this time. I'm expecting company, so I can't stay." Hopefully he couldn't read minds because her thoughts were definitely X-rated.

"Anyone I know?" He arched his eyebrows. "A gentleman friend, perhaps?"

Tara snorted. "Yeah, right. Nope, the woman from the antique store said she'd stop by this afternoon."

"Bonnie Brennan?"

"I guess. I don't know her last name. Why?"

A frown replaced the amused look on his face. "Nothing. Just…be careful."

Tara's frown matched his. "Why? She seems really nice."

"I'm just warning you, that's all. She isn't what she appears to be." He pulled the rag out of his pocket and scrubbed at an invisible spot on his left palm.

"Funny. She said the same thing about you. What's with the mutual admiration society; you break her heart or something?"

Lee looked at her for a long moment. "No," he said carefully, "I didn't break her heart. We used to…never mind." He picked up the ladder. "I have work to do. Enjoy your visit. Zelda, come!" The dog looked up, startled by his harsh tone, and reluctantly padded after Lee as he disappeared around the building.

Tara climbed into her truck and headed home, puzzled by Lee's sudden change in attitude. Men. She never would figure them out.

&

Surprisingly, the basement door hadn't relocked itself while she was gone.

Tara slid the new batteries into her flashlight, clicking it off and on a couple of times as though that would ensure the light would work when she was in the depths of the dark, scary basement. The rituals people cling to, believing that they'll protect them. Like not stepping on a crack. Or not walking under a ladder. Or not believing in ghosts.

She considered calling Sneakers to explore the basement with her. The cat growled at the door before; maybe he'd warn her of danger while they were down there.

Then again, what kind of danger could be in her basement? She was letting the whole haunted house thing get to her. Mariah was right: houses don't have wills of their own. There was no evidence that the house was anything more than just that: a house. Granted, a house with some strange characteristics, but maybe they were just the result of her overactive imagination.

It's only a basement. It's only a basement. Reciting that mantra, Tara flipped on the light switch. She reached for the handrail to guide her, but once again grabbed a handful of air. Making a mental note to install one, she boldly marched down the stairs. At the bottom, she turned on the flashlight, held her breath, and swept the bright beam around the room.

And discovered a normal basement. One large, musty room. Hard-packed dirt floor, masonry walls, cobwebs in the corners. A couple of light bulbs dangling from the ceiling. Metal heating ducts running overhead, once shiny but now dull with dust, held together by rusted screws. A light switch screwed to a support column. She flipped the switch, but nothing happened; hopefully these bulbs just needed replacing, too.

As she guessed, the windows were small and filthy, and the window wells overgrown with weeds. She explored the perimeter of the basement, making sure there were no secret rooms, no mysterious nooks or crannies, no false walls, no loose bricks. Nowhere anything could be hidden. But it was surprisingly empty. In fact, the room was almost sterile. Not a shred of paper, a scrap of cardboard, or a piece of rotten wood in sight.

So much for that idea. Tara was disappointed, but also relieved. She laughed at herself for being scared of a room. She turned off the flashlight and climbed the stairs.

The door was closed.

The wind must have blown it shut. Or maybe she closed it without thinking. She cursed her make-sure-everything-is-in-its-place nature and turned the doorknob.

It was locked.

She laid the flashlight at her feet and grabbed the doorknob with both hands. Shook it. Rattled it. Twisted it.

Nothing. The door was as secure as the first time she'd tried to open it.

Damn!

There was a logical reason this was happening. Just like the peanut butter, and the shutter, and the flagpole. It was a sticky door. It had done this before. All she needed was some leverage and she'd be able to force it open. Or maybe if she'd wait a minute, it would open again on its own.

Tara's mind was racing, trying to fend off the panic lapping at the edges. She wasn't trapped. She was merely stuck. In her own basement. Not with ghouls or murderers or rising floodwaters. With dirt and cobwebs. Nothing scary about that.

Then the light bulb on the stairs popped, and went out. She was left in total darkness. She turned and kicked the flashlight, which tumbled down the stairs and landed with a thump on the dirt floor.

Double damn!

That was stupid. Now not only was she locked in a basement, but in a *dark* basement.

Don't panic. First things first. Find the flashlight. She couldn't accomplish much without light.

Tara reached out cautiously with her left foot for the step below her, and missed it. Grabbed for the nonexistent handrail, lost her balance, and fell headlong down the stairs. She saw stars. And then, nothing.

&

The young women are sitting in a kitchen with red tile floors and golden oak cabinets. A fire blazes on the hearth, casting shadows around the room and filling the air with the smell of burning wood. They are arguing. Their exchange has a rhythm and pattern that speaks of habit and familiarity.

"San Diego?" the dark one asks. "What do you mean you're still going to San Diego?"

"You know I've been planning this for years. Mamai and Da would have wanted me to go."

"You're not moving to San Diego to go to college. You're moving to San Diego because you think they have better parties."

The redhead flips her curls over her shoulder. "You can't stop me. Stephanie is saving a room for me in her apartment." She doesn't add, 'on the boardwalk by the beach.' Her sister doesn't need to know those details.

"So, I'm supposed to take care of this place by myself?" The dark one glares at her.

"Like it's a big deal. The house practically takes care of itself." She smoothed nonexistent wrinkles from her short skirt.

"You know that's not true. One of us has to be here. Remember what Da said."

The redhead is quiet, remembering. Then she rises. "I never agreed to take care of them. I'm tired of worrying about them. You're the responsible one. I don't care if they all disappear."

"You don't mean that! You know what will happen if they're lost!" The dark one is almost frantic. "You can't abandon all that Da cared about, just to find a good time?"

"It's not my fault they drove off that cliff! I didn't ask them to leave us with... this!" She waves her hands to indicate the room they're in, and the house around it.

"Remember that day on the porch?" the dark one asks quietly. "Remember when he told us about the house? I think he knew he wouldn't be around to care for it. I think that's why he started teaching us early about our duty."

"I think he knew, too, that we both wouldn't be here," her sister responds. "I think he knew that I'd leave and you'd stay. Because that's what we do."

"Will you at least stay a few more months? You can start in the spring semester. Stay long enough to help me figure out how we're going to do this."

The redhead sighs. "Okay, for you." She hugs her younger sister and leaves the room.

Deep in the night, a figure slips through the silent house, curls bobbing with each careful step. She eases open the front door and disappears into the starlit night, leaving the door ajar. The warmth of the house seeps into the cold night like a frosty breath.

&

Tara didn't know where she was. She tried to sit and her muscles screamed, so she decided to lie quietly for a few minutes instead.

Her head hurt. Her body ached. She tasted blood. She could feel dirt under her fingers. Music whispered somewhere in the distance.

Gradually she remembered. She was exploring the basement. She fell down the stairs. And the door was locked.

She gingerly moved each limb. Amazingly, nothing seemed to be broken. Although she was going to be very sore the next morning.

Then she remembered the dream, or vision, or whatever it was. She could recall everything: the emotion in their voices, the sound of the hinges squeaking as the door opened, the smell of the night air.

The women must have been Deirdre and Mary, but they were so young. Deirdre mentioned someone driving off a cliff. Tara knew her grandparents died in a car accident, but not the details.

She didn't realize how young her mother and aunt had been when their parents died. How would Tara have handled that kind of loss at 16? Although her own loss at eight probably rivaled it.

And what were the girls discussing, protecting 'them?' Whatever 'they' were, Deirdre didn't seem too excited about it. And apparently, Mary didn't want to carry the burden alone.

Tara eased herself into a sitting position, ignoring her screaming muscles. Her headed pounded; hopefully she didn't have a concussion. She felt for the steps and slowly began to crawl up them. It seemed like hours before she extended her arm and hit something solid: the door. And as her hand brushed against it, it swung open.

The setting sun painted the kitchen a rosy hue. How long had she been unconscious? Tara crawled across the threshold and collapsed onto the cold tile floor.

Next time she would listen to her gut. Next time she wouldn't explore the basement alone. Next time she'd take the door off the hinges before she went downstairs.

Next time she wouldn't inherit a haunted house.

She finally had to admit it. There was something different about the house. Whether inhabited by ghosts or with a will of its own she wasn't sure, but she could no longer deny the facts. Maybe once she accepted it, the house would take the next step and help her understand what it was trying to tell her, instead of playing with her mind. If indeed the house was trying to tell her something, and not kill her.

"Are you a good witch or a bad witch?" Tara whispered, gazing around the dusky kitchen.

~ 21 ~

A knock on the front door startled her. Tara was stretched out on the couch pretending to read, but was actually deep in thought, so didn't see the headlights come up the driveway. She dragged herself to her feet and limped into the hallway; her muscles had grown stiff, and every step hurt.

But when she tried to open the door, it wouldn't budge. "Just a second!" she called, bracing her feet and pulling on the handle. "You'd better push from that side." Tara almost lost her balance when it finally popped open.

Bonnie stood on the porch, shaking raindrops from her tight curls. "Stupid weather!" the store owner said, laughing. "You'd think after living here my whole life, I'd remember to carry an umbrella." She walked into the hallway, and nodded toward the hole in the wall. "Big termites."

Tara laughed. "I told you I had to enlarge the hole to get to the sword."

"When you said you bashed the wall, I didn't think…well, you really *did* bash it, didn't you? Remind me never to piss you off when you have a sledgehammer in your hand."

"It was just a regular hammer," Tara said with a sheepish grin.

"You did that much damage with a hammer? Now I'm definitely not going to piss you off!" They both laughed as Tara hung Bonnie's pink slicker in the laundry room, and gave her a tour of the house.

"You're limping," Bonnie said as they climbed the staircase.

"I had a fight with the basement stairs. I lost."

Bonnie winced and laid her hand on Tara's arm, but Tara shook her head. "I'll be fine. Nothing broken; my pride's just a little bruised."

As they walked through the master suite, Bonnie stopped to study the jewelry lying on the bureau. "Is this yours?"

"No, it was my aunt's. Everything's pretty much where she left it; I haven't been able to work up the nerve to deal with her possessions." Tara touched the silver earrings. "I wish I knew the story behind some of this stuff."

"No kidding. Like where she found these." Bonnie picked up the gold earrings. "They don't match the other jewelry."

"Maybe they were a gift from an old boyfriend."

"The last gift from an old boyfriend," Bonnie said. "They're ugly enough to ruin any relationship."

They laughed, and Tara limped back down the hallway. Bonnie took a long look at the earrings before returning them to the bureau, and then followed her.

They stopped in front of the figurehead at the bottom of the staircase. "And this is Ariel," Tara said.

"Oh my God, this is amazing."

"She is, isn't she?" Tara said, adjusting the lei around Ariel's neck.

"I've seen a lot of figureheads, but this one is in incredible condition. They're carved from soft wood, so are usually destroyed by the rocks as they wash ashore. Unless the ship wasn't wrecked, but was dismantled in port. But that doesn't happen very often." Bonnie ran her hands over Ariel's face, hair, and body. "She's magnificent."

"See the mirror and comb in her hand? I think she's a mermaid."

Bonnie bent down and studied it closely. "Yep, you're probably right. Although having a mermaid as a figurehead would have been extremely rare. Seamen generally distrust them because legend has it they lure ships onto rocks and sailors to their deaths. Not what you'd call a good luck charm."

"I'd love to know where she came from, and how she ended up here," Tara said. "Hopefully I'll find something hidden in the walls that tells her story, and not just swords.

"And speaking of swords, here's mine," she continued as they walked into the dining room. "See what I mean? It's exactly like the one in the picture."

Bonnie gently unwrapped the weapon, withdrew the blade from the scabbard, and sighted along the edge. "Someone put a lot of effort into crafting this."

"Is it real?" Tara held her breath, waiting for the answer.

Bonnie acted as though she hadn't heard, running her fingers lightly across the engraving. "Definitely female. A kelpie? Impossible. It couldn't be — could it?"

"Bonnie?"

She looked up. "What?"

"Is it real?" Tara asked again.

"I'm sorry. I can't say for sure, but I can do some research. It's most likely a higher-end replica. I hope you didn't plan on selling it and retiring on the proceeds." She handed the sword back to Tara, who carefully laid it on the table.

Tara shrugged, trying to hide her disappointment. "Not really." Bonnie didn't need to know about her money problems.

"Have you found anything else?" Bonnie asked.

"No. But to be honest, I haven't looked. There were a bunch of holes in the walls when I moved in, but I was scared I'd find dead mice and other creepy stuff in them, so I patched them." Sneakers appeared and wound through Bonnie's legs. Tara started to shoo him away, but Bonnie stopped her.

"No, it's fine. I love cats. Where did you get him?"

"He showed up on my doorstep one day as I was complaining about mouse droppings in my cereal and the pitter-patter of tiny feet keeping me awake at night."

Bonnie picked up the cat, and he gently patted her cheek with an oversized paw. She spread his toes and counted. Six.

"That's what I thought," she said. "Polydactyl."

"Poly-what?" Tara asked.

"Polydactyl," Bonnie repeated. "Means they have more than five toes on the front paws and more than four on the rear. It's a genetic mutation. If you know anything about Ernest Hemingway, there are a slew of polydactyl cats at his home in Key West. Rumor has it the extra toes act like thumbs, so some of them can even open cabinets and doors."

"I've never seen one before." Tara knew Sneakers had big paws, but since she wasn't a cat person, she didn't realize they were larger than normal.

"Sailors liked having them on their ships; they believed they were good luck. But you usually find them on the east coast or in England. I wonder how this little guy ended up way out here."

"You know a lot about them," Tara said, and Bonnie shrugged.

"A head full of useless information." Bonnie hugged the cat and returned him to the floor, ignoring the black hair on her white sweater. "I'd better get going. Thanks for the tour. Sorry I can't tell you any more about your sword."

"I'm glad you came by. I don't have many visitors."

As she opened the door, Tara heard the sound of an engine coming up the hill. "Who in the heck…" They walked onto the porch as a Jeep Cherokee pulled into the clearing and stopped at the end of the flagstone path. It was too dark to tell its color, but Tara was pretty sure it was red. And when Lee climbed out, she was very sure.

"Good evening," he said as he climbed the steps. Tara was pleased to see the third step didn't buckle when he put his weight on it; maybe she had a future as a handyman, after all.

"Good evening yourself," Tara replied. Raindrops dappled the shoulders of his leather coat. Bonnie stood next to her, closing the snaps on her coat with more force than necessary.

"Bonnie," Lee said. Tara flinched at the ice in his voice.

"Didn't realize you moonlighted with the Welcome Wagon," Bonnie said.

"And you're, what, selling Girl Scout cookies?" Lee towered over the petite woman. Their eyes locked and held. The porch suddenly felt too small to hold them all.

Tara held her breath.

From inside came a crash and the sound of Sneakers howling. Tara hesitated, decided they wouldn't kill each other before she got back, and ran inside.

"This one's mine," Bonnie said, leaning on the porch railing.

"Like hell. Stay away from her."

"Still pissed about losing the last one, Lee? How about we share?" She winked.

"You know I'm not into that any more. I'm tired of seeing you hurt people," he said.

"Oh, right, you've suddenly developed a conscience. Tell that to someone who doesn't know you like I do."

"You don't know me at all, Bonnie. You never did."

"Does she…"

Tara returned with the cat. Two sets of eyes turned toward her. She could feel the tension in the air.

"I better get going," Bonnie said, forcing a smile. "I'll see you again soon, Tara." The woman walked to her car.

As Bonnie disappeared down the driveway, Tara turned on him. "You did that on purpose! You came here just to be mean to her." Sneakers squirmed in her arms and she dropped him, and he ran into the dark forest.

"I came here because I thought you might need backup." His eyes were still blazing.

"Backup? For what?" she said, crossing her arms. "To protect me from Bonnie? She can't weigh ninety pounds with rocks in her pockets. What's with you two, anyway?"

Lee's gaze wandered past Tara's shoulder into the hallway. "What's that?" he asked, staring at the banister.

"Ariel. Stop changing the subject."

He tore his eyes from the figurehead and stepped closer, his features softening. "I was worried. I thought I'd stop by and make sure everything was okay. That woman is trouble."

Tara's anger disappeared as quickly as it came. It had been a long time since anyone cared enough to worry about her. She felt the wall around her heart slip an inch or two.

When she was sure her voice wouldn't break, she said, "Well, thank you. It's nice to have someone looking out for me. But I really don't think there's anything to worry about."

Lee reached out and tucked a strand of auburn hair behind her ear. "Just trying to be neighborly." They stood for a long moment, staring at each other. Then he bent down and softly kissed her in a very un-neighborly way. Tara tasted peppermint and smelled a familiar cologne: Obsession. Robert's favorite.

All she could think of was slipping her arms around Lee's neck, pulling him down, losing herself in him. Finding the closeness they had in her dream. Letting someone else be strong for a change. But that definitely was not the smart thing to do. And Tara always did the smart thing. So she pinned her arms to her sides, took a shaky step backwards and said, "Well, um, thanks."

Lee shoved his hands in his pockets. "I'm sorry. I shouldn't have done that. It's just…"

"Just what?"

"It's just that…you look so much like her."

"Like who?"

He shook his head and hurried toward the Jeep.

What was that about? She watched his lights disappear down the driveway. He comes roaring up here to protect me, kisses me, and leaves with a cryptic statement about another woman. And speaking of other women, what was his problem with Bonnie?

Once again, a man had proven that his species was impossible to figure out.

Tara went inside, still shaken by the kiss, and picked up the sword. "Well, at least Bonnie didn't say it wasn't real. Let's hope she calls with good news; I could sure use some." She slashed at the air with the cutlass. "Take that, Black Jack! Avast ye, ye scurvy dog!" Then groaned as the muscles in her shoulder screamed. "Okay, give me a break. I'm just having a little fun."

She carefully placed the sword on the mantelpiece and wandered to the kitchen in search of spaghetti and garlic bread. Maybe a pan of warm brownies. And later to bed, to dream of Johnny Depp and pieces of eight. And blond men with hazel eyes who tasted like peppermint.

~ 22 ~

A steady drizzle fell outside Tara's window, and she wondered how many words there were to describe rain; in Oregon, there should be hundreds.

She tried to focus on the clock next to her bed, but the numbers were fuzzy.

And her damn phone wouldn't stop ringing.

She had no idea where it was. Usually she left it on the nightstand, but that only held her clock, an empty glass dish, and a paperback. Something was missing, but she couldn't think of what it might be.

She didn't remember going to bed the night before. Maybe she *did* have a concussion. Or maybe it was the tequila she pulled out of the freezer after dinner. There was something refreshing about ice-cold tequila. Although that wasn't why she drank it last night. Admitting that your house wasn't your run-of-the-mill dwelling — not to mention Lee's kiss — was a little unnerving, and drove her to reach for Courage in a Bottle. She should have stopped at two shots, though.

Ring, ring, ring.

Damn!

Tara tried to stand, but her body complained — loudly. So she carefully rose to a sitting position, which was better, and leaned against the headboard. She carefully scanned the room, searching for her phone. Sneakers, curled at the foot of the bed and *not* in his cozy basket, ignored her.

There it was. On the bureau, next to her bear. She kicked at the flannel sheets around her legs and slowly stood. Her muscles screamed and her head pounded as she deliberately put one foot in front of the other, until she reached the phone.

"Ms. Davies?" a familiar voice asked.

"Yes?"

"Sergeant Wells of the Surfside Sheriff's Department, returning your call."

"Thanks for calling, Sergeant." She closed her eyes, hoping it would ease the pain in her head. She would never drink tequila again. Or fall downstairs.

"I'm sorry it took so long to get back to you. Someone put the message on my desk and…well, you've seen my desk." He laughed a little sheepishly, and Tara thought about the disaster that he called a desk. It was the only light moment in her visit to the police station, when the sergeant told her they believed her father was guilty of murdering Deirdre.

"That's okay. I'm just trying to find my aunt's personal effects," she said.

"Personal effects?"

"You know, purse, jewelry, clothes, the items found on her the night of the…attack." She rested her chin on her hand to see if that would make her head hurt less.

"Oh, of course. Well, the morgue would have all of that."

She cringed at the thought of having to go to the morgue. "I should have thought of that. I'm sorry I bothered you."

"It's no bother. I'm happy to help. Do you need the number?" He read it to her and then said, "I hope you're doing okay."

"As well as can be expected. I'll be a lot better when you find whoever did this."

There was a long silence. "Ms. Davies, we aren't looking for anyone else. We're convinced your father was responsible for your aunt's death. The doors were locked. We found no sign of forced entry, no indication of anyone else having been there. We've filed charges with the District Attorney's office, and your father will be arrested if — when — he regains consciousness."

"I see," Tara said, although she didn't. "Do you know how she was killed?" She hadn't had the nerve to ask that question before; she wasn't even sure she was ready for the answer now.

"Strangulation. The autopsy confirmed it."

She was glad he didn't go into further details. Tears filled her eyes. "Thank you. I…I just wondered."

"I'm sorry," he said. And Tara believed him.

&

Now what?

Tara crawled back into bed and pulled the comforter across her legs. She wanted the sheriff's department to find the person who attacked Deirdre and her father, and make him pay for his crime. For destroying her chance for a normal life. They were convinced her father was guilty because the house was locked, but someone could have picked the lock and relocked it on his way out. It could have been a burglary gone wrong. Even a jilted lover or crazed ex-husband; Tara didn't know what Deirdre's life had been like during the years she was gone.

Heck, for that matter, the house could have locked itself. At this point, she believed it could be capable of just about anything.

Tara knew her father wasn't a murderer. She just didn't know how she was going to prove it.

She called the morgue and, after a few minutes on hold, found that they did indeed have Deirdre's personal effects. The clerk offered to send them to her, but she arranged to stop by and pick them up the next day instead. Who knows how long it could take for them to be delivered, and she really needed the keys.

Her head still throbbed. Maybe caffeine would help. She studied her reflection in the mirror as she pulled on her robe. With her red eyes, puffy cheeks and scowl, she looked like an 'after' picture designed to convince teenagers of the dangers of drinking. Unfortunately, she hadn't had the fun that usually comes before the hangover.

Winnie the Pooh leaned against the mirror in his trademark red jumper. Both he and the jumper were frayed from years of loving. When Tara unpacked the stuffed bear days earlier, she placed him precisely in the center of the bureau, keeping everything in balance.

Now he was perched at the far end of the bureau. Very out of balance.

She didn't move him. The wind couldn't have moved him; she hadn't opened the window in days. And Mariah hadn't been in that room. Hadn't been upstairs at all, for that matter. So she couldn't have done it.

Maybe she moved him in her sleep. Maybe he did the Teddy Bear Strut and moved himself.

Maybe she was making excuses because there was no logical explanation for how it could have happened.

Tara started to reposition him, then slowly pulled back her hand. Whoever — whatever — put him there might get mad and take him completely if she interfered, and she couldn't face losing one of the few things that her father had given her that she had left.

Filing it in the 'this defies logic, I'll figure it out later' category — which was already way too full — she staggered downstairs to look for caffeine. And her sanity.

As she sipped her coffee, Tara wandered into the study and studied her latest work-in-progress. The Kegel family. Fourth generation, living on land their great-grandparents homesteaded in the 1800s. They gave Tara pictures that had been in their family for decades, sepia-toned images of unsmiling men and women in severe clothing and unnatural poses. One of the benefits of staying in one place: pieces of your history didn't disappear.

Three moves is as bad as a fire, Granny Davies used to say. And Tara knew that all too well: she had very little left of her past. Each time she moved, something was lost or broken. Living a simple life was one thing, but living a barren one was something else entirely. And even though she didn't have a lot of good memories from her past, sometimes she wished she had kept a few souvenirs.

So she sat at her desk and, for a while, lost herself in the Kegels' story. And, for a while, pretended that she was a part of their story, part of something solid and strong, predictable and rooted. Part of a family.

Hours later, she stood and tried to stretch the ache from her muscles. Another book finished; another check in the bank. Another family's history preserved for future generations to treasure. Or maybe to use as a doorstop.

Now she could buy a few gallons of paint: robin's egg blue, perhaps. She would start in the bedrooms first, and work her way downstairs.

Tara was making progress. All of the holes in the walls had been repaired. Except the one in the hallway: it would take more than drywall mud to patch that one now, after her sword-seeking destruction spree. The shutters were hung, the steps repaired, the flagpole reinstalled. The fireplaces were scrubbed and vacuumed, although she needed to call a chimney sweep: she refused to climb on a wet metal roof in the middle of an Oregon winter to clean them herself. She didn't think Deirdre expected her to risk her life to restore the house. Although some days, just living there was risk enough.

She heard scratching, and figured it was the branch brushing against the window. Until a fat black paw appeared in the gap underneath the closed study door, and slid from side to side.

"I guess that means you want to come in," she said, opening the door. Sneakers padded into the room and jumped onto the desk, and started washing his face.

"So when do you think this place will be considered 'restored'?" Tara asked the cat. "I guess Mr. Edison will be the one to decide that." Which reminded her, she still needed to see if he had found any loopholes in Deirdre's will.

With calls to make, she shooed the cat out of the study, grabbed her sweater off the back of the chair, and started looking for her phone.

&

They say no news is good news. But sometimes, no news is better than bad news. An hour later, bad news was all Tara had.

She wandered along a winding path through the cedars east of the house, lost in thought. The fresh air and majestic trees were supposed to clear her head and help her to process the latest twists and turns in her life. So far, it wasn't working. Maybe the forest was mad at her for not visiting more often; on this property, that wasn't as crazy as it sounded.

There were no loopholes in Deirdre's will, so Tara couldn't access the funds to pay for the repairs.

It would take an incredible sum of money to keep the house from going to auction, and she didn't have much time to find it.

Deirdre's mail had arrived, and with the mail came bills. There would be bills in her mail, too. And her father's.

Why couldn't she find more treasure in the house? Why wasn't there a chest of gold hidden in the walls?

Gold. The evergreens faded, and she was driving through the Jackson valley in a red convertible with the top down and cash in her pocket, ignoring the bite of the early fall air. The aspens were turning gold on the surrounding mountainsides and the Grand Tetons wore a dusting of white. A frosty mug of beer and rack of ribs waited for her at the Snake River Brewpub in Jackson. Window-shopping in the stores around the town square. And an incredible mountain sunset to end the day.

But she wasn't in Jackson. There were no ribs waiting for her. And she had no cash in her pocket.

She headed back to the house, kicking at the pine needles and branches with her scuffed sneakers. She could really use some good news.

Someone was knocking on the back door as Tara walked through the front. *Does good news knock?* She heard the door open and Mariah call, "Can I come in?" The girl always wore the same outfit, although her clothes always looked clean. Maybe she owned an entire closet of faded blue jeans and pink sweatshirts.

She rolled into the kitchen and Sneakers went crazy. Fur on end, he hissed, backing away from the girl.

"Sneakers! Mind your manners!" The cat retreated into a corner, spitting and growling.

"Where'd he come from?" Mariah asked.

"He showed up a few days ago. He must have been outside the last time you were here. I don't know what's wrong with him. He's never acted like this before."

"Maybe he's scared of my chair. Did you find any more treasure?"

"No, not yet. I was waiting on you."

Mariah studied her. "You're a mess. What happened? Did somebody beat you up?"

"Just the basement stairs." And she explained.

When Tara was finished, Mariah said, "You think the house did it, don't you?"

"Do you blame me? The door was locked, then it wasn't, then it was. The light was on, and then went off just as I realized the door wouldn't open. My flashlight bounced down the stairs at the same time, too."

"That doesn't sound like a house attacking you. It sounds like you being a klutz. Maybe you bumped your head harder than you think you did. Did you go to the doctor?"

Tara laughed. "No, my head is fine." Except for a hangover, but she didn't say that. "I don't think a doctor could help with this." If she started telling people that she thought the house had a will of its own, they'd send her to a very different kind of doctor.

"Whatever," she said, dismissing Tara. "What are we doing today?"

Tara twisted her hair into a bun and stuck a pencil through it. "I really want to find the box, but I can't think of any new places to look. I bought stick-and-press linoleum tiles for the laundry room. I've already pulled up the old ones, so all I have to do is lay the new ones. And there's still that huge hole in the hallway that needs to be patched."

"You want me to choose between searching for treasure and patching holes? That's a no-brainer." Mariah gave Tara a look that reminded her of being a teenager herself, faced with the stupidity of adults. "You do the boring stuff. I'll look for the box."

Mariah headed for the study, and Tara tackled the laundry room floor.

But half an hour later, Tara was in tears. The room wasn't square, so she had to trim the tiles. But the blades she bought for the X-Acto knife were the wrong size. Damn useless clerks at that damn chain hardware store.

As she tried to cut one of the tiles by holding a blade between her fingers, it slipped and sliced deep into her thumb.

"Shit!" she screamed. "Damn it to hell!" Once again, she was bleeding on the laundry room floor. "This damned house!"

Suddenly it was all too much. Every bruise, every cut, every hole in the wall and every noise in the night. The anger she'd barely kept at bay boiled over. She picked up the stack of tiles and flung them into the kitchen, then hurled the blade as hard as she could toward the door. Just as Mariah rolled through it.

The blade skimmed over the girl's head and clattered into the hallway behind her.

"What was that?" She looked over her shoulder and saw the blade, and looked back at Tara, her violet eyes wide. Her face, usually pale anyway, was a deathly white.

"I am so sorry, honey!" Tara said, rushing toward her. "I didn't know you were there!"

"Are you crazy? You could have killed me!" Mariah said, finding her voice. "That could have hit me in the eye or in the face or…"

"I know, I know. I'm sorry." Tara hovered, not knowing what to say.

Mariah did. "You've got to get a grip," she exploded. "You think the house is alive, you're mad all the time, you hide up here on this hill…do you have any friends besides me?"

Tara fell into a chair at the kitchen table. She couldn't meet Mariah's gaze.

"I might be just a kid, but even I know something weird is going on here. What *is* your story, anyway?" She glared at Tara.

How much to reveal. The last thing Tara wanted to do was tell Mariah about Emma. But she owed her something.

She took a deep breath. "I did something really bad when I was a child, younger than you, and my parents never forgave me for it. My mother was pretty mean to me. My father tried to protect me from her, but he didn't do a very good job. So I left home when I was seventeen, and haven't had much of a relationship with them since."

As she said it, Tara realized she had never admitted this before, that her father bore some responsibility for the way she was treated. He only protected her when it suited him. Her heart sunk and tears filled her eyes as the image of her perfect father faded and was replaced with that of a flawed one.

"So you're mad at your parents for being mad at you? That's it?" Mariah asked.

"I guess that's a simple way to put it, yeah."

"Don't you know anything? When you're mad at someone, the only person it hurts is you. You have to forgive people. No wonder your karma sucks and you feel like everyone hates you. You hate yourself."

"I do not! I like who I am." Tara shredded a paper napkin, the tiny pieces piling up like a snowdrift on the table.

"No, you don't. That's why you hide up here. That's why you make other people's lives pretty, because you don't know how to do it to your own."

From the mouths of babes.

"So if I forgive people, I won't be mad or sad any more?" Tara asked.

"Yep."

If only it were that easy. "Why should I take advice from a thirteen-year old?"

Mariah shrugged a faded pink shoulder. "Because I'm right. And you know it." She rolled into the hallway and picked up the blade, and handed it back to Tara.

Tara walked to the fireplace and jabbed it into the mantelpiece. "I'll leave it here to remind me of what you said."

"Whatever. I'm going to look for treasure." She rolled toward the study muttering, leaving Tara alone in the kitchen.

The girl made it sound so simple: forgive. Yet Tara knew it wasn't that easy. She'd been hurt and angry for so long, it had become a part of who she was. That, combined with her guilt over killing Emma, colored her every action, her every thought. What would she be if she weren't wounded?

She had become a victim. Why did it take a child to point that out? Because Tara never got close enough to anyone for them to do so. Mariah was one of the first people in years she had shared her story with. Well, except for Lee.

Something about this town was making her open up to total strangers. Or maybe it wasn't the town. Maybe it was the house.

Tara looked down; her thumb was still bleeding. Deeply shaken, she wrapped a paper towel around it and returned to the laundry room, while Mariah tapped.

The pile of white shreds blew off the kitchen table and fluttered to the floor.

&

Sandwiches taste best when eaten on a blue-checked tablecloth. Especially when the sun's hot on your arms and a breeze blows your hair away from your damp face. Tara takes another bite of bologna and cheese, and the white bread sticks to the roof of her mouth. Daddy remembered that yellow cheese is her favorite kind of cheese when he made her sandwich. And that she likes mustard better than mayonnaise, that white slimy stuff.

Mama and Daddy are sitting in folding chairs under a big tree, laughing. They are drinking iced tea, but won't give her any. They call it longisland iced tea. She doesn't know what longisland is, but it must mean only for grown-ups.

The baby is trying to lick the ants stuck to her fingers, and makes a funny face when they wiggle on her tongue. Tara wipes the jelly from the stubby fingers, and Mama tells her she's a good big sister. Mama gives her two Oreos and a hug.

Tara pulls Emma onto her lap and they play with the Hey Diddle Diddle wind-up toy while Mama and Daddy whisper. Emma laughs when Tara copies the animal sounds. Tara laughs just because she's happy.

~ 23 ~

At one time, Tara loved cities. She loved them for the anonymity they offered, but also for their energy. The restaurants, the stores, the lights, the people. She craved city life like a drug, tolerating her time in other places until she could return to Tokyo, Vancouver, Buenos Aires, Cape Town.

But in the past year, she was surprised to find that she was starting to appreciate the pace of small-town life. First, Merrow Bay, which was nothing more than a handful of homes and small businesses clustered along the rocky shore of a sheltered cove. She came to love her quaint cottage, the tangled garden with its fragrant wisteria and riotous columbines, the crooked path that led to the crooked gate in the crooked fence. She planted a garden in the spring and in the summer harvested cherry tomatoes, green peppers, string beans, and summer squash.

And now, Surfside. She loved the town square, the cobblestone streets, the quaint shops downtown. Of course, there was the usual sprawl of fast food restaurants and chain stores on the outskirts. But it was still a small town.

Tara hadn't run into any more hostility, and had actually talked to a few shopkeepers and found them to be friendly. She even risked going into town a couple of times without her baseball cap to hide beneath. Maybe her reputation hadn't caught up with her yet; she couldn't imagine that it finally ceased to matter.

More and more, she dreaded leaving her new haven to make the trek to Portland. It would be different if her father was conscious, but since that wasn't the case, she didn't have much to look forward to. So each time she'd steel herself: she'd visit him, check his house, and get the heck back home as fast as she could.

&

Sitting by Ethan's bed, the machines humming around them, Tara launched into yet another one-sided conversation. She no longer tried to hide that she was living in Surfside; since everything she did revolved around the house and the repairs, she didn't have much else to talk about. The deputies had finally given up their post outside his room; they must have realized that he wasn't going anywhere — although she was sure they were still monitoring him from afar.

"I found a sword in the wall, Daddy. I thought it might be some kind of treasure, but when Bonnie — she's an antique dealer and I really like her, in spite of what Lee says — when she saw it, she said it probably was a fake. So I guess that's not what Deirdre was talking about when she said I would find what I was looking for in the house. Although I sure could use the money, if it *is* real. And I'm still searching for the secrets Mama said the house is hiding, but some days I think I'm just chasing ghosts."

The machines continued to monitor his heartbeats and brainwaves. Nothing she said or did affected him, since that first time. He was gradually ceasing to exist.

"I'm thinking of staying in Surfside for a while," she said, picking at the bandage on her thumb. "I know you'll be surprised, but I kind of like the town. I've met a couple of nice people, and I even got a cat. It feels like home, more than any other place I've been. I don't think I'll start dating just yet, but maybe in time I'll be ready to jump into that mess again. Once I figure out how to forgive myself for Robert."

Robert. Another innocent victim of her mother's disease. The man who taught her how to love, after a childhood spent in a home where unconditional love was a dream.

But Tara didn't believe he could forgive her for Emma. Her parents didn't; how could she expect anyone else to? So she hid her truth from him, until the lie grew big enough to destroy the fragile thing that existed between them.

Even after they were engaged, she didn't tell him; couldn't risk the pain of his rejection, the look in his eyes when he saw her for what she truly was. Fear ate away at her, convincing her that she didn't deserve him. Finally, the night before their wedding, fear won. Tara ran, leaving their warm bed deep in the night, running long enough and hard enough that he couldn't find her. Knowing she'd never find that kind of love again. That she didn't deserve to.

Two hearts were broken that night; she hoped one of them had healed.

"Oh, Daddy, come back to me," she whispered, wiping her eyes. "You're all that I have left."

&

As she was leaving, Dr. Chambers stopped her and ushered her into the empty waiting room with, "There are things we need to discuss."

The doctor verified what Tara feared: her father wasn't showing any improvement; in fact, the machines were most likely keeping him alive. Dr. Chambers told Tara that she would soon have to decide what the next step would be. She could move him to a facility that would maintain him in this state indefinitely, or she could choose to turn the machines off and let nature make the final decision.

"It's possible that his body will return to normal function, but we won't know unless we turn off the machines. And there's the risk of brain damage occurring before we can turn them back on, if he doesn't start breathing on his own."

Tara stared at her hands knotted in her lap. "Isn't there a chance he could wake up?"

"There's always a chance. But you have to decide how long you want to wait for that to happen. You'll need to consider the cost of the facility and the fact that his body *will* degenerate over time, as long as he's connected to the machines. And," the doctor placed her cool hand over Tara's worried ones, "you have to decide how long you want to prolong your own pain, waiting for something that might never happen."

"Do I have to decide now?"

"No, we have a couple of days before we need to do anything. Call me if you have any other questions. I want you to be very sure of your decision. I'll support your choice, whatever it is." She hugged Tara and walked away.

Tara huddled in the vinyl chair, surrounded by old magazines and plastic plants, stunned by the responsibility that Dr. Chambers had just placed in her hands. Deciding whether her father lived or died. Determining his fate.

&

A car pulls into the clearing and stops. A figure steps out, walks to the porch and up the steps. Starts to knock, stops, and examines the brass bell hanging next to the door. Reaches out to rub at a spot and peers closely at the result. Tentatively taps the bell and listens to the rich peal. Knocks on the door and waits.

When no one answers, the figure pulls out a tool and fiddles with the doorknob and the dead bolt. The door remains closed. The figure strides across the porch, stares through the window into the living room for a long moment, and then does the same in the dining room. And the study.

The figure circles to the back of the house, and the sound of a door being kicked and shaken echoes through the clearing. Then returns to the front of the house and gazes up at the second story windows, breathing heavily. The morning light is blinding, reflecting sharp and clean from the leaded panes. Inside there is a groan and a clatter, but the figure doesn't react.

The figure slowly backs toward the car, continuing to stare at the house, starts the engine and disappears down the driveway. A branch breaks free of the canopy overhead and crashes onto the road. But the car is already gone.

&

At the morgue, Tara picked up a brown paper bag with a Post-It note stapled to the top that read 'Destroy if unclaimed by Dec. 25.' She propped it in the passenger seat, deciding to wait until she was home to look through it.

As she drove, wipers squeaking, radio tuned to her favorite station, Tara thought about her conversation with Mariah. She had to admit that much of what the girl said was true. Tara had been angry with her parents for as long as she could remember. And while she felt that she had a right to be, maybe that wasn't a good enough reason any more.

There was a chance, for example, that the scene in the hardware store was a product of her overactive imagination. Maybe the clerk meant something totally different, and the other shoppers were merely reacting to her overreacting. Maybe she repeated this scenario over the years, misreading an innocent situation, assuming the worst.

While she couldn't believe that the years of moving and upheaval were for nothing, she *could* believe that sometimes she moved for the wrong reasons. Knowing that, maybe it would be easier to stay in one place. Maybe that place could be here.

In the background, Kenny Chesney sang about praying for forgiveness and a brand new start. Her stomach rumbled. Lee's Place was ahead.

Tara hadn't seen Lee since he kissed her. Admittedly, she had been avoiding him. She really didn't need another uncomfortable situation in her life, especially with someone who, so far, accepted her completely. If she just showed up and pretended nothing happened, maybe everything would be okay.

Except…there it was again, that damned door. Luckily, an elderly couple arrived at the same time she did, so she followed them through a surprisingly warm drizzle toward the bar. As she hurried across the parking lot, she lifted her hands to feel the rain, and the raindrops tingled as they kissed her bare skin. She smiled to herself, and promised that she'd stop and appreciate the little things in life a little more often.

Tara chose a seat in a corner of the crowded room and pulled her cap low over her face. Two young waitresses scurried between the tables and she could see a rotund man in a stained cook's coat hustling around the kitchen. A dishtowel hung over his shoulder, and occasionally she'd hear him call to one of the girls.

"Babydoll, you comin' get this burger 'fore it get cold?" She smiled at his accent, part Italy, part New York. "I give you a dollah you come get it now so's I don't look bad." Then he'd laugh, a rich sound that bubbled out of the kitchen, poured over the bar, and flowed across the room.

Tara ordered a Corona with orange and something the Specials board listed as a 'croque monsieur,' which the waitress said was "really a ham and cheese sandwich, only Lee thinks this sounds fancier."

When he read the order, Lee looked up and saw Tara, and brought her beer himself. She watched him cross the room, his face tight, his movements awkward.

"Hi," he said. "Didn't know if I'd see you again." *Are we okay?* he asked silently.

"I was afraid you'd ordered a bushel of oranges just for me, and I'd feel guilty if they went to waste." *Yes, we are.*

He smiled, the tightness in his face easing. "I'd whip up a batch of sangria and convince my regulars it was the Mexican version of Budweiser. What brings you out at this time of day?"

"Besides the desire for a croque monsieur?"

He chuckled. "Anyone can serve ham and cheese. Only a high-class joint offers a croque monsieur."

"With a straight face."

"That's not my problem, that's theirs." He nodded toward the waitresses.

"They think you're old and weird."

"And they'd be right." He looked around the crowded room. "Sorry, I need to get back to work."

"Go ahead. I know you're busy." She watched as he walked back through the room, stopping to talk, shake hands, laugh. He looked a lot more relaxed than he had a few minutes earlier.

After she finished her meal, Tara walked to the bar to pay her tab. "I don't suppose you'd be willing to give me a hint?"

"About what? Oh, you *still* haven't figured out my door? I thought you were more than just a pretty face." They were back on solid ground with each other. Although there was a new warmth in his eyes; she'd have to think about that later.

It was her turn to raise an eyebrow. "Is this any way to treat one of your best customers?"

"Okay, one hint. The answer is different for everyone."

"That's not much of a hint. How about telling me the magic word?"

He stopped counting her change. "There are pieces of our lives under our control, Tee, and pieces that aren't. We have to figure out which ones we can control, which ones we can't, and which ones we shouldn't."

"Are we still talking about the door?"

"Of course," he said and walked down the bar, grinning.

Tara ran to her truck, muttering, "Why couldn't he just tell me the stupid password?" And wondered if there was something otherworldly about every building in Surfside.

&

Tara dropped the paper bag on the kitchen table. She hung up her wet cap and jacket, turned on the burner under the kettle, changed into old gray sweats and soft pink slippers. Picked up a few pieces of silverware that somehow ended up on the floor. Stirred cocoa powder into a mug of hot water and took a sip.

Finally, she ran out of ways to delay the inevitable. She pulled out the staples from the bag and poured two plastic Ziplocks onto the table. She was surprised, and disappointed, at how little there was in them.

The first bag held Deirdre's purse. Tara felt as though she were trespassing as she went through it. It held the usual items: pens, change, a comb, chewing gum. The driver's license was a new one, issued in Oregon. But what *wasn't* in the purse was more important: no address book, no business cards, no pictures in the wallet, no credit cards. Nothing to tell Tara where Deirdre spent the last forty years, or why she returned to Surfside.

The second bag held two tortoise-shell combs, one with a strand of red hair tangled in its teeth. A delicate silver anklet. Four silver bangles, etched with intricate patterns. A pair of amethyst earrings. And what must have been the contents of her pockets: Chapstick, a cell phone and, most importantly, a San Diego Zoo keychain with two keys, one silver and one gold.

Tara opened the phone and tried to turn it on, but the battery was dead. And of course her charger wouldn't work on it, so she set it aside to deal with later.

She could hear Sneakers padding down the staircase, leaping over one particular tread, past Ariel, and into the kitchen, stretching and yawning. When he spied the paper bag lying on the floor, he stuck his head and then his entire body inside it.

Tara watched, laughing, as the bag shimmied and rattled across the tile floor.

Then the cat emerged, strode regally to the back door, and stared over his shoulder at her.

"So, now you want to go outside and torment the woodland critters." She opened the door and the cat dashed into the yard as if something were chasing him. "Go get 'em, tiger! Just don't bring any strangers home with you. And while you're out there, move that branch out of the driveway." It seemed that every time she left the house, she returned to find a branch blocking the road. At this rate, there wouldn't be any left on the trees.

She slipped the gold key into the deadbolt on the back door, and it turned with a soft click. *Finally.* Then she slipped it into the doorknob, with the same result. She tried the locks on the front door and it worked in them, as well. As she inserted the key, she noticed scratches on the locks. That was strange; she could have sworn they weren't there before.

But when she tried the key in the basement doorknob — which was locked again — it didn't fit. Of course it didn't. She couldn't be *that* lucky.

She ran to the garage through the rain, hopping over puddles, and tried the key in that door. And it opened. But when she flipped the switch, the lights didn't work. Of course they didn't. She stumbled a few feet into the dark garage, hands held out in front of her, and bumped into a car.

It was getting late. She was cold and tired. Her body still ached from falling down the stairs. In spite of her curiosity about the car, Tara really didn't feel like dealing with it tonight. It could wait until morning, when she could see what she was doing.

She ran back to the house, forgetting about the puddles, and stepped in the middle of the biggest, deepest. *Damn.* As she ran through the back door, toes squishing in her slippers, Sneakers dashed between her legs.

"Watch out, cat!" Her wet shoes slipped on the linoleum and she fell, landing on her barely healed wrist, which buckled under her weight. "Ow! Shit!"

She sat in the middle of the floor for a minute, rocking and cradling her hand, waiting for the pain to subside. And noticed black scuffmarks on the back door. Did someone try to break in while she was at Lee's?

Maybe it was the attacker. But she quickly put that out of her mind; it was probably just kids. She stood gingerly, and trudged into the kitchen. Stared at the items spread on the table, and thought about all of the things that she needed to do.

Her muscles ached. Her wrist hurt. And someone might be lurking in the woods, watching her.

"I give up," she told Sneakers, who sat at her feet, gazing up at her innocently.

Twenty minutes later, hot water lapping at her chin and lavender-scented bubbles tickling her nose, Tara settled into the deep bathtub and thought about Lee's secrets. About what he might be hiding. And about her dream.

She slid under the water, moving her head from side to side so her long hair flowed through the water, pretending to be a mermaid.

&

A man and a woman, whispering in the night. No faces. Just outlines.

Bodies intertwine. He wraps her long hair around his hand and closes it into a fist. His voice is indistinct; hers is clear.

"Careful, she'll hear you." A giggle. "That's enough. We can't."

He laughs. Tugs her head back with her hair, a small jerk.

"I'm serious. Stop." She starts to rise, but he covers her with his body.

"Get off me." Her voice loses its teasing quality. "I said no."

He releases her hair to grasp her hands. Fingers link. He pins them over her head and quiets her with a kiss. Not a gentle kiss. She begins to struggle, but he is too strong.

She starts to speak, but he cuts her off. His voice is now clear. "Be quiet. Do you want her to hear us?"

"You're hurting me!" Fear in her voice.

Skin strikes skin, and she cries out in pain. "You've been asking for this for a long time, college girl. Now shut up, or I will *hurt you."*

For a few moments, there are only sounds. Grunts. Gasps. Muffled whimpers. Panting. Then a long groan.

He stands and looks down at her. "I know you won't say anything, baby. Who's she going to believe, you or me?" He disappears.

The woman curls into a ball, her body shaking with silent sobs.

~ 24 ~

Tara's head pounded. She tried to open her eyes, but the sunshine made her headache worse. But when her eyes were closed, the images from her dream haunted her. Why was she suddenly remembering her dreams? Especially now that they were getting worse, and she'd rather *not* remember them. What were once dreams had now become nightmares.

She crept into the bathroom and opened the medicine cabinet. She had taken more aspirin in the last few days than she had in years. Maybe she was allergic to something in the house. She wrapped her aching wrist in an Ace bandage, popped a couple of pills, and eased down the staircase.

Maybe caffeine would help. She turned on the coffee maker, and the rich aroma and soothing murmur soon filled the room. Two cups later, she could turn her head without feeling that it would explode. The images of the rape would be much harder to erase.

Needing a distraction, she pulled an old sweater over her faded pajamas and wandered out to the garage. Maybe she'd find something there that would lead her to the box; she was starting to feel like time was running out.

But all she found in the garage was a baby blue Dodge Phoenix, in perfect condition. She slid the silver key into the ignition and the engine coughed once, and roared to life. Choking on the exhaust, she quickly turned it off. Running her fingers along the sleek lines, she wished she knew more about classic cars. Maybe it was worth something. Tara wondered where Deirdre had gotten it and, once again, wished she knew more about her aunt's life.

Tara looked around the garage. Everything of value was gone, down to the paneling that at one time sheathed the walls; all that remained were bare studs and a few scraps of insulation. Besides a couple of battered cabinets and one rusted toolbox, the building was empty — except for the fireplace poker lying on top of the cabinets, out of sight.

Deirdre's phone charger was in the glove box; Tara tossed it into her truck so she could charge the phone the next time she drove into town. She pulled her truck into the garage and parked it next to the Phoenix; it'd be nice not to have to scrape the windows on those admittedly rare frosty mornings.

Damn. Tara really hoped she'd find the box in the garage — although deep down, she knew it wouldn't be there. She walked back to the house, shaking her head.

&

"Where in the hell is it?" she asked Sneakers, who was lying on the heating vent in the kitchen. The furnace groaned and she jumped, and then laughed at herself as she slid a plate into the microwave. Her nerves *must* be on edge, to be so jumpy. Hot air rippled the cat's black fur as the smell of warm dust, and then warming brownies, drifted through the room.

Two gooey treats later, Tara was no closer to finding an answer. She believed the box was the key to finding the secrets. The more effort she put into searching for it, the more of an obsession it became. She didn't want to admit that there was no box, but that conclusion was becoming harder and harder to avoid.

As she licked chocolate from her fingertips, she remembered what Lee had said. 'Secrets can rule your life, if you let them. And ruin it.' Didn't he also say that some secrets should remain hidden? Lee seemed to be the voice of reason in her otherwise unreasonable life.

Maybe she wasn't supposed to find the box. Maybe she was wasting her time, looking for something that didn't exist; after all, a woman with Alzheimer's and a ghost told her that it did. Or maybe the house was just fulfilling its charge, hiding the treasure from her. She hadn't found a single clue as to where the box might be hidden. And she had run out of places to look.

Maybe Lee was right. Maybe some secrets are better left alone. Maybe she should focus on the more pressing issues in her life, like finishing the repairs and paying the bills. And figuring out how to forgive herself, if her father couldn't do it for her.

Maybe it was time to concentrate on aiming for goals she could reach, instead of tilting at windmills.

"I guess I wasn't cut out to be Don Quixote," Tara said to herself. She sighed. She would let the box — and the treasure — rest in peace. It wasn't a decision she was happy with, but at this point, it made the most sense. Maybe someday she could look for the box again, when her life calmed down.

And maybe now, the house would finally leave her alone.

Sighing, she reached for a third brownie while Sneakers watched, his tail twitching.

&

Tara sat at her desk, where two more families waited for her to do her magic and 'make them pretty.' The ever-present wind rattled the glass in the French doors, and the ever-present branch tapped an erratic beat. Sneakers settled into her lap and purred as she worked. Which is where they were when the phone rang.

She knew it was ridiculous to hate the phone, regardless of how often it brought bad news. Recently the calls hadn't been too painful, so she was trying to learn to answer it without clenching her teeth.

Maybe she stopped too soon.

The display read 'restricted call.' "This is Tara," she answered cautiously.

"Tara, Craig Morris."

"Hi, Craig!" She remembered watching the man stumbling through the parking lot, and felt sorry for him all over again. "Are you okay? How's your landlady?"

"Evelyn? Oh, she's fine. She's home. Thanks for asking."

"I'm glad. Can I do anything to help?"

"Help? No, you can't. Listen, I have some people in town who are interested in the house. I'd like to bring them up after lunch."

Her smile faded. "Interested in the house? What do you mean? In *my* house? For what?"

His voice dropped to a whisper. "Tara, look, give me a break. These people…I …well, I owe them. I need to show them…they expect something from me. Could you just help me out, let me bring them up there? I'll make it up to you, I promise."

"Let me get this straight. You want me to lie to these people because you've gotten yourself in trouble. And when they find out the truth, then what happens?"

"No, that's not it at all. Look, we both know you can't pay that tax bill. Help me, and I'll work out a deal with you. Save yourself the embarrassment of losing the house at auction. Believe it or not, I do want to help you. If you'll help me."

"You call this helping? This house is all I have left." Tara was close to tears. "You had me fooled. Not only do you not have a heart, you're a liar, too. I was right about you the first time."

"Tara, wait…"

She jabbed at the off button and slammed the phone on the desk. Sneakers jumped out of her lap and dashed through the door. How could a man be so gentle and caring with his landlady, yet still try to steal her home from her?

The phone rang again, but Tara turned it off and shoved it into a desk drawer.

The secret inner wall that shielded her from pain, the wall that had been gradually receding, slammed back to full strength.

Blinking away tears, she returned to her work with a renewed passion. She needed to sell more memory books. They were her last defense against Craig Morris.

&

"I know your secrets." Mary pours another drink.

Ethan looks up from his plate. "You do?"

"I do. You don't think I know, but I do. Now, you owe me."

"What do I owe you?" His tone is gentle, patient.

"You always think it's me who needs you. Well, mister, now it's you who needs me." She stumbles across the kitchen and falls into a chair next to him. Ice cubes clink in her glass.

"I always need you, Mary."

"You need me to be quiet. The things I know will get you in trouble."

He doesn't reply.

"I could tell your secrets now. But this works out better for me. Just remember, as long as I know, she's safe."

Ethan carries his plate to the sink and rinses it before sliding it into the dishwasher. Then picks up the empty vodka bottle from the counter and drops it into the trashcan.

"I'll remember, honey."

&

The rays of the setting sun, peeking below ominous clouds, poured across Tara's sleeping face. Two completed memory books rested on the desk in front of her, next to an empty mug that smelled of chocolate and cinnamon.

Sneakers jumped onto the desk with a soft meow and marched across Tara's laptop, lifting first a black and then a white paw, and placing them deliberately on clusters of keys. Once across, he paused to stare at Tara, then reached out to pat her cheek. Once, twice. The third time she flinched.

"Meow."

Tara opened her eyes. "Huh?"

"Meow." The cat was nose to nose with her.

She jumped, and her head pounded. "Ow, damn it!" Sneakers leapt off the desk and stood by the door as Tara grabbed her head, wincing at the bitter taste of pain in her mouth.

This was getting old. But now she knew that she woke up with a headache every time she had a dream, so thought for a moment. And remembered it.

Was her mother drunk? Stupid question. But sometimes Mary made more sense drunk than sober.

So maybe her father had secrets, too. Mary. Deirdre. The house. Even Lee had secrets. For that matter, so did she.

The dreams must be trying to tell her something. Something was at stake. Something bigger than a metal box. Something important enough that Deirdre reached out from her grave to lead Tara to it.

She couldn't stop looking for the secrets. Even though it seemed to be the smart thing to do, apparently someone — or something — thought otherwise.

So much for abandoning Don Quixote. She would keep tilting at the damn windmills.

She noticed Sneakers patiently waiting at the door. "I take it you need food. And I need more aspirin." She bent down to pick up the cat one-handed and carried him into the kitchen. "Then I guess we need to start looking for the friggin' box again."

Sneakers yawned. Or maybe it was a smile.

&

Tara wandered along Surfside Beach, her feet barely leaving a mark in the wet sand. A lone seagull cried as he rode the thermals. Rock monoliths towered in the distance, looming black against the pinks and purples of the setting sun.

Sunset was a bittersweet time for Tara: a time to reflect on the past and look toward the future. To reflect on mistakes made yesterday, and vow to do better tomorrow.

As the fiery ball kissed the horizon, she slipped out of her sneakers and waded into the ocean. She gasped as the cold sliced into her flesh; she never got used to the shock. The sand under her feet felt like broken glass. She waded deeper, waiting for the pain to change to pins and needles and then, to merciful numbness.

Finally, she stopped. Shivering, she buried her face in the armful of paperwhite narcissus blossoms she carried, inhaling their dizzying fragrance before scattering them on the waves that lapped at her thighs.

On this day every year for the last thirty-one years, she repeated this ritual in the waters of the world. Always facing west, always at sunset. Always paperwhites: December's flower, Emma's favorite.

"Happy birthday, little one."

She watched the sun until it sank out of sight, wishing her sins could disappear as easily.

Legs aching, Tara staggered out of the water, slipped on her shoes, and trudged back up the beach. One more anniversary marked. One more reminder of a debt she couldn't repay.

~ 25 ~

Tara parked in front of Bonnie's store and tossed her cap on the dashboard. Sleigh bells jangled as she opened the glass door. The smell of dust and age tickled her nose and she sneezed.

"Now what do you want?" Bonnie snapped from somewhere nearby.

"Uh, hello, Bonnie?" Tara thought maybe she should sneak back out the door.

"Oops!" Bonnie said, appearing around a massive armoire. "I'm sorry, Tara, I thought you were someone else." Her smile didn't reach her eyes.

"Are you okay? Did I interrupt something?"

"Nothing important. What's up?"

"I'm craving pizza, so thought I'd see if you wanted to join me for lunch. But I can come back later, if it's a bad time."

"To be honest, I was just leaving. But it's sweet of you to think of me. How about tomorrow instead?"

Tara explained that she was going to Portland the next day to clean out her father's house and return his Explorer.

"Do you need help?" Bonnie asked.

Tara couldn't remember the last time someone offered to help her. "I don't suppose you would be able to give me a ride home?" she asked, ready to be turned down.

"Sure. I have some errands to run in the morning, but I could meet you at your father's house in the afternoon. Would that work?"

"Wow. That'd be great. Thanks!" Tara hugged her and gave her the address. "I really appreciate it, Bonnie. I didn't know how I was going to do this alone."

"Happy to help. And it'll give us the chance to visit without interruption," she said as the phone rang.

"See you tomorrow," Tara mouthed. Bonnie waved and disappeared into the depths of the store, talking on the phone.

Tara returned to her truck, with errands to run and pizza to buy before she could return home. Wondering if she had finally found a friend. It wasn't a familiar feeling. But it was a nice one.

&

A white sedan stops in the clearing and two women step out: one short, one tall. They leave the engine running so the car will be warm when they return. Wool coats, white gloves, sensible shoes. They stride toward the house through the light drizzle carrying colorful pamphlets, engaged in quiet conversation. At the top of the steps, the tall one taps on the front door, and they wait.

Behind them, the sedan silently moves forward. Two feet. Five. Stops twenty feet from its original position.

Now the short one taps on the door, a little louder. After another long minute, she walks across the porch to peek through the bay window.

A horn sounds. They turn to see the car sitting in the middle of the lawn. Pamphlets fall from gloved hands, forgotten.

They stare silently at the sedan for long moments before cautiously moving down the steps toward it, one sensible shoe at a time. They huddle on the flagstone path, trembling, watching. The car waits, engine purring.

Finally, they cautiously approach it. The tall one slowly reaches for the handle. Opens the door and quickly backs away. The car continues to idle, blue smoke oozing from the tailpipe and curling into the still winter air.

They circle the car at a safe distance until the drizzle turns into a downpour. Hair dripping, makeup running, they hesitantly open the other door and ease into the blue vinyl seats. Close the doors. And the car slips down the driveway.

The rain stops. A light breeze ruffles the pages of the pamphlets lying forgotten on the porch.

&

Since Craig kept wavering between good guy and bad guy, Tara decided she should probably do the research on the house after all. So once again, she walked through the imposing doors of the library and headed for the reference desk, where a woman in her late sixties thumbed through a copy of VIBE magazine. Her tie-dyed blouse and dangling earrings didn't match the pince-nez glasses suspended from the rhinestone-studded chain around her neck. Which didn't match her orange crew cut. Her nametag read 'Edith,' with a yellow smiley face.

"Excuse me," Tara said. She was feeling brave, and left her cap at home.

Edith looked up and smiled. "Hello, my dear. How can I help you today?" she said, reeking of patchouli oil.

She *sounded* like a librarian, anyway.

Tara explained about the mermaid. "It's a relatively unique feature. Someone must have written about it at some point," she ended. "I'm hoping to find something that would help me fix it in history."

"Which house is this again?"

Tara gave Edith the address.

"I've lived in Surfside my whole life and I've never heard tell of a figurehead in town. Are you sure it's not something someone carved in their garage?" Edith sifted the chain through her fingers like worry beads. "I've heard tell of folks whittling a chain from a block of wood. All of the links connected. I don't know how they do that. I can't peel an apple without the peel breaking."

So she was a chatty librarian.

"It really does appear to be something that came from the sea," Tara said. "Can tell me where I could find the books on local history?"

"We don't have a lot of writers around here, dear. Lots more in Cannon Beach — they're so artsy down there, you know — but those folks don't write about anything up here. Nope, apparently nothing significant happens in Surfside. Although there was that time a beluga whale beached itself on Seaman's Point. Now that was pretty exciting. Poor thing flopped around for hours before someone from Marine Rescue arrived and took care of it. I'm sure we have pictures somewhere." She perched her glasses on her nose and started flipping through a drawer of index cards.

Tara glanced at her watch. "That's okay, I need to get going. Thanks anyway."

Just then, Edith pulled a yellowed card from the drawer. "Well, looky here. You said figurehead? From a ship?"

"That's right."

"Here's something I didn't expect to find. Someone must have misfiled the card." She looked up at Tara. "Which was probably me, since I'm the one who does the filing. Whoopsy!" She laughed, a horselaugh that caused the library patrons to look up from their books.

Tara thought it prudent not to ask why the library didn't have an electronic card catalog.

"Anyway, give me a minute." Edith disappeared into the stacks behind the desk. Tara waited. Listened to the clock behind the desk tick off the minutes. Five, six, seven. Wandered toward the spot where the librarian had vanished and peered around the bookcases. Where did she go?

"Found it!" Edith squealed in Tara's ear, and she jumped. "Betcha thought I got lost!"

Tara smiled. Backed up a little. In her white polyester pants and red Keds sneakers, Edith looked like an attempt to cross a hippie with a senior citizen that had gone dreadfully wrong.

She handed Tara a bound document. "It's not a published book, but it's sort of the same thing. A doctoral thesis on the figureheads of pirate ships. Written by one of the founders of Surfside. Or at least I think that's who she was. Maybe she's the granddaughter of one of the founders. Boy, I miss my memory some days. It probably says in here." She started flipping through the pages, and Tara bit her tongue to keep from screaming.

"I can look through it," she said, reaching for the book.

"Of course you can!" Edith replied, laughing. "That's me, always trying to be helpful. Anyway, I just need to see your library card, and we'll get you checked out and on your way."

Tara didn't have a card, so Edith read her magazine while Tara filled out the paperwork. When she was done, the librarian glanced over the form. Looked up at Tara. Looked down at the form again.

"Davies?" Her cheerful voice suddenly developed an icy coat.

Tara nodded. Edith glared at her and entered the information into the computer, jabbing at the keys, and shoved a card and the book at her. And stormed back into the stacks.

Tara took the thesis and hurried out of the library, head down. So much for feeling brave. Although her cap wouldn't have helped her. Someone would always be ready to judge her. Maybe someday that would stop. But apparently, not today.

She was almost to her truck when she heard someone shout, "Wait just a minute!" Tara turned and saw Edith standing in front of the library door, hands on her hips.

Now what? Tara walked back to the foot of the steps, steeling herself for the inevitable attack. "Yes?" she asked, looking up at Edith's pursed lips, narrowed eyes, and squared shoulders.

"You tell that no-good son of yours the next time he shaves my Fluffy, there will be h-e-double-el to pay! I have *had* it with him. And you! How can you let that hooligan run the streets unsupervised? You should be ashamed of yourself!"

"I don't…"

But Edith had already stomped back into the library, letting the door slam behind her.

Tara stared after her in stunned silence. Then burst into relieved laughter and returned to her truck. She tossed the thesis on the passenger seat and drove home, glad the wrath of Edith was aimed at someone else, for a change.

&

Tara had been accountable for far too long. It was time for a road trip. Even a short one would recharge her batteries, help her forget about responsibilities and obligations, finances and house repairs. Not to mention headaches and wounded wrists.

So she filled a cooler with root beer and a couple of peanut butter and banana sandwiches, and drove south. She heard about the beauty of the Oregon Coast Highway for years, but never found the time to drive it; returning to Oregon wasn't high on her list until recently. And the miserable weather over the past few weeks hadn't made beach-wandering very enticing, anyway.

The road meandered along the rugged coastline, past scenic beaches and vast sand dunes, ducking into lush evergreen forests and through fields filled with cows, sheep, and even goats. It hugged rocky cliffs, and crawled through small coastal communities and larger inland towns. She wished it were summer, with blackberry bushes crawling up the banks along the sides of the highway, laden with ripe berries.

Tara sang along with the radio, not thinking about anything but the ocean, and the sun, and the surf. A couple of times she stopped and wandered empty beaches, chasing waves, feeding scraps of bread to the seagulls, and laughing at the sand squelching between her toes. The air smelled of sea and spruce and faraway places, and she filled her hungry lungs with it.

When she passed a sign pointing toward one of the state's many lighthouses, she turned off the highway and followed the gravel road to a crushed shell parking lot. But instead of a typical white tower with a rotating light, there was a two-story wooden house topped by a red lantern. After browsing the exhibits and climbing to the watch room to check out the view, she wandered along a paved trail to a bluff and found a young girl huddled on a bench, her long blond hair rippling in the breeze. She was underdressed in her thin pink sweater and paisley cotton skirt; the sun might be hot, but the wind was biting.

"Aren't you cold?" Tara asked her.

The girl smiled. "A little. But the view is so pretty, I don't really think about it." She reached out her hand and Tara took it. She must be more than a little cold, she thought: her skin was pure ice. "My name's Muriel. This is one of my favorite places in the whole world. There just can't be anywhere more beautiful than this."

Tara thought about the places she'd been that took her breath away: Yellowstone, San Francisco, Tahiti. But at this moment, with the sun sparking on the water, the salt air tickling her nose, and the sea birds calling overhead, she had to agree.

They sat quietly, watching the waves roll into the shore, until Tara's fingers grew numb. "I'm going to head home. Is your house near here?" she asked, thinking of the empty parking lot.

"Oh yes, just along that path."

"You're lucky. This would be a beautiful place to live."

Muriel smiled. "Yes, it would be."

Tara thanked the girl for sharing her bench and left Muriel sitting on the bluff as she returned to the warmth of the lighthouse. She ran her hands under the hot water in the ladies' room until her fingers thawed, then wandered into the gift shop and studied a map of the park, but saw no homes on the property.

"Do many families live in the park?" she asked the clerk, who stopped wiping imaginary dust from a shelf of model lighthouses.

"No, just the lighthouse keeper. He lives upstairs, but his quarters aren't open to the public."

Tara frowned. "I just spoke with a girl who said her home was nearby. Maybe she meant she lives in a nearby town."

The woman looked at Tara through Coke-bottle lenses. "Long blond hair? Pink sweater? Sitting on the bench furthest from the lighthouse?"

Tara nodded.

"Well…she doesn't live anywhere. Muriel is our ghost."

"Your *what*?" She thought about the girl's ice cold hand.

The clerk smiled and shrugged. "Our ghost. Legend has it she was a sea captain's daughter who snuck into the lighthouse during the years it was abandoned, and was never seen again. Some say it's only a legend, but once you've seen her…

"Anyway, not many people get to talk to our Muriel. You're lucky; there must be something about you that attracts spirits."

Tara wasn't sure "lucky" was the right word.

She walked to her truck and slowly drove home, wondering if there was a way to tell real people from ghosts. Maybe she needed to learn.

~ 26 ~

Stress is all about perception. If she could cross some of the items off her to-do list, Tara believed her life would feel less frantic and she would be less stressed. At least it sounded good in theory.

So even though the repairs on the house weren't complete and clients were impatiently waiting for their books, she got up early, stopped for a chocolate-glazed donut at the Surfside Bakery, and headed inland. On the floor of the Explorer were a couple of colorful pamphlets she found lying on the porch; she had no idea where they came from.

She stopped at the hospital to check on her father, but the nurses were bathing him and suggested that she come back later. She didn't ask if there was any change. Some days she had to force herself to visit him; she was growing tired of watching him die. Although she couldn't admit that to anyone. On most days, she couldn't even admit it to herself.

After her conversation with Dr. Chambers, Tara had resigned herself to the fact that her father would never be coming home. At least not to his house. If — when — he did emerge from the coma, he'd have to spend time in a rehabilitation center: he would need months of therapy. Then Tara might be able to bring him to her house, as long as he had round-the-clock nursing.

Assuming he wasn't in prison.

Tara knew she was grasping at straws. But she couldn't give up hope that he was going to recover. It was all she had.

So, she decided to start clearing out his house. While she couldn't sell it without the power of attorney, she *could* store what she felt he might need, and get rid of the rest. As much as she didn't want to sort through the wreckage of her childhood, someone had to.

It was a relief to finally park the Explorer in her father's garage; now she wouldn't have to look at it in her driveway every day. She could decide what to do with it later.

It was also getting a little easier to walk into his house. Maybe the ghosts had moved on — or she was getting used to them. She opened the drapes, turned up the furnace, and started sorting through her parents' lives.

Marge soon arrived with her teenaged son Tony and together they packed every dish, every towel, every knickknack and picture. Cleaned out every closet, every drawer. Tara tackled her father's office, stuffing folders and stacks of paper into cartons; she'd take them home and go through them at her leisure, rather than rushing through them here and missing something important. There was a fireproof box tucked behind a row of books on the bottom shelf of a bookcase, but it was locked. Thinking they'd come across the key as they packed, she dropped that into a carton, too.

After she finished in the office, Tara walked down the hall and slowly opened the door to the master bedroom. On the lace-covered bureau sat jewelry, perfume, and a silver brush and comb set. Dresses and skirts still hung in the closet, and the floor was cluttered with shoes. A paperback romance lay on the nightstand next to the bed.

Nothing had changed in the year that Mary had been gone.

Why hadn't her father gotten rid of his wife's things? It was as if he thought she'd be back. Or maybe he just couldn't deal with the emotional strain of the task. Whatever the reason, it was eerie. Tara fought the urge to look over her shoulder, expecting her mother to walk in and demand why Tara was in her room.

She picked up the book. An old postcard was tucked somewhere near the middle, marking a forgotten place. She studied the card; it was a picture of the Taj Mahal. Tara remembered the brash young boy in torn pants and stained shirt who sold her the card, and how a mass of frantic vendors swarmed her afterwards, recognizing an easy mark. She bought her souvenirs from shops instead of street urchins after that. Tara thought her mother threw away the postcards she sent over the years without looking at them. She slipped it into her pocket, along with a few strands of hair from the brush.

Dealing with her father's things was hard enough; she couldn't face her mother's, too. She backed out of the room and decided to let Marge handle that task.

As she emptied the other rooms, Tara set aside a few items. A few of her father's books from the dusty shelves in his office. Her mother's favorite Christmas angels that she displayed all year. And smaller things: an earring, a bottle of Old Spice, a picture of her parents from the refrigerator door.

There were no signs of Emma anywhere.

Marge suggested they have a garage sale to sell what Tara didn't want to store or donate, and volunteered to organize it. Tara gratefully agreed. She didn't need to be present while strangers haggled over the pieces of her parents' lives.

The sun was setting by the time Tony dropped off the last bag at Goodwill. Tara thanked Marge again for handling the sale.

"Don't you worry your pretty little head about it. Me and Tony will take of it, won't we, honey?" Tony, looking bored as only an eighteen-year old could, nodded imperceptibly.

"You just get back down to Surfside and take care of your auntie's house. I'll be in touch." She patted Tara's hand and shooed her son out the front door.

Tara smiled at Marge's mothering, considering they were around the same age. Some people were natural mothers. Mary hadn't been. Tara didn't know if she was. She wished she could have had the chance to find out.

After they left, she wandered through the house, footsteps echoing on the bare hardwood floors. When she came to her old bedroom, she gathered her courage and peeked through the open door. She took a few things with her when she left at seventeen, not caring what happened to the rest. She wasn't surprised to find the room had been sanitized of its former occupant and turned into a guest room. Nothing remained of her in this house. Not even memories.

Tara hesitantly crossed the threshold and walked around the double bed to the closet. She slowly opened the door. But, like the rest of the room, it was empty. A few wire hangers dangled from a metal rod and a stray button nestled in a dusty corner. A plastic air freshener lay on the shelf, its fresh citrus scent a distant memory.

She could still picture the pillows piled in the corner, the shelf where she kept her small flashlight. Still remembered the hours spent in fear, praying her mother would pass out instead of come looking for her. Home was supposed to be a child's safe place; what a comment it was on her life that for Tara, her safe place had been a closet.

She pulled her sweater closer around her, touched her necklace, and firmly closed the door. Maybe there were still ghosts here after all.

&

A vehicle pulls into the clearing and stops. A figure emerges and walks up the path. As it approaches the porch there is a noise, loud as a sonic boom. The figure flinches, trips over one of the flagstones and pitches headfirst into an empty flowerbed, striking its head on a moss-covered rock.

The figure lies on the ground motionless, then slowly sits up and brushes dirt from hands and face. Looks around and notices the vehicle silently rolling backwards down the driveway, gaining speed. The figure jumps up and runs down the gravel road after it.

&

Tara was sitting on the front porch surrounded by cartons, watching the sky turn orange, when a sleek black Mercedes roadster pulled up.

"Nice car," Tara said, plodding down the steps. After a day spent wrestling with ghosts, she was exhausted.

"It's my boyfriend's," Bonnie said. "When he's out of town, he lets me babysit. I'm only supposed to drive around Surfside. But when he pisses me off, I go on little road trips." She grinned. "Like this one. Hop in!" They stuffed the cartons into the trunk, and Tara noticed a deep scratch on the rear bumper.

"That's nasty."

Bonnie glanced at it. "Yeah, someone keyed it last week. Dumb kids." They climbed into the car and headed west.

As the miles slipped beneath the wheels, Bonnie told Tara about growing up in Surfside, her stay-at-home mother and blue-collar father, and learning the antique business from her pack rat uncle. Tara shared tales of the Amazon, the wine country of South Africa, the beaches of the Caribbean.

"Your life is so much more interesting than mine," Bonnie said.

"It's 'the grass is greener' syndrome. Anyone can travel. Not many people are lucky enough to have a family like yours."

"I guess everything has its good and bad points," Bonnie said. They drove in silence for a few minutes. "How about your family?"

Tara wanted to trust Bonnie. She was the first person she'd met in a long time that might be a friend. If Tara was going to put her old life behind her and start fresh in Surfside, she would need friends. Lee didn't shun her when he learned her secret. But Bonnie wasn't Lee.

So instead, she told Bonnie about her father's engineering business and birdhouses, and threw in a couple of stories about Deirdre — stories about how she thought Deirdre lived, anyway — gradually turning the conversation back to the house. Maybe someday she could tell Bonnie about her mother, and Emma. But today wasn't that day.

"Speaking of the house, has anything else popped out of the woodwork?" Bonnie asked, shifting gears smoothly as the sports car hugged the winding turns of Chinook Road.

"Not yet, but I haven't had much time to look." Tara told her about Craig and the back taxes. "So I'm trying to make enough money to pay the taxes before I lose everything."

"We can't let that happen. I have some friends who might be able to help."

"Oh, thanks, but I don't know how anyone can help, unless they have a treasure map." Tara laughed shortly. "Or you're wrong about my sword, and someone wants to pay me an obscene amount of money for it."

"Maybe you'll find something that *is* worth big bucks. In the meantime, I have feelers out about the sword. Worse comes to worse, I could take it off your hands. But like I said, just don't get your hopes up."

"I'm trying not to." They unloaded the cartons and stood next to the car. "Thanks so much for the ride. It was fun," Tara said. And meant it.

Bonnie hugged her. "Any time. Let me know what happens with the evil developer."

"Will do. I'll stop by the next time I'm in town. Maybe we can grab a glass of wine or something. If your boyfriend doesn't mind, that is."

A shadow crossed Bonnie's face. "Oh. Right. No, he has nothing to say about it. I'll see you later." She gunned the engine and disappeared down the driveway, gravel flying.

&

After stacking the cartons in a corner of the kitchen, Tara stared at them. It had been a long, emotional day; she didn't have the energy to go through her them right now. Then she saw the thesis from the library lying on the table. That, she could do. Grabbing a fistful of oatmeal cookies, she collapsed on the couch and started reading about figureheads.

And discovered that Bonnie was wrong about sailors thinking mermaids were bad luck. The crew of at least one ship believed mermaids were good luck — or brought the kind of luck they wanted, anyway. It was a pirate ship, captained by a woman who commissioned mermaids as figureheads because she liked the idea of their luring innocent victims to their deaths.

Surprisingly, there were a number of female pirates throughout history. Most seamen believed having a woman on a ship was bad luck, so women pirates dressed as men until they earned the respect of their male counterparts through their fighting and drinking prowess, then they could reveal their true identities. Men also feared the women for their unpredictability. Tara laughed at that.

History was vague on which female pirate captained this particular ship. Some said it was Mary Read, but others claimed it was Anne Bonny; the women had sailed together for a time. Eventually Mary was captured and executed, but a pregnant Anne escaped and history lost track of her. So Anne could have cruised the Pacific, and her ship could have been wrecked off the Oregon coast. And Ariel could have come from her ship. Anything was possible. Maybe this would be enough to convince the city fathers to help her save her house.

Tara tossed the thesis on the chair next to her purse and wandered into the hallway to kneel beside the figurehead. She gazed into her emerald eyes. “So, Ariel, could you really be a pirate in disguise? Want to tell me where you hid your treasure?” Laughing, she rose and walked into the study.

Ariel continued to stare into the distance, guarding her secrets.

~ 27 ~

A figure slips out of the woods, hurrying between the raindrops. Crosses the clearing to peek into the garage and peer through the bay windows. Taps on the front door. When there is no reply, slips a tool into the lock and, after a struggle, the door swings open.

Inside the house, the figure darts from room to room, looking under furniture, peeking behind pictures, searching kitchen cabinets, rapping on walls. Rattles and twists the basement doorknob, which is locked. Pounds a fist into the wood with a muttered curse and disappears into the study, where desk drawers are opened and slammed shut again.

Finally, the figure stands in the hallway, glaring into a gilt-framed mirror. Then turns and pulls open the front door, which swings too easily and smacks the figure in the face.

From the window seat in the living room a black cat watches, tail twitching, as the figure reels backwards, hand to face, stumbles through the door, and disappears into the woods.

&

There was never enough time, Tara thought, as she drove the foggy roads from Portland. How did people with families and jobs pay bills, run errands, mow the lawn, make dinner, hug their kids, love their spouses, and still have time to pursue a career and play darts with the boys or drink wine with the girls every Tuesday? As much as she longed for a family, she didn't know how she'd fit one into her life. Maybe she'd have more time when she wasn't restoring a house. Wasn't running from her past. Wasn't looking for a box of stars.

Even though she was feeling rushed, she swung into Lee's; she could make time for a quick beer. Maybe he'd cheer her up. His Jeep Cherokee sat in its usual spot. She ran to the door through the rain, wishing she had an umbrella.

What did Lee say? Pieces of lives we can control, pieces we can't, and pieces we shouldn't. She shook her head. What did that have to do with opening the stupid door? The man was a nut case.

Something echoed deep in her memory, as disconcerting as a déjà vu moment. A conversation about souls. Pieces of souls.

Pieces sometimes are ripped away and sometimes discarded without thought. Lose a piece and the soul grieves until 'tis found again.

She remembered something else, something about transgressions and forgiveness. But the memory was gone as quickly as it came. She didn't know where it came from, and wished she could remember more.

Maybe Lee would be able to explain it to her. Maybe Lee's Place had its own ghost. So she banged on the door and waited for him to open it, water coursing off her hood and dripping into her face.

But he didn't answer. After pounding for a few minutes, she gave up. Maybe the music was too loud for him to hear her. Maybe he wasn't there after all. Too bad; she really could use cheering up.

Tara slowly pulled back onto the highway. She didn't see the curtains in a rear window move slightly.

&

Sometimes opportunity knocks. Sometimes it just walks in.

"Whatcha doing?"

Tara jumped up, knocking over her chair and banging her knee on the desk. Sneakers fell off her lap and retreated into the far corner, hissing.

"Mariah! You scared me to death. Sneakers, shut up!" The cat made a wide berth around the wheelchair and dashed out of the room.

"Sorry. I thought it'd be okay if I just came in. The door was open." The girl hung her head and stared at her feet — or at her sneakers, anyway. Her chair was dry; the rain must have stopped.

"I'm not mad, honey. You just surprised me, that's all. Of course you can come in if the door is unlocked." Although Tara swore she locked it. Then again, she thought she locked it when she left that morning, but it was unlocked when she got home. There were more scratches on the lock and what looked like footprints in the hallway. She was trying to convince herself the house was just playing tricks on her again, since nothing seemed to be missing.

"I wanted to look for the box some more," Mariah said.

"I honestly don't know if there *is* a box, Squirt. If something is hidden in here, we should have found it by now." Tara rubbed her knee; that was going to leave a nasty bruise.

"Do you care if I look anyway?"

"Of course not. Maybe you'll be luckier than I've been. I need to do some painting upstairs. Will you be okay down here by yourself?"

"I'm going to find some treasure today if it kills me." Mariah rolled into the living room. Tara climbed the staircase, noticing that the weak tread sagged more each day. Maybe she should move 'fix step' higher on her to-do list.

She finished rolling blue paint on a wall in the master bedroom and was admiring her handiwork when she heard a scream. Running downstairs, she found the basement door open and the light on. And Mariah's chair at the top of the staircase, empty.

"Mariah!" Tara called. "Are you okay?"

"Of course I am. Why wouldn't I be?"

Tara looked down the stairs and saw the girl sitting on the basement floor. "Well, you screamed. Hang on a minute." She ran outside and found a rock, wedged it against the open door, and positioned the wheelchair to block the opening. She wasn't going to be trapped down there again. Only then did she hurry down the stairs.

"How did you get down here?" she asked the girl.

"On my butt." Mariah's jeans were dirty, the empty legs tangled beneath her. Tara looked up and saw the girl's sneakers and a pile of rags lying on the top step. "I didn't think you'd get weirded out if I took off my legs."

Tara laughed, though she was still concerned. "No, I'm not weirded out. But why did you scream? You scared me."

"Sorry, but I was excited. Look what I found!" She held out a dirty hand. Resting in her palm was a gold star. Granted, it looked like a plastic Christmas ornament covered in gold glitter. But it was still a star.

Tara took it from her and examined it. “Where’d you find it?”

“Right here, at the foot of the stairs. I put my hand on it when I got down here. It was sticking out of the dirt. Sometimes it’s good not to have legs.”

Tara hadn’t found anything in the basement. Not a shred of evidence that anyone had been down there in years. Certainly not a star.

“You think it’s a clue? To the treasure?” Mariah asked, brushing her dirty hands on her even dirtier pants.

“It could be. What do you think?”

“You told me the box was full of shiny stars. And I found a star. Maybe it’s like Hansel and Gretel and the breadcrumbs. Maybe if we follow the trail of stars, they’ll lead us to the box.”

“Makes sense to me. You want to keep looking down here?”

“Sure. But it would help if I had more light.”

“My flashlight is down here somewhere. Can you see it?” Tara asked.

“Nope. I can’t see anything. I need a flashlight.” Mariah giggled at her own joke.

“Funny girl.” Tara glanced around the room. “Are you okay staying here alone while I go upstairs?”

“I was here alone before you came down,” she said, using her ‘duh’ voice.

“Good point.” Tara handed the star to Mariah and ran upstairs.

New light bulbs solved the problem, and soon the basement was flooded with light. Tara left Mariah scooting around in the dirt, although she offered to bring down her wheelchair. “Your mom might be upset if you get your clothes dirty.”

“No, she won’t.”

Mariah never mentioned her parents. Maybe there was a reason Mariah spent so much time here instead of at home. Maybe her home life was similar to Tara’s when she was a girl.

Deciding to pursue the topic later, Tara once again climbed the stairs. Sneakers crouched at the top, growling.

“Now what?” Tara asked. “The last time you did that, I tried to save you and ended up falling down the stairs. Stop it. There’s nothing down there but Mariah." She left the cat pacing in front of the open door and walked to the sink to wash the paint from her hands.

Stars. Why would the house show her a star? The obvious answer would be that it wanted her to keep searching for the box. Which she had already decided to do. It made no sense. Well, assuming that a house consciously doing anything made sense.

Then she heard Mariah call again. "I found it!"

"What?" Tara walked to the top of the stairs.

"Your flashlight!"

"Where was it?" she asked as she jogged back downstairs.

"Behind this pipe." Mariah pointed toward a piece of copper that ran the length of the basement.

"How the heck did it get back there?" Tara asked.

"Dunno. It must have rolled."

There was no way the flashlight could have rolled up and over the pipe.

"There aren't any other stars down here," Mariah said, a note of dejection in her voice.

"Maybe there are more hidden in the rest of the house. We weren't looking for anything that small before. Next time, we can look in star-sized places instead of box-sized ones."

Mariah scooted up the steps, Tara close behind her. The girl gathered her sneakers and rags, hopped into her chair, and rolled toward the front door. "Sorry I didn't find the treasure," she said, offering the star to Tara.

"You keep it, and think about what it's trying to tell us."

"Really?" Her eyes shone. "I can keep it?"

"You betcha. Finders keepers." Tara leaned down to hug the girl. "Are you sure you'll be okay going home alone? It's getting dark out there."

"Oh, I'm fine. See you later."

Tara watched her disappear into the evening and closed the door, noticing that the gilt-framed mirror that she hung over the hole in the hallway was crooked. As she reached out to straighten it, long red curls and emerald eyes smiled back at her.

Tara had straight auburn hair and blue eyes.

She blinked and looked again, and her own reflection peered out at her. Although the face in the mirror now was drawn and pale, as if it had just seen a ghost.

&

Ethan enters the living room, where Mary is changing a squirming toddler's diaper.

Three-year old Tara is hiding behind the couch. "Look for me, Mama, look for me!" she chants.

"In a minute," Mary says. "Let me finish with your sister."

Tara starts crying. Emma joins in. Mary shifts Emma to her shoulder and paces, gently bouncing the baby into sniffles. "Ethan, can you get Tara, please?"

Ethan holds a piece of paper. "It's from Deirdre," he says, paying no attention to Tara, who cries louder.

Mary stops bouncing. Emma starts crying. "From Deirdre?"

Tara crawls around the couch and hurls herself at her father's legs, whimpering. He absently pats her head, watching his wife. Mary starts mindlessly bouncing again.

"Let me see," she says, reaching for the letter with her free hand.

He holds onto it. "She wants you to take care of her baby for a while."

"What baby? She has another one?"

He nods. "A boy. Two months ago. Says she needs to take care of some business. She'll bring him up here and be back to get him as soon as she can."

She glances toward Tara, clinging to his leg. "Like she did last time?"

He shrugs. "At least this time she's giving you a choice."

Mary looks at him. "I can't do it again."

"I know." He starts to crumble the letter.

"Give it to me," she says. He hands her the page. "I'll read it later." She slips it into her pocket and places the baby in a playpen by the fireplace. Tara crawls onto the couch and sucks her thumb.

"Why do you want to keep it? I told you what it says."

"It's all I have of her," Mary says.

~ 28 ~

A dark cloud appears on the horizon. Another joins it. Soon the sky is blanketed in black. The breeze that stirs the winter branches strengthens into gusts that shake the trees to their very roots.

A rumble in the distance. Another, stronger, closer. The air grows heavy. Dogs pace restlessly. Birds fall silent.

A ray of light pierces the gloom, enters the house, and illuminates the silent figure at the foot of the staircase. Her emerald eyes blaze in the eerie glow.

Some storms announce their arrival with thunder and lightning. Some sneak up silently. Both can be deadly.

&

Tara awoke and checked the clock. Nine o'clock. That was a surprise; she never slept past seven. She looked out the window and saw that it was still dark. At this time of year, even when the winter showers obscured it, the sun should be up by now.

She walked to the window to greet Emma and study the sky. The clouds hovering overhead were black and thick with rain. A long rumble shook the house. Then another.

"Looks like a doozey of a storm," she told Sneakers, still snuggled deep in the comforter. "You might want to stay in bed today instead of pursuing your usual hectic schedule. Oh, wait, that *is* your usual hectic schedule." Tara stroked the cat before slipping on her robe and heading downstairs.

Sitting at the kitchen table, mug in hand, she remembered the dream. But for the first time, she didn't have a headache. Maybe there was so much aspirin in her system, she had become immune to the pain. But her wrist still ached, so that wasn't true.

She thought about the dream. Were they really dreams, or had she somehow found a way to peek through a fold in time and see events that occurred in the past? Maybe it was ghosts, trying to communicate with her. Or just her overactive imagination.

Regardless of whether it was a dream or a vision, Tara now knew that Mary helped Deirdre raise one of her children. This was the first she heard of Deirdre having a family; why didn't her parents mention it?

If Deirdre had children, that would mean Tara had cousins. If they were still living, that is. She might have a family after all, after years of being alone.

Tara was almost forty years old, yet never had a real family. No husband to cherish her, no children to love and need her. Her father neglected her, her mother abused her, her aunt abandoned her. She destroyed her one chance of finding true love. And killed the only person who could have been her ally.

It always came back to her mother and her disease. Mary's drinking colored Tara's life from the day she was born. And was still doing so.

Her fortieth birthday loomed. And she'd be spending it alone. Again.

"*Damn it!*" Tara hurled her mug across the kitchen, coffee spraying the room. The ceramic cup smashed through the window, sending shards of glass flying into the sink and onto the floor around it. The rain that threatened all morning began falling furiously, blowing through the broken window.

Tara huddled at the table, crying for the life she never had.

&

But pain eventually subsides. And this was familiar pain. So after a few minutes, Tara raised her head, wiped her eyes, and stumbled to the sink.

"Good job, Davies. Now you have another window to fix. And a mug to replace." She taped a garbage bag over the broken pane and started wiping up the coffee with a dishtowel. But as she did, her thoughts returned to Deirdre.

She wished she knew more about her aunt. There must be neighbors, friends, *someone* who knew how Deidre spent the last forty years.

Then again, Tara didn't have anybody, so maybe Deirdre didn't, either.

She continued cleaning up the mess, thinking about how similar she and Deirdre were. And wishing, once again, that she had known her aunt. All she could do now, besides find Deirdre's children, was honor her by restoring her home and building a life in it.

Which meant protecting it from Craig.

&

Tara felt like she spent more time driving between Portland and Surfside than working on the house *or* her memory books. So to cheer herself up, she bought a couple of mochas and headed to Bonnie's. Her passion for chocolate verged on an addiction; knowing that she most likely had inherited Mary's addictive personality, Tara avoided overindulging in anything. Except chocolate, that is. Considering the substances she *could* be addicted to, she wasn't too worried about it: you didn't hear of many people dying from an overdose of cocoa.

With the cardboard cups burning her hands and her wet hair sticking to her face, Tara backed through the glass door with 'Antiques' painted on it in fancy script. "Bonnie?"

"Back here!" came the reply, and Tara continued to the rear of the store.

"Ouch!" she said as she sat the hot cups on the glass counter. "They took me seriously when I asked for extra hot."

The petite woman appeared in the office door, smiling. "I smell a mocha. How did you know that's my favorite?"

"Anything that combines caffeine and chocolate can't be bad," Tara said, blowing on her reddened fingers. Then she looked up and saw Bonnie's black eye. "What on earth happened to you?"

Bonnie shrugged. "I was carrying some boxes and tripped over that carpet I warned you about. Smacked my nose pretty hard, and woke up with a shiner."

Tara raised an eyebrow. "You can tell me to mind my own business, but this doesn't have anything to do with borrowing your boyfriend's car, does it?" She took the top off her cup and blew on the coffee; she didn't want to burn her tongue, too.

"Oh no, of course not!" Bonnie answered too quickly. "I'm just a klutz. He would never do anything like that. Sometimes he gets mad over stupid stuff. But he'd never hit me." She sipped the hot drink, her eyes not meeting Tara's. "I love your perfume, I keep meaning to tell you. What is it?"

Tara wasn't going to let Bonnie change the subject that easily. "Heavenly Angels. Victoria's Secret. Promise me that if you feel like he's going to hurt you, you'll call me — or someone."

Bonnie looked at Tara over the rim of her cup. "Okay," she said simply.

After the women agreed to meet for lunch the next afternoon, Tara ran back into the rain, vowing that if anyone laid a hand on her friend, she'd hit him with more than a flagpole.

&

Tara sat in the Stop 'N' Shop parking lot, chewing her thumbnail. She forgot to grab her baseball cap when she left home. And it was pouring, so she couldn't wear sunglasses without drawing even more attention to herself.

She longed for the days when buying groceries was a pleasure instead of something to fear. No one had been mean to her since the scene in the hardware store; she'd even met some nice people. But she hadn't been brave enough to venture into town without her disguise very often, either.

It'd be okay. It would only take a few minutes; what could happen in a few minutes? Grasping her necklace for courage, she walked through the supermarket doors, trying not to cower.

Shoppers scurried through the aisles, intent on getting home at the end of a long day. "O Holy Night" played in the background. Tara grabbed a basket and hurried through the store, tossing in the essentials. She'd come back later in the week when she could shop incognito. But so far, everyone was ignoring her. So far, so good.

As she finished filling her basket with oatmeal, brownie mix, and cocoa, and was starting to believe she'd make it out of the store without any problems, she heard a man call, "Hey lady!" She lowered her head and kept walking, eyes on the scuffed linoleum. He couldn't mean her.

"Hey! You in the red coat!" He *did* mean her. She hurried around the corner, and found herself in a maze of tortilla chip and beer displays.

She was trapped.

Tara dropped her basket and turned to face her pursuer, fists knotted. To hell with the groceries. Maybe if she attacked first, he'd back down. Give her a chance to escape.

She heard footsteps approaching. Held her breath.

"Hi, Tee," Lee said as he rounded the corner. "Whatcha doing back here? Sudden craving for nachos?"

"Damn it, Lee!" she said, her heart pounding. "You scared me to death. Why didn't you say it was you?"

"If I knew you were going to pull an O.J., I would have." Then he stared at her. "Hey, hey, are you okay? Why are you shaking? I didn't mean to upset you."

Tara raised her chin to stop its quivering. Now the danger was past, she could let her guard down. "I'm fine, really. You just scared me, that's all." Her voice broke.

He wrapped his arms around her. "I'm sorry. I didn't think." For a moment they stood quietly, Tara struggling not to cry.

"Let's get you out of here." He squeezed her cold hands, picked up her basket, and waited while she checked out. They walked to her truck dodging lake-sized puddles, put the bags in the front seat, and stood looking at each other. Tara noticed a barely healed cut on his forehead.

"Sorry for falling apart," she said.

"No apologies needed. My fault entirely."

After another awkward pause, Tara stretched up on her toes and kissed him softly. Lee slid his hand behind her head, tangled his fingers in her hair, and kissed her. Not so softly. Then he released her and stepped back.

"Well, um, I'd better go," Tara said. "Thanks for taking care of me." She climbed into her truck, the taste of peppermint strong on her lips.

"Any time, Tee," Lee said as he watched her pull out of the parking lot. "Any time."

&

Once she was home, Tara forced herself to focus on something besides the smell of Obsession lingering on her fingers. Something mundane, like checking phone messages. She reluctantly called her voice mail. The first message was from Craig, obviously left right after she hung up on him the other day.

"Tara, listen. This is not what it seems. I know you don't believe me, but I'm trying to help you. If you give me a chance, I can explain. Will you call me, please?"

Although it sounded interesting, she was still suspicious. Maybe she'd call him later.

Then she turned on Deirdre's phone, which was finally charged. As she expected, it didn't reveal much. A few calls to Surfside numbers. A couple to Information in San Diego. And one to a Portland number: her father's. She checked the date and time. The call was made the day she died.

Why was Ethan in Surfside? Maybe Deirdre wanted him to help renovate the house. For that matter, why did he ask Tara to come? Maybe it was a surprise, so she could finally meet her aunt.

Or maybe they were meeting the person that attacked them. Maybe it wasn't a stranger. Maybe it wasn't a random crime. Tara realized she might never know.

According to the symbols on her phone, Deirdre's voice mailbox was empty. So there were no answers there, either. Someone must know where she'd been and what she'd been doing all those years. Sighing, she turned off both phones and left them on the desk, and went upstairs to paint.

~ 29 ~

The wind was still howling, the rain still falling. Tara could hear the bell by the front door clanging with each gust. Blue paint freckled her ponytail and eyebrows, splashed across her T-shirt, dripped down her jeans. Even Sneakers had paint on his paws and nose. But she was almost finished. Although the air was so damp, she didn't know how long it would take the walls to dry.

All that was left to paint was the downstairs hallway. With the damned hole. She hadn't tried to patch it after she found the sword; it would probably just pop open again anyway. So she covered it with the gilt-framed mirror and hoped that nothing creepy would crawl out. She imagined long tentacles snaking out of the wall, oozing from behind the mirror, weaving their way down the hall and up the stairs and…

"Stop it!" she said. "You're scaring yourself. Pretty stupid thing to do when you live alone."

"Who are you talking to?"

Tara screamed. Mariah screamed. Sneakers, asleep on the stairs, leapt to his feet and hissed.

"Oh no, I did it again," Mariah said. "I forgot I was supposed to knock." She sat in the kitchen door, water dripping from her yellow slicker.

"Not necessarily knock, but at least holler when you come through the door so I know you're here. Cut it out, cat!" Tara tried to scoop up the cat, but he dashed up the staircase, leaving little blue footprints on every tread but one.

"I'm really sorry," Mariah said again, close to tears.

"Don't worry about it, honey. It'll clean up."

"I wanted to look for stars." She sniffed and unsnapped her raincoat. "Have you found any more?"

"No. I decided to let you look for them. I'm trying to get the painting finished." Tara hung the dripping coat in the laundry room, leaving spots on the linoleum.

"Can I check upstairs?" Marian asked. "I know you said you did already, but maybe I'll find something you missed."

"Sure. Do you need help getting up there?"

"Nope. Although it would be easier to get around if I had my chair." So Tara carried the chair upstairs and Mariah started searching again.

Half an hour later, the painting was finished. Brushes were clean, hands washed, paint-spattered clothes in the laundry basket. But, as Tara feared, the walls weren't drying; she already had to retouch a couple of spots where she had bumped into the wet paint.

Maybe a fire would help. Hopefully there weren't any nests, or other surprises, hiding up there. She cursed herself for forgetting to call the chimney sweep.

She bought a few bundles of firewood the last time she was in town. With the newspapers from her father's house and a box of twigs she collected in the forest, she was ready. She could almost smell the sizzling sap and feel the soothing heat.

Smiling at the thought, Tara spread crumpled newspapers on the hearth in the living room, wiping the black newsprint from her fingers on her jeans. She arranged a small pile of kindling on the paper and balanced a few larger sticks on top. Then reached for the poker, but it was missing from the tool set; she'd have to use the shovel instead.

The date on one of the papers caught her eye: December 1. Her favorite month, since her birthday and Christmas fell a week apart. Not to mention Emma's birthday.

She planned to do something special for her fortieth birthday. Rent a villa in Tuscany. Climb the Great Wall of China. Maybe take a barefoot cruise through the Caribbean.

Instead, she was restoring a house in Surfside, Oregon. Not exactly Beijing or St. Croix.

Oh well. Maybe she'd celebrate her landmark birthday next year instead. By next year, her life would be different.

It had to be.

Tara found her matches in the pocket of a sweater. As she touched one to the striking surface, her father's voice echoed in her head: *Is the damper open, Squirt?*

The damper. She always forgot to open the stupid damper. Tara couldn't count the times her father reached through black smoke, coughing, to open it. He always gave her a look of pretended disapproval, and she always apologized.

But this time, she remembered the damper. And as she did, realized that the thought of her father hadn't crippled her this time. Mentally patting herself on the back, she reached into the chimney for the handle. Felt around.

No handle.

She sighed. All she wanted was a lousy fire. She pulled back a soot-covered hand.

Where was her flashlight? After searching the obvious places, she found it upstairs in the bathroom. As she passed the master bedroom, she saw Mariah looking through the closet.

"These aren't your clothes, are they?" the girl asked her.

"No, that's my Aunt Deirdre's stuff."

"What happened to her?"

"She's the one who I inherited the house from. She died a little while ago."

Apparently, Mariah didn't read the newspaper. "Oh, I'm sorry. That sucks. What are you going to do with her things?"

Oh, for the innocence of a child. "I haven't decided yet. It's hard for me to think about doing anything with them right now."

"Maybe I shouldn't be in here, then." She started to move her chair.

"No, it's okay. If you find anything interesting, let me know."

Flashlight in hand, Tara went back downstairs. The paint would be peeling by the time she got the fire started.

She shone the flashlight up the chimney and found the handle, tucked almost out of reach. Grabbed it and gave it a tug.

Nothing.

Maybe it was rusted shut. She placed the flashlight on the floor, and pulled on the handle with both hands.

A flash of lightning lit the room, followed by an ear-splitting boom. The walls of the house shook. Another flash. Another boom.

Tara had turned on the lights earlier, to help pierce the dark day. With the next lightning strike, they went out.

Now she needed the fire for warmth *and* light. Flakes of rust fell onto her hands as she fought with the handle. She cursed her sore wrist, but kept working.

She heard a crash upstairs. Then another boom of thunder.

Finally, she felt the handle move slightly. With one last pull, the damper opened, and something fell onto the hearth. As Tara reached for the object, she heard another crash, this one much louder. And a scream.

"Tara! Help!"

She dashed up the stairs two at a time. The house shook as the storm raged. She could hear items tumbling off the shelves in the kitchen. Maybe it was an earthquake. Mariah's screams drowned out her thoughts.

"Where are you?" Tara yelled. She cursed her flashlight, lying on the living room floor, and ran through the dark hall toward the master suite.

The screams suddenly ceased.

Tara stopped at the bedroom door. A flash, and she saw the massive chest of drawers lying on the floor, Mariah's empty wheelchair next to it. Another flash, and she saw Mariah lying beneath the chest.

"Mariah!" She grabbed a corner of the chest and tried to lift it. In the next flash, she saw Mariah's face, still and white. She braced herself against the wall and shoved. The chest moved slightly. She shoved again. One final push, and she could see most of Mariah's body. She grabbed the girl's arms and dragged her from beneath the massive piece of furniture, picked her up, and rushed downstairs. The chandelier at the foot of the staircase creaked and swayed as she ran under it.

It felt like they were under attack. Tara could hear dishes breaking in the kitchen. The mirror in the hallway crashed to the floor as she reached the front door and grabbed the doorknob, which came off in her hand. *Damn!*

She ran through the kitchen, tripping over toppled chairs. Grabbed her raincoat as she ran through the laundry room, and threw it over them both. Prayed the back door would open. If she had to, she'd break a window to get out of the house.

But the door opened. And she dashed into the storm.

They needed to get as far from the house as possible. So, she ran down the driveway through the rain, Mariah clutched to her chest, until she reached the highway. She laid the unconscious girl on the reasonably dry ground beneath a huge cedar tree and examined her. Tara cursed the need to move her, hoping it hadn't make her injuries worse, and thought about flagging down a car to take them to the hospital. Just then, Mariah opened her eyes.

"What happened?" she croaked, looking around. "Why are we outside?"

Tara felt a rush of relief. "Are you okay?"

"I think so. My head hurts."

"Is that all? You don't hurt anywhere else?"

Mariah struggled to sit up. "Not really. Just my head."

"That's good. I was really worried." Tara wrapped her arms around the frail girl and held her for a long moment.

"You still haven't told me why we're out here," Mariah mumbled into Tara's chest.

Tara released her and sighed. "You won't believe me."

"Did the house do something?" She grimaced; maybe she really *was* hurt.

"Yes. I'm afraid to go back, but I know we can't stay here forever."

Mariah looked around. "Where's my chair?"

"In the house."

"I need it, so we have to go back. Don't worry; it'll be fine."

Tara smiled at the girl's attempt to console her. "I sure hope you're right," she said, knowing they really didn't have a choice. She hoisted Mariah onto her back and started up the driveway.

"Do you remember what happened?" Tara asked. She was amazed at how light the girl was; it felt like carrying a sack of feathers.

"I was trying to get one of the drawers open, but I guess it was stuck. I remember pulling really hard, then…I don't remember anything else."

"The chest fell on top of you. Maybe the house didn't want you to see what was in the drawers," Tara said.

"What were *you* doing? Maybe the house didn't like what you were doing and it punished me instead?" Mariah said.

Tara didn't point out that Mariah was starting to believe that the house was capable of doing things. "I was trying to start a fire, but the damper was stuck. When I finally got it open, something fell out of the chimney."

"What?"

"I don't know. I didn't have the chance to find out."

"Could it be the treasure?" Tara could hear the excitement in the girl's voice.

"Maybe. We'll find out in a couple of minutes."

When they reached the top of the driveway, Tara stopped to study the house. It sat peacefully in the clearing. Sometimes she questioned how much of this was actually happening, and how much was her imagination.

"See?" Mariah said. "It's just a house. Let's go inside. I'm freezing." The rain had stopped, and the temperature was dropping quickly.

Tara carried the girl to the back door, which stood partially open. As they stepped into the house, the lights blinked on. She laid Mariah on the couch and went upstairs to get the wheelchair. When she reached the master bedroom, she stopped and peeked through the door.

The chest of drawers was still on the floor. Maybe Mariah *did* pull it over onto herself. Maybe it wasn't the house after all. Maybe Tara needed a long vacation. In a padded cell.

She pushed the wheelchair into the living room. Mariah sat on the floor in front of the fireplace. "No wonder the house was pissed at you," she said. "Look!"

Nestled among the crumpled newspaper and twigs was a metal box, with rusty hinges and traces of a once-colorful pattern on the lid.

"Is this *the* box?" Mariah asked.

"It could be." Tara didn't want to get the girl's hopes up. Or her own.

"Open it! Let's see if there are stars inside!" Mariah squirmed with excitement.

Tara took a deep breath and slowly opened the box. The squeak of the lid sounded like the one on the ghost's box.

She peeked inside, but there was no golden glow. No stars. Just a worn leather book and a couple of folded pieces of paper, yellow with age.

"Is it the treasure?" Mariah asked, peeking over her shoulder.

Tara tried to hide her disappointment. Although she knew there wouldn't be a galaxy in the box, she hoped there would be something equally as thrilling. "It looks like someone's diary, and a couple of letters."

Mariah sighed. "That's not very exciting."

"No, not really. But they could be important."

"Well, maybe the real treasure is still hidden in the house somewhere." Mariah crawled into her chair. "Thanks for saving me," she said with a shy smile. "I don't know what would have happened if the house had more time to beat me up."

"You're probably right: you pulled the chest onto yourself."

"Yeah, like I'm strong enough to do that. I'll come back later to look for more stars."

"You're always welcome," Tara said. And realized that she meant it.

The girl rolled through the back door and disappeared, humming to herself.

Tara walked through the hallway, stopping to slide the doorknob back into place and hang the mirror back over the hole. She cleaned up the mess in the kitchen and fixed a cup of cocoa, then carried the box into the study, spread the items on the desk, and unfolded the first page.

It was a report from a medical clinic dated thirty-nine years earlier, addressed to her mother. It listed information on blood types and Rh factors that she didn't understand. But the final sentence was clear.

There is a high degree of probability that Ethan Davies is the father of the child, Tara Marie Davies.

Why would her mother have a paternity test done on her own child? And if there was one for Tara, why wasn't there one for Emma, too?

The next document was an official-looking certificate. Embossed, raised seal, watermarked. It was a birth certificate. For Tara Marie McCarthy.

But Tara already had her birth certificate. And her last name was Davies, not McCarthy.

She studied the document again. The space for her father's name was blank. And her mother's name was not listed as Mary McCarthy Davies, but as Deirdre Susanna McCarthy.

~ 30 ~

Tara stared at the document clenched in her trembling hand.

She laid it on the desk, climbed the staircase, and pulled a metal box from beneath her bed. Opened it and withdrew her birth certificate, then returned to the study and laid the two documents side by side on the desk.

Both were printed on heavy yellow paper. Both had raised embossed seals and watermarks. Both were issued in Surfside. The only difference was the names typed on them.

Years earlier, when she discovered she had been born in Surfside, Tara asked her father about it. He said they were driving through the town when her mother went into labor, and he was afraid they wouldn't make it to Portland in time, so stopped at the hospital in Surfside. Tara never had a reason to doubt his story.

One of the documents could be a fake. But they both looked official. There were no dates on them except her birth date, so she couldn't tell which one was issued first.

She realized that she was focusing on unimportant details instead of facing the truth.

Ethan was her father. The paternity report proved that. Although Tara never had a reason to doubt that.

But who was her mother?

If Deirdre was her mother, Mary must have suspected that Ethan was Tara's father. Hence the paternity report.

So if Ethan really was her father, he and Deirdre must have had an affair. Or at least a one-night stand. During which Tara was conceived.

And somehow, Mary knew.

Tara's head was spinning. She laid the papers aside and reached for the leather-bound book. It was a diary, as she suspected. The cover was worn, the pages folded and dirty.

When she opened it, a small bundle fell out. Envelopes addressed to her, tied with a faded pink ribbon, with 'return to sender' scrawled across each one in her father's handwriting. She slid open the flaps and found birthday cards and Christmas cards, cards for a child and then for a teen, yellowed with age. Signed, "Love, Deirdre." Not aunt. Not mother. Just Deirdre.

Tara studied them for a moment, and slipped them back into the box. She would read them later.

The writing in the diary was cramped and small, and hard to read, especially by the dim light of the study lamp. Tara found a stronger bulb in the kitchen. She barely noticed her fingers burning as she changed the hot bulb. Then she leaned back in the chair and started reading.

&

Tara closed the diary and checked her watch. Three A.M. The storm was long since over, the night deathly still outside the windows, except for the ever-present tapping of the branch. She rested her head on the back of the chair and closed her eyes.

While many of her questions were answered, she now had a set of new ones.

The diary was Deirdre's. Although the entries only started a few months earlier, it began with a summary that explained the preceding years. How she lived. And why.

Instead of a life spent traveling the world as Mary claimed, Deirdre struggled with addictions. While Mary thought Deirdre was on safari in Africa or shopping in Paris, she was actually unconscious behind a dumpster in San Diego. Her days — and years — were a journey from fix to fix, bed to bed, man to man.

A year earlier, Deirdre finally hit rock bottom, as the lucky ones do, and began the long struggle to find herself again. And her family, although she harbored no hope that they would welcome her into their lives. That they would forgive her.

By the time she found the courage to contact Mary, it was too late. Deirdre described the pain she felt when she visited her sister at Fairhaven and Mary treated her like a stranger, inviting her to join her party of cardboard cookies and make-believe tea.

Tara turned to the last entry. It was dated the day she died.

I called Ethan today. I tried to explain where I am now, but he didn't want to hear it. I guess I need to get used to that kind of reaction. People back away from addicts. It's like they're afraid they'll catch something. They don't understand that we can't give our demons away, no matter how hard we try. They live inside us, never giving us a moment's rest. I guess the up side is that we're never lonely. But the down side is that we never get to be alone, to learn who we are. We never get any peace.

He agreed to come to the house. I need to explain what happened. I need to find my children.

The next lines confused Tara.

Now that Mary's as good as gone, I have to protect Tara. I have to make sure he knows that I know, that I'm continuing where Mary left off.

I need to warn her about him. That she shouldn't trust him. That her life depends on it.

Tara paced the worn carpet in the small study. What — and who — did Deirdre need to warn her about?

Fragments from her dreams came back to her. Deirdre left a baby with Mary and Ethan. That baby must have been Tara. Mary and Ethan must have adopted her; that would explain the other birth certificate. But Deirdre said 'children.' Maybe that was the baby Deirdre wanted Mary to take care of, the one she mentioned in the letter. There were two girls in the dream when Ethan read the letter, so Tara knew the baby wasn't Emma. Could Deirdre have abandoned two babies? And if so, where was the other one?

Mary wasn't her real mother. The realization overwhelmed her. The years of pain, of abuse, wouldn't have happened if Deirdre had raised her. Her eyes filled with tears. All the years she dreamed that Deirdre would save her, whisk her away from the hell that was her childhood, she wasn't so far off base. Her real mother wasn't the woman abusing her, scarring her soul.

But this was where reality intervened. Her real mother was passed out in an alley, high on heroin or crack. Not exploring

Paris, London, Vienna. In San Diego, National City, Chula Vista. Selling her body for a fix.

The lesser of two evils. If she had a choice, which mother would Tara have chosen? She needed to remember that she had Ethan. Even when Mary was at her worst, Tara knew Ethan would protect her. She wouldn't have had that same chance if Deirdre had taken Tara with her when she left.

Now what?

Tara stared unseeing out the French doors, into the night. Her mother wasn't her mother. Her aunt wasn't her aunt. Her father was her father, but not in the way she thought. He betrayed her mother. And Mary knew, yet she stayed with him. She raised Tara as her own daughter, never revealing Ethan's sin.

Maybe that was one of the reasons Mary drank, to drown that knowledge. And maybe the Alzheimer's helped her forget when the alcohol couldn't.

Mariah said Tara needed to forgive her parents. Tara didn't think that forgiving Ethan would be hard, but she didn't know how she could forgive her mother.

Now, Tara saw Mary in a different light. She raised a baby that wasn't her own; that was, in fact, the child of her husband's betrayal. She didn't have to do it. But she did.

If she tried, Tara could remember good times before Emma's death. And, if she tried, she could probably remember good times after Emma's death: memories she chose to forget because they didn't mesh with her image of herself as a victim.

Why was it so hard to see Mary in any light but a drunken haze? Tara always had clean clothes to wear and food on the table. Her mother made cupcakes for her school bake sales. She invited Tara's friends over for dinner and was the life of the party, although Tara prayed they didn't realize her mother was drunk.

Forgive and forget. Could she? The wounds ran deep; Tara had nurtured them for years.

She needed to think. It was the first step toward healing those rifts. Small steps. Baby steps.

Tara turned from the window and stumbled on a wrinkle in the worn Persian carpet. When she knelt to smooth it, she saw something wedged under the desk.

It was another gold star.

&

Questions. Some had been answered, but there were still so many left. Tara tucked the star into the box and went upstairs, hoping for a few hours' sleep.

But sleep wouldn't come. Her mind was racing. No wonder she looked more like her aunt than her mother; she still didn't know how to refer to the two women, both mother, both not. A father who had fallen in her esteem, although she needed more details before she could condemn him outright.

And a brother, somewhere. If he was still alive. The thought of having cousins was exciting enough; to know that she might have a sibling was even more thrilling. To finally have a family. To finally belong.

Now Tara knew why Deirdre had been in Surfside. But she was still no closer to knowing who killed her.

She tossed and turned, sweat-dampened sheets tangled around her legs. Deirdre said she needed to tell Ethan that she knew. Knew what? Could it have anything to do with his secrets, the ones Mary threatened to expose? Mary's words echoed in Tara's head. *As long as I know, she's safe.* And Deirdre's words. *I have to protect Tara.*

Tara was starting to believe that Ethan's presence in the house the night of the attack didn't have anything to do with a renovation. And once again, she wished her father would wake up, but now for very different reasons.

So Mary was right, after all. The house was protecting secrets. Not just golden trinkets, although maybe there were more of those hidden in the walls. Treasure could take any number of shapes and forms.

Eventually exhaustion won and Tara fell asleep, to dream of stars.

&

In the dark, a figure moves across the clearing and stops in front of the garage. Tries the handle on the side door and finds it locked. Slides a tool into the lock and opens the door. Silently slips inside.

After a few minutes, there is a crunch and a muffled cry. The figure staggers out of the garage, dragging a leg, and disappears into the darkness, leaving the door swinging in the still night air.

~ 31 ~

Tara stared at the ceiling, wondering what woke her. Sneakers snored in his customary spot at her feet. It was still dark; even the birds weren't awake yet. But something dragged her from dreamless slumber.

Or was it truly dreamless? It seemed that her nights were busier than her days, crowded with familiar people and unfamiliar events. Tara didn't know if they were ghosts, or echoes from the past. But she believed the house was causing her dreams — dreams that she now remembered perfectly, that caused more pain than joy.

She still didn't know what the stars signified. Obviously, they weren't in the box. And obviously, they stood for something. And now, she was finding them all over the house.

Tara couldn't deny it any longer. She knew what the house wanted, why it kept showing her images from her past.

It wanted her to figure out what the stars meant.

In a minute. She nestled deeper under the soft down comforter, not wanting to leave her warm bed. She'd think about it in a minute.

&

Ethan carries Emma into the master bedroom and lays her on the bed. A trail of bloody drops follows them. He arranges her arms next to her still body, straightens her clothing, wipes a fingerprint from her shiny black patent-leather shoe. Then he steps back and studies her for a long moment, his face expressionless.

Her eyelids flicker.

Leaning over the child, he touches her neck and finds a pulse, hears her ragged breath.

He selects a pillow from the head of the bed. Positions it over her face. Presses down with both hands. Watches and waits as she struggles, struggles, and finally stops.

He removes the pillow and checks again for a pulse, a breath. Fluffs the pillow and carefully returns it. Brushes a strand of hair from the child's pale face.

He descends the staircase and enters the living room, where his wife sits.

"We have a problem."

Her eyes slowly swivel toward him. An empty glass drops from her limp hand onto the carpet.

"It's Emma. I've called the ambulance, but I think it's too late. Tara killed her." He waits to see her reaction. His timing is perfect; she frowns, struggling to understand, but then her head nods, her eyes close.

He sits on the couch, watching the fire dance as his wife snores softly. After a few minutes, he picks up the telephone.

&

Tara sat up, gasping for breath. Her head was pounding, but she paid no attention, grabbing for her necklace. She couldn't have seen what she thought she just saw.

She knew that she killed Emma. It was the one fact that defined, and destroyed, her life. The moment she was transformed from beloved daughter to pariah. After that day, her family changed. Her mother became bitter, her father silent. There was less laughter, less love. She lost her best friend. And she knew it was all her fault.

Or did, until this moment.

Maybe the house was playing games with her. Until now, she had no reason to doubt any of the images it showed her. But now — well, she had doubts. This affected the very fabric of her life.

If Tara were to believe this dream, everything she knew to be true was a lie. The burden of guilt she carried was misplaced. The shame, the anguish, running from town to town, hiding from people who hated her for what she had done — all for nothing.

And worse. Her father. The one constant in her life. The one person on whom she could depend, the person she trusted and loved beyond reason. Could he really have killed Emma, and blamed the crime on her?

"Why did you show me this?" Tara screamed at the walls around her. "What am I supposed to do with this?"

&

Later — maybe minutes, maybe hours — Tara huddled on the porch steps. She was still in her nightgown, too numb to notice the cold. Squirrels and chipmunks scurried around the yard in the morning sunshine, oblivious to her presence.

She couldn't bear to be in the house. Even the porch was too close. But she had nowhere else to go.

She needed to act, to make decisions, but didn't know where to start. How do you rebuild a shattered life?

Deirdre's words rang in her head. *The house will help you find what you seek, but the price can be steep.* Her aunt was wrong. Tara had paid the price most of her life. It couldn't get any steeper.

Eventually, she forced her brain to work. First, she decided to believe the dream. The house hadn't lied to her yet, as far as she knew. She didn't know why it would. And she needed somewhere to start. She could no longer hide from the world. Hell, apparently she didn't have to.

She couldn't repair her reputation; it was too late to change the past. All she could do was start fresh, knowing that she wasn't a murderer.

She wasn't a murderer. Tara never thought that she would utter those words. She couldn't keep up with the sensations: relief, despair, joy, anger.

A reprieve from a life sentence. A life of running, of hiding, of regret. Wishing every day that she could undo the damage she had done to her family, to herself. To Emma.

All for nothing. It was all a lie.

It would take time to figure out how to go on, no longer bent double by the burden of grief she had carried for far too long.

What doesn't kill you makes you stronger. She would be stronger, wiser. She would rebuild her life on a foundation of truth instead of lies.

And on the foundation of the house. Which seemed to be showing her the way, painful though it was.

What was the house trying to teach her, with all of this pain? It must have something to do with her parents: every dream revolved around them and the decisions they made.

Tara stared into the dark forest, searching for answers. Once again, she thought about Mariah insisting that Tara forgive. If Mariah could forgive her parents for the loss of her legs, could Tara forgive hers for the loss of a normal life?

Maybe there was no such thing as normal. Maybe what she needed to do was create a life that fit her, rather than longing for something that never existed in the first place.

She tucked her feet under the hem of her nightgown. Maybe Mariah was right. Maybe forgiveness was the answer. Forgiving her parents — all of them — for the lies they told, for the mistakes they made. For being human.

And forgiving herself for believing their lies. For not protecting Emma. For wasting too many years regretting things that she couldn't change.

It was ironic. She had put so much energy into preparing to ask her father for his forgiveness, when he should have been begging for hers.

Forgive. It sounded so simple. But sometimes the simplest answer was the last one you found. Although she knew it would take time to completely forgive them — especially her father — she could at least start the process. Start believing that she could actually do it.

Tara crossed the porch, her bare feet silent on the cold boards, and walked into the house. Took the first steps down the path toward the rest of her life.

She didn't notice the garage door standing partially open. Nor did she see the shooting star fall through the early morning sky.

~ *32* ~

So far, Tara's new life looked very much like her old one. She started working on a special memory book. She fed the cat and cleaned the house. But mechanically, as she tried to fit the pieces of the puzzle together. As a result, she almost forgot her lunch date with Bonnie. Luckily, she remembered just as she was sitting down to eat a peanut butter and banana sandwich. She wiped off her chocolate milk moustache, changed out of her sweats, and rushed into town.

The door was locked. A "Sorry, We're Closed" sign hung in the window.

Tara checked her Pooh watch. She was only a couple of minutes late; Bonnie couldn't have given up on her already. They didn't discuss where they were going, so she couldn't meet her at the restaurant. And since they hadn't exchanged phone numbers, she couldn't call to find out where she was. Or if she was okay.

Maybe she was running late. Tara watched a few snowflakes whirl down the street while she waited. But after fifteen minutes, she had to admit that Bonnie wasn't coming. She thought about the black eye, and hoped that nothing had happened to her.

Disappointed and worried, she returned to her truck and headed home.

&

When Tara pulled up to the garage, she noticed the side door was open. She always locked that door since she kept her truck in the garage; it was one of the few things she owned that was worth anything, and she didn't want anyone messing with it.

The open door was unnerving. Maybe it was just the house, screwing with her again. She wished she had a weapon as she cautiously pushed it open. Or tried to; it would only open partway.

She peeked through the opening, and saw Deirdre's car jammed against the door.

Tara had seen a car roll when an emergency brake failed on an incline. Sometimes a child left in a car released the brake and drove through a storefront. Heck, even dogs had taken cars for unintentional joyrides. But she couldn't remember hearing about a car moving across a flat surface on its own.

Even though she was getting used to the strange happenings in the house, this one gave her the chills.

She gathered her courage, opened the overhead door, and eased around the car. And found a black sneaker wedged under the left front tire.

It wasn't the house screwing with her, after all. Someone had been in the garage. Someone who left without a shoe, but maybe with a few crushed toes.

Who had been here? No official, like a meter reader or George the mailman, had any reason to be in her garage. And she didn't have any friends who would stop by unannounced.

Then she thought about the scratches on the locks and the footprints in the house. The scuff marks on the back door. And now, the sneaker.

Someone had trespassed on her property. More than once.

Tara glanced toward the house standing silently in the clearing amidst a dusting of snowflakes. Maybe they were inside, waiting for her.

She could call the sheriff's department, but they'd probably laugh at her for thinking that a sneaker and a few scratches meant someone was after her. But she couldn't stay out here in the cold forever, either.

Wishing once again that she didn't have to face every challenge alone, Tara slowly approached the house. She quietly unlocked the door and stood at the foot of the staircase, listening.

A noise. Coming from the kitchen.

Damn.

Feeling exposed, she flattened herself against the wall, listening for another sound.

Something brushed against her legs. She screamed, and Sneakers darted up the staircase and disappeared around a corner.

Tara collapsed on the bottom step, her heart pounding. *Stupid cat!* If Sneakers felt comfortable wandering around the house, there probably wasn't anyone there. Although she'd never heard of people using cats as watchdogs.

"Sorry, kitty," she called. "Didn't mean to scare you. Although you scared the pants off me." Even though she was reasonably sure the house was empty, Tara walked through each room checking for footprints or anything out of place. Everything was as she left it — except the plate of oatmeal cookies teetering on the edge of a kitchen counter, thanks to her curious cat.

She fell into a chair, still shaking, and waited for her heartbeat to slow.

So, how did the car move? She knew the answer: the house did it. It was comforting, in a twisted way, to know that the house was trying to protect her, not just screwing with her mind. Although other people would question her sanity if they heard her describe this scenario as 'comforting.' Tara was discovering that everything is relative.

It was unnerving to know that someone had broken into her home. But she didn't know what she could do about it, since locked doors didn't stop them. They didn't do any real damage, or steal anything. In fact, she couldn't prove that anyone had been there, so there was no reason to call the sheriff.

What could they be after?

Maybe she should get a dog. Maybe she should get a gun.

&

Tara decided that the first step in forgiving her parents was to tell them what she had decided. So after breakfast, she headed into Portland, her hands damp on the steering wheel again. She wasn't sure why she was nervous, since neither of them would understand what she was saying. But it was vital to her, and to her new life, that she at least try.

At the hospital, Tara perched on the green recliner next to her father's bed. "I have something I need to talk to you about, Daddy." Taking a deep breath, she started. And didn't stop until she told him everything she learned: from Deirdre's diary, from the paternity report, and from her dreams.

"So now I have questions, and no one to answer them. I don't know what happened between you and Aunt Deirdre. Or why you never told me she was my mother. But worst of all, I don't know why you killed Emma and blamed it on me. Do you know that you ruined my life?" Her voice broke, and she wiped tears from her cheeks.

"That night I was supposed to meet you in Surfside, I was going to ask you to forgive me. I thought if you did that, we could have a normal relationship, and I could have a normal life. But I didn't know that you should have been begging me to forgive you instead."

She paced around the room, running her hands through her tangled hair. "I've done a lot of thinking, and have decided that none of it matters. The only way I'm going to be able to get on with my life is to let it go." She stopped and faced the bed. "So I wanted to tell you that I forgive you. For everything."

It felt good to say it, even if she wasn't sure it was true. She wished he could respond. Explain why he did what he did. Tell her he was proud of her. Apologize. Something. Anything. But there was nothing.

She stayed for a few minutes, just in case. But when the nurse came in with his medication, Tara slipped out.

Back in her truck, she realized she didn't have the energy to face her mother, too. Although she was anxious to get it over with, that conversation would have to wait. So she headed home, both elated and exhausted, knowing that she did the right thing, but not sure where to go from here.

&

Tara stopped at Bonnie's store as she passed through town, but it was still closed. Now she was really worried. She jotted a quick note asking her to call and slipped it through the mail slot, trying not to picture her friend lying injured somewhere. Or worse. Maybe she should stop at the sheriff's department. But what would she report? That she was afraid Bonnie's boyfriend was beating her? Tara didn't even know his name, or where they lived. Better to go home and wait for Bonnie to call. And try not to imagine the worst.

~ *33* ~

Tara was playing 'chase the shoelace' with Sneakers in the study when she noticed her father's answering machine sitting on the corner of the desk, and idly pressed 'play.'

"I know…taking over where Mary left off…protect her. Don't think about hurting…tell the sheriff…make you pay…watching you…."

Wait a minute. Tara played the message again, and reached for the worn leather diary. Opened it and read Deirdre's final words.

Now that Mary's as good as gone, I have to protect Tara. I have to make sure he knows that I know, that I'm taking over where Mary left off. I will make him pay.

They were the same words.

The message was from Deidre.

She played the tape over and over, memorizing the sound of her aunt's voice. Then carefully took the cassette from the machine and stored it in the top drawer of the desk. It might be silly, but it was one of the few pieces of Deirdre that she had left.

She sat back and rubbed her temples. Her concerns about Bonnie faded as she thought about the night of the attack, and wondered if there hadn't been an intruder, after all.

A crash outside startled her. Sneakers disappeared upstairs to hide under a bed. Tara looked out the French doors and saw the firs swaying in the late afternoon light. Another crash, which she followed to the back door. Pressing her nose to the cold glass, she could see branches littering the yard and black pines bent almost to the ground. She opened the door a crack; the air was thick with the smell of rain.

Another storm. Tara hadn't spent a winter in Oregon in years, and forgot about the frequent storms. She loved thunder and lightning, loved the thrill of watching Mother Nature crack her whip. As long as the power stayed on, she'd be fine.

Another crash, and the lights went out.

She didn't have any candles, of course. And no idea where she left her flashlight. She stood for a moment and stared out the door, watching the first raindrops fall.

What began as a shower quickly turned into a steady downpour, then a deluge. The wind-driven rain sounded like pebbles striking the windows. Maybe it was hail. The Portland weatherman had predicted freezing rain, but that was inland; surely it wouldn't freeze here on the coast.

It was already dark outside. And darker inside. Tara felt her way through the kitchen, stubbing her toe on a chair in the process, trying to remember where she last saw her flashlight.

The smart thing would be to sit quietly and wait for the power to come back on. Although if a tree took out the lines, it might be hours before Pacific Electric could repair them. But of course, Tara couldn't do the smart thing. So she stumbled around the house, looking for a light in the darkness.

The occasional bolt of lightning helped her search downstairs, and then upstairs. No luck.

She was getting frustrated. And cold. Fumbling through her closet, she found her favorite sweatshirt and eased back down the stairs, pulling it over her head. As she descended, she tried to remember which step was the one she needed to fix. Just as she decided it was one more step down, she put her full weight on a tread and her foot crashed through the weakened wood.

Tara lurched to the left and lunged for the handrail, but as she grabbed it, the rail disintegrated and she fell backwards. Her leg twisted in the hole in the step, and the shattered wood ground into her ankle. Her head smacked against the wall. She collapsed on the steps, a piece of broken rail clutched in her hands.

She lay for a few moments, afraid to move. Her left foot was stuck in the hole, twisted at an awkward angle. Her left knee throbbed. Her head pounded.

When she lifted her head, her body screamed with pain. She slowly dragged herself into a sitting position and pulled her foot out of the hole, tearing the fragile skin of her damaged ankle.

"Ow! Damn it!" Blood trickled down her instep. More than trickled. Flowed.

She tried to pull herself up using the figurehead for support, but her leg wouldn't hold her weight. The wind and rain beat against the house as she slowly slid down the stairs.

Tara inched along the floor, dragging her foot, grimacing each time she moved. Through the dark hallway, into the kitchen. Finally, she reached the table. Pulled herself into a chair and sat for a moment, trying to think through the pain.

Light. She needed light. She fumbled through her purse for the matchbook she hoped was buried in the bottom, and found it. Her first lucky break. It took a few tries before she could light a match. But eventually she did, and held it near the floor to study her foot.

There was a long ragged gash across her anklebone, bleeding freely. The ankle itself was beginning to swell. As was her knee.

Now what? The first aid kit was upstairs. She couldn't climb the staircase, so she grabbed a dishtowel and tightly wound it around her ankle. That should stop the bleeding for now.

She couldn't work the clutch on the truck, so couldn't drive anywhere. And she needed to find out what tore her ankle, but that would be difficult without light. If it was a rusty nail, she'd need a tetanus shot.

She didn't have Mariah's number. She didn't have Bonnie's number. She was desperate enough to call Craig, but didn't know where she put his card.

Wait. She could call Lee. His number was in her phone.

Then she realized she didn't know where her phone was. She cursed her habit of leaving the damned thing wherever she last used it, and started searching. Luckily, she found it in the side pocket of her purse where it belonged. But when she opened the phone, there was no signal.

The weather didn't usually affect cell phones. Unless the storm had knocked out the cell tower. *Great.* She tossed the useless phone on the table and winced. She must have wrenched her shoulder, too.

They would probably fix the tower by morning. If she kept her foot elevated and tightly wrapped, the bleeding should stop.

Her leg would be swollen, but that wouldn't kill her. All she needed to do was get through the night.

One night. How hard could that be?

She could crawl down the driveway, but that was insane. She'd do even more damage. Probably catch pneumonia. And where would she crawl to, anyway? Lee's was miles away, and she didn't know any of the neighbors except Mariah. And she had no idea where the girl lived.

She should stay put. As she should have done in the first place, instead of roaming around in the dark.

And after all that, she still hadn't found her flashlight.

Her leg ached. Her head pounded. She just wanted to lie down. She dragged herself into the living room and onto the couch. Carefully extended her leg, pulled her grandmother's quilt over her, and closed her eyes with a sigh.

The house echoed in the silence between the rolls of thunder. She couldn't hear the rain pounding on the roof any more, although the wind was still howling. The silence gave her time to think. About her parents and their lies. Her childhood, or lack of one. The choices she had made, avoiding relationships, denying herself the chance to be a wife and a mother, to fall in love, always running from what other people thought she was.

Everything she knew to be true was a lie.

She couldn't forgive her parents. It was too much to ask. They hurt her too severely. The damage they did couldn't be undone. She was doomed to exist in this limbo forever, seeking but not finding, never at peace. And since she couldn't forgive them, she could never forgive herself.

"Sneakers?" she whispered, hoping for the comfort of the little cat. But he was nowhere to be found.

Cold, hurt, lonely. Confused, betrayed, abandoned. Facing a birthday, a Christmas, a life, alone.

Gripping her necklace, the storm raging around her, Tara sobbed, pierced by a shattered heart.

~ 34 ~

An hour passed. Maybe two. Tara couldn't sleep. She was cold and scared. Her body hurt. Her heart hurt.

Maybe a fire would lift her spirits. She couldn't bear to lie here all night like this.

But the matches were in the kitchen. She tried to stand, but quickly realized that wasn't a very good idea. Her muscles had stiffened as she lay on the couch, her knee wouldn't bend, and her ankle throbbed. The towel around her foot slipped as she dragged herself toward the kitchen, and the bleeding started again.

Lightning flashed as she glanced through the window. The world was sparkling. Every branch, every rock, every bush, was frozen in a crystal embrace. Freezing rain. That's why she couldn't hear the raindrops hitting the roof. The weatherman picked a lousy time to be right.

She heard a crack and a crash, and realized the weight of the ice was breaking branches. In the forest. And probably on the driveway. She wouldn't be able to get down the hill, even if she could drive. It would be a skating rink. A branch-littered skating rink. She found the matches and crawled back to the living room, feeling even more trapped.

The crumpled newspaper and tinder were still on the hearth. She just had to light the paper. But the matches refused to work. She tried one after another, only to have each one stubbornly slide across the striking surface without a spark and eventually disintegrate. Soon there were only two left.

Tara wanted to throw the matchbook across the room. Scream out her frustration, pain, and anger through the cold, dark house. But she couldn't fall apart now. Instead, she took a deep breath, tore out one more match and swiped it, with a small prayer to whatever gods were listening. There was a spark, and a flame jumped from the match head. She tossed it into the fireplace. It landed in the dry newspaper, which caught fire immediately.

Smoke began to billow out of the chimney. The damper must have closed itself again. *The damned house!*

She dragged herself to her feet, balanced on her good leg, and reached through the smoke for the handle. She grasped it and tugged. But the combination of sore wrist, wrenched knee, and sprained ankle prevented her from getting any leverage.

The smoke was burning her eyes, filling her lungs. Tara yanked the dishtowel from her ankle. It ripped away from the wound, and she screamed. She wrapped the towel around her mouth and tucked the ends into the neck of her sweatshirt, and grabbed the damper handle again. She pulled harder. Desperately.

Suddenly, the handle released. She lost her balance and fell backward, landing heavily on the hardwood floor.

And the fire exploded.

Flames shot across the room. Sparks flew onto the rug, the furniture, and the curtains, which caught fire immediately.

Coughing, Tara crawled away from the hearth. She had to get out. But the flames were spreading, cutting off her escape. The living room filled with smoke. She couldn't find the door. The air was so hot.

She couldn't see. Couldn't breathe.

She needed to get out.

Out...

She saw red curls and a flash of blue as something covered her face, and the world went dark.

~ 35 ~

Air. Clean, smoke-free air.

Tara's lungs screamed as she drew first one ragged breath, then another. Each one ended in a hacking cough. She concentrated on breathing. In. Out. Cough. In. Out. Cough.

After a few minutes, Tara opened her eyes. She was sprawled across the seat of a pickup truck. If she could have smelled anything besides smoke, she would have smelled years of dust and dogs inside the cab. The dashboard was scratched and scarred. The truck was old, but clean.

She felt strong arms around her, a damp flannel shirt soft on her cheek. She looked up. Craig Morris stared down at her; she could see a crooked scar hidden under his chin.

"How…?" she croaked.

"Welcome back." He smiled, but it was shaky. "You okay?"

She struggled to sit up, and he helped her. When she moved her leg, she bit back a scream.

"Here, take a drink." He handed her a bottle of water and she took a sip. Coughed, and sipped again. Like the air, the cool water burned as it touched the raw tissues of her throat.

Questions formed in her mind. She tried to decide which one to ask first, but her brain was fuzzy. She picked the easiest. "What happened?"

"The house was on fire. By the time I found you, the place was engulfed. I can't imagine there's anything left but smoke and ashes by now. Good thing you got to the porch before you passed out, or..." He didn't finish the thought.

"The porch? How'd I get out there?" She didn't remember crawling to the porch. All she remembered was the flames in the living room, and the smoke. She coughed hard, and winced. Then she remembered the flash of blue. "Did you put…something over my face?"

"There was no need to. We were out in the fresh air. I just grabbed you and ran."

So if Craig didn't cover her face, who did?

"Did you call the fire department?"

He looked at her sadly. "Honey, your house isn't in a fire district. The Department of Forestry can protect the forest, but they can't fight structural fires. All they can do is hose down the trees, and watch the buildings burn. I'll call them on the way into town, but there's very little fire danger with all this rain and ice. I need to get you to the hospital."

"No hospital. I'm fine." She looked at her torn ankle, blood and bruises marring the skin. And at her swollen knee. Coughed again. "I'm just fine."

"No, you're not. You inhaled a lot of smoke, and your leg looks pretty nasty. Humor me. Let me take you to the ER."

"No. Just want to sleep. I'll see a doctor in the morning." She continued to cough with each sentence.

He scowled. "You sound awful. I don't like it."

"You don't have to. I'm a big girl."

Craig sighed. "You're also a stubborn one. Tell you what. I'll take you back to my place. That way, I can keep an eye on you. If I don't think you're improving, we're going to the emergency room. Agreed?"

Tara nodded, although she had no intention of complying. They could fight about it later. Craig put the truck into gear and they rode in silence. She watched the wipers trace a semi-circular pattern across the windshield as raindrops splattered onto the cracked glass; the temperature must have gone up. She couldn't tell if there was ice left in the trees.

Then something occurred to her. "Why were you at the house? Trying to get me to sell it again?"

He looked over at her, his face unreadable. "No. I left a message on your voice mail. Didn't you get it?"

She shrugged. "Hadn't decided if I was going to call you back."

"You hadn't..." He shook his head and took a deep breath. "Mariah called me."

"Mariah? You said you didn't know her."

"I don't. I got a call from someone who said her name was Mariah, and that you needed help. So I came."

"How would she know...?" She trailed off, puzzled. Then, "Why did you come?"

"Why wouldn't I?"

She closed her eyes. "I don't know. Can we argue about this later?"

"I don't want to argue with you at all, Tara. I just want to get you into bed."

Tara raised an eyebrow and he groaned. "Don't worry, your virtue is safe with me. You're too sick to be much fun, anyway."

She glared at him, and he winked. She looked around the cab. "Whose truck is this, anyway? Where's your fancy convertible?"

"This is my normal rig. The convertible's just for business; people expect a developer to look successful."

"Mariah thinks you look sleazy." She coughed.

He laughed. "Nice. Who is she, anyway?"

"The girl in the wheelchair."

"Oh, the one I couldn't see?"

Tara had forgotten about that. "Oh yeah. That's her."

Craig stopped in front of an older two-story home in the center of town. It could have won first prize in Surfside's "Best-Decorated Home" contest. A massive red velvet bow graced the front door, evergreen garlands wound through the railings of the wraparound porch, and a single candle glowed in each window.

He got out of the truck, opened her door, and carried her into the house. Once inside, he laid her gently on a sectional couch. It felt soft, like microsuede. The coffee color suited the rest of the apartment, which was decorated simply, in muted colors.

"Nice place," Tara said. It was like Dr. Jekyll and Mr. Hyde: she never knew which Craig was going to show up.

"Thanks," he called from the kitchen. "One of my aunts is an interior designer; I used to help her during my summer vacations. And Evelyn pretty much lets me do as I please with the place." He carried two steaming mugs and a first aid kit into the room. "Not bad for a bachelor, huh?"

She cradled the mug. Cocoa. Nirvana. "Thank you. No, not bad for a bachelor. How is Evelyn, by the way?"

Craig shrugged. "Holding her own. She won't talk about it, although she's letting me help her a little more than she used to."

"You called yourself a bachelor. You mentioned a wife…?"

He bandaged Tara's ankle, fed her a couple of painkillers, and fell onto the love seat across from her. "Ex-wife. That was a long time ago. I also have a daughter. Somewhere."

"Somewhere?"

He hesitated. When he continued, his voice was husky. "They awarded her mother full custody. I was…busy. I didn't see her as often as I should. Now I don't see her at all. I've never been a part of her life; I doubt she'd want me to start now." He emptied his mug in one gulp, like downing a shot of whiskey.

"How old is she?"

"Twelve."

"A girl always needs her father. Especially at that age." Tara tried not to think about her own father.

"I don't know where to start looking for her. Her mother and I lost touch years ago."

"In today's wired world, you could find her, if you wanted to. You have to decide that for yourself. Just don't wait too long."

He studied her. "You sound like you know something about the subject."

She sighed. "It's a long story. Maybe I'll tell you someday."

"I'd like that." He walked to the couch and perched at her feet. "There's something else we need to talk about."

"Now what? Did you buy my house and are evicting me?"

"Will you forget about the house? Believe it or not, there is more going on in my life than your damned house."

"Sorry." She was quiet for a moment, and then leaned toward him. "I really want to like you, Craig. I like the caring man that you let out in bits and pieces. I just don't see him often enough."

"I know, and I apologize. Like I said, I let my work get in the way of my common sense sometimes. It's a bad habit that I'm trying to change.

"Anyway, I *do* have something I need to tell you." He paused for a moment. "You know I came to Surfside to find my mother."

"Yes."

"Well, I found her. Or at least I found out who she was."

"She died when you were a baby, right?" Tara said.

He stood and paced around the room. "That's what my father told me, that she died soon after I was born.

"Jimmy — my father — was a gambler. Not your stereotypical father figure. He met my mother in San Diego, before the Gaslamp Quarter went from porn to trendy. They lived together for a while, and I was the result.

"Once my mother was gone, my father left me with his sister and headed to Vegas. I was pretty much raised by aunts and uncles. He stopped in from time to time, bringing me presents, sometimes taking me with him to Vegas or Atlantic City, or wherever he thought the tables would be kind to him.

"Luckily my aunts didn't let him take me very often, so my childhood was relatively stable. Plenty of strong men and women to guide me, even if they weren't my parents. But I always knew I was missing something."

"Anyway, he died last year. Lung cancer. Too many years of secondhand smoke in the casinos, not to mention his own fondness for unfiltered Marlboros. I see my aunts and uncles when I go home. And my mother…like I said, I thought she was dead."

"You thought? You mean she isn't?" Tara winced as she tried to find a more comfortable position.

"No, she is. But not in the way that I thought. One of my aunts told me. My dad found a note on the kitchen table from my mother a couple of months after I was born. Said she had some loose ends to tie up and she'd be back soon. He never heard from her again."

Why did that sound so familiar?

"Anyway, after doing some poking around, I finally found out who she was." He stopped.

"And?"

Craig watched Tara as he said, "It was your aunt, Tara. Deirdre McCarthy."

~ *36* ~

"Deirdre? *Deirdre* was your mother?" Tara stared at Craig.

"Yep. I'm having a hard time believing it myself, and I've known for a couple of days now."

"How did you find out?"

Craig sat on the end of the couch again. "I tried to find her for months, but got nowhere. So I finally hired a private eye, who knew what questions to ask. He found out pretty quickly. I can show you his report, if you need proof.

"I don't plan to do anything about it," he continued. "I just thought you should know, since apparently we're cousins."

"But," Tara said, struggling to organize her thoughts, "you're her heir. You should inherit part of her estate."

"Which is…what? The house? You're saying your house is — or was — rightfully mine? In spite of what you think of me, Tara, I wouldn't take your home away from you."

"Not the whole house. Just half of it."

"What?" he asked.

Tara paused for a moment, and then said, "Deirdre McCarthy wasn't my aunt, Craig. She was my mother."

"*Your* mother?" He stood and stared down at her. "What the hell are you talking about?"

"I know, I know. It's a long story. The short version is, I found my original birth certificate, and it listed Deirdre as my mother."

Craig fell onto the love seat. "Holy shit. Can I see it?"

"It was in the house." The diary, the birth certificates, Ariel, the box — everything was in the house. Everything was gone.

They watched each other for a few minutes, suddenly awkward. Finally, Craig shook his head. "It's times like this I wish I still drank. Are you hungry?"

"Do you have any chocolate?"

"I meant real food."

"Chocolate isn't real food?" She smiled, although she was only half joking.

"I'll see what I can find." Craig disappeared into the kitchen. Tara leaned back into the soft couch and closed her eyes, trying to wrap her mind around this new twist.

Craig was her brother. He was the other baby that Deirdre wanted Mary and Ethan to raise.

She had a family.

Tara's head was spinning with questions. But although there was a lot more of the story that she needed to hear, the pills Craig gave her did their job and she fell asleep.

Craig walked out of the kitchen carrying grilled cheese sandwiches. "Sorry, no choc…" Seeing her asleep on the couch, he quietly placed the plates on the coffee table and sat on the love seat, and watched his sister sleep.

&

Tara woke and looked around. She was in a strange bed. At least she was alone — not that that was anything new. She sat up and groaned. Her body ached. Her hair smelled like smoke. Her clothes — she looked down. She was dressed in a man's oversized sweatshirt and pants. Where were her clothes?

Then she remembered. The shirt must be Craig's. Hopefully Evelyn helped him…no, probably not. *Great*. Even if they were family, she wasn't ready to deal with the knowledge that Craig Morris had seen her in her underwear.

She limped into the living room and found him asleep on the couch, a single ray of sun highlighting his tousled auburn hair.

Tara lowered herself onto the love seat and propped her leg on the coffee table. She thought about all that happened, all that she learned. Now she needed to decide what to do with that knowledge.

First, she needed to see the house, or what was left of it. She needed closure, to convince herself that it was really gone. She reached up to touch her necklace. At least she hadn't lost that.

She needed to call Mr. Edison and discuss what would happen to the bank account now that the house was gone. They also needed to decide how to share the inheritance with Craig, in spite of what he said about not wanting it. It was only right. Tara wondered if Craig's existence would be a surprise to Mr. Edison, considering his reluctance to discuss Deirdre's family. Maybe the attorney knew more than he was willing — or able — to admit.

And she needed to decide where she went from here. Without the house, she had no reason to stay in Surfside.

Except for the man sleeping across from her.

He stirred and opened his eyes. "Morning," he said.

"Good morning. I'm sorry you had to sleep on the couch."

He stood and stretched, and leaned against the breakfast bar, his left food propped on his right shin. "No worries. I often sleep here. When I'm watching television," he added quickly, "not because I'm drunk or anything."

"Relax. I'm your sister, not your mother. You don't owe me an explanation." She noticed how he was standing. "Do you do that often?"

"Do what?"

"Stand like that."

He looked down at his legs. "How am I standing?"

"With your foot propped on your shin. My mother and I both do it. I remember pictures of my family standing in the kitchen — my grandparents, Mama, Deirdre — everyone with their left foot propped on their right shin. We used to laugh about it. It's a McCarthy trait."

Craig deliberately lowered his foot to the ground, smiling. "I'll have to pay attention to that. Speaking of legs…"

"It's fine. I'll live — thanks to you."

"Stubborn."

"Yep." Then Tara said, "Um…thanks for the clothes."

Craig blushed, and smiled. "Don't worry, I closed my eyes."

There was a moment of silence, and then Tara said, "If you don't mind, I'd like to go back to the house and see what's left. I know," she said, holding up her hand as he started to speak, "I'm grasping at straws. But I need to see it, to convince myself that it's really gone. So I can move on."

He nodded. "Sure. Let me change clothes and we'll head out there. I don't have any coffee; do you mind cocoa again?"

"A man after my own heart." She hobbled into the bathroom to pull herself together, and found a tray filled with cufflinks. She chose a pair of simple silver ones, slipped them into the pocket of her pants, and turned on the shower.

~ *37* ~

As they drove to the house, Tara fiddled with her necklace.

"Are you okay?" Craig glanced at her. The sun was shining and birds were singing; aside from a few broken branches, there was no evidence of last night's storm.

She shrugged. "Everything I owned was in that house. I just hope there's something left."

"I don't mean to be insensitive, but the place was an inferno. I can't imagine anything's left but the chimney."

"You're probably right. Most of the time I'm a realist, but today I'm trying to be an optimist. Maybe I'm turning over a new leaf."

As he reached the bottom of the driveway, Craig stopped. "What happened to the branches?"

"What branches?" Huge gullies ran down the center of the road, but Tara didn't see any branches.

"The road was a sheet of ice last night, with huge branches strewn across it."

"So how did you get up the hill?"

He smiled sheepishly. "I hiked in. I'm a rock climber, remember? I keep my gear in the truck — including ice crampons."

"Wait a minute. You *carried* me down the road? Wearing crampons?"

He nodded. "Didn't have a choice. Good thing you're little."

She shook her head. "Not that little. I owe you even more, then." And looked back at the driveway. "What a mess. It's going to take a ton of gravel to fix this."

"Are you going to rebuild?"

"I don't know. Maybe. I don't have a lot of other options."

But she did. Honolulu. New Zealand. Jost Van Dyke. All options that once she would have jumped at, rather than choosing something that would tie her down. But things were different now. Now she had a reason to stick around.

"We need to discuss the taxes at some point, too," Craig said. "My business does pretty well; I can help you pay them."

Tara sighed. "We'll talk about it later. I guess they'll still exist, won't they? Even if the house doesn't. And I guess your condo plans are toast now."

He shook his head. "I wanted to talk to you about that, but you never gave me the chance. I never planned to gut your house. You made me so mad, I said crazy things."

"But the people you wanted to bring up…"

"I didn't say they wanted to buy the condos. They own a construction company. I thought they could help you with the repairs. I owe them a favor, so was trying to drum up some business for them. If you called me back, I would have told you that."

"Well, if you hadn't pissed me off…"

Craig held up his hands. "Stop. Truce. We agreed we weren't going to do this, remember?"

Tara laughed. "Old habits die hard." The truck crested the hill and Tara gasped.

"What the hell…?" Craig said.

The house stood in the clearing, awash in lemon sunlight. Intact.

They sat for a minute in stunned silence. "This is very weird," he said. "The house was engulfed. It should be gutted."

Tara sighed. "I guess I need to explain the rest to you."

Craig turned to look at her, and she told him about the peculiarities of the house. The dreams. And the treasure. But not about the box of stars.

"You have Deirdre's blood running through your veins, too," she finished, as the truck idled in the clearing. "I'm guessing the same magic that affects me, affects you."

"So now I'm going to start seeing ghosts?"

"No idea. You might have to sleep here to find out. I didn't dream last night, for the first time in weeks." Maybe Craig would be lucky; maybe the house didn't have anything to teach him. "But I think the house will stop attacking you once it knows who you are." She opened the door of the truck.

"Do you want me to come in with you?"

"No, thanks. Hopefully the house is all out of lessons. But I have to find out for myself." She leaned across the seat to kiss his cheek. "Maybe we can have dinner. We have a lot to discuss."

They agreed to talk later, and Tara watched Craig disappear down the driveway. She wondered how he was going to deal with these ghosts. With his mother leaving him. With having a family. Hopefully knowing what it felt like to be abandoned by a parent would help him decide to look for his daughter, and be a part of her life again.

Like Tara, Craig had a lot to forgive.

There would be challenges: they were both strong-willed people, used to getting their own way. But they would learn. She was willing to do almost anything to be part of a real family. Hopefully, Craig felt the same way.

Tara limped to the porch using a crutch that he lent her — a souvenir from a rock-climbing accident, he said — and cautiously climbed the steps. She tried to sense any hostility, any reason for the fire. But felt nothing.

She opened the door and crossed the threshold. Past Ariel, gazing at distant horizons. Past the gilt-framed mirror, hiding who knew what secrets. And into the living room, where the fireplace looked exactly as it did the day before, a fire ready to light.

"Okay, 'fess up," she said, addressing the room in general. "What's going on? Do I have to be asleep or unconscious for you to explain things to me?" Not that she expected an answer.

She continued into the study and checked the desk. The box was gone. "So you were mad because I found the box, you pretended to burn yourself down, you almost killed me, and now you've hidden the box? Are you mad because I haven't learned whatever lesson you're trying to teach me?"

The branch tapped against the glass and Tara walked to the window. "And I'm going to chop down that friggin' tree because the tapping is making me nuts. Sorry if it pisses…"

There was no tree. Nothing close enough to the window to tap on it. A shiver tiptoed down her spine. She truly was losing it. Was anything about this house real?

She coughed and winced. Her throat was raw. That was real enough. She limped through the hallway and examined the staircase. The step and handrail were still in pieces. That, too, was real. As were her twisted knee and torn ankle.

She knelt to run her hands across Ariel's hair. Had it always been so tousled? "You're looking a little disheveled, m'lady. What mischief have you been up to?" Then she trailed her fingers along the figurehead's shoulders. Shoulders that used to be covered by a blue shawl, but were now bare.

An image flashed through her mind: something blue being draped over her face.

She must have dreamed it. Craig was the one who saved her from the fire. Although he did mention how lucky it was that she made it to the front porch.

But she didn't make it to the front porch. The last thing she remembered was the smoke, and the fire, in the living room.

It didn't make any sense. Then again, what about the house did?

She knelt to stare into the figurehead's green eyes. "I thought mermaids lured sailors to their death, not saved them from it. Maybe I need to thank you for saving my life."

Tara hobbled into the kitchen and sat on one of the chairs, lost in thought. If folks thought she was crazy for believing a house had a will, they'd surely lock her up for thinking a piece of wood saved her life.

Sneakers bounded into the room and onto her lap. "Thank God," she said. "I guess the fire didn't affect you, either. Looks like it's just Deirdre's children who see things that aren't there."

She wished she still had the diary, though. Maybe if she learned whatever lesson the house was trying to teach her, it would return the book, too.

Tara leaned back and thought about what she had been doing when the fire started. Besides trying to light it, that is.

She had been thinking about forgiveness. When she considered forgiving her parents, the box appeared. And when she decided she couldn't forgive them, the box disappeared, and the house burned — or made her think it did, anyway.

She found out about Craig and his past as a result of the fire. And forgave him for trying to take her house, once she knew the details of the situation.

But how did Mariah figure into all of this? Besides being the one who showed Tara what forgiveness truly looked like, and urging her to do the same with her parents?

Tara stroked the purring cat. The peculiarities of the house notwithstanding, inheriting it changed Tara's life. She now knew who her real mother was, and understood what Mary went through to raise her. She knew she didn't kill Emma, which allowed her to consider staying in one place and creating a normal life for herself. And now she had the family she longed for, in Craig. And hopefully his daughter, too, someday.

Maybe she could let herself care for someone again. Maybe even have children of her own.

Could she forgive Deirdre for abandoning her? Mary for abusing her? Her father for neglecting her and, worse, for killing Emma and letting her take the blame? That was a lot to ask. But she realized that she would have to forgive them before she could begin her life again. It had to be all or nothing.

Tara took a deep breath. She could do this. She needed to. She could forgive them. And, in turn, forgive herself.

She waited for the fireworks, for a burden to lift from her shoulders, for awareness and insight. Instead, she felt — tired. Maybe awareness and insight would come later.

The back door creaked, and Tara reached for the crutch lying next to her chair.

"I'm hollering!" Mariah called as she rolled through the laundry room. "Tara, I'm hollering!"

"I hear you. Thanks for not scaring me to death this time."

The girl rolled into the kitchen, a faded denim jacket spread across her lap. She studied the crutch, Tara's bandaged ankle, and the baggy sweatpants. "What in the heck happened to you?"

Tara shook her head. "You'll never believe me. Let's just say I had a whopper of a dream."

"That made you smell like smoke and hurt yourself?" Mariah rolled her eyes. "You're right; I don't want to know." She parked her chair next to Tara's. Sneakers hissed and jumped out of Tara's lap, disappearing through the kitchen door.

"I wonder why he does that," Tara said. "He sure gets weird when you're around."

Mariah shrugged. "Did you find any more stars?"

"Actually, I did. There was one in the study, under the desk." Which appeared after she found the box. And read the diary. And considered forgiving her parents.

Mariah grinned, her eyes sparkling. "Did you figure out what they mean yet?"

"I think so. I think maybe I'm supposed to do what you said: forgive my parents. And forgive myself. Stop punishing myself, and try to lead a normal life."

"I'm smarter than I look, aren't I?"

Tara slid her arm around the girl's shoulders. "You *are* as smart as you look, Squirt." The jacket slipped to the floor and Tara saw a brown paper bag in her lap. "What's that?"

"Something that needs to be returned to you." The girl placed the bag on the table. "Open it after I'm gone."

She rolled back her chair. "I came to thank you for saving my life."

Tara started to speak, but Mariah held up a small hand. "With that action, you paid your debt. You've learned the lesson. I've been caring for the house long enough; it's your turn.

"I wanted to say goodbye. That I love you and forgive you. And that you've always made me proud of you. But I'm taking my ring. You won't need it any more."

"What do you mean, paid my debt? What lesson? *Your* ring?"

Mariah grinned and started humming a tune. Tara listened for a minute, and froze when she recognized it.

It was a lullaby. One that she made up when she was a child.

One that she sang to Emma.

Tara stared at the girl who winked, blew a kiss, and vanished.

"Mariah! Wait!" There was no response. Only the faint echo of a song suspended in the air.

As Tara looked at the space where Mariah — Emma — had been, Sneakers padded into the room, jumped back onto her lap, and began purring again.

"I don't know what just happened, kitty," Tara finally said, "but I think there was a good reason Craig couldn't see her. And why you didn't like her." She'd have to do some research on cats' reactions to ghosts.

Her mind was whirling, thinking about the times Mariah visited. She was the one who first mentioned that Tara should forgive her parents. And now, Tara understood how Craig knew to come to the house and save her.

Mariah found the first star. But Tara still needed to figure out why it was in the basement. There were a lot of things she still needed to figure out.

But now she knew that Emma forgave her for not protecting her. And Emma wanted Tara to forgive their parents. She knew about Ethan, obviously. If Emma could forgive him for what he did to her, then Tara could, too.

Tara reached for the chain around her neck, but it was empty. She felt a deep sense of loss. Then she noticed the bag on the table, opened it, and withdrew a box.

The box.

She lifted the lid and found the medical report. Both birth certificates. Deirdre's diary. And the star she had given to Mariah.

When she lifted the book out of the box, something slipped from between its pages.

It was a picture. A picture of her and Emma as children. Playing with dolls. And laughing.

~ 38 ~

Tara sat in the kitchen, cat in lap, picture in hand. Dust danced in the rays that streamed through the windows. For the first time in weeks, her mind was clear. She didn't feel the burden of finding secrets, of worrying about bills, of being alone. The path of her life stretched before her — one that she was excited about following.

She could feel the ghosts of her family around her. But they no longer tormented her. Instead, the thought of them gave her peace.

Was it really that easy, that all she had to do was forgive them for their mistakes? For being human? She expected so much of herself, and of others, that she missed the simple truth of allowing people to be who they are, and to love them for it.

It was so obvious, yet she couldn't see it herself. It took her family — the very ones she blamed for her problems — to show her the answers. Maybe she hadn't been alone all of those years, after all.

Tara would go on. She'd create memory books and finish restoring the house. Maybe fall in love. Her future was promising, now she could give it a chance. Now she could finally stop beating herself up for things she couldn't change.

It was freeing, this letting go.

Deirdre was right. She did find what she was seeking in the house. Tara thought about the years behind her, and the years ahead. It was definitely worth the price.

&

Now what?

Tara looked for something to do that didn't require standing or walking. She wanted to change clothes, but couldn't face climbing the staircase. Bonnie still hadn't called, and she was worried about her friend. When she went into town, she'd stop by the sheriff's department and file a report.

The cartons filled with her father's paperwork were still in the corner of the kitchen where she left them. She limped across the room, eased herself onto the floor, and opened the first one.

A couple of hours later, there were two piles in front of her: stuff to toss, and stuff to save. Talk about a pack rat. Her father kept every invoice, every cancelled check, every scrap of paper he ever received. Thankfully she didn't inherit that trait, and was throwing away far more than she was saving.

She reached into the final carton and touched something cold and hard: the lockbox. She had forgotten about it. And realized that they hadn't found the key.

It probably held his passport, or birth certificate, or whatever else Ethan deemed important enough to secure. She shook it and heard something solid bump against the sides. Something that didn't sound like papers.

Now her curiosity was piqued. But she needed the key; it wouldn't be as easy to break into as the house had been. And even that had its drawbacks, she thought, as she examined the barely healed cut on her wrist.

Reluctantly, she balanced the box on top of the 'save' pile; she'd call Marge later, to ask if she'd seen the key.

As Tara broke down the cartons to stack in the recycling bin, something clattered onto the tile floor. She picked up the object. It was a third gold star.

Why would there be a star in her father's papers? She thought the star in the study was her reward for considering forgiving her parents. This one must have something to do with her father: maybe rewarding her for deciding to forgive him, in spite of how his actions colored — ruined — her life.

But the star in the basement. The one that Mariah — Emma — found. Tara didn't know what that one meant, since they didn't find anything of interest down there.

Unless they missed something.

Leaning on the crutch, Tara hobbled to the basement door. She reached for the knob, and stopped. Wasn't the knob on the other side of the door before? She remembered propping the door open with a rock — which was gone, by the way — and shoving

Mariah's wheelchair in front of it. But that wasn't possible if the door opened in this direction: the wall was in the way. She shook her head and passed it off as yet another example of her bad memory. Or maybe another trick played on her by the house.

She turned the knob and the door swung open.

Since the door wasn't locked, she must be supposed to go downstairs. It occurred to Tara that she was accepting very strange things in a very calm fashion, but it was a matter of self-preservation. If she continued to question every out-of-the-ordinary event she experienced in the house, she'd go crazy. Denial was her new best friend.

She pressed the switch, and light flooded the stairs. So far, so good. Leaning awkwardly on the crutch she limped down, cursing the missing handrail. Then again, the last time she grabbed for a handrail it didn't turn out so well, so maybe relying on inanimate objects in this house wasn't such a great idea.

Although Tara was learning to trust people, she was also learning to be more judicious in how she applied that trust when it came to the house. Sometimes it helped her, while other times it fought her with every board and nail. Maybe it was conflicted, torn between hiding its secrets and honoring its charge to protect them. Or maybe it was just pissed at being left alone for forty years, and was taking it out on her.

Whatever the reason, the house appeared to be on her side.

Once Tara reached the bottom of the staircase, she tried the next switch and those lights came on as well, illuminating the corners of the basement. She limped around the empty room, pushing on walls, peering in holes, rattling pipes. Everything was solid. No hidden doors, no hiding places.

Thinking perhaps the star fell down the stairs at some point in the past and was really supposed to be upstairs, Tara hobbled back to the bottom of the staircase and looked up.

The door was closed.

"Are you kidding me?" she said. "I do *not* believe I let you do this to me again! I've fallen down every staircase in this stupid house, and I will not do it again.

"I'm going to sit right here and wait for you to open that damned door. This is ridiculous." And she flopped onto the bottom step, tossing the crutch into the dirt at her feet.

Great. Just great. Tara shook her head incredulously. How could she fall for that trick again?

Maybe there was a reason the house wanted her to stay down here. She closed her eyes, trying to be receptive to whatever message she was supposed to receive.

The lights flickered and went out.

When she opened her eyes to curse the house again, she saw them.

Stars.

Or, more accurately, golden points of light. Hundreds of them. Maybe thousands. Some large, some small. Hovering throughout the basement. Floating like fireflies on a gentle breeze. Shifting, glowing, twinkling Tinkerbells. Just like the ones she had seen in the box.

Tara sat frozen, as they drifted around her. She tentatively reached out to touch one, but it danced away. But not before she felt its heat.

"They're souls, me love," a voice said from the top of the staircase. She turned to watch an auburn-haired man descend, the stairs lit by the glow. Golden lights danced around his head. "Or pieces of them, anyway." He lowered himself onto the step beside her. "The house protects them, ye see."

"But what are they, really?" she asked. The appearance of a strange man in her basement no longer surprised her. Especially when surrounded by golden stars. "And who are you?"

"As I told ye, they're pieces of souls. Lost by those refusin' to forgive the transgressions of others."

"But have they been here the whole time? Why couldn't I see them before?"

"A person shouldna have to bear more than one burden at a time. Ye shed the one ye carried, so now are ready for another. " He rose and paced the basement floor, puffs of dust rising with each step. "When me great-great-grandfather built this house, he charged it with protectin' the family that dwells within its walls. But the house also protects the souls — at least the pieces that find their way here.

"The pieces belongin' to our family are the strongest, and the ones the house will fight the hardest to keep. So we bear a special burden of guarding our souls more carefully, for we might not be able to wrest our pieces back."

"But how do people lose them?" Tara couldn't take her eyes off the stars, which had begun to whirl around the man like a slow-motion tornado.

"Pieces can be lost in many ways. Forsakin' a dream. Betrayin' a love. But 'tis the refusal to forgive that pains the soul the most, and tears away the biggest pieces.

"Do ye not question why Deirdre" — he rolled his Rs — "left ye this house, darlin'?"

"Of course I do. I didn't even know her." The dust floating around the basement tickled her nose, and she sneezed.

"But she knew ye. And she knew ye would be the one to bear the burden, once she was gone. 'Tis your birthright, Tara."

"What burden? And you still haven't told me who you are."

He smiled down at her. "Do ye not recognize me? True, we never met, but ye'r ma must have pictures of me amongst her things."

Then she knew. The same auburn hair, the same smile she saw reflected in her mirror — on the mornings she found something to smile about. Deirdre's dimple. Her mother's eyes.

"Grandpa McCarthy?"

"The very same, me love." He sat beside her again. "'Tis time ye knew the house's secrets, for 'twill be ye'r duty to help it fulfill its charge from now on."

"My duty? Why me?"

"The magic flows strongest through our women. Ye'r brother will have some of it, but 'tis ye who will feel the power."

"And what exactly am I supposed to do with this power? For that matter, what am I supposed to do with this house?" Tara's butt was numb from sitting on the wooden step, and her leg throbbed.

"Ye have already started, lass. By residin' within its walls. By healin' it, and protectin' it."

"But the house acts like it's mad at me half the time. Are you sure it's going to accept me — what did you say — helping it fulfill its charge?"

"It's been left alone a good while. Perhaps it's forgotten how 'tis supposed to behave." He closed his eyes for a moment, and

Tara saw his lips move. Then he opened them again. "There. I've reminded the house of its charge, and of who ye be. 'Twill be no more misbehavin.'" He smiled. "Although I canna say the same for ye'r brother. Ye will have ye'r hands full with that one."

"You said the stars are pieces of souls that are lost when someone refuses to forgive. So, what happens if that person changes his mind, and does forgive?"

"Then the piece will return, and their soul will be whole again. But," and his expression became solemn, "the house must retain some pieces to survive. Each time a piece leaves to return home the house feels it, and 'twill mourn a little. Although 'tis a happy time for the soul, for 'twill be whole again."

"Is there any chance of all the pieces disappearing?"

He shook his head. "'Twould be a blessing if they did, me love. But people bein' what they are, I fear there's no danger of that happening." He rose again. "'Tis a heavy burden ye bear, Tara love." Her name sounded exotic, colored by his brogue. "But ye don't bear it alone."

"I don't?" She stared at the man towering over her.

"Do ye not know by now that ye'r family resides here? This is our home, too. We have a life separate from yours, in this very place. When it suits us, we show ourselves. If ye need guidance, just think upon us and we'll be there."

He started to climb the stairs, but stopped to look down at her. "Follow ye'r heart, me love. Forgive as much as ye can. But remember, there are acts too foul to be excused. Know the price ye pay when makin' the decision not to forgive, though. For 'tis both good and bad will come of it."

"Wait!" Tara said. "Why is there a mermaid in the hallway?"

"The one ye call Ariel? 'Tis said that spirits dwell within the figureheads. If a ship sinks, the spirit of the figurehead guides the sailors' souls to the Land of the Dead. To sink without a spirit condemns their souls to haunt the sea forever. Ye'r Ariel is merely doing her job — protecting the souls. And ye."

"But why a mermaid?"

"Ask her." He stood at the top of the staircase, winked, and vanished. The lights came on. And the stars disappeared.

Tara looked around, searching for the golden lights, but saw only cobwebs and dust. But when she reached out, she felt something warm brush against her fingertips, as if she had dipped them into the healing waters of a sulfur spring. And she smiled.

&

Tara was exhausted. So much had happened in the last few days, she didn't know how to begin dealing with it. She decided the best way to start was with a nap. The rest could wait.

She limped into the living room on the crutch. Stared suspiciously at the fireplace, then curled into a corner of the couch, pulled the quilt over her, and closed her eyes. Opened one eye and peeked around the room to see if anything had changed. The fireplace sat cold and still, waiting for a match. Fat chance of that. Closed her eye again.

A noise woke her. It was dark. How long had she been asleep? Then she heard the noise again: voices. In the room with her. Tara slumped on the couch, hoping they wouldn't see her.

"I warned you." A woman's voice, low and taut. "We both have. You have to stop."

"You can't stop me." A man's voice this time, a familiar one. "I should have finished this years ago. I can't risk you spreading your vile disease any further. I've already taken care of the others. You two are all that's left."

"It won't end with her. I have a son, who you'll never find. And my sister lives, in spite of your best efforts. Damaged, but alive. We will continue. *It* will continue."

"The disease doesn't transmit through men," he said. "Just women. I've done my research. Years of thorough research, making sure there are no loose ends."

"You can't research magic. It follows its own will. How do you know she hasn't passed her power onto someone else? Bloodlines are the strongest links, but there are other ways. Which you won't find in your 'research.'" She was mocking him, her voice growing stronger with every word.

"She would have told me. She trusts me." He laughed, but there was no joy in the sound.

"You're too late. I've already warned her. She knows."

"You're bluffing. You haven't seen her for years," he said.

"You can believe that if you want. Anyway, I've paid for my mistake," she said. "You can't hurt me with it any more. She'll forgive me. She has to."

"You won't get the chance. This ends here."

"You've already raped me and killed my niece. And tried to kill my sister. Driven me away from my family. There is nothing else you can do to me."

There was the sound of a struggle and a piercing scream, cut off. The sound of something heavy falling — or being dropped — onto the hardwood floor. And then, nothing.

Tara sat frozen, petrified. She heard heavy breathing. And, finally, a whisper. "One more. It ends tonight."

Suddenly the house groaned, just as it did when Tara found the box. Then, she thought the storm was shaking it. Now she knew it was the house itself, angered by her discovering its secrets. By its charge being betrayed.

This time its rage was palpable. It shimmered in the air like heat waves. Tara covered her head with the quilt as the house unleashed its fury.

She could feel the turmoil in the air as the house attacked the man. His moans and screams cut through the air like shards of glass, and turned her blood cold. She prayed to her ancestors, to her family, to whoever could protect her from the violence that was shattering the night.

His screams ripped through her head until Tara knew she would go insane from the sound. Until suddenly, finally, they stopped.

The air was hot — too hot to breathe. It seared her throat. She gasped, trying to pull enough oxygen into her damaged lungs to survive. Just as she believed she would be consumed by the house's rage, it ended. The air cooled. There was silence.

Deathly silence.

She uncovered her head and looked around. The living room shone in the early afternoon light. Birdsong echoed through the forest. She peeked over the back of the couch, but found the room exactly as it was when she entered it. No bodies, no destruction.

It was another dream.

If what she saw was true, she just witnessed Deirdre's death at Ethan's hands. And the house attacking him in return. Fulfilling its charge. Protecting its own.

~ 39 ~

Tara was still trembling from the house's fury, even though it hadn't been directed at her. The knowledge that the house avenged Deirdre's death was both fearsome and comforting.

She had to admit that her father was responsible for Deirdre's death. Even though she found it hard to believe, the evidence was damning. Ethan a murderer. Hell, more than once, apparently.

And how did the souls figure into this? Maybe that's why her father was in the coma: he gave up too much when he took Deirdre's life. He had, in effect, sold his soul, and was paying the price.

Her thoughts were interrupted by the phone. It was Marge.

"Honey, I got a call from the woman who bought your father's desk at the garage sale. She found a key; sounds like it fell from some hidey-hole. I didn't know what it could be for, but I had her bring it over anyways."

"It is a small key?"

"You betcha. Like for a padlock."

"I might have an idea what it goes to," Tara said.

"Tell you what. Tony is driving down to Lincoln City; I can have him stop by your place on the way. Assuming that bucket of bolts he calls a car makes it that far." In Marge's laugh, Tara could hear the long-suffering mother of a teenaged boy. "'It's a classic,' he says. Classic piece of crap, I'm thinking."

"How about I meet him at Lee's Place, on the highway south of Surfside? I'm not sure he'll be able to make it up my driveway." She wasn't sure her little truck could get down it, with the damage from yesterday's storm.

"Good idea. I'll have him drop off the check from the garage sale at the same time. We did pretty good for selling a bunch of junk. Oops, sorry."

"No reason to apologize," Tara replied. "It *was* a bunch of junk. I appreciate your taking care of it for me."

"My pleasure, sweetie. Have to confess that I kept a few things for myself, for old times' sake, you know. That Ethan is a dear, dear man. I'll surely miss him."

They agreed on a time to meet and Tara hung up, thinking how Ethan had fooled so many people over the years.

Unless the house had shown her false images. Maybe it had something against her father and wanted her to be angry with him, too.

Maybe the house could distort her dreams to suit its purposes. She had no concrete evidence that her father did any of the things her dreams showed her. Maybe the house was jealous of him, or viewed him as an enemy, taking Mary to Portland. Maybe it blamed him for Deirdre leaving, for being abandoned for so long.

This was crazy. She was trying to figure out the motives of a house. But it was something to think about, considering all of this was so unlike the father she thought she knew.

Maybe she needed to rethink blaming him for Deirdre's death, and for killing Emma. Although that would mean that, once again, she herself was guilty…

Tara was overwhelmed. It was too much to think about. A beer would calm her nerves. And if it eased the throbbing in her leg, that would be good, too. Then she could decide what to think about everything she'd just seen.

But she couldn't go anywhere in Craig's sweats. So she gathered her strength and crawled upstairs to change clothes.

As she passed Ariel, Tara said, "I'll deal with you later," and hobbled to her truck, praying it could make it around the gullies, and that her ankle would work long enough to get her to Lee's.

She really needed that beer.

&

Distracted by the pain in her foot and the thoughts tumbling through her mind, Tara forgot to stand at Lee's door and fret about how to open it. Instead, she just walked — limped — in.

She was stroking Miss Gertrude's leathery ears before she realized what happened. She stared at the door in surprise. "How the heck did I do that?" she asked herself.

"What's changed since your last visit?" Lee was standing behind her, a grin on his face.

She snorted. "How much time do you have?"

"Let's start with the relevant stuff. What were you thinking about when you came in?"

"About how much my ankle hurt. And how good the beer was going to taste. And…other stuff." She didn't feel like telling him about the last few days just yet. It was still too fresh.

"What *weren't* you thinking about?"

She opened her mouth for a snappy comeback, then stopped. And smiled. "How to open the damned door."

"You assumed it would open, and it did. You stopped wanting it."

"That's the big secret? If I stop wanting the door to open, it will?"

He laughed. "Open it a few more times and I'll decide if you're ready to know the rest of the secret."

"I've had my share of secrets this week, thank you very much."

Lee looked at her bandaged ankle, red eyes, and crutch. "Did looking for secrets do that to you?"

Tara shrugged.

"Whatever," he said. "I've got a Corona here with your name on it."

She was relieved that he gave up so easily. In spite of Bonnie's warning, she had decided to trust him. But she didn't feel like talking about it just yet.

It was a strange sensation, this trusting people.

As they walked toward the bar, Tara noticed that Lee was limping, too. "What happened to you?"

He grinned sheepishly. "Told you I was a klutz. Fell off the damned ladder after I saw you the other day. Next time I'll follow my own advice and let someone more coordinated do my home maintenance projects."

"When did you…" Her phone buzzed with a text message. *How do I get in the stupid bar?*

"Can you do me a favor?" she asked Lee. "There's a boy outside looking for me. I'd hobble out, but he might die from old age by the time I get there. Can you send someone out to meet him?"

He winked, and reached under the bar. "Or I could press this button and let him in."

Tara's jaw dropped. "You have a button under there that opens the door?"

"Yep, and a closed-circuit camera. I wouldn't have any customers if I didn't have a way to circumvent the system."

"So I didn't have to figure out how to open the stupid door, after all?" She wanted to smack the grin off Lee's face.

"Oh no, you did. I make important people earn their way in."

Important people?

He slid a cold beer across the counter as Zelda appeared. She sniffed Tara's ankle, gently licked the bandage, and flopped at her feet.

"Here's to secrets," he said, holding up his mug.

"How about something a little less…" she started.

"Less what, Tee?"

She saw a strange light in his eyes. "Less vague," Tara said, ducking his thrust. "Here's to beer. And maybe peanuts." She took a long drink, avoiding his gaze. She had enough of secrets for now.

"To beer." He sipped from his mug and placed it on the bar. "Where's your cap today?" he asked. "I barely recognize you without it."

"Turning over a new leaf," she said. That would be something she'd have to get used to, as well — not donning her disguise every time she left the house.

A waitress handed Tara a long thin envelope with her name printed on it in block letters. Lee spoke to the young woman and she disappeared into the kitchen, where Tara could hear the cook's hearty laughter.

"I love his laugh," she said, slipping the envelope into her purse. "Maybe I should eat here more often."

Lee looked at her for a long moment. "Maybe you should." Then continued. "Are you going to tell me what happened to your ankle?"

She took a swig from her bottle as the waitress returned with a fat cheese sandwich, oozing tomatoes and mustard and garnished with an orange slice, and hoped that not answering was answer enough.

"I warned you that some secrets are better left alone. I'm guessing you didn't follow my advice," Lee said.

"Why should I?" The pain in her leg was making her irritable.

"Because believe it or not, I know what I'm talking about. Dee didn't listen to me either, and look how she ended up." He shoved a glass into the sink, splashing himself and the surrounding area with dirty water. "Shit!"

Tara remembered her mother referring to Deirdre as Dee. "That's right; I never did ask why you were at her funeral. How did you know her?"

He wiped the water from the counters, not looking at her. "She stopped in a few times. We were…friends." The way he said it made Tara think that maybe they were more than just friends. Not that Deirdre's personal life — or Lee's, for that matter — was any of her business.

"I'm slowly learning about her. And her secrets. They're mine, too, you know," she said.

Lee shook his head. "Don't. No good will come of it. I don't want to lose another friend."

"It's my birthright," she said, wondering about his use of the word 'friend.' "You know that I'm her niece, right?"

"I figured you were related. You look like her." He scrubbed at an invisible spot on the bar.

"Is that why you kissed me?"

"No," he answered slowly, looking up at her. "I knew who I was kissing. And why."

There was an awkward pause as they stared at each other. Tara was the first to look away. "Well, I just found out that I'm not her niece, after all. I'm her daughter."

He froze, towel in hand. "Her daughter? Are you kidding me? How…?"

She sighed. "Long story. More than one beer. Maybe a case."

"Will you tell me someday?"

"Yes. When we have more time."

"Promise?" he asked.

"Promise."

She bent to pick up the crutch, patted Zelda, and rose. Lee walked her to the door, his arm draped lightly around her waist. "Be careful," he said. "I'm worried about you up on the hill by yourself. There's something not right about that house."

Boy, was that an understatement. She wondered if Deirdre had said anything to Lee about the house; did it have lessons to teach her aunt, as well? "It may sound strange, but the house isn't dangerous. At least not to me. But that'll take a lot more than a case of beer to explain. Anyway, thanks for caring. I'll be back."

"I'll be here." He reached out to touch her cheek; she could see flecks of gold in his eyes as he looked into hers.

Tara covered his hand with hers for a long moment. Then she walked out the door and into the fading light, knowing that he would be there when she was ready. Counting on it.

~ 40 ~

As Tara pulled into the clearing, her headlights shone on a car parked in front of the garage. A classic Oldsmobile Cutlass. But it was empty.

She hobbled to the front door. It was unlocked. She had locked it when she left. Now she really wished she had a gun. The crutch would only get in her way, so she dropped it on the porch and grabbed the flagpole instead. It served her well enough when Craig visited.

As she approached the front door, she noticed that a patch on the brass bell had been polished. A burglar who stopped to clean before robbing a house? She peered at the spot and could see a word engraved into it: *Alma*.

Tara quietly opened the door, limped across the hallway, and peered into the dining room. She didn't turn on the lights; she knew the way around her house in the dark better than a stranger would. The porch light was bright enough to illuminate the dining room, and she could see that no one was in there. She crept into the room and found a huge hole bashed into one of the walls, plaster and dust everywhere.

The porch light didn't shine into the study, so she decided to skip that room and continued to the living room. Where she found more holes in more walls.

What she didn't find was the sword, which should have been on the mantelpiece.

The sword might not be real but it *was* sharp, and could do more damage than her flagpole. She crept into the kitchen, her heart pounding.

No intruder. But more holes in the walls. *What the hell?*

She exchanged the flagpole for a carving knife, and knotted her hair into a ponytail to keep it out of her face. But as she headed for the hallway, intending to check upstairs, she heard a crash in the basement. And a curse.

Someone was after the souls.

She limped to the door and twisted the knob. It opened easily. Raising the knife in her shaking hand, Tara yanked open the door and stepped back, but no one jumped out.

She cautiously reached for the switch and flipped it, and stepped back as light flooded the stairs.

"Goddamned house." A voice floated up the staircase.

Tara listened over the frantic beating of her heart. "Bonnie?"

Silence.

"Bonnie, is that you?"

"No, it's the fucking Easter Bunny."

Tara looked down the stairs into the dark basement. "What are you doing down there?"

"Hiding Easter eggs." Bonnie groaned. "I think my leg's broken. Turn on the damn light and stop asking stupid questions."

Tara hobbled down the stairs, still wielding the knife, and flipped the switch.

"Why didn't the lights work when I did that?" Bonnie lay crumpled on the floor, her leg bent at an unnatural angle, cold sweat bathing her face. Tara could see the jagged edge of a bone sticking through the flesh and quickly turned away. But not before she saw the sword, and Deirdre's gold earrings, lying in the dirt next to the woman.

Tara didn't think it was a good time to explain how the house worked. "I asked what you're doing down here. How did you get in?"

Bonnie let her head fall back onto the dirt floor. "Through the front door, of course. Looking for something." She groaned, and Tara saw blood staining the dirt around her leg. How long had she been lying there? It didn't take long for a person to go into shock after a severe injury.

Tara was surprised that the house let Bonnie in. Then again, maybe it had a reason. After all, it exacted its price from her in the end. "What are you looking for?" She sat on the steps, out of Bonnie's reach.

"Can we discuss this later? Goddamned leg is killing me." Bonnie wrapped her arms around her chest, shivering.

But for once, Tara didn't let her soft heart overrule her head. "No. Answer my questions and then I'll get help. Otherwise, I'll let you rot down here."

Bonnie was quiet for a minute, and Tara thought she had passed out. Then she said, "Sword. It's real. The bell. The mermaid. All point to the treasure."

"The bell? Are you the one who rubbed the spot…?"

"Needed to see the name on it," Bonnie said. Tara suddenly remembered where she had seen that name before. It was mentioned in the article at Bonnie's store: the sister ship to the wreck where the sword in the picture was found.

"Rumors of a pirate stash around here for years." Bonnie paused between sentences, as though talking was an effort. "Spent most of my life looking for it. Saw that carving and knew it must be here. She was the figurehead…Alma del Mar. Whoever built this place had to know about the treasure."

The gaps between Bonnie's sentences were getting longer, and Tara was afraid the woman was going to pass out. "So, are you really an antique dealer?"

"Please. Call help. I feel…awful."

But Tara wasn't about to stop now. "I'll call when I'm good and ready. Answer my question. The antique store?"

Bonnie's cough was ragged; maybe she had internal injuries, too. "Searching for treasure is expensive. And I like my…toys. You'd be amazed...how many ways...make antique business profitable...easy scam. Ask your friend Lee.

"Treasure's here somewhere," she continued. "But every time I tried to find it, something happened. Damned house kept attacking me."

"So the black eye wasn't…from your boyfriend?"

"Boyfriend?" She snorted and groaned again. "You're too dumb to see what's right in front of you. I don't do boys."

Tara thought about Bonnie's hugs, the touches. How naïve could she be?

"Your stupid car…broke my foot." Bonnie's voice was barely a whisper. "Still don't know how it started rolling. Sorry I missed our 'date.'" Her sneer turned into a grimace. "What kind of locks…on your doors? Pain in the ass…to open."

Tara thought about the scratches. The house, protecting its secrets again. "Why would you waste your life chasing a rumor?"

"Not rumor. Anne Bonny. Female pirate. I'm named after her. She's my forefather...foremother...whatever the fuck she is.

Treasure's from one of her ships, so it's my birthright. And you better not try to steal it from me, or you'll be sorry!" She struggled to sit up, and Tara stood.

"I told you I'd get help, but if you're going to threaten me, I'll leave you here. No one will find you for weeks."

"Yeah, right."

Tara turned off the lights and started up the staircase.

"Wait a minute! You can't be serious!" Bonnie's voice held a note of panic.

"Try me."

"Okay, I'll play nice. Just…help me."

Tara turned the lights back on. Bonnie's skin was a bluish white, and Tara suspected the last outburst drained what was left of her energy.

"Was anything you said true?" Tara asked. *Were you really my friend?*

Bonnie closed her eyes and shrugged.

&

Tara called an ambulance, and sat on the front porch to wait for it. She couldn't bear to go downstairs again. Her heart ached, and she fought back tears.

Once again, someone she trusted betrayed her. Someone she thought was a friend. Someday she'd learn to tell the difference between the Lees and the Bonnies of the world.

If Bonnie was telling the truth, and there really *was* treasure hidden in her house, Tara had to decide what she was going to do about it.

Pirate treasure in her house…how many more secrets were there to find?

&

The ambulance took Bonnie to the hospital, but when the sheriff tried to file a report, Tara refused to press charges. She could see the headlines: Woman Searching for Treasure Attacked by House. Oh yeah, she needed that kind of publicity.

Bonnie had a long road ahead of her; it would take months for her leg to heal, if it ever did. Tara was pretty sure the house wouldn't let Bonnie inside again, so there was no danger of her stealing the treasure. Her injuries, coupled with losing the treasure, were punishment enough; Tara didn't need to add to her grief, even though Bonnie hadn't shown her the same consideration. A court case would just prolong the whole miserable situation — one Tara would just as soon forget.

Besides, if it hadn't been for Bonnie, she wouldn't know about the treasure. Now she had a better understanding of the value of what the house protected — along with the souls, that is. Although she still wondered how the treasure wound up in the house in the first place. Some questions would probably remain unanswered. Unless the house chose to tell her.

Or maybe someone else would.

Tara knelt next to Ariel. "So, why are you here, anyway? Grandpa McCarthy said to ask you, so I'm asking. What's a mermaid doing in a house in the woods?"

She waited for a response, feeling foolish. And of course, didn't get one.

But wait a minute. Maybe she already knew the answer. Although legend accused mermaids of luring sailors to their deaths, it also said they fell in love with the sailors and took them to live in their kingdom beneath the sea. Perhaps Ariel lured the pieces of souls to the house to protect what, to her, was a valuable, yet elusive, treasure.

Treasure.

Maybe Bonnie was wrong when she thought there was pirate's loot hidden in the house. Maybe the gold she sought for years was actually the golden stars: the souls. It wouldn't be the first time a treasure-seeker discovered, to his chagrin, that the treasure he lusted after was actually something intangible, yet infinitely more precious than gold and jewels to the owner. After all, what was more valuable than a person's soul? Although Bonnie probably wouldn't agree.

Ariel and the house were inextricably intertwined. Grandpa McCarthy said figureheads were guardians of souls, didn't he? Maybe Ariel lured the souls here, and helped the house protect them. Although understanding that didn't make the unique nature of the house any easier to accept, let alone explain to anyone else. Unless she wanted a permanent reservation at the funny farm, Tara would have to keep that as one of her own closely guarded secrets.

"So," Tara continued to address the figurehead, "it'd save me a lot of trouble if you'd just tell me whether or not there's more stuff hidden in the house. Or is the treasure you're guarding really the souls?"

Ariel silently gazed into the distance. Tara followed her gaze, and realized she was staring at the gilt-framed mirror that still covered the hole in the wall.

"I already found the treasure in there, Ariel. Remember the sword? There's nothing else; I looked."

So much for thinking wooden figures could solve mysteries.

But then, a golden spark slithered from behind the mirror, danced along the hallway, and slipped through the window next to the front door. Tara ran to the door and watched the Tinkerbell spark float into the night sky, growing smaller and smaller, until it disappeared into the galaxy of stars overhead.

She turned to gaze at Ariel with tears in her eyes. "Did that one go home?" She knew that somewhere, someone's pain had eased. And that the true treasure Ariel — and the house — protected had nothing to do with swords and chests of gold.

&

Tara swept up the chunks of plaster and made a note to buy more wallboard, to cover Bonnie's holes. Although this time, she'd be sure to look into them first. Just in case.

After she returned the broom to the closet, she remembered the key. Determined to think about something other than Bonnie's betrayal, she hobbled into the kitchen to find her father's lockbox. It probably held something mundane and predictable. But Tara felt as though she finally was nearing the end of her search, had finally discovered all of the secrets. Except this last one. Once this last mystery was solved, she could get back to her real life — whatever that looked like.

The lockbox sat in the middle of the table. She collapsed into a chair and pulled it toward her. Tore open the envelope and shook a small key into her palm. And slid it into the lock, where it turned with a soft click.

Tara opened the lid and pulled out a pocket-sized spiral notepad. Her father always had one in his pocket; he used pads like this for everything from taking notes during meetings to making detailed to-do lists. But those were usually battered; this one was pristine, as though it had never seen a pocket. What could be so important about this book that he kept it safely locked up?

Tara opened the cover and saw her father's precise handwriting. His years spent as an engineer, meticulously printing on blueprints and plans, were evident in the neat block letters. Her heart twisted, seeing the familiar writing.

She settled back into her chair and started flipping through the pages, expecting to find notes on his investments or confidential details about his clients.

After a few minutes she sat up, her hands trembling. Because what she just read had nothing to do with investments or clients.

Instead, it listed his reasons for needing to kill women.

Not just any women. The women of her family.

Emma.

Deirdre.

Mary.

And Tara herself.

~ 41 ~

It was his life's work.

The book held a detailed explanation as to how and why he needed to eliminate the women in the McCarthy clan.

How he suffocated Emma, after Tara pushed her. How inconvenient it was that Tara didn't kill her, forcing him to finish the job himself. Letting everyone believe that Tara killed her. He was pleased at how well that worked out, with the media circus focused on Tara instead of him.

How he recognized Mary's addictive personality — probably inherited from her father — and encouraged her alcoholism. And regularly added a hearty dose of lead to her meals to make sure her mind was destroyed, in case the vodka didn't do the trick.

How he planned to meet Deirdre at her house — a place he loathed and that loathed him — and his careful plans to strangle her and set fire to the house, cleansing the earth of its warped magic.

And how he would invite Tara to meet them at the house, killing two birds with one stone, so to speak. Ending the McCarthy lineage. Destroying the hated house and its secrets.

Tara stared in stunned silence at the detailed map to Deirdre's house. Scripts of what he would say in each situation. Drawings of graveyard plots. His engineer's love of detail and design came through in every deranged illustration.

His last lines hurt the worst.

They are all cursed. I am the only one who can stop them.

It ends tonight. With their deaths, their line is done. It will be finished.

The house has always hated me. So I will destroy it, as it has tried to destroy me.

I hate what they stand for, the secrets they harbor. I hate them all.

I will cleanse with fire. And with it, I will cleanse the world of their disease. My work will be done.

The pad fell from Tara's stiff fingers onto the table. She stared at her hands as if they belonged to someone else. For long minutes she sat, stunned.

Slowly, her mind began to work. She could almost feel the wheels straining to turn, trying to believe the unbelievable.

The fragile image of her father — the image she struggled to maintain in spite of the mounting evidence against him — shattered and fell in fragments around her heart. The trust she worked so hard to build. The belief in him as the only person she could rely on. Her need to beg forgiveness for destroying their family.

All lies.

Her mother might be an alcoholic, but her father was a madman.

She stood on unsteady feet and limped to the back door. The night was impenetrable; all she could see was her reflection in the dark glass. The empty eyes staring back at her pierced her soul.

Forgive, she could hear Mariah whispering. You have to forgive.

She couldn't. She wouldn't.

She had forgiven so much already. And although she knew it was the right thing to do, that by forgiving him she would keep her soul complete and know true peace, it was impossible. She couldn't stretch that far.

Tara remembered her grandfather's words: *There are acts too foul to be excused. Know the price ye pay when makin' the decision not to forgive, though. For 'tis both good and bad that will come of it.*

Tara knew the bad: her soul would forever be missing a piece. She could feel the pain of the piece tearing away as she stared into the darkness. But she also knew that the house needed the pieces to survive, especially those of her family. That was the good part: she would be nourishing the house, helping it fulfill its charge, helping it survive.

If her grandfather was right, she had already lost so many pieces of her soul. Forsaking dreams. Betraying love. Maybe that's what she'd been searching for all of these years, those missing pieces, not knowing that they were safe, patiently waiting here for her. Maybe if she could earn them back, repair the mistakes she made, she wouldn't feel the absence of this piece so keenly.

Some things she couldn't forgive. Wouldn't forgive. That was a decision she would have to live with. It was a price she was willing to pay.

Tara limped back to the table, slid the notepad into the lockbox, and locked it. She would decide what to do with the box later. Maybe Lee would help her. They had things to talk about, anyway. Like treasure. And secrets.

It was too late to do anything tonight. Tara stumbled into the living room and curled up on the couch to wait for the dawn.

&

The next morning, Tara rose from the couch. Pulled on her jacket. Walked slowly to her truck. Dodged the gullies, and drove through a downpour to Portland. The miles passed unseen as she thought about what she read in her father's notepad. How could he, she kept asking herself. How could he?

She may never know the answer to that question. But she did know what she could do about it.

At the hospital, she rode the elevator to the fourth floor. Walked past the nurses' station to where her father lay motionless under a white sheet, machines humming. The daisies she brought on her last visit wilted on the nightstand, and the cards and pictures she taped to the walls smiled down on him haphazardly.

Tara studied his face, searching for any remnant of the man she loved. Trying to find compassion in her heart for him. Anything that would help her understand his actions, and the decisions he made.

She recalled his words. And then repeated her grandfather's.

"There are acts too foul to be excused."

She called the nurses' station and asked for Dr. Chambers, who arrived a few minutes later. Tara hugged her, apologized for disturbing her, and thanked her for all she had done.

Then she fulfilled her final duty as Ethan's next of kin. Took responsibility for determining his fate, as he tried to determine hers. Gave the doctor her decision and ended his twisted reign.

"Turn off the machines. All of them. Now."

And walked out of the room without looking back.

~ 42 ~

As Tara drove back to Surfside, she resolved not to think about her father. She would have plenty of time to grieve for the relationship that could have been. Hopefully some day, she'd be able to remember the good times with him, and not his treachery. Right now, the pain was too fresh, the wounds too deep.

Instead, she tried to focus on her future. She had a life to plan. A new life with a new family. Another chance to find love.

She would return to Portland and make her peace with her mother. Once the doctors knew that Mary's dementia could be caused in part by heavy metal poisoning, they might be able to treat it. Maybe Mary would recover some of her memory; maybe they could have some kind of relationship, after all.

She would visit Emma's grave to thank her for forgiving her, and for teaching her to forgive. For freeing her.

And she would place white roses on Deirdre's grave, honoring the mother that she never knew.

But she knew their spirits lived on. Their souls were still in the house, nourishing it. Dancing in the basement.

Tara was working on a special project: a memory book for her own family. She had rose petals from Deirdre's grave; Mary's earring; Craig's cufflinks; the postcard from her mother's book. Strands of the sisters' hair. Tissues with Mary's and Deirdre's perfumes. The picture of her and Emma. She would decide later if she would include anything of her father's.

The second half of the book was empty, waiting to be filled with Tara's and Craig's lives as they unfolded. His daughter's life. Maybe her daughter's.

Then there was the treasure. Could there really be more hidden in the house, or was she right in thinking that the souls were the true treasure? Tara — and Craig — would have to decide if they wanted to demolish the place searching for mythical pirate's loot, or finish the restoration and get on with their lives, knowing that the house might still be hiding something.

She would take the sword to a reputable antique dealer, though; she wanted to know more about the weapon, especially the figures engraved into the bell guard that looked suspiciously like mermaids. Although she had no intention of selling it, now that she knew its origin.

Maybe Tony would like Deirdre's car. She owed Marge a little peace of mind in return for all she'd done for Tara, and her father.

She'd even brave the local hardware store and buy a Christmas tree.

And she would patch the damned hole in the hallway, once and for all. The house might finally let her do that. Unless something else was hiding in there.

Someday she'd travel again. But now, she looked forward to putting down roots. To belonging. Maybe the world would wait for her to gain her feet before calling to her again.

When Tara arrived at Lee's Place, she slowed and turned into the parking lot. It was time to tell him her secrets. And find out about his. Maybe she'd stay for dinner. And dessert. Maybe he'd show her the rest of his tattoo. Maybe she'd find out how accurate her dream was. A small smile played across her face as she remembered the taste and feel of her blond-haired man. Yes, definitely dessert.

And tomorrow, she'd go into town and buy a new trinket for her chain. Maybe a small gold star.

&

On the hill, under a mantle of twinkling lights, the house stands tranquil in the clear winter night. Inside, three gold stars rest on a mantelpiece next to a pirate's sword. A silken lei graces the neck of a water sprite gazing at distant horizons, searching for soulless ships and lost sailors. And a golden glow radiates through the basement, its secret safe once again.

A memory book sits on a solid oak desk, its pages spread to reveal rose petals, pictures, samples of perfume, strands of hair. A cluster of Tinkerbell sparks float across the room, hover for a moment above the book, and descend in a swirling dance to disappear between the carefully crafted pages.

Outside, the combination of light and dark, of bright and shadow, forms the picture of a house contented. All sins forgiven. Pleased with what it has achieved. And with what lies ahead.

A house can't cry. But it can surely smile.

&&&

Want more? Here's a sample from my next book. Enjoy!

Forget Me Not

When Alexandra Bailey reached across the bed toward her husband, her drowsy hand came back filled with memories.

She looked at the clock. Four fifteen. Glanced at Brett's side of the bed — he slept on the side closest to the door to protect her from monsters, he said — but it was empty. His head should be resting in its familiar divot in his too-soft pillow, hand fisted beneath his chin, tousled hair framing his sleeping face. She should hear his breathing, deep and even, until the sun peeked through the bedroom window. She should see his body stretched out next to her, one leg flung over hers: he always needed to touch her.

But his pillow lay uncreased, the early morning rays falling on silky sheets neatly turned back, waiting for him to slip silently between them.

He should have been home by 1:00 a.m. 2:00 at the latest, if they begged him to stay. He knew she'd be asleep, so the extra hour wouldn't steal from their time together. But not 4:15. Never 4:15.

Relax. There was a rational explanation. His car probably wouldn't start again, and he spent the night with Frank instead of calling her for a ride. Or he fell asleep on the couch watching an old movie. There was nothing to worry about.

Alex wandered from the bedroom into the living room, a golden retriever padding behind her, a touch of gray on his nose, but the television was silent and the tired couch empty. She found the cordless phone shoved between the cushions again and cursed the dead battery. Pulled her cell phone from her purse and called Brett, knowing his phone was probably in his car, in spite of trying to teach him to keep it in his pocket. She listened to it ring.

"Darn that man," she said to Riley, who answered with a single thump of his feathery tail. She was learning to pick her battles, although he knew how important this one was to her. He was always contrite when he finally remembered to look at his phone, and discovered she'd been trying to reach him. But he was a slow learner.

When it switched to voicemail and she heard his lazy drawl — he said he qualified as a southerner since he was from Southern Colorado — she left a brief message for him to call her, and hung up. Although she knew he wouldn't get it: she hadn't been able to teach him to check his voicemail, either. She walked across the cold linoleum floor and slid her finger down the list of numbers taped to the refrigerator, stopping at one near the bottom labeled 'BC Inn.' Dialed. And waited.

No answer. Still no reason to worry. She'd drive to the bar and see if his car was there. Maybe he was asleep in the back seat.

Maybe there were too many maybes.

"Come on dog, let's take a ride," Alex said, returning to the bedroom, Riley at her heels. She pulled on a brightly patterned skirt and pink tank top, and winced when she bent over to pick up her flip-flops. An evening out with the girls usually meant too much laughter, too many nachos and, last night, one too many margaritas.

She had driven home humming the song, "Tequila Makes Her Clothes Fall Off." Not clothes last night, though, just a fuchsia high-heel that she found on the passenger seat this morning. She pitched it into the back seat and urged the dog into the rear of the slate blue Jeep Liberty.

The sun was peeking over the San Juan Mountains; sunrise arrives late in this part of Colorado, even in the summertime. Soon the streets of Alamosa Springs would be busy with tourists gawking, locals grumbling their way to work, and kids celebrating the freedom of a July morning. But now the town slept and she cruised the silent streets, enjoying the peace and the sweet smell of summer.

The Bear Creek Inn was as quiet as the rest of the town, a lone car parked in the lot behind the gray barn-like structure. It was barely light enough to identify the car, but it had to be Brett's.

When she pulled into the lot and realized it was a Subaru Outback, Alex's heart fell. Brett owned a…well, she didn't know what it was; she didn't pay much attention to that kind of stuff. But his car definitely wasn't an Outback.

Oh well, at least he wouldn't come home with grease under his nails and another bill from the auto parts store.

Alex parked next to the carefully polished car, walked to the heavy steel door and pulled it open. The smell of last night's spilled beer and fried food was hard on her empty stomach and she swallowed uneasily. Damned hangover.

The owner of the Subaru had his back turned to her, swinging his mop to a beat that Alex couldn't hear. His silver hair was Brylcreamed in place and his black nylon sneakers gleamed. He hummed as he danced around the room with his soggy partner.

She didn't want to scare the man into another heart attack, so Alex stomped on the scarred pine floor as she crossed the room. But it didn't help; he jumped when he felt the vibration and searched the room until he saw Alex, and smiled.

"Alexandra." He pulled out the iPod earpieces and carefully tucked them into the top pocket of his worn overalls. "You startled me. I was doing the two-step with Dottie West. Why are you out and about so early on this fine, fine morning, precious?"

"You know I'm always up early, Ralph. The creative juices seem to flow strongest before noon."

"And that boy of yours is still asleep so you can work without distraction, I'll wager." He winked.

"Yes, he can be a distraction." She smiled, thinking of how he distracted her yesterday morning, pulling the covers over their heads and pretending they were in a high mountain meadow, loving her slow and long and hard in the midst of the imaginary wildflowers. "Speaking of which, he didn't come home last night. I don't suppose you know where he is, do you?"

Ralph leaned on his mop. "Sorry, Alex. I've been here since 4:00, and his car and guitar were both gone when I arrived. Should I make a call or two, and see if any of the staff know where he might have been bound when he left?"

Alex shook her head. "No, don't wake anyone. I'm sure he's fine. It's just not like him to forget to come home." He might forget to pick up milk at the store or put gas in his car, but he didn't forget to come home. Well, not any more.

"He's probably there already, waiting for you with those big ol' puppy-dog eyes of his, begging you to forgive him for running a little late. I'll pen a note for Frank, asking him to give you a jingle when he arrives for his shift."

Alex thanked the old man and left him to his imaginary partner. She called Brett's cell again as she walked to her Jeep, and again the call when to voicemail.

Ralph was right; he was probably at the house by now, fast asleep. Or went home with a musician friend after the last set and lost track of time. Their jam sessions could stretch far into the wee hours, with no one to pull them out of their rock and roll reverie. Not that she could stay mad at him for long; Ralph had Brett pegged, with those puppy-dog eyes.

Anyway, it was Wednesday, their day to meet for lunch at Susie's, and he never missed their date. Especially not today. If only she could figure out how to set that internal alarm of his for other, more important events, like doctors' appointments and dinner with friends. But for now, she was content there was at least one place she knew she could always find him.

"Home, James," she said to the dog panting in the rear of the Jeep. And headed west, one eye on the road, the other searching for an ice-blue sports car.

30546048R00170

Made in the USA
Charleston, SC
19 June 2014